MALIBU

Malibu

William Murray

Coward, McCann & Geoghegan, Inc.
New York

For Alice

The author gratefully acknowledges permission from Metro-
Goldwyn-Mayer to quote lyrics from "We're Off to See the
Wizard," Copyright © 1939, renewed 1967 Metro-Goldwyn-
Mayer, Inc. Rights throughout the world controlled by Leo
Feist, Inc. All rights reserved. Used by permission.

Library of Congress Cataloging in Publication Data

Murray, William, date.
  Malibu.

  I. Title.
PZ4.M982Mal.   [PS3563.U8]   813'.5'4   79-14308
ISBN 0-698-10978-3

Printed in the United States of America

Gatsby believed in the green light, the orgiastic future that year by year recedes before us. It eluded us then, but that's no matter—tomorrow we will run faster, stretch out our arms farther. . . . And one fine morning—

—F. Scott Fitzgerald, *The Great Gatsby*

I

The Third Week in June

1

Both the Harvey boys were tough to teach. Peter, thirteen, the older one, was a big solidly built kid who could hit with power, at least off the forehand, but he was overweight and slow and frequently off-balance. Anthony, though still only ten, would clearly never be able to play well. He was uncoordinated and held the racket like a soup ladle. He cried easily if you pushed him too hard, and he hated physical exertion of any kind. It was like trying to teach figure skating to a couple of paraplegics, Art Bonnell reflected, but was it really fair of him to feel that way?

What Art should have done, of course, was be honest with the Harveys. Your kids will never be tennis players, he should have told them, so why waste time and money trying to teach them the game? Why not send Peter to a camp for fat kids, where they'd take some weight off him and make him at least look and feel better, if nothing else. And why not turn Anthony over to a shrink or give him hormone shots or discuss a sex change for him with the family sawbones? Wouldn't it have been kinder all around?

Sure, Art Bonnell told himself, flicking the ball back across the net to consume the minimum of energy, sure, of course it would have been kinder and far more honest, and then where the hell would the summer go? The Harveys were rich, they were here for the season, and they wanted their boys to take tennis lessons every day, an hour a day, at thirty dollars an hour. Go and throw that kind of easy money out the window. Not likely, no, indeed. "Nice shot," Art said as Peter, more by accident than design, hit one down the line that luckily picked up a piece of the corner. "That's it, Peter. But off the right foot, got it? Otherwise you'll always be off-balance. Okay, let's try a few backhands now. . . ."

Boy, it was hot. He could feel the sun beat on the back of his neck, searing the exposed skin between the collar of his shirt and the turned-down brim of his canvas hat. Already he'd had two clusters of sun-crazed malevolent cells cut out of there, and today, of all days, he'd forgotten the protective lotion he usually wore. He was getting more forgetful in his old age. Patiently he went on plunking easy shots toward Peter's backhand, only to watch the returns, always badly undersliced, fly off and away from the court, too far from even his reach to be kept in play. "Peter, take it easy!" he called out. "Turn your body and bend the old knees and pull the racket back! Like this!" And he'd show him, for the tenth, or twelfth, or twentieth time—who could remember anymore? What a way to make a living, even for him. Art glanced at his watch. Ten minutes to go, then a break, and a quick run home to get his lotion. "Here, now, get down low, Peter!" Art shouted. "Put your whole body into the shot!"

"Hi there," Lee Harvey chirped, coming through the wooden gate behind the court, with Anthony trailing disconsolately after her. "How's it going?"

"Oh, hello," Art said. "Not bad. He's coming along."

"I thought I'd watch for a few minutes," she said. "That okay?"

"It is with me," he told her, then sent a ball bouncing toward Peter's forehand, so Mommy might at least see that she was getting something for all this money they were spending. "That's it, Peter," Art said, "but don't let the ball get in back of you. Anticipate, anticipate. And try to hit it at the top of the rise."

"Very nice," Lee said after a few minutes. "He really *is* coming along. I thought he was kidding me."

"Okay, that's it, Peter," Art said, coming over to towel off. "We'll work on the backhand more tomorrow. Pick up the balls now."

Peter obviously liked that part of the lesson best of all. He pushed the clumsy-looking little yellow cart around the court and beamed as it gobbled up the balls and fed them one by one into a wire basket from which the pro could select them later without having to stoop over. Art sat down beside Lee Harvey; he decided, too, that he really liked the looks of her long brown legs, capped by brief white shorts and extended now to pick up the sun. "It's hot as hell," he said. "Crazy weather for June here."

"Wonderful, isn't it?"

"For some people," he told her, grimacing, "but not for old tennis pros. You're looking good, Lee. Malibu agrees with you."

"Thanks. Art, I wanted to ask you something. We—"

"Hey, Mom," Anthony complained, "do I have to have my lesson?"

"You bet," she said, "but I want to speak to Mr. Bonnell first."

"I hate tennis," the boy mumbled.

"Anthony, hit some with your brother for a few minutes," Art said. "I'm going to get my sun lotion. Maybe you could give me a lift, Lee, and we'll talk. All I have is my bike."

"Sure thing."

"I don't want to hit with him," Peter said. "He can't get them back."

"Fuck you, I don't want to play with you either!" Anthony yelled.

"Boys," Lee said, "you do what Mr. Bonnell tells you, or else."

"I'll be right back, guys," Art said, ushering Lee out toward the cream-colored convertible Mercedes parked in back of the court. "No goofing off, now."

"It's Sid's idea," Lee explained as she settled herself behind the wheel. "He thinks they ought to learn to play tennis as a social accomplishment, the way I had to study piano as a kid. Do you really think they'll ever be able to play?"

"Sure," he lied. "They'll never make it to Wimbledon, but they'll be able to play socially, all right. They don't have much desire yet, but maybe that'll come."

"You know how I control them? I unplug the TV sets and force them to read *books!*"

"Horrible," he said, "a prospect to intimidate anybody. What kind of books?"

"Printed ones," Lee said, "with real words in them."

Art Bonnell laughed. He liked this woman. She had a nice sense of humor to go with the legs, and it wasn't her fault she had a couple of sissy kids and a hairy, overly ambitious husband who had made tons

11

of money selling or manufacturing something useful. Or that they came from a cold manufacturing town somewhere in northern Wisconsin, where it was winter nine months of the year. Not everyone could live the golden California life year-round. That's why people came here for the summer, to get a sniff at least of the truly good life in the sun.

The big Mercedes eased itself over the steep ridges in the road, artificial bumps placed there years before to impede speeders and protect the Colony's smaller fauna, then purred past the guardhouse and turned left up the Old Malibu Road. "Where are you?" Lee asked.

"Just beyond the last of the Colony houses," Art explained, "around the first bend and up about a quarter of a mile. Nice of you to do this."

"No problem. Where's your car?"

"Laura has it. Hers is being serviced, and she had to go into Beverly Hills to do some shopping."

"I don't know how you do it."

"Do what?"

"Teach tennis all day long. Don't you ever get bored?"

"Sure, often," he admitted. "But I get more bored not eating. What's on your mind, Lee?"

"Sorry, have I touched a nerve?"

"Not at all," he lied. "But I thought you wanted to ask me something."

"I do."

"Well, shoot."

"It's about this party we want to give on the July Fourth weekend."

"What about it?"

"Well . . . I suppose this is going to sound funny."

"You can make a U-turn just beyond the fire hydrant and park in front of the garage, over there," he said, indicating the back of their house, tucked between two much larger ones and almost invisible even from where the road straightened out again. "I'll be right out. Then we can talk."

"Can I come in a second?" she asked. "I could use a glass of water."

"Sure thing."

She parked, got out, and allowed him to open the gate for her. "What a cute place," she said.

"I'd better lead the way." He trotted briskly down a flight of narrow wooden steps leading to the deck of the house, a small rust-colored bungalow thrust on angled beams out over the incoming surf. "Come on in," he said, opening the back door into the kitchen.

"Hey, I like this," she said, smiling at him from the doorway.

"Ice is in there," he told her, waving at the refrigerator. "I'd drink from the cooler, if I were you. The tap water's undrinkable here."

"I found that out."

"I'll change my shirt and pick up my lotion, okay?"

"Okay," she agreed, making no move yet to do anything but just take in the whole scene; she seemed oddly delighted by the incident, as if it constituted something of an adventure for her, or at least the beginning of one. "This is so sweet. I mean, this whole place—it's darling."

"Yeah," he said, and fled into the interior of the house. That was just what he needed in his life then, he thought, an affair with the mother of his two most lucrative pupils. Oh, yes, he needed that badly, he did. Like hell. "I won't be a minute."

"Take your time," she called out after him. "The boys can keep busy."

Sure they can, he thought as he closed the bedroom door and peeled off his sweaty shirt. Sure. And she did have very nice legs. . . .

"Don't take it personally," George Alcorn told Laura Bonnell that morning, "but I did have somebody younger in mind."

"You didn't say so in your ad," Laura answered, "and I do take it personally. You make me feel a thousand years old."

Alcorn blushed and scratched his cheek. "God, that isn't what I meant. I mean, I had in mind some young kid just out of school, somebody I could train."

"Why?"

"Why?" He looked confused. "Well, I don't know, really. I just assumed . . ."

"Would you like to know how old I am?"

"No, of course not. I mean—"

"I'm forty," she said, "and suddenly I'm feeling every day of it."

Alcorn groaned. "Look . . ."

"We don't have to do a whole number on each other," she said. "I know I'm a good-looking forty."

"You sure are."

"And I don't mean to put you in an embarrassing position," she continued. "I'm applying for this job because I think I can do it, and I think I can do it better than some teenage kid just out of school."

"It doesn't pay much."

"I know, but it's a start," she said. "You can train me in the production part of it just as fast as you can train some kid, and I do have experience in dealing with people. And if the job works out, I won't quit to live with some guy or to go back to school or, God forbid, get married and raise kids. Or maybe not show up on you one morning just because I'm bored or something."

"You've got a point. But what's your situation? Are you married?"

She nodded. "Twenty-one years, to one husband. I'm a freak."

He smiled. "I'm just out of my second attempt to make that work," he said, "but, unlike the song says, it wasn't better the second time around."

"I'm sorry."

"Don't be," he assured her. "It wasn't that sensational at any time. I guess I'm not a husband."

"I want this job," Laura said.

"Why? You obviously don't need the money."

"Well, I do, as a matter of fact," she answered. "Who can't use money? I'm assuming the job could work into something really interesting eventually."

George Alcorn nodded and glanced down at her letter. "You live in Malibu," he observed. "Isn't that a long drive in for you?"

"What are your hours?"

"Nine to five, like everybody else's."

"Not such a long drive," she said, "but it is a nasty one." She shrugged. "Still, everybody in L.A. drives to work. At least I don't have to go from La Cañada to downtown or from Sherman Oaks to Long Beach. Compared to that, Malibu to Beverly Hills is a snap. And I have a little Japanese car that gets thirty miles to the gallon. I'll learn to love it."

"What about home?"

14

"My son's twenty and pretty much on his own," she explained. "My husband's out most of the day."

Alcorn nodded. "Look," he said, "can you give me a couple of days to think it over? Will you call me Monday?"

"In other words, no," she said, standing up. "You want somebody else."

He looked startled. "No, I have no one really in mind," he objected with a laugh. "Dammit, sit down a second. I'll be right back." And he suddenly left the room, closing the door behind him.

She sat down again and looked more carefully around his office, liking what she saw. It was on a top-floor corner of a four-story colonial-style brick building, two blocks south of Wilshire, and it was full of light, with a nice view down a residential street of well-kept private homes shaded by oaks and sycamores now in the full green leaf of early summer. The room itself was furnished simply but in good taste, with several old English horse prints on the walls and, over Alcorn's desk, a huge Piranesi showing a section of the Imperial Roman Forum. The room was designed to be pleasant and functional, not to impress visitors. That was comforting to her, because she'd seen too many rooms designed to flaunt the possessions of some show-biz princeling. Hollywood infected everything it touched.

Before seeing the ad in the L.A. *Times*, Laura had heard of Alcorn-Hyland; she knew it was considered one of the best small ad agencies in town, with a limited but classy roster of accounts. The room confirmed this impression, though she hadn't yet quite made up her mind about George Alcorn himself, whom she'd be expected to work for. He distracted her a little. Too much Hollywood about him. Too much thick, perfectly-moulded, prematurely white hair; too many shining even teeth, perfectly capped; too much of a tan, an excess of which she had learned to distrust in middle-aged men; too expensively tailored a suit, though at least it was a suit, with a real tie, and not some mod unisex costume draped in chains and speckled with flowers. She still wanted the job, she decided; she needed it.

Alcorn now ushered in a willowy, gentle-looking bearded young man he introduced as Carlo Rozzi, his art director. "You'd be working with Carlo, too," he explained. "I wanted him to meet you."

Carlo was gay, no doubt about that, she decided, and he seemed

15

genuinely nice. He spoke in a very slight accent, a legacy from his childhood in the Veneto, and clearly he knew his job. He asked her very specific questions designed to find out exactly how much she knew, if anything, about layouts, paste-ups, typography, production in general, then smiled, shook her hand very formally, and skipped out of the room. "A brilliant kid," George Alcorn said. "He designed the whole Fountain campaign last year around that symbol of the black-gloved hand holding a silver spoon, remember?"

"Yes, I do."

"It was his idea, and a super one. I pay him a lot of money."

"I guess he's worth it."

"You bet he is." He sat down behind his desk again and looked sharply at her. "You didn't tell me you could do paste-ups."

"You didn't ask me," she explained. "I worked part-time for about a year for a little newspaper down in Laguna, where we used to live."

Alcorn looked puzzled. "Laguna?" He glanced again at her letter. "You aren't related to Art Bonnell, the tennis player?"

"I'm married to him."

"I'll be damned!" Alcorn exclaimed. "I knew he used to teach down there. Wasn't he the pro at some big private club?"

"Yes," she said, "the South Bay."

"I didn't know he'd left."

"We've been in Malibu nearly five years."

"What's Art up to?"

"Teaching privately, mostly."

"Say, he was a hell of a player!"

"Yes, he was."

"I saw him twice at Forest Hills. I was there the day he took Rosewall to five sets in the semis."

"I gather you play tennis," she said without enthusiasm.

"Do I ever," he answered, smiling. "Art Bonnell, boy, he had the best-looking game I ever saw, the most classic style. It was too bad about his shoulder."

"Yes," she said, "but it's all right now."

"I'm glad to hear it."

"Well . . ." She stood up to go again. "I'll call you Monday."

"Don't bother," George Alcorn said. "Just come in at nine."

"I've got the job?"

16

He nodded. "Yep. I can pay you six dollars an hour on a tryout basis, for the first six weeks, after which, if we like you and you like us, we'll talk yearly salary, benefits, and all that. Okay?"

"Yes," she said. "Thank you."

"You don't seem overjoyed. Did I say something?"

"No, not really. I was just wondering whether you're doing this because you think I can do it or because you found out I'm Art Bonnell's wife."

"A little of both," he admitted. "I'm being honest."

"Yes, I appreciate it," she said. "I'll see you Monday."

Maybe he felt sorry for her, she thought as she walked out of the room, maybe he thought it must have been tough to have had all that money and all that glamour and to have to look now for a job. Especially at forty, with no real experience, though she still did have her looks, yes, she certainly had those. Alcorn should have seen her at nineteen, when she first met Art and married him.

When Art Bonnell reappeared in his living room, Lee Harvey was outside on the deck and looking down at the waves breaking on the rocks below. "It's such a nice house," she said, coming inside and tugging the glass doors shut behind her. "I'm not sure I could take the constant roar of the surf right under me, but it's a beautiful spot."

"Both Laura and I find we sleep better," Art said. "So well, in fact, it's hard to get to sleep when we're away from it."

"It's what you're used to, I guess. I grew up in the country and never heard the insects, but we had crickets in the summer that deafened visitors." She waved a hand around the room and smiled. "All this, it's your wife?"

"Mostly," he admitted. "The tennis trophies and old photographs over the bar, that's me. The rest is hers."

"She has good taste."

"The couch we bought a couple of years ago, at an auction," he explained. "The rest of the pieces are family heirlooms, Laura's, of course. My family heirlooms were bricks and cement." For some reason he couldn't yet pin down, all this praise, this discussion of furniture, made him jumpy. Was she patronizing him or was he becoming paranoid in his middle age? He headed for the door. "Come on. I've got a pupil waiting, remember?"

"I hope they haven't killed each other by this time," she said, strolling past him and up the outside steps.

You've got terrific legs, he wanted to tell her, *and I'd like to work my way up them from the heels. And maybe you'd like that, too, wouldn't you, rich lady? Does the hairy tycoon, with his wheeling and dealing, keep you satisfied, or are you going to have yourself an aging tennis pro this summer?* "We'll have to get you and Sid over," he said instead. "Laura would enjoy meeting you."

"Listen, *that's* what I had on my mind."

"Meeting Laura?"

"This party we want to give."

"Oh, yeah?"

"The problem is, we don't know anybody," she explained. "I mean, we've been here a couple of weeks now and we've met a few people, but, well, it's like the summer is going to slip away before we get to *know* anybody." They got into her car again and she swung carefully out into the road, then headed back toward the Colony. "We'd like to invite quite a few people, kind of break the ice."

"So what's the problem?"

"Well . . . I mean . . . people we don't even know, would they come?"

"Why not? That's one of the things people do here in the summer—go to parties."

"Sid insisted on the July Fourth weekend, but I thought there might be a conflict or something and nobody would come to our party." She laughed nervously. "It sounds ridiculous, doesn't it?"

"No," he answered. "But why don't you check with Billie Farnsworth? Didn't you rent your place through her?"

"Yes."

"Well, she knows everybody," he said. "Not only that, but she's the biggest and most reliable gossip on the beach."

She laughed. "I kind of figured that. That's why I'm asking you. Sid and I figured you must know nearly everybody. We don't want just the summer people. We'd like to invite the regulars, too."

"Well, you'll also have to go to Billie," he told her. "It would be a big mistake if you didn't."

"I suppose."

"She'll know if there's a conflicting brawl, and she'll give you the names and numbers of all the players. As for me, I can turn out some of the tennis crowd."

"Oh, good. Sid, by the way, really wants to get into a regular game."

"I'll see what I can do."

The Mercedes turned past the Colony gates and guardhouse. Lee waved to Wally, plump and inscrutable as ever behind his desk, then eased the big car over the first of the traffic bumps. "I forgot about these one day," she said, "and I almost took the bottom out of the car."

"How well does Sid play?" Art asked. "I only saw him rally once."

"He's a real hacker," she said, "but lots of determination."

"I'm running the tournament, you know. You and Sid going to be in it?"

"Sure thing. I'm no good at all, though. Sid won't play with me."

"You've got company, don't worry. Anyway, it's a good way to meet people," he said. She pulled up beside the Wharton court, where the boys were rallying sullenly. "Coming in?"

"No. Just send Peter out. I'll pick Anthony up in half an hour. And thanks."

"For what? You'll see," Art said, "the Colony comes on like a very exclusive place, but it's all just folks, really."

Art Bonnell watched her drive away, with a last wave and a smile. He thought about the long brown legs again and how the rest of her might look naked against clean white sheets; then he shook his head and went back to work. The first ball hit at Anthony bounced past him without the kid even touching it. It was one hell of a way to make a buck. No wonder Laura and he were so miserable with each other these days.

2

The summer began for Billie Farnsworth with the phone call from Lee Harvey. It woke her up, which was a bad way to start the day, because until her second cup of coffee Billie found it difficult to carry on a conversation. "What time is it?" she mumbled into the receiver.

"It's nine o'clock," Lee Harvey answered. "God, Billie, I'm so sorry. People with young kids get to believing everybody gets up at the crack of dawn. Shall I call you back?"

"Yes," Billie said. "No. I'll call you. You home?"

"Yes."

Billie hung up and fell back against her pillows. After a few minutes she forced herself out of bed and went into the kitchen to put the coffee on. While waiting for it to percolate, she tottered out to the living room and collapsed into the sofa, from where she could stare out her picture window at the beach. The back of Billie's house jutted out over the sand, and from that end of the curve she could look up toward the packed array of Colony houses nestled together against the sand, or she could turn her head and gaze south toward the public beach, where already a couple of dozen surfers in wet suits were in the water, black specks on white splinters speeding on the crests of waves toward the shoreline. It was a cold and foggy

21

morning, with a nasty chill coming in from the icy offshore current. Not a good beach day, Billie thought, but a good day for Jay R. Pomerantz and the Carey house. The guy had sounded so eager on the phone that she was dying to meet him. Ever since their first conversation, Billie had been telling herself that she ought to get out of the business if she couldn't sell him that house. He sounded like the most assured client she'd handled in years. But then, everybody wanted to buy or rent in Malibu these days; she'd been making pots of money.

What was it about Malibu and the Colony, anyway? People all over the world had heard about the area, but so few really knew anything about it or its history. To most outsiders it was one of those places at the end of the yellow-brick road. Once inside, they'd find the wizard who could work real miracles, if they were willing to pay to make their dreams come true, and who wouldn't? If they couldn't find the wizard and their dreams turned out to be illusory, why, then, just like Dorothy, they could all go home again.

Billie Farnsworth knew all about Malibu and she could answer most of her clients' questions about the place. She'd immediately impressed Jay R. Pomerantz with her knowledge, but then, wasn't it her business to know? How the hell could you sell anybody a million-dollar house, she wondered, if you couldn't answer the simplest sort of queries about not only the property itself but the whole surrounding area? Especially if the name had a magical sound to it. Malibu. It conjured up visions of the golden life, even as the word itself sang in your ears. Malibu. *And we're off to see the Wizard, the wonderful Wizard of . . .*

The original Rancho Malibu, Billie had found out, consisted of about thirteen thousand acres, a narrow strip of land squeezed between the mountains and the ocean. It began at a point about twelve miles north of Santa Monica and extended up the coast of southern California for about twenty-six miles. The whole parcel had been bought in 1891 for ten dollars an acre by one Frederick Rindge, a millionaire who had moved to California from Cambridge, Massachusetts, four years earlier. He and his wife, Rhoda, had lived on this estate like feudal barons and dedicated themselves to defending it from all outside encroachment.

After Rindge died in 1905, his widow fought a seventeen-year legal battle to keep the Southern Pacific Railway and federal- and state-highway interests from pushing through her domain. She built fences and hired armed guards to scare off surveying parties, but of course she was bound to lose. She beat the railroad, but eventually a superior-court decision granted the state a right-of-way to build a road through the property, and rising taxes began to squeeze Mrs. Rindge into surrender. In 1927 she began to lease out parcels of land, including a short sandy crescent just north of Malibu Creek that became known as the Malibu Motion Picture Colony.

The first star to come and build a summer home there was Anna Q. Nilsson. She was soon followed by Warner Baxter, Jack Warner, Clara Bow, Barbara Stanwyck, Ronald Colman, Dolores del Rio, and others. What they sought was privacy, and they got it. Malibu was a long way from Hollywood, with a lot of still-open country between the beaches and the city. The movie people built what they called bungalows and thought of the place as a weekend refuge and summer home. And the Colony became famous as a locale for the sort of lavish parties that distinguished the social and drinking life of the 1920's.

The fad for the area as a weekend and summer resort faded with the Depression, but Warner Baxter and a few others kept at least the tradition alive through World War Two. During the postwar boom years, with the population swelling and the city of Los Angeles pushing westward toward the beaches, the character of the Malibu Colony changed. Most of the houses were bought and built by middle-class citizens who wanted to raise families and live in suburban tranquillity. As late as the mid-sixties there were still empty lots between many of the houses, and the only resident big-time movie star was Lana Turner, who was rarely seen outdoors and became really visible only at Halloween, when she dispensed candy by the fistfuls to trick-or-treating neighborhood kids. Houses rented for as low as four hundred dollars a month, and little of the old movie glamour had survived. In fact, all of Malibu still seemed fairly remote. The coast highway was a narrow, intimidating road; the surrounding hills had not yet sprouted condominiums; there were few public facilities, only one supermarket, and not even a movie theater. People still rode horses up and down the beach and swam in Malibu Creek.

This was the Malibu Billie Farnsworth had found when she and her husband, Winston, arrived in the early fall of 1958. The price of

23

real estate didn't really begin to soar until a few years later, at just about the same time the celebrities rediscovered the Colony. In 1969, a movie columnist named Rex Reed spent a few weeks there and wrote a scathing story for *Holiday* in which he observed that the "cesspool of (L.A.) culture empties somewhere in the vicinity of Malibu." He wrote about Nureyev teaching Barbra Streisand how to dance on the beach, dropped a lot of other big names, and described endless parties in which people smoked and drank themselves into temporary insanity. The Colony became a gathering place for stars and jet-setters who "for as long as the summer lasts get stoned on pot, barbecue everything but the delivery boys from Western Union, and work like hell to make their summer rent money pay off."

Reed's piece was inaccurate (Western Union doesn't deliver telegrams to Malibu), attracted a lot of attention and made Malibu sound like a terrific place to be for all those people tired of hanging around St. Tropez and the bathhouses of Bangkok, but it startled the locals. The Malibu *Times*, a homey little country weekly, devoted practically two whole issues to the article and admitted that the Colony had in the past been the scene of some pretty splashy parties, but moralized that one man's party was not necessarily somebody else's pot-smoking orgy. Billie Farnsworth had never met Rex Reed and she couldn't recall anybody saying they'd ever seen or spoken to him. And Billie, of all people, even then—well, she'd have heard *something* if Rex Reed had been around the Colony all that much.

When you're a woman of fifty-two, she reflected, widowed, with your best days behind you and living alone, you tend to live your life vicariously. Billie had always known as much as anyone about what was going on, partly because she'd made it her business to know, and also because she enjoyed the gossip. It was Rich Bentley who had once offered to nail her ears up over her tongue above the Colony entrance as a logo to sort of define the whole atmosphere of the place. She'd overheard Rich Bentley suggest it at a party a couple of years before, shortly after he and Mary Wharton had broken up, and the image stuck. But she wasn't really to blame, Billie told herself, because people just seemed to want to come up and confide in her. They'd tell her the most incredible things, even people she hardly knew. It was a quality Billie had; people trusted her. And why wouldn't they? She'd never betrayed a real confidence, never. If she heard a good story, she'd tell it, but she also knew when to keep her mouth shut. She had to know that, or she wouldn't have been able to stay in business.

The smell of freshly brewed coffee lured Billie back into the kitchen, where she poured herself a cup, then returned to her perch and the view. My God, she thought, it was incredible what people would pay to buy or rent a Colony house these days. The summers were especially wild. People from as far away as Ohio and Michigan and Illinois, who may never even have visited California, would begin calling in February and March to find out what was available and to get their bids in early. Summer rentals averaged between five thousand and seven thousand dollars a month, but the better places went for as high as ten thousand, often sight unseen. Billie could never understand why, either.

The houses in the Malibu Colony were big, often luxuriously furnished, but they were packed side by side like books on a roughly mile-long shelf of sand fronting the ocean. From the air the place looked like just another older and very crowded development, two rows of houses on either side of a single paved road, with here and there a tennis court to break up the monotony of rooftops. The beach itself was narrow and not very clean, the water full of rocks and floating kelp, and traffic along the Pacific Coast Highway made it difficult to go anywhere, especially on weekends. Periodically the highway would be closed to all traffic, occasionally for weeks at a time, by falling boulders and landslides along the stretch that skirted the cliffs between Big Rock and Topanga, and then the drive into town became a nightmare forty-mile detour through the canyons. The natives put up with such inconveniences, but for the kind of loot these summer visitors were spending, they could have gone around the world or rented whole islands of their own. But Malibu had the sound and the feel of magic, Billie had discovered early on, and that was what got them every time.

When Billie Farnsworth had started her business ten years before, it had still been possible to buy something in Malibu for as little as a hundred or two hundred thousand, but that had changed drastically over the past few years. Prices had really skyrocketed lately, and the average purchase price of a home in the Colony had soared to between five hundred and seven hundred thousand. A few weeks earlier, Billie had sold a one-bedroom place up on the Old Malibu

25

Road, not even within the Colony gates, for five hundred and fifty thousand dollars. This particular day she had two houses available inside the gates for a million each.

One of them, the old Carey place, had been built forty years ago. It had rotting plumbing, a leaky roof, and no central heating. Billie had doubted all along that she'd be able to get anything like the asking price on this one, but that had been before she'd heard from Jay R. Pomerantz. She smiled as she raised the cup to her lips again and felt the hot steam against her face. Old Carey had paid twenty thousand for his place back in the late thirties and left it to his four children, who had used it for many years as a summer camp for themselves and their horde of savage, destructive offspring. That the house had survived at all was a miracle of sorts.

Billie still worried a lot about what the real-estate boom was doing to Malibu, even though she was profiting by it. She knew that it was chasing out some of the nice middle-class families who had moved there since the war because they'd wanted to live quietly in a country atmosphere. Quite a few of these people were friends of hers. When she and Winston had bought their own house back in the late fifties, Malibu had still been a rural hideaway, as remote from smog-bound central Los Angeles as if separated by a mountain range and linked to the city only by a dirt road. The flat fields behind the Colony, on the other side of the highway, had been full of flowers that stretched like a gaudy carpet to the hills, where only a few houses nestled among groves of eucalyptus. Crosscreek Road had been a narrow winding lane shaded by old overhanging sycamores, and the Serra Retreat, once the old Rindge place, had dominated from its hilltop an approximation of the gentle wilderness that had once been Rancho Malibu. Billie's son, Dave, had grown up riding horses over those fields and swimming in the creek that wound out of Malibu Canyon.

All that had changed. It seemed to Billie now that it had begun to change immediately after her husband had so ungraciously and thoughtlessly put a bullet into himself and bled to death on the floor of his den, where she had found him. Winston had always had a very poor sense of timing, in life as well as in bed. He'd killed himself and died land-poor and broke just as the boom was about to explode and solve all their troubles. He'd left Billie his debts, a little life insurance, and a four-year-old Mercury with sixty-eight thousand miles on it. Billie had had to go to work.

26

Luckily, she'd had a flair for it. It hadn't taken her more than a couple of months and a little studying to figure out that she was a great saleswoman. After a year with her first agency, she'd struck out on her own and done fabulously well. Her friends had helped, of course, mainly by sending her clients, but after those first few weeks on her own, after her first million-dollar sale, she hadn't needed much help. She was good. She knew how to sell. She could charm the birds off trees and clients out of their life savings. If anyone wanted to buy or rent a house in the Malibu Colony, Billie Farnsworth became the person to see, everybody knew that. And with all the money she'd begun making, Billie had been able to send Dave through college in style, then later get him started as an architect with his own firm and his own clients.

Billie had bought her own Colony house, too, with its own tennis court, and become a real power in the community. Not only that, but she was having a hell of a good time. She was happy with her life, now that the fires in her had cooled and she'd learned never to trust another human being ever again. She lived well, made a point of it, in fact, because she'd also found out what some people had always known—that nothing else mattered but the senses and the immediate pleasures. Every day Billie Farnsworth revenged herself on life, a little.

It was lucky Billie had never thought of herself as a crusader and embraced any causes, because basically she hated what the real-estate boom had been doing to Malibu, even as she contributed to it. She despised the cold architectural lines of the new Civic Center, for instance, all glass and stone and steel, so out of sync with the beauty of the hills that framed it. She hated the way people just built in any style they wanted, regardless of whether it harmonized with the terrain or not. The last big brush fire, seven or eight years ago, had leveled the old Serra Retreat and swept away many of the more elegant, older homes in the hills and on the other side of Malibu Creek. Most people had rebuilt, but in poor taste. The lower ridges, all too visible from her back patio, were speckled with unimaginative ranch houses and split-levels and boxes thrust out on stilts above the steeper slopes, while cancerous clusters of condominiums overwhelmed entire hillsides.

Most of all, Billie hated the Pepperdine campus, which looked to her like a minimum-security prison. That huge stone cross they'd erected above Malibu Canyon Road advertised not love or mercy but money and arrogant intolerance, the loud-mouthed pushiness Billie had always associated with Christian fundamentalism in all its unmerry guises. These Pepperdine kids, with their short hair and their bland smiles, seemed throwbacks to her, clones from the Eisenhower era, when the whole country had gone to sleep.

Billie made no secret of her hatreds, and she could get away with saying almost anything in public, mainly because most people liked her. Her big mouth helped her sell, too. She'd discovered very early that she could always loosen up a client merely by making him laugh. The hard sell was not her line. She often disparaged her properties and pointed out their defects. For some mysterious reason this made people trust her, and occasionally Billie would find herself actually trying to talk a customer out of a deal or getting him at least to delay long enough to give himself time to think it over. Billie lived in Malibu, and she didn't want unhappy ex-clients for neighbors.

By the time Billie Farnsworth called Lee Harvey back that morning, she'd finished her second cup of coffee and was ready for her. Billie had already found out from Art Bonnell that Lee and Sid wanted to give a big party on the July Fourth weekend and that Lee would be calling her, so the request came as no surprise. "Lee, honey," Billie told her, "as far as I know, nothing's going on that weekend. Usually, with a tennis tournament, people will throw spontaneous parties, but a big formal bash like yours . . ."

"Not that formal," Lee Harvey said. "I want a big friendly get-together. We want to meet everybody."

That made Billie laugh. "Everybody? You'd better get a caterer."

"We plan to. Sid thought we could set up a tent over the beachfront, have a band and all. Dancing. What do you think?"

"I think it's a terrific idea."

"What I mean is, will you help? See, we really don't know a lot of people. Art Bonnell said you were the one to call."

"I'll be glad to help, Lee," Billie said. "When do you want to get together?"

"Well, it's only a couple of weeks off . . ."

"I've got a client for lunch. Why don't you come by around five? I'll give you a drink and we'll make a list."

"That would be terrific, Billie. I really appreciate it."

"Forget it. I'm the Colony housemother. Didn't Art tell you?"

28

"Something like that."

"See you later, then."

"Oh, Billie, one more thing. The boys locked themselves into this weird little room over the garage yesterday. Like a padded cell or something. What is it? Did you ever see it?"

"Oh, honey, that's just the primal scream room. A while ago, some of the folks out here got into all that—you know, you shriek yourself into mental health. I forgot to tell you about it."

"That's a relief, I guess. I'd better take the lock off. Anyway, thanks again."

She seemed like a nice-enough person, Billie reflected, and she had these gorgeous legs. Billie knew about legs, because her own had always been considered pretty spectacular. After hanging up on Lee, Billie walked into her bedroom, took off her robe, and had a good look at herself in the full-length mirror on the closet door. What she saw did not entirely displease her. Not bad for an old broad. A lean body, no fat on it, and in a soft light it still looked terrific. All right, so my ass sags a little, she thought, and my tits droop a bit too much and my skin hangs a little loose and my face has taken too much sun over the years. So what? She was fifty-two years old and she couldn't complain. She was free and had money and she was going to give herself a few more good seasons in the sun before she'd allow winter to shut her down. What hadn't she tried for a while? Love? That was for kids.

3

Dorothy Ferrero heard her husband, Victor, drive into the garage and come into the house through the kitchen, and she waited for him to call out a greeting. He must have known she would be home, though he might have forgotten about the theater, so it surprised her when he neither called out nor came up the stairs to find her. Dorothy got up from her dressing table, put on a robe, and went out into the hallway. She could hear Michael coughing and a blur of voices from the TV set in his room, but nothing from downstairs. "Michael?" she said.

"Yeah, Mom?"

"Turn that thing down. Your father's home."

She heard Michael's door close; then she went to the head of the stairs and leaned over the banister. "Victor?" she cried out.

Still no answer. Dorothy walked down the stairs and peeked into the kitchen. It was empty. She turned away, went into the living room, and saw him. He was standing in the middle of the room and staring out the picture window at the beach and the rocks, over which the larger waves of a moderate surf broke in showers of fine spray. Two pelicans flew past, skimming the froth, their large, ungainly beaks poised like scimitars above the heaving water. And still Victor Ferrero remained motionless. The setting sun glared against the far corner of the glass and shed a golden beam across the foam. Victor, frozen in some darkness of spirit she had sensed in him only occasionally before, did not move. "Victor?"

"Yes."

"I heard you come in."

"Yeah." He didn't turn to look at her, but suddenly kicked off his shoes and headed out. "I want to walk a bit," he said, pushing open the door onto the sun deck and striking out across the sand toward the water's edge. She watched him go, then went into the kitchen for ice. When she came back into the living room, he had vanished from sight, so she made herself a drink, sat down, and waited for him to return.

Victor found her still sitting there when he came back twenty minutes later. He had been running, she guessed, because his face was flushed. But then she realized the color was one of grief, not health. Dorothy bided her time, steeling herself for news she knew she wouldn't want to hear. "Want a drink?" she asked.

"Sure." He sank into a chair across from her, groped on the coffee table for cigarettes. "A little vodka, on the rocks."

She got the vodka, dropped ice cubes into a tall glass, and poured a stiff one. He took the drink from her, exhaled smoke into the air around his eyes, and coughed. "I thought you were going to quit," she said.

"I did. Two days ago. I quit several times a month. That's how I know I can do it."

"For a doctor, you say the strangest things."

"I have no willpower," he explained, smiling faintly. "Like Oscar Wilde, I find that the easiest way to cope with my vices is to indulge them."

He looked away from her again, stirred restlessly, glass in hand, to avoid the unavoidable. "We have theater tickets," she said. "Something new at the Forum. Did you forget?"

"No. But I don't think I can make it."

"Maybe I can still give the tickets away. Want me to try? It's pretty late."

"You go. Call Billie or Dee. They're crazy about the theater. Maybe one of them can go."

"Billie's already seen it. She went to a preview. It's a new play."

"Any good?"

She shook her head. "Billie says no, but she only likes Neil Simon. I could try Dee," she said, "but I'd rather not. Why don't we just forget it, or maybe try to give the tickets away."

"I'm sorry. I had an emergency of sorts."

"Bad, huh?"

"Yeah." He looked away from her. "Where's the gang?"

"Michael's upstairs, nursing a creative cough. Terry isn't home yet. I don't know where she is."

He ran a hand over his face, shook his head, and crushed his largely unconsumed cigarette out in the nearest ashtray. "I still think you ought to go."

"I did want to see it, but we can go some other night," she said. "I'll ask the Kramers if they can use the tickets, okay?"

He didn't answer, but stared moodily into his glass, holding it out there in front of him like a delicate, fragile talisman of some sort. Dorothy started for the phone, but his voice, tight with suppressed anger and grief, stopped her. "I've lost him," he said.

She whirled on him. "Evan?"

He nodded.

"Oh, God," she said, sick with the knowledge of it inside her now and spreading like a foul stain over everything. "Oh, shit!"

"For Christ's sake, Victor, if there's nothing wrong with me," Evan Gilbert had said to him, "what the hell do I have to go into a hospital for?"

"I didn't say there wasn't anything wrong with you," Victor answered. "Just that I didn't find anything."

They were sitting in Victor's office, and Evan Gilbert looked amused. He could gaze beyond Victor up toward the Hollywood hills, where the sun had just begun to burn away the early-morning mist and turn it into smog. Victor had never liked that view and had arranged his desk so he could sit with his back to it. After all these years, he still thought and felt like an Easterner; all that lush greenery, all those palms, made him feel uneasy, as if they mocked his origins. Victor's office was practically bare, except for his desk, a couple of chairs, his medical books, and pictures of Dorothy and the kids. A single undistinguished hunting print adorned his walls. He liked the feeling of being in a cell; it was a place to work, not to bask in luxury like some movie producer. Evan Gilbert, who had known him for so long and so well, understood his uneasiness and its source. It made him smile.

"What's so funny?"

"Nothing," Evan said. "Well?"

"Evan, ordinarily I don't even do these basic little physicals like the one you just had. I'm a fancy surgeon. I worked this one up for you because you're an old friend."

"I appreciate that," Evan said. "I thought as long as I was in town . . ."

"Yeah, of course."

"The point is, roomie, you didn't find anything. You medical boys—"

"I don't need any of your testy little lectures now about what a bunch of hopeless quacks we all are," Victor said. "You can save that for your pop biology books and your wisecracks for the talk shows. There's obviously something wrong with you, and I'm trying to find out what it is."

"I'm getting old, Victor. So are you. We all have back pains, we all have to go to the bathroom a little more often."

Victor sighed and leaned back in his chair. "I can't make you do anything, old buddy. It's up to you." Irritated, he quickly tugged open the upper-right-hand drawer of his desk and produced a crumpled pack of cigarettes, then began groping around for matches. "Goddamm it. I can never find . . ."

Evan smiled and crossed one long elegant leg over the other. "And how many of those do you smoke a day?"

"Not more than two or three hundred," Victor growled, jamming an unfiltered butt into his mouth and producing a match. "Ah." He lit up and exhaled. "But only when I'm nervous."

"What are you nervous about?"

"You, Evan. You always make me nervous."

"My God, look at you," Evan Gilbert said. "And you call yourself a healer! I wouldn't let you trim my cuticles!"

Victor ignored the sarcasm and slammed the drawer shut. "Yes or no?"

Evan did not answer immediately. He scratched the tip of his nose with one finger and shifted about in his chair to avoid his friend's disconcertingly direct stare. "Well, yes," he said, after it became

34

clear to him that Victor was not to be put off. "I suppose that's why I came to see you, isn't it?"

Victor grunted and reached for the phone, but Evan suddenly stood up, caught himself, as if not quite properly balanced, then strolled casually to the window. "Is that it? That kind of thing?" Victor asked.

Evan nodded. "Yes," he said. "Sometimes it's worse." He turned to look out the window at the hazy hills. "Victor, what do you *think* is wrong with me?" he asked.

"I wouldn't presume to guess," Victor answered. "It could be nothing. Really. But we ought to find out."

The tall man leaned back against the windowsill, folded his arms, and gazed calmly at the doctor. "What's involved here?" he wanted to know. "A couple of days? I'm supposed to fly to Washington on Thursday for those committee hearings on genetics." He smiled faintly. "I'm preaching to our elected lower orders."

"You'll have to postpone," Victor said.

"Really? I'm not sure I can."

"Really. Make the time, Evan."

"What's so complicated?"

"You want details?"

"Of course," Evan said. "You know I'm a stickler for facts."

"We have to do an EMG and a special tap called a lumbar puncture," Victor explained. "I also want a myelogram."

"Which is?"

"We inject a dye into your spinal canal so we can X-ray it."

"It doesn't sound like fun."

"It isn't," Victor said. "If we did all these tests at once, we'd probably kill you, and Jennifer would sue."

"I supppose I could put off the Senate of the United States for you, Victor," Evan said. "But my God, what do you expect to find or to do about it if you do find something? In five thousand years of recorded medical history, you guys can't even come up with a cure for the common cold."

"Look, Evan, I'm not going to argue with you," Victor said, reaching for the phone again. "Go home. Get Jennifer to cook you up a great last meal. You won't be eating again for twenty-four hours."

Evan pushed himself away from the window and headed for the

door. "What's the *plat du jour* at this three-star slaughterhouse of yours? Tapioca?"

Victor laughed as he began to dial a number. Evan Gilbert waved to him and quietly shut the door behind him as he left.

"You're certain, Vic?" Dorothy asked her husband. "Even you make mistakes . . ."

"No mistakes. Not this time," Victor said. "Evan's going to die."

"But what does he have? Cancer?"

Victor nodded. "Yes, a very bad form of it."

"What, exactly?"

"It's called an ependymoma," he explained in a tight, hoarse voice. "It attacks the spinal cord and it's one hundred percent fatal."

"How much time does he have?"

"Hard to say. A few months, maybe, if he responds well to treatment. There are a few things we can do, but not many."

She went over then and sat down beside him, but she didn't touch him. She knew how tightly he was holding on to himself, and she couldn't make herself risk an outpouring of grief. Not yet. Not now.

"Call the Kramers," he said.

"I will."

"I'm sorry I told you like this."

"Is there an easier way? I'm glad you told me. I'd have worried about you all evening."

Victor suddenly bounced to his feet, fled to the bar, and there began an endless puttering among glasses and bottles and a myriad of small objects, anything to keep himself physically occupied, constantly in motion, like a dancing master tiptoeing over a floor strewn with carpet tacks.

"Victor, I feel useless," Dorothy said, not knowing then what else she could tell him.

The glasses rattled on the bar as his hand exploded against its polished surface; it shook the room. "We're *all* useless!" he said. "All this fancy training I had—useless! There's not a single thing I can do about it, not one!"

She suddenly couldn't stand it. She needed a moment or two by herself, so she ran upstairs and into their bedroom. She couldn't cry yet, not yet, but she stood by their window for a few minutes and looked out at the sea, at the endless dull, rhythmic wash of it over the sand, providing not relief but merely a plodding reminder of the present, of the reality and the boredom of time passing. This monotonous rolling in and out, this wash of gray water over so many billions of tiny stones and shells, fossils out of time, so immortal in their indestructibility. . . . *When did I first become afraid of death?* Dorothy wondered. *I was five years old, exactly. My father dropped dead on the bathroom floor, just like that. No warnings, no long lingering illness. I wasn't even there to see it. There was no viewing of the body, either. He was just gone.* . . .

When Dorothy walked back into the living room ten or fifteen minutes later, Victor was still there, staring. She sat down beside him again. "I'm sorry," she said.

He put an arm around her then and they sat there in silence for a long time. They both had a tight hold on their emotions, and maybe it would have been better, she thought later, if they'd let their grief surface right away, but they'd always prided themselves on their self-control, and to Victor it had become a professional necessity. No doctor could afford or could permit himself the luxury of too much grief; it would have torn him apart, made him useless to his patients as well as to himself. So they sat there, husband and wife, hugging each other in the twilight, and waited for the worst of it to pass. "You know, I don't remember ever wanting to be anything but a doctor," he said at last. "It made me feel . . . safe. *I* had the secret. *I* could beat the game. . . ."

She touched his cheek and was startled to feel how cold it was. "If Evan's going to die, Victor," she said as calmly as she could, "it's not your fault."

"Christ, I'm not blaming myself. It's just that sometimes I get tired of playing God," he said. "It's such a lousy charade."

"It's more than that, isn't it?"

"Oh, we can work a little magic," he continued, taking her hand and holding it very tightly, "a very *little* magic. We've mastered a few small, imperfect tricks. We've built some complicated little machines. But what we all want—ah, that one eludes us."

"Sweetheart," Dorothy said very quietly, "please stop it."

He squeezed her hand and stood up. "Okay, I know. Want another drink?"

37

"No."

"Let's go out to dinner somewhere," he suggested, "just the two of us. Michael's all right?"

"Oh, sure. He's got the set on and his eyeballs are turning red, that's all," she said. "He'll be okay tomorrow. His temperature's down. I'll leave Terry a note."

"Go get dressed, then."

"Where do you want to go?"

"We'll think of something. Somewhere quiet and dark."

She hurried upstairs to change. On her way back she stopped by Michael's room and stuck her head inside. The boy was flat on his back against the pillows, his eyes riveted to the screen, where some mindless fantasy cooked up by the TV geniuses was spinning itself out for his benefit. "Hi."

"Hi, Mom." His eyes never wavered from the picture. "Where's Dad?"

"Downstairs. He's had a very tough day," she explained. "We're going out to dinner. He'll be up later. Okay?"

"I guess."

"Are you okay?"

"Fine, Mom."

She blew him a kiss, shut the door, and started down the stairs. Through the closed door of the hall bathroom she could hear Victor heaving into the bowl. Dorothy waited until it was over and he had flushed the toilet, then hurried to meet him. He came out looking pale and old and very tired, and she took him in her arms. They stood there in the hallway and hugged without saying anything; then he took her hand again and they left.

They drove into the hills above Topanga, to a self-styled inn named after some consciousness-raising group, where the waitresses wore long folksy gowns and the emphasis was on health foods and organic cooking. The place was falsely rustic and the prices high, but the salads were splendid and they knew they wouldn't run into the tonier Malibu crowd there. They wanted very much to be alone, just the two of them together. And not until the coffee came and they could think of nothing trivial to talk about anymore did either of them mention Evan Gilbert again. It was Dorothy who broke the unspoken pact; she asked her husband if Evan himself had been informed.

"No," Victor murmured. "He's still in Washington. He'll be back next week sometime. They're supposed to move into the Weaver house over the Fourth."

"They're going through with that?"

"I suppose so. Why not? What difference will it make? It might be a good thing," he said. "He'll have the sun and the sea this summer. . . ."

"Yes, and Jennifer. She'll be a help. Thank God she's a young woman."

"She'll need more than youth. It's going to be very rough."

"I think she loves Evan very much. And she strikes me as a very strong person."

"I hope so."

"What are you going to tell him?"

"What can I tell him, Dottie?"

"He'll want the truth."

"Yes, I know," Victor said. "Yes, I'm afraid he will. I guess that's what I'm most afraid of right now. . . ."

4

Jim Wharton bent slightly at the knees as he took his position at the net facing his opponents' backhand service court. It was match point at last, in the third set of this grueling "friendly" weekend doubles match that had taken very nearly two hours to complete, and Jim Wharton reminded himself to stay loose but ready, his racket poised to punch the volley away for a winner if the ball should come his way. Behind him he could hear his partner, Burt Frankel, bounce the ball in front of him once, twice, three times before tossing it up into the air over his head for the service. Burt Frankel had a really good serve; it had not been broken all morning.

Across from Jim Wharton, Harry McKay waited, seemingly nonchalant but ready. On the forehand side, standing just behind the service line, Dan Lefkowitz looked grim and angry. Jim Wharton had all he could do to repress a smile. This victory would be sweet, sweeter than last week's skunking by far.

Burt Frankel threw the ball up at last, and his metal racket flashed in the air as it came down over the ball. The serve, sneaky fast, picked up the backhand corner line, and Harry lunged for it, sending a high, short lob toward Wharton, who measured it calmly, then smashed it at Lefkowitz' feet for an easy winner. Jim laughed. "Hot damn!" he said, and turned to shake his partner's hand.

Lefkowitz whirled on Harry McKay. "Goddamm it, Harry," he said, "he's been serving you in the corner all morning! Why weren't you ready?"

"Dan, you're a sore loser," Harry said very pleasantly as he headed for the net to shake Jim Wharton's hand. "We just got beat, that's all."

"Shit," Dan Lefkowitz said. "I still say we should take these guys easy."

"You haven't won a match off us in a month," Jim Wharton said, grinning now. "You played over your heads today just to stay close. You'll never beat us. We should go back to a round robin."

"I'll double-or-nothing next week," Dan Lefkowitz snarled. "You'll run out of luck one of these days, Wharton."

"You think so, Dan?"

Lefkowitz stormed toward the sidelines. "You're goddamn right," he said, retrieving his gear and heading quickly for the locker room.

"Next Saturday, same time?" Jim Wharton called out.

"Yeah," Dan said. "For four hundred."

"Not me, Dan," Harry McKay said calmly. "You're on your own. I don't like playing tennis for money."

"I'll carry us both," Dan Lefkowitz said. "Maybe, with no money riding on it, you won't choke."

Harry McKay shook his head deprecatingly, but Dan Lefkowitz was already out the gate on the way to his car.

"Wow," Burt Frankel said, "what a sorehead."

"Oh, he's all right," Harry said, sitting down on the courtside bench and toweling the sweat off the back of his neck and arms. "I enjoyed that. It was a good match."

"You guys *should* beat us, you know," Jim Wharton said. "You've got the best game of all of us, Harry, and Dan is a real competitor."

"Dan beats himself," Burt Frankel observed. "Stay close to him or get the jump on him, and he starts picking his partner's game apart. He may be a winner around the studios, but at tennis he's strictly a loser."

"Maybe he's right about me," Harry McKay said. "I really don't care who wins. I mean, nobody here is going to Wimbledon, right? I play for fun, and I don't like this betting thing we've gotten into, either."

"It was Dan's idea," Jim Wharton reminded Harry. "If he wants to spice it up betting, we'll let him. What the hell, we can all afford it, can't we?"

Harry shook his head. "That isn't the point," he explained. "It changes everything. Dan cares so much, it's like losing a deal or a client for him. I don't like it."

"Okay," Jim Wharton said, clapping Harry lightly on the shoulder as he prepared to leave the court, "after next week we'll stop. But Dan needs the lesson, and we're going to give it to him."

"Jim, you're a wonder," Burt Frankel told him, "a fucking marvel. You could make a moral case for the hatchet killing of somebody's grandmother. Here you are, gouging old Dan out of his pocket money just for the fun of it, and it's all because he needs a good lesson." Burt laughed. "Yeah, you're a wonder!"

"If you ever need a good lawyer . . ."

"You bet," Burt Frankel said. "I wouldn't want you against me in any courtroom. My God, you'd send me to the gas chamber for the good of my soul, wouldn't you?"

"Maybe," Jim Wharton answered, "maybe. For that *and* my fee."

They left the court together and headed for the clubhouse.

Dan Lefkowitz had already driven away, but Jim wasn't offended, and neither were the other two men. The four of them had been playing tennis together at the Malibu Racquet Club, where Jim was a member, every Saturday morning for two years, and they'd all become used to Dan's evil temper. Before the regular game had hardened into set teams with money riding on the outcome, Dan's bad sportsmanship and gloating when he won hadn't bothered them, though Wharton realized now, as he stood under the hot stream of water in the shower stall, that Harry was probably right. The game was turning ugly and perhaps wouldn't survive the next match, because he and Burt would surely win it. Harry would indeed choke if it was close, or Dan himself would blow it by losing his temper. There was no way, Jim reflected, that he and Burt could lose to McKay and Lefkowitz, not with money on the line, no matter how small the sum. Jim Wharton hadn't gotten to where he was in life by misreading people's characters.

The poor bastard wanted to win so badly, just to establish his own superiority, that he wound up beating himself. Behind a desk, with the phone glued to his ear and a big deal in the works, Dan Lefkowitz couldn't lose; on a tennis court, made to feel inadequate and out of his league, he couldn't win, not with Harry McKay for a partner.

Harry was exactly what Dan wasn't—tall, easygoing, a Gentile from Boston who had inherited money and a house in the Colony, married wealthily to a beautiful ash-blond Gentile wife, and had drifted through life on his looks and his unearned income, without ever having had to work hard or sweat for a dollar. Dan probably hated him, and how could you win in doubles if you hated your own partner?

Burt Frankel, on the other hand, was ten years younger than the other three, a Beverly Hills Jewish prince who'd played on the Stanford tennis team, gone to fat in his mid-thirties, never been married, and inherited a department store from his daddy, which meant he didn't have to work at all to live well, and quite simply didn't care about much of anything, including tennis. But he couldn't be rattled, and basically he despised Dan Lefkowitz for being too much like his own father, a ghetto product with ghetto manners, and so he enjoyed trouncing him, relished watching him make a snarling fool of himself when he lost.

No, there was no way Jim and Burt were going to lose to Harry and Dan, Jim was absolutely sure of that, and the more money they bet each week, the worse it would get, until Dan would either storm off the court for good or make such a scene that Harry would refuse to play with him anymore. And that would be the end of their regular game, but so what? They'd be able very easily to replace Dan, who didn't even live in Malibu and drove out there every Saturday morning from his pagan mansion in the Bel Air hills. Too bad. Jim had sort of liked Dan Lefkowitz when they'd first met, over two years ago now, after Jim had taken him on as a client in that plagiarism suit against Continental. A lot of fun that had been, yes, and an easy suit to win, too, the offense committed had been so patently obvious. Jim had liked Dan then, had admired his guts and his temper, his arrogant refusal to be intimidated even by a big studio, and with so much at stake. That had been the side of Dan Lefkowitz that Jim Wharton had admired, because Jim himself, if Dan had only known it, had also come up from nothing. He wasn't at all the Ivy League WASP Dan thought he was. No, he was a street fighter, too, with an instinct for the jugular, and Dan Lefkowitz, who had seen him in action in a lawsuit, ought to have understood that side of him better than he did. It made Jim lose respect for Dan, to have been misread like that. It was too bad, really.

44

When Jim Wharton finally stepped out of the shower, Harry McKay was sitting on the locker-room bench and putting on his shoes. He looked up at the lawyer and shook his head in a puzzled way. "You know, Jim," he said, "I've been sitting here trying to figure Dan out. I don't know what he wants from me, do you? I mean, I play a better game than he does. Half the time at least I make the winning shot. What more do you suppose Dan expects from me?"

"I'll tell you, Harry," Jim Wharton said. "Dan is a Jew, and he's short and not too good-looking. What he'd like to be is a tall, handsome Gentile. Now, if you can do that for Dan, your troubles with him are over."

Harry's jaw sagged slightly open, and then he began to laugh; he slapped his thigh, threw his head back, and roared. Jim Wharton grinned back at him, then finished drying himself off, dressed, and went upstairs into the clubhouse to look for his daughter.

Gail Hessian had been about to unplug the phone all morning, but had resisted the temptation. She wanted to work uninterruptedly on her novel, but she knew the station would call her, and she couldn't exactly pretend not to be in. She had foolishly promised them to try to set up an interview with Jim Wharton, and she knew that Alex West, her producer at *Dateline News*, would keep after her until she got it. The fact that Jim Wharton never gave interviews hadn't bothered Alex at all; he was certain that Gail would be able to get one. After all, she had never failed him yet, had she?

For nearly two hours now Gail Hessian had been sitting at her typewriter, trying to transcribe her tape-recorded notes and edit the copy as she went along, but it wasn't turning out very well. It was really a lot harder to write a novel than she had imagined when she first got the idea. She had talked it over with her agent first, and then her lawyer, before dashing off that twenty-two-page outline, on the basis of which some crazy New York publisher had actually offered her a contract. She'd signed it, of course, banked the first advance, and now here she was at last trying to write the damn thing.

It had seemed like such a good idea at the time, everyone had been so enthusiastic, so what had gone wrong? Gail had never doubted her ability to write a novel, and she did have a good story to tell. It was to be a thinly fictionalized account of her own career in this business, about how she had risen from being a schoolteacher in

Van Nuys to air-watch traffic reporter to weather lady and finally to anchor person on the top TV news show in L.A. Yes, quite a story, full of drama, humor, and pathos.

Gail Hessian had been the first woman in TV news to crack the male barrier in this town, to break out of being what women were supposed to be on the air when she'd started, either reporters covering the cutesy-pie side of the news or weather readers. She had made it, made it big, and with no help at all from the women's movement either, but entirely on her own. She had played the game then the only way a woman could play it in a man's world, by exploiting her looks and by coldly, ruthlessly climbing over the dead and dying until she had reached the top. It would make a hell of a novel, she knew that, and so did her agent and her lawyer and her editor. Now, why couldn't she seem to get it off the ground? That was the only reason she'd rented this apartment in Malibu and taken a month's leave from her job, wasn't it? It didn't really have anything to do with the fact that she and Alex weren't seeing each other anymore, except professionally, did it?

Gail Hessian had also sensed that her career at the station had sort of come to a turning point, that it needed a jolt, a push of some kind. Yes, she had a good contract; she made two hundred and twenty-five thousand dollars a year, and everybody liked her. But she was thirty-seven now. Younger women were coming up in back of her, and she tended to be a little paranoid about it. It was an insecure business; you always needed insurance. You had to be wanted, a usable commodity, or they'd drop you very quickly. Gail couldn't have stood that; she had no life, really, except this one that she'd made for herself. What middle-aged woman, except for Barbara Walters, had ever managed to remain a TV news star? No, she had to find something to keep her on top.

The novel had seemed a very good way to achieve that goal, especially if she could hit the best-seller lists with it, auction it off to the paperback houses for a handsome sum, then let some big studio buy the movie rights for an even bigger chunk of loot. She'd become a nationwide celebrity, not just a local one. The whole scheme had seemed like an unbeatable parlay to her, with the added delightful prospect of impending wealth. But nobody had told her anything about how tough it could be to write a book. It wasn't at all simply a question of talking it into a tape recorder and then transferring it to print. She'd been at it less than a week now, and she had nothing, literally nothing usable.

When they'd first discussed the book, her agent had mentioned the possibility of bringing in a ghost writer to help her, but Gail had resisted. She'd always done everything on her own, and this was going to be no different. What was the big deal about writing a book? All she needed, she'd assured him and herself, was the time to get it organized and off the ground. Once she had a chapter-by-chapter outline and fifty or sixty usable pages, she could go back to the station and her job and work on the book in the evenings and on weekends. That had been the idea, but it wasn't turning out that way for her. A week of her time had passed, and she still had nothing to show for it on paper. And Alex had been no help or comfort to her at all; what he cared about was the Wharton interview. The man was impossible. No wonder she'd walked out on the son of a bitch.

He called just before noon. "Hello, love, how are you?"

"You don't give a shit how I am," Gail answered.

"Not quite accurate, my sweet," he said. "I do care for you—"

"Alex, I'm working."

"How is it coming?"

"Terrific," she said, "just terrific. I've got this character in here who's a renegade limey who becomes the head of a TV news department. He's a real turkey. You'll love him."

"Do you think I shall?" he asked. "How nice."

"Good-bye, Alex. Don't call me, I'll call you."

"Just a minute, darling. What about our Wharton interview?"

"You know he won't give me one. We've already discussed this a hundred times."

"Sweetheart," he said, "I know you'll overcome this trifling difficulty."

"Alex," she told him, as if addressing a troubled but retarded relative, "I've already explained to you that my first job this month is getting my book organized."

"Easy," he said. "You'll have that in shape in another week or so."

"Horseshit," she said. "And secondly, Jim Wharton is smart, tough, and very well-connected. He stopped giving interviews twenty years ago, when he moved out here from Chicago and found himself labeled a Mafia lawyer in the press."

"Well, he is, isn't he?"

47

"*Was*, Alex, was. Now he's a respectable citizen who contributes heavily to charity and both political parties. Why would he want to talk to me?"

"You'll find a reason, I know," he cheerfully assured her. "You might begin by reminding him that his name keeps coming up over and over in connection with Rancho El Mirador, as well as every other big land grab we've ever done a story on, like that one about Vegas interests wanting to build the sports complex in the Valley. I should think he'd want to explain his position in these deals."

"He won't, Alex."

"You'll see him in the Colony, darling. You'll get to know him well."

"In three more weeks?"

"Gail, dear, I understood you'd rented the place month-to-month. Even after you come back to work—"

"I did take it, at least for the summer. But it isn't in the Colony, as you know damn well."

"Malibu is such a small, friendly community. I understand he plays tennis. Do you play tennis?"

"No."

"Buy a sweet little tennis outfit. Bill us for it. One that shows off your figure, love."

"Fuck you, Alex."

"No, love, not me. *Him*."

She started to scream at him, but he'd already hung up, of course. With shaking fingers she lit a cigarette, her first of the day, and walked out onto the balcony of her apartment to get a breath of air. From up here she could look down on the sunbathers and kids romping around the pool area of her condominium or up to the hills and the line of cars snaking down Malibu Canyon Road toward the beaches. God, how Alex's attitude infuriated her. All he wanted was this interview, even if she had to go to bed with Jim Wharton to get it. He'd made that clear enough, and from what Gail had heard about Wharton, that wouldn't be too hard to bring about, though it didn't mean he would talk to her. Surely the man didn't spill his guts out to the women he fucked; half the Hollywood hookers in town would be sure to know everything about him. Yes, he had *that* kind of reputation. Also, Wharton would know who she was. That might titillate him sexually, but it sure as hell wouldn't get him to talk. Alex was just being a creep about the whole business.

She exhaled smoke, flicked ashes away, and tried to get her mind back on her novel. It wasn't easy. She couldn't remember one single thing about it now, and the whole idea of having to get back to it filled her with despair. Tomorrow, she decided, she'd unplug the phone and leave it unplugged. That way Alex would have to come out and see her himself, if he had to talk to her. She'd like that, she decided. She'd like to see him ask her for something once, just once, without being in a position to order her to do it. That would be a novelty.

Jim Wharton was a big man whose size alone could intimidate people. He had been a three-letter man at Boston College, which he had attended on a football scholarship, and he moved with the heavy grace of an ex-athlete, so that some people weren't immediately aware of his bulk. At business meetings, however, or at union bargaining sessions, or when he rose to address judge and jury in a courtroom, he looked formidable. He had thinning blond hair that he combed straight back without a part, a round beefy face with a strong jaw and wide mouth, flat cheekbones, and small, icy light gray eyes that seemed able to peer through walls. He usually spoke softly, in a gruff, raspy baritone, but he always made himself heard. He had a not undeserved reputation for being tough, unforgiving, and ruthless where his own interests and those of his clients were concerned. People realized soon after meeting him that he could not be ignored and that you went against him at considerable risk. Now, as he stood lounging idly at the railing of the clubhouse terrace overlooking the court where his daughter was rallying with young Tad Bonnell, he seemed affable and harmless enough, but his presence could hardly pass unnoticed. The seven or eight other people on the club terrace all nodded or spoke to him. The girl behind the reservations counter came out twice to ask him if he wanted or needed anything. Both Julie and Tad spotted him immediately and waved to him, and he waved back. "Take your time," he said.

"Just five more minutes, Dad," Julie called up to him. "Tad's working on my backhand, and it needs it!"

Jim Wharton nodded and smiled. It was easy to see that he loved his daughter. He leaned on the terrace railing and never took his eyes off her, as she moved gracefully around the court returning the shots Tad Bonnell hit at her. She was a nice kid, Jim Wharton told himself, and smart, too, but perhaps just a little too fond of young

49

Tad. He'd have to keep an eye on that relationship. Julie was only eighteen, and Jim had plans for her, plans that did not include her getting involved with the penniless tennis-playing son of a penniless washed-up old pro. Jim had been too smart to oppose openly this romance between his daughter and young Tad. He'd figured it wouldn't last, but it had gone on, he realized, quite awhile now, over a year. There would come a day when Jim would have to break it up, and there were a lot of ways he could do that, but it could be risky. Jim had a good instinct for that kind of maneuver, and he knew it was not yet time, things had not yet gone too far. Jim would know when they had, and he would act.

"Hey, Mr. Wharton," Tad called out, "watch this!" The boy hit a long looping shot toward the backhand corner, and Julie turned her body, planted her feet, and stroked the shot back on a line cross-court. Tad barely got to it, and laughed as he lobbed it down the middle. Julie tried to get set for an overhead, but swung too soon. The ball hit the rim of her racket and bounced straight up into the air. Both the kids laughed.

"What the hell was that?" Jim asked, grinning.

"But did you see the backhand?" Tad answered.

"Sure. But now you'd better work on her overhead," Jim said.

"Oh, Daddy, you're such a drag!" Julie said.

"Three more," Tad told her, "then we'll call it a day." He picked up the balls and again hit one toward Julie's backhand.

"Hello, Mr. Wharton."

Jim turned. Terry Ferrero, the doctor's daughter, was standing beside him. She was dressed in tight terry-cloth shorts and a loose cotton shirt open nearly to her waist, and the sight of her startled him. "Hello, Terry," he said. My God, this kid was a beauty; she had a body on her like a goddamn movie star. "How are you?"

"I'm fine, thanks. Hey, there's a call for you downstairs. You can take it in Mike's office," Terry said. "He sent me up to tell you. How's Julie doing?"

"Improving," Jim said.

"Since she and Tad began seeing each other, boy, her game has moved up several notches," Terry observed. "I mean, Tad's terrific, isn't he?"

"Yeah," Jim said. "Excuse me."

"Oh, sure," Terry chirped. "See ya." And she moved off toward the Jacuzzi area, as Jim headed for the stairs.

Mike Kenmore, the nervous, bearded young man who was the manager of the club, saw him coming and stepped out of his office. "In here, Mr. Wharton," he said. "I think it's long distance. They called your house first."

"Thanks, Mike." Jim Wharton picked up the receiver from Mike's desk as the latter shut the door behind him to give Jim privacy. "Yeah? This is Wharton."

"Jim, we have a problem."

The voice at the other end of the line was one Jim had never heard before. "Who is this?" he asked.

"Kerrigan, Dudley Kerrigan. We've never met. I need to see you."

"I left instructions never to be called here. This is a public place."

"I'm afraid it's urgent, Jim. I'm new on this, but it's a company matter."

"How do I know that?"

"It's a three-three-o, Jim, concerning our investments down south."

"We're on a public phone," Jim snapped. "I never discuss business on the phone."

"I'm flying in tomorrow night."

"Sorry, Kerrigan, but I'll be in Las Vegas," Jim said. "I have a prior commitment I can't break. The company knows that."

"How about next Wednesday?"

"Fine. Six o'clock, the usual place."

"Jim, it's very serious—"

"We'll discuss it on Wednesday."

Jim hung up but remained in Mike Kenmore's office long enough to weigh the implications of such a call. It had to be an urgent matter, he knew that, but he hoped it wouldn't interfere with his summer plans. Jim would be fifty-five years old in August, and he'd begun telling himself it was time to begin slowing down a little. He'd paid his dues, hadn't he? Why couldn't they remember that back in Chicago?

5

It had been unreasonable, Charlie Wigham realized, to insist that Brian Golding, the head of a major studio, read the script himself. Golding was probably besieged daily by such requests and had hundreds of scripts piled up in his office. But Charlie had been upset by Golding's silence. There was an old studio maxim to the effect that no minion in the movie business ever lost his job by saying no to a project; they only got into trouble when they recommended something. So finally Charlie had written again to Brian Golding directly, calling on whatever reserves of credit he might have with him, and actually begged him for two hours of his reading time.

Two months had passed since Charlie had sent him the script of *Pale Moon Rising*, and he had heard nothing. Then, at last, Golding's secretary had called, around the middle of June, and now here Charlie was, on the Wednesday of that following week, sitting on the couch outside Golding's office at Continental Pictures, waiting to get in to see the great man.

When Charlie had first contacted Golding, he'd been full of confidence, but a lot of it had been eroded away in the interim, and Charlie was pretty nervous by now. He tried to look cool and unconcerned, but he didn't think he was fooling Golding's secretary at all. Her name was Velma, and it suited her. She was a plain, middle-aged woman with iron-gray hair, who looked as if she could type five thousand words a minute and who sat there, impervious to pain, flicking all ten fingers efficiently over her electric keyboard. She paused only to glance up at him from time to time with what Charlie was certain was faintly mocking pity. How many other suppliants Velma must have seen come and go over the years from her safe little perch, he thought, and how boring the routine must have become for her by now. Charlie uncrossed his legs again, shifted in his seat, leaned back, and yawned; that would show her.

Velma looked up and smiled. "He's still on the phone, Mr. Wigham," she said coolly. "It won't be much longer, I'm sure. I know he's been expecting you."

"Oh, that's okay," Charlie said. "No rush."

The hell there wasn't. When Charlie Wigham had gotten back to L.A. from his European vacation at the end of March, he'd found the movie business not in very good shape. During the two months he'd been away, lazing lavishly with his girlfriend Michelle from one pleasure center to another, the bottom seemed to have fallen out of everything again. Interest rates had gone up and money had become tight. All the major studios, despite some recent successes, were reportedly cutting back on production, and the independents were scrambling around to find any kind of backing.

Charlie should have been worried. He was out of a job, his personal financial reserves were low, and all he had to peddle was the shooting script of *Pale Moon Rising*, the movie with which Charlie hoped to establish himself as a successful independent filmmaker. But for some reason, he hadn't been worried at all. In fact, he'd actually been optimistic.

Charlie Wigham knew that movies were still being made and would always be made, and he was confident he'd find the money to make his. Sure, a few of the sources he'd been counting on might have dried up, but he had plenty of places to go, and he figured he had a lot of credit piled up where it was supposed to count. Besides, he'd reasoned, wasn't this the new era in Hollywood? The day of the independent creative artist who did his own thing and really got it on, for love, truth, beauty, and only tangentially, commerce?

Everybody had been saying that for several years now, and coming up with the statistics to prove it. About seventy percent of all the American movies produced the previous year had been made by independents. The studios still turned out their potboilers, disaster epics, and tearjerkers, but the heart of the business today was the independents. Unencumbered by studio overheads, union featherbedding, and old-fashioned ideas, they had revolutionized the industry and grabbed off the major share of the action. It was a great day for the creators, an exciting time for anyone with talent and ideas. People got to make their films in their own way and without compromising. It wasn't Hollywood anymore, but sort of a new Athens, where every idea man could be his own *auteur*.

Still, what about the money? It had to come from somewhere, either from a studio or a producing firm or an investor. The first thing Charlie had done when he got back from Europe was draw up a budget for *Pale Moon Rising*. It came to exactly $2,418,895, which made it, by studio standards, a real cheapie. But Charlie was confident he could make it for even less than that, if he had to. The figure included a nice fee for himself, a hundred thousand dollars, less money than he'd been making as a TV producer, but Charlie figured it was his first movie and he wouldn't be too greedy. The scripts had come out of mimeograph in early April, and for Charlie it had been magic time. He'd invited some friends over to his Malibu place, read the thing aloud to them himself, and the very next day he'd started out after the money. He'd decided, of course, to go to a major studio first. The six majors still accounted for most of the two-and-a-half-billion-dollar yearly gross, so it was only natural Charlie would go that route. He'd been very, very confident.

Charlie Wigham had had every reason to feel confident. After all, he wasn't just some fly-by-night newcomer with nothing going for him but youth and chutzpah. Charlie Wigham had an impressive track record. In 1974, at the age of thirty-one, he'd taken over an ailing TV series produced by Gemini Productions on the Fox lot and made a hit out of it. *Larkin*, starring Dan Gregory, had been thirty-fourth in the ratings, had never had a good review, and was about two million dollars in debt. Three years and seventy-eight episodes later, the show had risen to remain constantly in the top twenty, had acquired more than its share of glowing notices, and was no longer in debt. In fact, it had been one of only a handful of non-deficit-financed TV shows in the history of the studio. Charlie Wigham had been very big there for a while. In those three years he'd handled over eighteen million dollars in production costs, and the heads of the studio had let him know that he'd saved them maybe two million. He'd been given the equivalent of the production company's medal of honor, which was a pat on the back and a thank-you-very-much. Charlie had been well-liked there, as well as at the studio.

But Charlie had always been popular around the studios and in the industry in general. Before taking over *Larkin*, he'd been a press agent and an associate producer on half a dozen features. In ten years in the business, he'd worked his way up from a hundred dollars a week as an office boy to two thousand dollars a week as Dan Gregory's overseer. Charlie was very well thought of. He wasn't pushy and he didn't throw his weight around. This was because he'd been brought up in the industry and understood its class system, about how you deferred to stars and studio heads and got in the backs of cars and opened doors, things like that. Charlie had always gotten along well in that atmosphere. He'd been the only producer under forty at Gemini and the only one on the Fox lot who had ever been invited into the executive steam room. All the more reason to think that, when he decided to make his move, checkbooks would flutter open to him. Charlie Wigham was one independent film artist even the old studio dinosaurs could trust. He'd proved himself within the system, and now he had this project of his own, one he believed in totally.

The script of *Pale Moon Rising* had been written by Lester Markham, a sixty-eight-year-old veteran of the Hollywood wars who looked a little like Walter Cronkite and who was kind of a minor poet, Charlie liked to tell people, and a really lovely old man. Markham had directed and turned out some of the better *Larkin* scripts, and he'd responded warmly to the material Charlie had asked him to adapt, a collection of folk tales about a legendary mountain man called Luke, who traveled throughout the land combating evildoers, devils, ghosts, and witches, his only weapon a banjo with genuine golden strings. After a couple of false starts, Markham had turned out what Charlie felt was a really terrific script. "This character of Luke, with his golden-strung banjo, who in his odyssey through the West encounters the occult and mysticism, is authentic American folklore," Charlie had written to Brian Golding at Continental, while also pointing out where the loot was buried: "The marriage of today's country music and the big business of the occult and witchcraft in one script with a modest budget makes, it seems to me, this hip saga a strong commercial entry."

It had made a lot of sense to Charlie Wigham to approach Continental first, partly because Brian Golding, the head of production there, was a friend of his, and, more importantly, because Continental's record division had earned thirty million dollars last year, with artists like Tim Bigbee and the Hive, Cole Winchester, and Dave Spring on its roster. Charlie wanted a Tim Bigbee or a Cole Winchester for his leading role, and the tie-ins had seemed obvious. So, after a telephone conversation, the script had gone off by messenger to Brian Golding, who had promptly turned it over to the Literary Department and left for Europe a few days later without having read it. And now here Charlie Wigham was, two months later, sitting outside Brian Golding's office and about to find out at last what the fate of his script would be at Continental. Charlie had had some other rejections since he'd first written Golding, and he wasn't anywhere near as confident as he had been. It was pretty goddamn nerve-racking, in fact, to have to sit there outside Golding's office and watch Velma, the frozen typing machine, while he was waiting to be summoned into the royal presence. Charlie yawned again, shut his eyes, and leaned his head back against the wall. He wasn't going to let himself be intimidated, no, goddammit, he sure wasn't.

"You can go in now, Mr. Wigham," Velma said twenty minutes later.

Without even glancing at her, Charlie got up slowly and sauntered nonchalantly into Golding's office. "Hello, Brian," he said, closing the door behind him.

"Charlie, I'm sorry," Brian Golding said. "I've been on the phone with New York for a fucking hour. How are you?"

It was really spectacular in here, Charlie thought. It was so dark he could barely see Golding across the room, with all these Tiffany lampshades and the furs on the floor and draped over the couches and things. The place looked like some kind of elegant bordello.

Brian Golding, firmly in touch with the times, as always, had grown a beard since Charlie had last seen him, so their conversation began with a couple of moments on the significance of that, after which Golding said, "Charlie, I hated the script."

Charlie did not flinch, but merely smiled. "Gee, Brian, I'm sorry to hear it," he answered. "I was hoping that at least you'd be lukewarm so maybe I could try and do a sales pitch."

"Nope," Brian Golding said. "Supersoft."

"Well, okay," Charlie said. "I'm sorry the project got handled the way it did."

"Oh, the Literary Department loved it," Brian Golding told him, tossing a reader's report across the desk at him. "Here, you can have it. They didn't knock you out about it. I did. I just don't think it works, and I don't like it. I think it's a phony and has some bad laughs in it."

The whole interview took less than five minutes. Outside, in the parking lot, Charlie read the reader's report. "This screenplay is a joy," it began, and went on from there, with one encomium after another and concluding with a recommendation that it be produced. Charlie was stunned. In all his years at various studios he'd never read this glowing a report on any property ever. He had to suppress a wild impulse to run back upstairs into Brian Golding's office and wave the report at him and say, "What is this? How can you do this to me?"

But he didn't. Instead, on the long drive home, back through the smoggy San Fernando Valley toward Malibu, Charlie composed a long letter to Golding in his head. He would tell him, among other things, that he, Golding, was too hip a cat to play Jack Warner, but Charlie Wigham knew very well, even as he imagined what he'd say, that he'd never mail such a letter. Shit, he thought to himself, this picture might never get made, and he might need a job someday, and Golding could ruin him. Then Charlie comforted himself with the reasoning that Golding's judgment was questionable at best. As a producer himself, before coming to Continental, Golding had turned out two of the biggest bombs of the past five years, pictures that single-handedly had almost sunk two other major studios. Brian Golding had also gone on record that year, in the *Calendar* section of the L.A. *Times*, as saying that a director, a real director, had to be given total freedom. This was a policy, Charlie knew, absolutely guaranteed to bring in every picture late and over budget. Christ, Brian Golding was a wonderful example of how to fail upward in the movie business, Charlie told himself. What the fuck did Brian Golding know about anything? By the time Charlie eased off the Ventura Freeway and turned into Malibu Canyon Road, he'd pretty much put this disastrous meeting behind him and was feeling a little more cheerful. He'd just have to really get down to it now; there were a lot of other ways you could go these days to get your financing.

6

For several days, ever since the first minor heat wave of the summer, Lee Harvey had been seeing the same man walk briskly past her spot on the beach. She always sat about halfway down, facing the ocean, a book resting on her thighs, and she would look up at him as he passed and smile. From the first time she'd seen him, he had never failed to wave to her, and he seemed so friendly and nice. He looked vaguely familiar to her, and she guessed she had probably seen him on TV at some time or other. From his graying good looks and carefully manicured appearance, she had guessed he was an actor, and it flattered her that he would even take notice of her. But then, everyone she'd met in Malibu since she and Sid had moved into the Colony had been friendly; it was typical of the place, she supposed, and probably had nothing to do with her specifically. Both she and Sid had noticed this about Malibu, especially since they'd spent their previous summer on an island off the coast of Maine, where the natives had been closemouthed, surly, and as cold as the icy water that hemmed them in year-round.

On this particular morning, after Lee had waved back, the man turned and came strolling up to her. He was dressed in a bright blue warm-up suit and was sweating, but he was even handsomer than from a distance. He was in his late forties, she guessed, and was a few pounds overweight, but he had startlingly large green eyes, a strong chin, and a really charming, dimpled smile. He was almost too good-looking, she decided, a picture out of some liquor or perfume ad. "Good morning," he said. "Don't you know it's unlucky to read alone?"

"Really? I hadn't heard that."

"Of course," he said, "except in bed, where I find it's the only way to get to sleep. I hope I'm not intruding."

"Oh, no. I see you walking by every day."

"It's my answer to jogging," he explained. "You've probably noticed that everyone else here runs, but I decided last year, when I turned fifty, that I really don't look all that well running, even in my fanciest outfits. At my age, things begin to jiggle a bit here and there when you bounce up and down, so I decided the hell with it. Also, two friends of mine died last year overexercising, one of them on a tennis court and the other one running. Acts of folly, wouldn't you say?"

"Back home," she answered, "I go to a supervised exercise class, just to keep myself trim. I guess it's dangerous to overdo at any age."

"Back home? Where would that be?"

"Appleton, Wisconsin," she said, "on beautiful Lake Winnebago."

"Ah, then you're here for the summer."

"Yes," she said, waving vaguely at the air behind her, "my husband and I rented this place for the season."

"The Dennison house. They rent it every summer and go abroad," he said. "It's a very nice house. You enjoying it?"

"Very much. We really love it here."

"I'm so glad."

"Are you? Why?"

He smiled that dazzling smile at her again and sank to his haunches facing her. "Because that's one of the things about Malibu," he explained. "We all want everyone here to love it and us. Love me, love my life-style. It's so terrific living here, I suppose we feel a bit guilty about it and want outsiders to approve of us. Haven't you noticed?"

She laughed. "Actually, I have. Sid and I have talked several times about how nice everyone is."

"And what does Sid do?"

"He's a businessman," she said. "Paper products. He owns a whole forest of his own somewhere in Canada."

"A whole forest?"

"A small whole forest," she said. "But Sid does very well at it."

"So I gather. Have you noticed something else about Malibu?"

"What?"

"How people get really friendly right away and carry on very intimate conversations without even knowing each other's names?"

She blushed and laughed again. "I'm Lee Harvey," she said, holding out her right hand.

He shook it, then held on to it for a while, until she gently withdrew it. "I'm Rich Bentley," he said quietly.

"Oh, sure. I knew you were an actor. I remember you in that old CBS series. Wasn't it called *Roundup?*"

"Right you are," he said. "I had a good four-year run on that thing, plus all the residuals over the years. It made me financially independent, thank God. But how would you remember *Roundup?* You must have been in kindergarten."

"Not quite. I was in high school. My boyfriend and I used to watch it religiously. You were terrific."

"How sweet of you to say so. And you look very sweet, too."

She laughed a little nervously. *My God, he's coming on awfully fast,* she thought. *Is this the way Malibu works for lonely women on the beach?* "Uh . . . do you . . . do you live in the Colony?" she asked, blushing in spite of herself.

"Up at the other end," he told her, "the little green cottage squashed in next to the Weavers. It was one of the earliest of the Colony bungalows and the least pretentious. It belonged to some character actor from the silent days, who wouldn't have dared to build anything too fancy. I bought the place with the loot from the show, but for a lot less than I could get for it now. I must have you and Sid over."

"That would be very nice," she said, "and we're giving a big party of our own over the Fourth, just to kind of meet everybody. I do hope you'll come."

"I wouldn't miss it. Meanwhile, what are you reading?"

"Trash," she confessed, holding the Gothic paperback up so he could see the lurid cover. "I read these the way some people eat salted peanuts. I can't help myself."

He laughed. "Do they turn you on?"

She shook her head. "God, no. They're kind of fun, that's all. Some people do crosswords. Sid reads mysteries. What vices do you have, besides your daily beach walk?"

"None," he said. "I'm simply killing time. I had another show this year, but it wasn't renewed, probably because it was faintly literate and occasionally even believable, the cardinal sin on any network series. Did you ever see it? It was called *The Gentle Time*."

"No."

"The pilot was plagiarized from an old Kaufman-and-Hart comedy, but it was really too good for a run."

"Have you always been an actor?"

"Always, ever since college, when I starred in *The Admirable Crichton*. I was entirely admirable."

"I believe you," she said, smiling.

"Acting is so much easier than working," he said, "when there is work. Anyway, it's hiatus now, so I walk a lot. Speaking of which, how about joining me?"

She hesitated, but only briefly. "Why not?" she said, rising gracefully to her feet and brushing the sand off her legs. "Where are we going?"

"Let's go see what the surfers are up to, with their bony knees and their great lizard eyes," he suggested. "Then perhaps we can stroll out on the pier and watch the fishing. Ever been out there?"

"No."

"Come on," he said, taking her firmly by the elbow and steering her toward the water's edge. "It's better footing this way. And it's about time you saw a little more of Malibu Beach than the patch of sand in front of your house."

Later, as they stood and watched the surfers at the public beach working the long swells and swooping in toward the shore, Lee realized that perhaps she shouldn't have accepted Rich Bentley's invitation; he was so obvious about wanting her. All the way down the beach he had found little ways to touch her or brush against her, and twice he had taken her hand, until she had gently but firmly disengaged herself. And she felt completely undressed with him even now, because she knew he was standing a couple of feet in back of her only so he could feast his eyes on the lower half of her body, which was pretty much exposed below the shirt she had hastily slipped on over her skimpy sunbathing outfit. On Lake Winnebago or up in Maine, she would never have dared to wear it, even on her own beach. Here such near-nakedness passed unnoticed, though his greedy eyes had suddenly made her feel self-conscious.

It was ludicrous, really, she thought—he was almost certainly harmless. Rich Bentley undoubtedly came on like this with everyone; it was probably expected of him. After all, he was a Hollywood actor, had once even been a TV star with his own series, and she was just a nice-looking rich housewife from Wisconsin. He must have felt it was expected of him to make a pass, and surely he'd had success with it often enough. He was nice, really, and eventually, when he got the message that she wasn't just up for grabs, not even with an ex-TV star, he'd be a pleasant-enough summer acquaintance. If he'd just get his mind off seducing her.

But she'd keep her cool. She could never, in any case, take a man like him seriously. He was much too frivolously good-looking and too much of a pussycat. In fact, he made her want to laugh at him, which, she knew, would certainly have offended him. It was funny about some men, she reflected, how they simply assumed that looks and territory and power meant so much. She had never felt that way. She had really loved Sid when they'd begun dating, and he certainly had been no Adonis. She had admired his quick mind and appreciated his restless energy, had been sexually attracted by it, too. It was the below-the-surface tensions that appealed to Lee, the strength and turmoil of the male dealing with the complexities of life at every level. She had always sensed and responded to that quality in her men.

It was what had attracted her from the first to that tennis pro. He had so much going on beneath the surface, a whole secret world he was revealing, she felt sure, to no one else. Art Bonnell, she had found out from Sid, had once been somebody and would be somebody again. She wondered how he could tolerate the boring routines he seemed to have locked himself into. She wondered about his marriage and what Laura was like. Very beautiful, she imagined, some sort of golden girl from some golden place. How big a price had the man been forced to pay to keep himself and the fading golden dreams afloat? The roars of the watching crowds had become

63

echoes enshrined now in one small corner of his living room. Art Bonnell must have paid a price there, and Lee, for some reason, probably just simple curiosity, had decided to find out what.

"What are you so pensive about?" Rich Bentley asked as they headed up from the water's edge toward the steps leading to the highway and the pier.

"Oh, nothing," she said with a quick smile. "Just remembered some things I forgot to do. I'd better get back pretty soon."

"Sure," he said, "but let's take a quick look at the action. It may amuse you."

He held out his hand to help her from the soft, dry sand to the first rung of wooden steps, and again she felt him ogling her as her extended arm caused her shirt to open and gave him a glimpse of her breasts. The transparency of his lust made her want to laugh, but she resisted the impulse. No sense offending the poor dear; he had become for her a living cliché, the stereotypical Hollywood seducer. How Sid would laugh when she told him. . . .

"You haven't asked me about my job," Laura said to her husband. "Don't you care?"

"Sure, I care," he answered.

"Then why don't you want to hear about it?"

"What's to hear? What is there you need to tell me, Laura?"

She had come home to find him out on the terrace with a drink in his hand, staring out to sea. He'd waved at her, and she'd gone inside their bedroom to change out of her dress into slacks and a shirt; then she'd made a drink for herself and joined him. He had not moved, and for some reason his immobility, his strange passivity, had finally provoked her sufficiently to bring her own resentments out into the open. She would not sit down, but from her post by the open sliding glass doors she would confront him, force him at least to acknowledge her existence. "Arthur," she said, "I've been there a full week now. Not once have you asked me about it. What am I to think?"

"Nothing," he answered, "absolutely nothing."

"You don't care what I do?"

"Laura, you do what you want," he said. "It's your life."

"What a bunch of crap! What the hell are you trying to prove?"

"Nothing, Laura. I'm not trying to prove anything."

64

"You're mad because I didn't tell you about it, because I didn't ask your permission."

"No, I'm not. You're wrong."

"Am I?"

He looked at her then for the first time, but without anger, only more of the indifference that had recently been the chief characteristic of his attitude toward her. It was insufferable, really. "Oh, Christ," she said, whirling away from him and retreating into the house.

He did not follow her inside, not until the sun had finally set and, empty glass in hand, he strolled casually into the living room, shut the doors behind him, and sat down facing the television set. He reached out to turn it on, but she suddenly emerged from the kitchen, obviously still annoyed. "Why don't you want to talk?" she asked.

"The Dodgers are in San Francisco tonight," he said. "I thought I'd watch the ball game."

She walked into the room now and leaned against the wall, facing him. "Art, for God's sake," she said, "I can't do this alone."

Perhaps, she realized later, he really didn't know what to say to her, how to talk to her at all anymore. What she remembered best of that particular moment was that he sighed, his hand hesitating over the dial of the TV set, then sank back with a resigned look on his face and waited, as if for a blow. He had turned off the overhead light and all but one of the lamps in order to get a better picture on the screen, and in the now dim light of the room she could barely make out his features. He'd become incorporeal for her, as well as for himself, she thought, a ghost in his own house. "Arthur, I want you to ask me about my job," she told him very deliberately.

"Why?"

"Because, after twenty-one years, I have some claim to your attention."

"And you've never had that?"

"Not recently. And neither has your son."

"That's bullshit and you know it," he said. "I'm with Tad a lot."

"That isn't what I mean," she insisted. "You don't talk to him, either."

"How would you know?"

"I know."

"How?"

"Because Tad tells me you don't," she said. "Do you even know, for instance, that he's thinking of going to medical school?"

He looked shaken. "No," he admitted. "But why wouldn't he talk to me? We're together a lot."

"You play tennis, you talk baseball to each other," she said, "but you don't *talk*."

"Look," he said, "why are you trying to pick a fight with me? Why are you doing this?"

"Because I want you to care about us, that's why," she said angrily. "I want some show of concern from you, Arthur."

He opened his mouth as if to react with heat, then seemed to catch himself, to get his emotions under control, as if, perhaps, his very sanity depended on it. "All right, Laura," he said quietly, "I'll speak to Tad. I admit I may have been a bit casual with him lately. I've had a lot on my mind. Anyway, how *is* the job?"

"It's fine. I like it very much," she said. "I think I'm going to become very good at it, and I think they'll offer me a permanent place at the agency."

"That's wonderful," he said. "I'm very happy for you."

"Are you?"

"Of course. It's what you want."

"And that's all it means to you?"

"I know what it means to me," he said in that same detached way he'd been cultivating with her, "I know what it means, Laura, but I don't want to go into all that right now."

"Why not?"

"Because," he said, "the Dodgers are in San Francisco and I want to watch the ball game." His hand reached out again and turned the set on. The picture came immediately into focus, but the sound, luckily, was turned too low. Before he could adjust it, she came around in back of his chair and looked down at him from behind. "I took the job," she said, "because I'm tired of not quite enough money and, more importantly, I'm tired of being Laura Bonnell, the wife of a great athlete. I need to be something on my own, and we can use the money."

"Swell," he said. "What do you want, my approval? You've got it."

66

The batter on the screen took a vicious swing at the ball and missed. Art kept his gaze focused on the picture, but Laura stared down at the top of her husband's head, resisting a sudden wild impulse she'd had to smash both her fists down on top of it. "I'd have taken this job, or some other job, with or without your approval," she said instead, keeping her voice low and very controlled. "I don't need your approval and I don't want it. What I was hoping from you was some small acknowledgment of my existence, that something I do still means something to you. Is that unreasonable?"

"No," he said, "it's not unreasonable. Do you know what is unreasonable?"

"Tell me, Arthur."

"That I can't come home after a very tough day, have a drink, and watch the ball game in peace," he said. "That seems to me unreasonable." He reached out again now and turned up the sound. The roar of a large partisan hometown crowd filled the room, as the batter on the screen took another swing and this time hit the ball on a line over second base into right field. "McCovey," Art said. "I'd rather have him up there with men on than anyone else in the game, wouldn't you?"

But Laura had gone. As he had reached out to turn up the volume, she had walked out of the room. By the time he came to bed two hours later, she was lying on her side, her face to the wall and her back to him. He slid under the sheet without touching her, and lay quietly in the darkness until sleep came to him. He could have speculated that Laura wasn't asleep at all, but simply lying there in the darkness of their room, shielding herself from any further contact with him. He hadn't heard her breathe, which meant that probably she was still awake, but he had no stomach for more of a scene that night, and so he closed his eyes until he lost consciousness himself.

Had Laura left him in the middle of the night to go outside and sit alone in the darkness, or had he merely dreamed that? Art Bonnell never asked his wife about it, and she never mentioned it, even much later.

7

Jay R. Pomerantz was really too good to be true. Not only did he apparently have limitless supplies of money, but he seemed perfectly willing to spend heavily in order to get exactly what he wanted. It hadn't taken more than an hour to show him through the Carey house the first time, and Billie Farnsworth had worried about that, because he had seemed distracted and kept looking at his watch and talking about a business meeting he'd be late for, but then he'd called back that same evening and asked to be taken through the house again. He'd apologized for having had to be in such a rush the first time around, and of course, Billie had understood. Financiers like Jay R. Pomerantz were always on tight schedules and always rushing off to meetings. That was how the money got made, Billie knew, not by lounging around and strolling casually through life, waiting for the loot to fall into your lap, but by running after it and grabbing for it with both hands. You had to shake the tree, to choke life into surrender, Billie had found out, not wait for it to give in to you.

Pomerantz was an odd-looking bird, Billie thought. He was small and round, and from the rear he looked even chunkier than his five-foot-six, but he had long, delicate, manicured fingers, like those of a beautician, and his eyes were a little frightening. One was brown with flecks of green, and the other almost a pure gray. They peered out at the world through thick horn-rimmed eyeglasses, and they seemed to have a life of their own, quite independent of whatever else Jay R. Pomerantz might be thinking or doing. He'd smile often, and he obviously enjoyed a good joke, probably laughed a lot, but the eyes never seemed to flicker or cease their intense, very cold scrutiny of whatever it was Jay R. Pomerantz was concerned with at the moment. It was as if there were another, quite different human being locked up in there behind that soft-looking, benign exterior, but that feeling didn't bother Billie much either. In fact, it reassured her, maybe because it reminded her of the way her husband, Winston, had been when he'd been in control of his life and clicking on all twelve cylinders. You had to stay cool and clear back there, adding it all up in your head and making just the right moves at just the right times, or the game could get away from you and some son of a bitch would ride you down. Billie decided she was even more impressed by Jay R. Pomerantz the second time around than she had been at their first meeting.

He certainly wasn't in a hurry this time, and she wasn't about to rush him, either. They walked slowly through the whole house, inspected every corner of it, and by the time they got back to the living room, Billie had gone into her negative routine. "Look, Jay," she told him with a broad, sweeping gesture that encompassed the whole house, "what they're asking here is really ridiculous."

"I sure like the view from this window here," Jay said. "I like the way the room thrusts out, so you can see a ways up and down the beach. It kind of compensates for the way some of these Colony house are packed in so close together. Whoever designed this old house sure knew what he was doing."

"Well, it was one of the first," Billie explained. "But it's got some structural problems."

The strange eyes focused on her, but without alarm. "Yeah? Like what?"

"A lot of these old houses sit right on the sand," Billie continued. "I mean, the new ones, see, they're built on pilings, but these old ones just sit."

"Meaning what, honey?"

"In a storm or some of these high tides we get here in the winter

70

months," Billie said, "the ocean can cause some problems. If it gets up under the house or washes too much of the beach away, you could be in trouble. Last winter we had to do a lot of sandbagging."

"Here?"

"Well, no. Down at the other end mostly. The storm came up from the south. The houses down at this end didn't get the worst of it." Billie pointed out the window. "See those rocks? Well, there's a point of land out there. It kind of protects the houses at this end, but up at the other end they had a lot of trouble. The high tides came right up under a lot of the houses and took away the back decks and the patios."

"That old devil sea," Jay R. Pomerantz said, smiling. "But you say this house has been here how long?"

"It was one of the first built here," Billie said. "Maybe the fourth or fifth one."

"Then I got nothing to worry about, do I, honey?"

"Jay, that isn't all I'm talking about."

"No? What else, honey?"

"What I'm trying to tell you, I guess," Billie said, "is that the house also needs a lot of work and the asking price is really too steep. Why don't you make an offer that takes that into account, and I'll see if I can persuade the estate to accept it. They won't, but maybe we can agree on a compromise figure."

"Who did you say owns this place?"

"The property is managed by the lawyers for the Carey estate," Billie explained. "Steve and Irma Carey built this place back in the late twenties. He was a big director in silent films. They were killed in an automobile accident on Pacific Coast Highway nine years ago, and since then the house has been used as a sort of vacation campground for the Carey heirs and their families. The main trouble is, the Careys left a badly written will and the lawyers and the courts have tied everything up for years. Also, the heirs are fighting among themselves. There are ten or eleven of them. Anyway, they finally agreed to sell the house, had to because of taxes, but a million dollars is really an outrage, even at today's prices. With all the work you'd have to put into the place, half that amount would be about right."

Jay sighed and turned to look out the window again. "I sure do like this view," he said.

"The roof leaks and needs repairing," Billie went on. "The kitchen is a major disaster area, and the plumbing is in very bad shape. Last summer I rented the place to a family that found itself living over their own waste. The pipes were so rotten that everything leaked out onto the sand directly under the house. The cesspool is much too small and has to be pumped out four times a year, or it overflows. You need a whole new heating unit, and obviously, a good paint job inside and out. Want me to go on? I could, you know."

"Sure," Jay said, settling himself comfortably into the dingy armchair by the fireplace and grinning up at her. "Say, what kind of an agent are you? You talk like you're working for me, not those Carey folks. What did they ever do to you?"

"Come on, Jay," Billie said, "Do I look like a dummy? I live two doors down. I don't want to sell this house to somebody who's going to start screaming the day he moves in. I want you to know what you're buying."

"I always know what I'm buying, Billie."

"What did you say you do?"

"I didn't say, Billie. Investments. Land. Oil. Some cattle."

"You still live in Tulsa?"

"Nope. Haven't for years. Just keep an office there, you know. Close to where the money is, see." He laughed and slapped his hands on his pudgy thighs.

"And where are you living now?"

"No place, really. I have a suite at the Beverly-Wilshire."

"So you're living there?"

"For now. I've been traveling a lot the last few years, Billie," Jay said. "I deal quite a bit with two or three of what the press calls the emerging nations, you know. I'm getting kind of tired of living in hotels and airports. That's why I'm thinking of settling down here. Get me a nice home. Meet some nice folks. Maybe invest in some projects around here. We'll see. Anyway, if I decide to buy this house, or any house, I'll spend what I have to to fix it up. What do you think they'll take, Billie?"

"Why don't you make an offer?" she suggested. "I assume we could close the deal for about eight hundred or eight and a half."

"What makes you so sure? I guess the land alone is worth nearly that or more."

"Sure. That's really what you're buying. This house stands on a double lot. Waterfront lots are going for at least a quarter of a million now, assuming you can get the Coastal Commission to let you build on them."

Jay R. Pomerantz giggled with delight. "It's funny, you know?"

"What is, Jay?"

"Why, shit, for that kind of money, Billie, I could buy me a whole county in Oklahoma and own the sheriff to boot."

She smiled sweetly at him. "Why, Jay, honey, that's Indian territory, isn't it? Who in hell would *want* to live in Oklahoma?"

"By God, that's right, Billie," he roared. "The goddam Indians ought to take it back, once we get all the oil out of it."

"Seriously, Jay . . ." she began, hoping he would rise now to the bait.

"Billie, offer them six hundred thousand."

"You bet. I'll get back to you as soon as I have a reaction. It may be a week or so. All the heirs have to be contacted."

"Ain't that a bitch," Jay observed. "If we do close a deal, how long before I could get in here?"

Billie looked thoughtful and measured her words carefully. "We'd have escrow to go through, of course," she said. "Then all these heirs and the lawyers and the banks." She sighed. "It might be a month or two, Jay."

"Damn," he said. "I suppose I could move in before that, though."

"I could always ask."

"Well, you do that, Billie. 'Cause if I'm spending this kind of money, I sure ain't going to pay rent on this place, and I don't want to miss the whole summer."

"Let's see if we can agree on a price first," Billie said. "The rest will fall into place."

Jay R. Pomerantz stood up and rocked happily back and forth on his feet. "Well, I guess I can fix this place up," he said happily. "Don't you sell it out from under me, now, hear?"

"I hear," Billie said, and turned to lead him out again. "But don't worry, even with the market as hot as it is right now, nobody's going to pay a cool million for this house."

Out in the Colony street again, Jay R. Pomerantz took a last look at the old Carey house before heading for his car, the huge silver-

and-blue Rolls convertible parked up against the closed garage doors next to Billie's Mercedes. "I'll fix it up real nice," he said. "It'll be the showplace of the Colony when I get through."

"And I've got just the architect for you," Billie said.

"Who's that?"

"My son, Dave. He's remodeled quite a few of the Colony houses."

Jay laughed. "You got it all locked up, Billie."

She laughed with him. "You don't have a family, Jay?" she asked as he settled himself in the driver's seat.

"Never had the time," Jay said, beaming. "Maybe someday I will."

"So what do you need such a big place for?"

"Billie, honey, you sure are nosy. Hell, I entertain a lot."

"Well, you've sure come to the right part of town."

"That's what I figured," Jay said, easing the big car noiselessly out into the road. "I'm going to love it here, Billie, and you're sure a nice gal."

She watched him drive away, taking the Rolls carefully over the speed bumps. From the rear Jay R. Pomerantz looked like an overweight elf, his tiny hands gripping the steering wheel of the huge car tightly, as if he were afraid the machine had a life of its own and just might be too much for him. He must have just bought the car, Billie thought, and was trying to get used to it. He was kind of cute, despite those weird eyes, but it would be interesting to know where all that money came from exactly. Somehow she'd find out, Billie told herself. The little guy liked her, she was sure of that, and maybe, just maybe, he'd like to play a little. It was going to be a good summer, whether he did or not—that much Billie was sure of.

II

The Fourth of July

8

Art Bonnell was one of the last to arrive at the Harveys' Fourth-of-July party, which, he could tell immediately, was turning out to be a huge success. There must have been well over a hundred guests packed into the premises. Out on the patio, overlooking the beach, a huge blue-and-white-striped tent had been erected by the caterers to accommodate the gyrations of a small horde of dancers bouncing up and down to the rock rhythms of a local teenage band hired for the occasion. Art was no dancer. What he needed was a drink, but he had to quite literally push his way through the crowded sunken living room to get to the bar. He wanted to be sure he had some booze in him before having to cope with any Colony party chatter or any more of the complaints, bitchy remarks, and small social crises that had characterized every Colony tennis tournament, at least since he had been running them over the past two years.

The three-day competition had taken its usual spiritual toll of him, and he really didn't think he was up to one more scene, how-ever insignificant. He wouldn't even have come to this party if he hadn't had to, but really he had no choice. On his slow progress through the room, he nodded, smiled, mumbled greetings, and waved at people, not pausing to talk until at last, double Scotch in hand, and with the first swallow of liquor coursing warmly through him, he turned to face the social music. Not surprisingly, he found himself confronting Lee Harvey, who had seen him arrive from her post by the kitchen door and followed him. "Hi," she said, beaming. "Isn't this terrific?"

Art grinned. "I told you everybody would come."

"So you and Billie said. I guess we got lucky."

"How's that?"

"Nobody else gave a big party this year."

"Well, the Fourth being on a Tuesday might have made some difference, I guess."

"How are you, Art?"

"I'm fine, Lee, just fine."

"Sid's ecstatic, but I suppose he told you."

"About getting to the finals? Yeah."

She laughed. "You set it up, didn't you?"

"Sort of," he admitted. "See, the whole secret of these things is matching the players. You put strong ones with weaker ones, and the handicaps level things out. Now, Sid's very determined—"

"'Aggressive' is the word."

"You said it. And he gets the ball back most of the time, he keeps it in play," Art explained. "So if you pair him up with a really good player, like Wharton, who's really an A and not a B, well, you've got a winning combination there."

"Until they ran into Tad."

"The kid's good. Too good, maybe, for these Colony wingdings. I shouldn't have let him play, but we were a man short."

"Yes, he's really tournament caliber. I mean, real tournaments," Lee said. "That guy, what's his name, his partner . . ."

"Wigham, Charlie Wigham."

"He could hardly hit a ball at all."

Art nodded. "Tad's thinking of going out on the pro circuit," he said, "but Laura and I want him to finish school first."

"Of course."

"Anyway, you enjoyed yourself, too, didn't you?"

Lee laughed. "Oh, no," she admitted. "I was too busy worrying about this party and whether anybody would come. About the only ones who didn't are Redford and Newman, but I didn't really expect *them* to show up."

"They like to play in the tournaments," Art said, "and sometimes they'll show up for a party. It's early. Maybe they'll still come."

"Sid was funny," Lee told him, looking quickly around to make sure her husband wasn't in earshot. "He'd never been on a court with a bunch of celebrities before. I even thought he might get too nervous to play. But after he got over it, he played better than I've ever seen him play before."

"He's a real competitor, all right."

"Is that your biggest headache, Art?"

"What?"

"Having to handle a bunch of celebrities in a social tournament like this one?"

Art shook his head. "No, ma'am," he told her. "The toughest part is trying to remember which couples are still together and which aren't when you set up the mixed doubles. Also, who will absolutely refuse to play with whom, and on which court. The celebrities are easy. They just want to have fun, mostly."

She giggled. "You know what happened on our court?"

"No."

"Mary Wharton got paired up with that actor . . . what's his name?"

"Rich Bentley."

"Yes. Well, she said she wouldn't play with him. She announced—pretty loudly, too—that he was a limp dick in everything, not just tennis. And she stalked off the court."

Art sighed. "I heard about it."

"What's her problem?"

"Right now, the immediate one is booze. The main one, though, is being married to Jim Wharton."

"I don't like him. He's too slick," she said. "Who is he?"

"I'll tell you sometime. This isn't really the place."

"I guess not," Lee said, suddenly turning serious. "Art, I want to see you—"

Before she could tell him exactly what it was she wanted to see him about, Sid Harvey joined them. He was a chunky, heavyset man, muscular and hairy, who bounced on the balls of his feet when he talked, and he absolutely radiated energy. Art admired that quality in him, though he imagined it had to be difficult to live with. It also

79

made him wonder how he and Lee could have produced two fat, effeminate kids, but then, the genes held mysteries that defied rational analysis. Or maybe it wasn't a question of genes at all, but simply an absent father and an inattentive mother.

"Excuse me," Lee said, patting her husband on the arm and moving off through the crowd. "I'd better see what's happening in the kitchen."

Yes, Lee did give that impression of having her mind rather firmly fixed on other possibilities in life than merely the running and managing of her husband's domestic affairs, Art thought, watching her go. Then he turned back to Sid, who stood in front of him, gently bouncing. Sid told Art what a great time he'd been having and how much he appreciated what Art was trying to do for his kids and how swell it had been of Art to turn out so many really nice folks for their party and how terrific meeting all these Hollywood types had been for him and Lee, because they were just like real people and not phony at all, and how he owed the success of the summer so far to Art and Billie and all the wonderful guys and gals they'd met since moving into the Colony and about how he was even thinking of moving out here permanently next year, since he now did most of his business by phone anyway. Maybe Art could make real tennis players and men out of those two kids of his. And Art nodded and smiled, and smiled and nodded, while across the room he could now see Laura deep in conversation with that guy Alcorn, her boss. What was that all about, anyway?

"That kid of yours sure plays a hell of a game," Sid Harvey said to him.

"What? Oh, yeah," Art answered, "he does. Chip off the old block."

"You bet. Say, Art, this must be a pretty tough racket for you. I mean, running these tournaments and all," Sid Harvey said. "I mean, you were a hell of a player yourself, and you missed out on all the big money in the game today."

"That's right," Art answered, "I did."

And now he watched Alcorn lean over to whisper something in Laura's ear, and he saw her look up and smile at him and shrug her shoulders.

"Art?" Sid Harvey said.

"Yeah?"

"That is your wife, isn't it? She's a beauty. I'd sure like to meet her."

"You will, Sid, you will."

A few minutes later, after Sid Harvey had moved on to greet other new friends, Art looked across the room again and noticed, to his surprise, that Laura and Alcorn had vanished. Where had they gone? Out on the beach? To dance? *What the hell's the matter with me anyway,* Art asked himself, even as he smiled and chatted with some other Malibu people he didn't know very well. *What the hell is happening here? I think I'm just tired, that's all, just really tired. . . .*

Lee arrived in the kitchen just in time to quiet an argument between her caterer, an elegant black exquisite named Oswald whom Billie had touted, and the wetback Mexican maids she had hired, also at Billie's suggestion, to help serve the food and clean up. She never did quite sort out what the trouble was about, something to do with the clumsy manner the Mexicans had of overloading each tray with food, which offended Oswald's obviously highly cultivated aesthetic sensibilities, but she was able to smooth things over, mainly by permanently banishing the surliest of the Mexicans to the living room, where she was assigned to empty ashtrays and retrieve dirty dishes and glasses.

By the time Lee had achieved a degree of uneasy harmony and was ready to rejoin her guests, she found herself confronted in the kitchen doorway by Mary Wharton, who had been drinking straight gin over ice and seemed bent on self-destruction. It was too bad, Lee thought, because Mary had once obviously been a very beautiful woman, and now, only in her late forties, she had clearly let go and begun putting on weight. Billie had tipped Lee off that Mary had become a lush, so her appearance and behavior fortunately hadn't taken Lee by surprise. "Hello, Mary," Lee said a bit tentatively. "Can I get you anything?"

"Ice," Mary said, holding out her glass. "You just ran out."

"Oh, Lord, we have plenty of ice," Lee answered, taking Mary's glass and heading for the corner where the vats of store-bought ice cubes had been stored. "I'll send more out." She filled Mary's glass and returned it to her. "I hope you're having a good time."

Mary Wharton shrugged. "These Malibu parties are all the same," she said. "It's always the same faces."

Lee laughed a bit too graciously. "Well, not to me, of course. We're new here."

Mary took a large swallow of her gin and smirked cynically at her. "And are you loving every moment of it?"

"We're enjoying ourselves, yes," Lee admitted. "I hope that's not against the rules."

"Oh, no," Mary Wharton said. "It's one of the obligations of living here. Meet any celebrities yet?"

"A couple. We were hoping one or two might show up," Lee confessed with a laugh. "We heard a rumor Charlton Heston was in the vicinity, because he plays tennis, but I haven't seen him. Anyway, everybody's welcome."

"You've met our resident show folks, I gather."

"Who do you mean?"

"Rich Bentley, for one."

"Oh, yes. He introduced himself to me on the beach the other day. He seems very nice."

Mary Wharton laughed harshly. "He wants to fuck you," she said. "He wants to fuck everyone. Don't worry, he can only get it up about ten seconds at a time, like a rabbit. It's all over before you know he's even done it."

"Mary, I honest to God wouldn't know, and I don't really care."

"No, I can see you're a nice girl," the older woman said. "How about the oopsy-daisy queen? You met her?"

"Who's that?"

"Dee Stauffer."

"Oh, yes, I was introduced to her. What did you call her?"

"Her acting name used to be Dee Francesca, before she married poor old Ed Stauffer. She used to be a Mouseketeer."

"You're kidding."

"When she grew tits and started fucking her way up, she got this one part in one of those beach pictures they used to make back then, remember?"

"No."

"*Beach Bash Bongo*, I think it was called," Mary continued. "Dee had this one number in it. She sang and danced in a bikini and bumped her hips, 'oopsy-daisy,' with this big squeal and all. She can't dance and she can't sing, but she thinks she was a star. Luckily for her, she grabbed onto poor old Ed."

"What happened to him?"

"He keeled over dead at the Daisy one night. Dee threw him a birthday party and invited everybody from Malibu. That was it for Ed. He went out feetfirst, and Dee got half the loot. She settled with the children from his first marriage, even though he'd left her everything in his will."

"That was nice of her."

"Don't you believe it," Mary said, draining her glass. "She didn't want the estate tied up in litigation for ten years with the fucking lawyers. Jim represented her, and she came out with a lot of loot. Ed was very rich. He was a retired exec from some subscription book company back East, but he made a ton of loot in real estate out here. Smart guy, but dumb with women. Dee's a real cunt."

"Charmingly put, Mary," Jim Wharton said, looming up behind her. "Come on, I'm taking you home."

"It's early . . ." Mary started to protest, took a backward step, and almost fell. Jim reached out, caught her by the arm, and held on.

"Come on, honey," he said gently but very firmly as he led her away. "It's time to go home." He shot a backward glance at Lee and winked. "I'll be back," he mouthed silently at her.

Lee nodded and waited until they had safely gone before rejoining her guests. Life in Malibu, she had begun to realize, was not that much different, except in degree, from life on Lake Winnebago. The aging, unhappy rich got drunk and went to pieces the same way everywhere, except that back home you had the names and numbers of all the players down pat, along with their lifetime averages. Out here in Malibu, it was all up for grabs, because there seemed to be no rules and no precedents to go by. Everybody here had once come from somewhere else, shedding past lives the way snakes shed skins. And certainly, back in Wisconsin, you would not be told by a perfect stranger that one of your guests couldn't get it up for more than ten seconds and that another one had once been a Mouseketeer. No, that at least was very different. Lee giggled and made her way back into the main action of their now very noisy, very active party.

Art hadn't realized how much Scotch he'd consumed until Laura and George Alcorn found him and he tried to get up to greet them. For over an hour, or maybe two, he'd been sprawled in a corner of the large circular couch facing the fireplace and talking first to Dee

Stauffer, then to anyone else who had come into his small orbit. Mostly, he'd just been drinking. When he saw Laura and her smiling, flushed-looking boss, he tried to get up, but almost couldn't make it. At the last moment, he stuck a hand out and propped himself up against the mantelpiece. "Wow," he exclaimed, grinning foolishly. "I must be bombed."

"Why don't you eat something?" Laura asked.

"Good idea. I will."

"You said you wanted to go home early. Want me to drive you?"

"No, it's okay," Art told her. It was true, he was feeling better; all he needed now was some food in him. He let go of the mantelpiece and stuck his right hand out toward George Alcorn. "Hi there. You're Laura's boss, aren't you?" he said. "You're also a pretty good tennis player. Did you enjoy the tournament?"

"Sure did," George Alcorn said. "I'd always meant to play in one of these. Finally, this year, I made it."

"Yes, you did."

"You're a pretty fair player yourself, Art," George Alcorn said. "One of the best I've ever seen."

"Thanks." Art looked around in order to pin down the exact location of the buffet. He finally spotted it across the room against the wall, then glanced back at his wife. "Guess I'll eat something."

"Why don't we go?" Laura said. "I'm ready."

"I don't think *I* am," Art said. "Go on home if you want to."

"How will you get home?"

"I'll get a ride, don't worry."

"Your wife's a hell of a dancer," George Alcorn said.

"Yes, she is," Art agreed. "A terrific dancer. I can't dance, never could."

"Art, I'd really like to go home."

"Go ahead, honey, who's stopping you?"

"I can drop you off, Laura," George Alcorn volunteered.

"Yeah," Art said, "why doesn't George drop you off?"

"You're drunk," Laura snapped at him. "You can't drive."

Art grinned. "Sure I can." He laughed. "It's a mile from here, exactly one mile, and I'll do it all in second, okay?"

"Arthur—"

"It's all right," George Alcorn said, "I'll take you home, Laura. I really have to go, too."

84

"Why don't you stay and dance some more?" Art suggested, but he did not wait to hear an answer. He began to push his way through the crowd toward the buffet; then, feeling just a little too dizzy, he quickly changed direction and let himself out a side door leading to the beach. He jumped down from the deck onto the sand, kicked off his loafers, and loped heavily toward the water. The waves washed up around his ankles as he leaned over and heaved. Behind him, from inside the blue-and-white striped tent, glowing and pulsating with life in the summer night, the heavy rock beat continued to hammer at the darkness.

After a few minutes, when he felt better, Art splashed cold salt water on his face, rinsed out his mouth, and started back toward the house. Halfway there, out of the darkness, Dee Stauffer suddenly confronted him. "Arthur, are you all right?" she asked.

"Yeah. What are you doing out here, Dee?"

"You looked a little green," she told him, smiling. "Just thought I'd make sure you're okay."

"I'm fine."

He started to move past her, but she caught his arm and turned him toward her. There was no moon, and it was very dark, with only the reflected light from the dancing tent and the orange glow from illuminated windows on either side casting pale reflections on the sand. Art couldn't make out Dee Stauffer's face, but she was dressed in white, all in white, and her man's shirt had been slashed open to her waist. The golden strands of her heavy jewelry glowed in the dim light. Art remembered very clearly now when he had last really seen Dee Stauffer or talked to her, only a month or so ago. She had been naked then and lying on her back on the yellow satin sheets of her bedroom. She had a good body, firm and tight for a woman of forty-one, and still available to him, right there on the sand, if he wanted it, between the Harveys' party tent and the line of foam at the edge of the narrow beach. She obviously wanted him to want her, and Dee Stauffer was used to having her own way in everything.

Art backed away a step. "Dee, it's no good anymore," he said. "It's over."

"Is it?"

"Yes, it is."

"You're going to be unapproachable and virtuous now?"

"No, it's not that."

"I should hope not."

"I think I tried to explain this to you," he said. "Maybe you weren't listening."

"And maybe I was, Arthur."

"If you choose not to believe me . . ."

She smiled. He could see the flash of her white teeth in the darkness, and it made him think of her suddenly as some sort of carnivorous animal. "I believe what I can see, smell, and touch," she said.

"Dee, what happened, happened, okay? I think I tried to explain it to you sometime back," he said, "but evidently it didn't take."

"You told me you love your wife," Dee Stauffer said. "Wasn't that the gist of it?"

"I suppose."

"How trite, Arthur. Really."

"Yeah," he said, "and like so many trite sayings and clichés, it happens to be true." He again tried to move past her, and this time she let him go.

"Arthur?" she called out.

He didn't answer her, but kept on toward the house, his bare feet sinking into the cold sand.

"Arthur?" she called again. "I don't want your love, baby. I just want to play around a little."

"I'm sorry," he said, still moving.

"Like your wife and that guy she spent the whole evening with," Dee Stauffer said. "What's wrong with a little fooling around, baby? You're so good at it."

9

Charlie Wigham had come to the party early, determined to have a good time. So far he had managed to succeed, and without once talking shop. Michelle had warned him she would leave him on his own that night if he did; she was tired of hearing Charlie hustling on the phone all day long and then having to listen between calls to his endless speculations on possible new sources of financing for his production of *Pale Moon Rising.* "This is so boring, Sharlie," she told him that very morning. "I cannot bear more of it, you understand?"

Charlie had understood and had promised that, at the Harveys' party at least, he would not once mention *Pale Moon Rising.* He and Michelle would just go and have a hell of a good time eating, drinking, and dancing. Charlie would maybe talk a little tennis—after all, he and young Tad Bonnell had won the tournament, hadn't they?— but not anything to do with *Pale Moon Rising* or the Industry in general. Charlie was quite aware that in these past two weeks he had pushed poor Michelle to the breaking point. And he did not want to lose Michelle, who, in her own kooky, sweet French way, had become as essential to him as his career. Well, almost.

My God, that very morning he'd been turned down by Paramount, the last of the major studios he'd approached. "I don't know what you're trying to get at in this script," this dumb schmuck of a producer there had written him. Bud Lavin, his old boss at Gemini, where Charlie had flourished as a *wunderkind,* had also written him a second polite rejection note, after Charlie had turned to him for help, at least with seed money. "In these tough and unpredictable times," Bud Lavin had dictated solemnly to his secretary, "we can't take a chance on the dubious possibility that this script has what it takes to guarantee success at the box office." This was the guy Charlie had made millions for by salvaging *Larkin.* Fuck him.

"Where's the gamble? What chance is he taking?" Charlie had shouted, more to himself, actually, than to Michelle, who had emerged wide-eyed from the kitchen, frying pan in hand and dressed only in her string bikini bottom, to stare at him. "I mean, I don't understand these guys!"

"What guys, darling?" Michelle had asked. "Who is being naughty to you now?"

Charlie had explained it all to her, because it seemed to help; he had to get it off his chest, didn't he? Look, here he was, he told her, a bright young man with impeccable credentials and bubbling over with talent, and these studio heads and their flunkies apparently now chose to regard him as some kind of wild nut touting an artsy-craftsy sure loser. "All I want, honey," he'd said, "all I want is to make a successful motion picture."

"Well, of course, that is normal, no?" Michelle had answered.

"Yeah," Charlie had continued. "If I could bring it under budget and get a G rating, they could bail out just on a TV sale. How bad could they get hurt? Where's the downside risk, baby?"

"I don't know, Sharlie, where is it?"

"Honey," he'd said, "don't you see?"

"See what, Sharlie?"

He had started to tell her and then thought better of it. Michelle knew nothing about the movies except that she enjoyed going to them. She was a child, really, just a child, whom Charlie had whisked out of a French restaurant in Westwood one night. She had been a waitress there, and Charlie had quickly established that she was the daughter of one of the owners' cousins, back in Bordeaux, that her delightful French accent and her innocence about life in general were both genuine. She had gone to bed with him almost immediately, but only because she liked him and not because she was natu-

88

rally promiscuous. No, Michelle was a child of nature, the genuine article, and she had moved in with Charlie three days after their first formal date. Her distant relatives at the restaurant had stopped speaking to her, but Michelle, who had also fallen out with her parents over her free and easy sex life back in France, couldn't have cared less. Sharlie, as she called him, could make her laugh, and that counted more than anything with her. Best of all, from Charlie's point of view, she had the body of a young Bardot, no inhibitions, and, as if that weren't bonus enough, she had no desire whatsoever to become a movie star. What Michelle wanted was to have a good time, to enjoy herself to the fullest. What Charlie was afraid of now was that the good times would stop, and very abruptly, unless he could get *Pale Moon Rising* off the ground.

What he hadn't realized right away was that the studios were playing their old, old game of follow-that-trend. Ever since the success of *Star Wars* and *Close Encounters*, everything had to be either sci-fi or fantasy-horror. "You see, honey," Charlie had said to Michelle later that same morning, "I'm being turned down because they think nobody gives a shit anymore about kids and music and finding yourself. They think I'm behind the times. Michelle, I'm *ahead* of the times, don't you see?"

And that was when Michelle had revealed to him that she found this "so boring, Sharlie." He'd immediately clammed up. It was bad enough he couldn't stop thinking and talking about his movie; if he lost Michelle because of his obsession, the whole summer, the whole year, would turn out to be a total loss.

Charlie steered Michelle carefully through the party, avoiding all those people who might be expected to ask him what he was up to. He concentrated on tennis instead, and told wonderful stories about matches he had seen, exploits he had witnessed, debacles he himself had participated in, such as the time he'd missed an overhead during the Labor Day tournament the year before and thrown his metal racket so hard on the court that it had bounced up and cracked him under the chin. That had cost him the match, the racket, three stitches, and his self-esteem, though it *had* gotten the biggest laugh of the weekend and turned him into an instant Colony celebrity, at least for that one weekend.

Charlie was a born raconteur and told all these stories very well, but even so, he could sense, after an hour or more of this kind of chatter, that Michelle was getting restless. "Want to dance?" he suddenly asked her.

"Oh, Sharlie," she squealed, "I thought you would never, never ask me!"

Hand in hand, they pushed their way out of the living room and onto the patio, where the band was going full blast and a couple of dozen sweaty couples were hard at work. Charlie was a lousy dancer and knew it, but Michelle was sensational. He simply turned her loose to do her thing and contented himself with just bouncing up and down in place, while she whirled giddily about him, a half-smile of pure contentment on her face, lost to the beat of the music.

Billie Farnsworth happened to witness the epic meeting between Rich Bentley and Charlie Wigham's girlfriend, Michelle. Billie had been talking to the Kramers, who had just left her to go after refills, when the actor came up beside her. "Billie, darling," he asked, "what is this swill they are serving at this lousy party instead of wine?"

"I don't know, Rich," Billie answered. "And it's not a lousy party. What's the matter with your wine?"

"It looks like wine," Rich said, "and at first sip it even tastes like wine. After that, my dear, it's old socks. Who's been trampling their stuff? Unwashed Chicanos inspired by Cesar Chavez to undermine the grape industry?"

Billie took a sip from his glass. "Oh, come on," she said, "it's just some perfectly harmless California jug Chablis. What did you expect, for Christ's sake? Pouilly Fuissé for a gathering this size? You've drunk worse, I'm sure."

"Not recently." He started to walk away from her, but suddenly caught himself. "Good God, who's that adorable little creature?" he asked.

Billie had to agree that Michelle, who had just returned from the dancing tent, really did look smashing. She was dressed in white slacks and a silk Pucci blouse, and her long straight blond hair fell to her shoulders. She was slender, almost boyishly thin, but her face was adorable. It had a gamin quality that was really enchanting, and when she smiled, as she did now at Billie, she revealed a set of perfect dimples and an absolutely exquisite little mouth with pouty lips and gleaming teeth. "I want to meet her," Rich Bentley said.

90

As if she had read his mind, Michelle threaded her way toward them. "Michelle," Billie asked, "have you met Rich Bentley?"

The girl looked faintly puzzled. "Bentley?" she asked. "He is rich, you say?"

"That's his name, honey," Billie explained quickly. "He's one of our resident celebrities. Rich is his first name."

Michelle giggled sweetly. "Oh, no, I have not. How do you do."

"Well, I've just introduced you," Billie said. "Look out for him, Michelle."

"You should, you know," the actor said, smiling. "I'm extremely dangerous."

Michelle laughed. "Really? How nice."

"Actually, he's a pussycat," Billie observed.

"I adore pussycats," Michelle confessed. "I have once owned a pussycat at home."

"How sweet," Billie said. "Well, I don't want to cramp your inimitable style, Rich, dear . . ."

"How could you do that?" Rich asked. "Don't go, Billie. Finish your drink."

"Are you rich, then?" the girl asked.

"It's my name, you dear thing," he said, again focused on her. "I'm not. I'm an impoverished actor."

"How sad. Money is so important, don't you think?"

"You better believe it, honey," Billie said. "It's crucial."

"I do think it's important," Rich agreed. "What do you do, Michelle?"

"Do?" she asked, puzzled. "I do nothing."

"You're not in show business?"

"Oh, goodness, no," she said. "Sharlie—you know Sharlie?"

"Wigham?" Bentley replied. "Oh, sure."

"I am with him."

"I see. And you are French, I gather?"

"From Bordeaux."

"Have you been here long?"

"About an hour."

"No, no, no!"

"Oh, you mean in this country?"

"Precisely."

"Not very long. I come for a visit to my cousins here, where they are owning a bistro, and then I meet Sharlie. It's very nice, no?"

"Yes," Rich Bentley agreed, "very nice. Where is Charlie?"

She shrugged. "I do not know. We were dancing, you see, and then I have enough and I come in here for a while. You are a star?"

"Of sorts. Would you like to look at some?"

"What, please?"

"Stars. Real ones. Outside," Rich Bentley explained. "Don't you think it's hot in here?"

"All right, then. Why not?"

On their way out, as if it were the most natural thing in the world, Billie watched Rich Bentley take Michelle's hand, ostensibly to expedite their progress. Oh, dear God, Billie thought, didn't he ever quit? Did he have to go after every single woman he ever met? He was so transparent. How could any woman be fooled by him? The answer, of course, was that no real woman was, only the child people, like this curious little French waif poor Charlie had picked up somewhere.

As he continued to bounce up and down to the heavy beat of the music, Charlie Wigham was reconsidering his whole life-style. He still had his rented twelve-hundred-dollar-a-month house on the beach, his Jag, the wardrobe from Carroll's in Beverly Hills, a taste for dollar cigars, and seats on the fifty-yard line to Rams home games. And he liked to entertain and drink good wine. Other than that, Charlie told himself, he really lived very modestly. Aside from Michelle, his only other recreation was playing a lot of tennis, but this was done on other people's courts, where furnishing an occasional can of balls was his only expense.

Austerity, he realized, might, however, be leering around the corner. Charlie's monthly expenses also included hefty alimony and child-support payments to his ex-wife, and now the income had stopped. He and Michelle had blown a huge wad in Europe, where they'd indulged themselves in the best hotels and restaurants. By midsummer, he figured, he'd be down to his last ten grand. And most of that would have to be set aside to meet his basic obligations to his ex-wife and kids for a year. He'd almost certainly have to give up his house, sell the Jag, and move into an apartment. That late in the summer he could probably get a small place somewhere in Malibu for half what he'd been spending, though almost certainly it wouldn't be on the water.

Michelle would understand. After all, he'd been more than generous so far, and he'd already explained to her about the ups and downs of the movie business. He'd come back, he'd make his movie. Like a fighter getting into shape for a title shot, he'd just have to peel away the fat in his life, concentrate totally on the challenge at hand. The only essentials to wheeling and dealing in L.A. were a car and a phone, and those he'd always be able to afford. Charlie anticipated that by mid-August he'd be down to his last two thousand dollars, but he also knew of a very rough Monday-night poker game he could get into right away. Charlie was one hell of a poker player, and he was pretty confident he'd be able to stay alive off that game for months, if he had to. He'd done it twice before, hadn't he? And this game, he knew, had been started by Wilson Mahoney, a big loser at contests of skill and chance, especially after the booze took hold. Mahoney may have been a good director, but at cards he was a dope, the kind of patsy you could sandbag out of at least one big pot a night, and that would probably be all Charlie needed to carry him for a while. He'd play his cards very, very well, because adversity and pressure always brought out the best in him, Charlie reassured himself. So what was to worry about? With the luxuries eliminated and the essentials accounted for, however precariously, Charlie would find himself free to maneuver, without having to worry about heavy bills. Yeah, he had it figured out, all right. . . .

The music stopped and the lights came up briefly. Charlie looked around. Where was Michelle? Jesus H. Christ, had he been dancing here all by himself? And for how long? What had happened to her? Where the hell had she gone?

10

Jim Wharton showed up at the party only because, as president of the Malibu Colony Association, he felt he really had no choice. This summer couple was giving the first big bash of the season, and Jim knew that practically everyone in the Colony would attend. He couldn't *not* go, that was the point. But what the hell, he told himself, the job was elective, and he'd be out from under it by the end of the year. You had to serve when it was your turn, especially when you functioned as a prime mover in the community and were active in local affairs.

He had a big role to play in this small pond, as well as in the much bigger ones, Jim believed. There were standards to be maintained and appearances to be kept up. He knew all about every aspect of his part and what it meant; he'd spent practically a lifetime preparing himself for it. And he'd built himself an image he intended now to honor, as substantially as if it reflected the truth about himself. But what was the truth? "The truth," he'd once told a wavering witness in a court case, "the truth, you asshole, is what I tell you it is, and don't you ever forget it."

Well, he wouldn't have to hang around this party too long, though he did want to be present for the fireworks display. He had to be absolutely sure these new clowns he'd hired to put it on would show

95

up on time and not botch it. Last year those guys from downtown, those two old Chinamen and their dingbat assistants, had first somehow wound up in Trancas, ten miles up the coast; then, two hours later, they'd blown up the whole arsenal right there in front of his house, practically setting it on fire. It had been a miracle no one was killed by those two crazy slants. This year, through his political connections downtown, Jim had hired the Long Beach outfit, which seemed to consist of one elderly, surly Italian and two long-haired beachboy helpers, but Jim had been assured they were reliable. No way to supervise it, of course, except by being present, so Jim had come prepared to stick it out until the display, scheduled for ten o'clock sharp, was over, after which he'd get the hell out of there. Anyway, his host, Sid Harvey, wasn't too bad a guy. Not much of a tennis player, but at least he could keep the ball in play. Now, if only Mary would stay sober enough . . .

"Jim, you were terrific," Sid said to him, handing him a drink as he walked in. "We should have won it."

Jim Wharton forced a smile. "We ran into a ringer."

"You can say that again. That kid's a demon on the court." Sid Harvey grinned. "I gather he and your daughter have been dating or something."

"Mostly something," Jim said, forcing a smile. "Nothing serious, Sid. They're just a couple of kids."

"Oh, yeah, I know. They're here, by the way."

"I figured. Probably out where the music is."

"Right. How's Mary?"

"Fine, fine. She's here somewhere."

"Oh, yeah?" Sid said. "Funny, I haven't seen her."

"She's probably well on the way to getting bombed. Mary's having some problems, Sid," Jim said.

"Hey, I'm sorry, Jim. I didn't mean to pry or anything."

"It's okay, Sid. It's no secret, you know. Few things are in the Colony. You probably already heard it from Billie."

"I had no idea—"

"Skip it, Sid."

"Yeah, yeah."

As Jim moved casually through the party, chatting about this and that while accepting compliments on his tennis game, he kept an eye out for Julie. He didn't find her in the tent or elsewhere on the premises, so he guessed she must have gone out on the beach with Tad, maybe to keep a close eye on the fireworks. The old Italian and his helpers were going to set off the display from a point at the southern end of the Colony beach, well below the last of the houses. There would be sheriff's deputies there to keep people away and make sure nobody got hurt, and a lot of the kids would have gone down there by now, especially the younger ones. Of course, maybe Julie and Tad had gone off on their own somewhere, to be alone with each other. Jim was a realist; he wouldn't have bet a dime they hadn't gone to bed together yet. Still, that possibility disturbed him more than it should have. Maybe the time *had* come for him to take some action, he told himself; maybe this thing *had* gone too far.

"You're Jim Wharton," the voice said. "I've always wanted to meet you."

He turned and found himself confronted by a very attractive woman in her middle or late thirties. She must have been worried about her age or had a bad complexion, because she wore a little too much Pan-Cake makeup, but she was still a fine-looking specimen, with, Jim noticed at once, a slender, very nicely proportioned figure. He knew he'd never met her before, but her face was definitely familiar to him. "Hello," he said. "We've met somewhere, I'd bet."

"Nope," she told him, smiling, "I'm Gail Hessian, *Dateline News*." She laughed now as she saw his expression go blank. "Don't panic. I don't want to interview you."

"I don't give interviews."

"I know that. I just wanted to meet you."

"Why?"

"You're an interesting man. And a hell of a tennis player."

"Don't tell me you play tennis," he said with mild sarcasm. "Come on, Miss Hessian."

"Not a stroke," she said. "I look great in a tennis outfit, but I can't hit the ball worth a shit."

He laughed. "What are you doing here, then?"

"I rented an apartment for the summer." she said, "in one of those phony Mediterranean villas up on Malibu Canyon Road. You must know the place."

"Sure."

"I'm working on a book, a novel," she explained. "I took some time off from my news stint."

"How's it coming?"

"Terrible. I always thought writing was easy," she said. "Once we took a sidewalk survey for the program, you know. We asked about thirty people we picked at random whether they thought they could write a book. Every single one of them said yes. They all had this great book in them, if they could just find the time to get it down on paper. You know what I've discovered? It ain't easy, Jim. It's goddamn hard. I'm getting nowhere with it. Know a good ghost?"

Jim studied her shrewdly. He believed her story, as far as it went, but there was surely something else involved. He liked her—the way she talked, the way she looked—but he knew better than to trust anybody in the news business. "I could get in touch with one, or an agent who could get you one," he told her. "I've had a couple of Hollywood clients who used ghosts to write their autobiographies. Never fiction, though. The trouble is, Gail, the good ones want a cut of everything."

"Well, sure," she said. "Why not? They're entitled, aren't they?"

"I got the ones for my clients for a flat fee," he said. "Writers are mostly greedy bums. You don't want them cutting in on your royalties."

"At this point, I don't care," she said. "What I've got right now is seventy-three really terrible pages. I didn't know I was an illiterate until I started to write."

"Don't you write your own stuff at the station?"

"Hell, no, not if I can help it." She smiled. "We have some underpaid hacks who do that. I just sit in front of the cameras looking sexy and sweet and do my little number. It's show biz, Jim, nothing else. You know that."

"I heard you wrote your own stories, Gail. I haven't watched you lately, but as I remember, you had your own special features."

"I reported them, Jim, I didn't write them," she said. "Big difference. I always thought I could, of course. Fact is, I can't write my name on toilet paper, it turns out. Where'd you learn to play tennis like a pro?"

"When I moved to California, back in the early fifties," he said. "Took it up for exercise. It turned out I had a talent for it. Strictly a club player, though. That kid who wiped us out of the finals, that's a tennis player. Different levels of the game, Gail."

"I got the picture. Still, you play well."

"Not bad," he admitted. "Tell me, what's your novel about?"

"Me," she said, "little old me, very thinly disguised. It details, or will when I get somebody to help me, exactly how much shit I had to eat and how many people I had to fuck to get to the top, or wherever the hell it is I am today."

"It sounds interesting. Is it true?"

"Oh, yes," she said. "I may even have to tone it down a bit. When I started out in this business, women on the air read the weather or gave traffic reports from helicopters hovering over freeways. I was the first anchor lady in California, or maybe the second. I didn't get there on talent alone, Jim. Did you?"

"No. Nobody gets there on talent alone, Gail."

"That's what my book's about."

"How is it going to help your career?"

"I don't know," she said, shrugging. "And you know what? I don't care. I just want to write about it. Get it off my chest. And I've got a publisher and an advance."

"You've got a very nice chest."

"I'm glad you like it." She raised her wineglass to eye level and toasted him. "Tell me, Jim Wharton, didn't you ever want to get anything about your past life off *your* chest?"

"Never," he said quietly. "And as I told you before, Gail, I don't give interviews, on or off the record."

"I got the message," she said. "Can I call you about ghosts? I'm serious."

"Sure," he said. "Anytime, kid."

"Kid? Flattery, Jim Wharton, is sure as hell going to get you somewhere," she told him. "Is your phone number listed?"

"Nope," he said. "But you can call my office number and leave a message or call the guardhouse and leave your number there. I'll get back to you."

"I'll do that. Try to get the message to me in person," she said, starting to move away from him. "It's more fun that way."

"I just might take you up on it," he told her.

This could prove to be a little risky, Jim Wharton realized, but he thought he could handle Gail Hessian without too much trouble. His only serious weakness in life, he knew, was women, but he'd coped in the past with far more demanding and dangerous specimens than this one. Anyway, his basic plan going in was always to take everything and give as little as possible. He was attractive to most women of all ages, and he'd rarely failed to take advantage of it. The only ones you had to watch out for, he'd learned very early, were the loonies, the young cunts with their brains addled by youth, not the careful, cunning climbers like this Gail Hessian, an ambitious, slightly overripe news lady. Still, he would have to be careful, a little more careful than usual, especially after last Wednesday. . . .

The man they'd sent to see him had been a revelation to Jim Wharton. Dudley Kerrigan was in his mid-thirties, but looked younger, with a thick head of well-groomed light brown wavy hair, not too long but not short either, obviously cut and kept trimmed by an expensive professional. He wore a perfectly tailored English custom-made three-piece gray suit, carried a black-leather briefcase with his initials stamped in gold on the lid, and spoke softly but distinctly in a fancy Ivy League accent that sounded authentic. He had a round, open, pleasant-looking face, with a delicately chiseled nose and a dimpled chin. But his light blue eyes, shielded by clear wire-rimmed glasses, were as dead as those on a wax model, and he apparently didn't know how to smile. He also saw no reason to waste time on amenities or casual conversation. "Jim, we're upset about the El Mirador situation," were his opening words as he sat down in Wharton's small corner office overlooking Wilshire Boulevard in Beverly Hills. "There is so much concern, in fact, that I had to come myself."

"That so?" Jim said. "We've had nothing but trouble with that place from the start. It was inevitable, of course."

"I wouldn't know about that."

"You obviously haven't been around the operation that long, or you would know," Jim said. "The Rancho El Mirador has had bad press from day one."

"I know that. What I don't know is why it was inevitable," Kerrigan snapped.

"Listen, son, I'm not going to explain it to you now," Jim said kindly. "If they thought it was important for you to know, they'd have told you. What's the problem?"

"We've found out the attorney general's office here has had informers planted inside El Mirador for at least six months," Kerrigan said. "A girl in the spa itself, one of the reception clerks in the main hotel, and a telephone operator. Maybe one or two others."

"I'm listening."

"One of these informers tipped off the police to the presence at El Mirador of two friends of ours," Kerrigan continued. "They were there, under cover, of course, until we could make other arrangements for them. Both were arrested."

"They must have been careless."

"Yes. One of them had a friend . . ."

"A woman?"

"Yes. They evidently had an argument, the woman made a phone call, talked too freely, and that was it."

"Where are they being held?"

"In San Diego."

"Out of my area."

"Yes. We're taking care of the matter. The bail is too high, but we're negotiating. We have a judge we think we can count on."

"I know him."

"I guess you would."

"What can I do, Kerrigan?"

"I think we have to find a way to remind the attorney general's office that we have been contributing to his political campaigns since 1972," Kerrigan said. "He seems to have lost sight of that fact."

"Somebody goofed, that's for sure," Wharton agreed. "We arranged for a twenty-five-thousand-dollar one last year and a large charitable contribution two years before that through my sources at the bank, the San Diego branch, I believe."

"Right," Kerrigan agreed, opening his briefcase. "We have some useful documentation. You can use it as you see fit." He extracted a large sealed manila envelope and dropped it on Wharton's desk. The older man made no move to pick it up. "I think you ought to know that the company feels you should have been on top of this matter. It should never have gone this far."

Jim Wharton's face flushed slightly, but otherwise he displayed no emotion. "As I told you, Kerrigan, the El Mirador situation has been a fuck-up from the start," he said evenly. "The financing for the whole complex down there was clumsily arranged. It was bound to surface, and when it did, the press picked it up and has been fucking

101

around with it ever since. If you ask me, it was pretty goddamn dumb to try to stash anybody away there. You had to figure somebody would have an informer planted on the premises, or a newspaper guy. Somebody in Chicago goofed, not me. I wasn't even told."

Kerrigan's face remained expressionless. He quietly snapped the briefcase shut and set it on the floor beside him. "I wouldn't know about that," he said. "I'm just telling you what our position is."

"I understand that," Wharton told him. "The operation inside El Mirador is almost certainly a leftover from the previous administration. Our man probably doesn't even know about it, or I'm sure he'd have put a stop to it. I'm sure we can find a way to terminate it. We'll get the funds cut off. But it may take a little time. Meanwhile, the company has to forget about El Mirador for a while. Tell them that in Chicago."

"I'll certainly do my best."

"Anyway, in about two months we'll have the resorts in Palm Springs and Acapulco open. And the Bahamas deal is in good shape. That should take some pressure off. At least we have the financing well arranged for those projects."

"Fine," Kerrigan said, suddenly standing up. "I don't want to take up too much of your time, Jim." He stuck out his hand. "It was a pleasure."

Jim Wharton shook hands with the younger man, nodded to him, and waited until he'd gone before sitting down again, after which he sank back in his chair and tried for a few minutes to get his thoughts in order.

El Mirador again. Were they never to be out from under that botched-up deal? From the time it had leaked out that the resort complex had been built with money from the Teamsters Central State Pension Fund and those Nevada banking interests, you might as well have kept a spotlight focused on the place. The police had had undercover people in there before from time to time, especially on prostitution charges, but this was more serious. How could the company be so careless as to use El Mirador as a hideout? Jim hoped Kerrigan would take that message back to Chicago with him. Meanwhile, what sort of trouble was he in? Jim asked himself.

Not serious, he estimated, but it wouldn't do to take too much for granted. No. The mere fact that they'd seen fit to send this guy

Kerrigan, somebody he'd never met and knew nothing about, was a little ominous. Jim Wharton had good friends inside the company, but somebody had decided to deal with him on the matter on a strictly businesslike basis. He was being held partly responsible, that much was clear. But he was confident he could handle this matter fairly easily, just as he'd handled so many others for them. Only, they'd have to shape up back there. They'd have to stop taking his territory for granted. The political scene had shifted, people had come and gone, some hitherto safe avenues had been closed to them. All this Jim had faithfully relayed to them, but evidently they hadn't been listening. It was a damn good thing he was in a position to move quickly and effectively in this matter, but what really annoyed him, Jim realized, was that, after all these years and all he'd accomplished, he was still being taken for granted in Chicago.

He sighed and reached for the phone. Somebody back there needed to be reminded that Jim Wharton had paid his dues to the company, and then some. "Hello, Donna," he said into the receiver, "set up a lunch for me with Mort Lewis, his first available date."

When the old Italian's first rocket exploded above the Colony beach at 10:04 P.M., Jim Wharton was standing with a couple of dozen other people at the edge of the sun deck, just beyond and to the left of the tent. He pretended to be as delighted by the display as the others in the group, but actually the spectacle bored him. He was pleased, however, that his confidence in the old man had not been misplaced. Unlike last year, this display went off without a hitch and without even one injury—a real bonus, if you were to recall the mishaps, minor and major, of past summer seasons. For this success Jim Wharton would take full credit; he could resign his unpaid, time-consuming task as president of the Malibu Colony Association at the end of the summer in a small blaze of glory. He'd have done his social duty by his Colony friends, and done it well. What more could they ask of him?

The rockets went up and exploded with a satisfying bang above the ocean, then showered multicolored flowers of light over the horizon. The flashes intermittently lit up the long curve of white sand, where a sizable crowd had gathered, gasping and squealing its pleasure, as shouting kids and barking dogs romped excitedly about, tripping, tumbling, and falling over each other in the sand. The waves broke in showers of silver foam, bouncing reflected light toward the onlookers.

The display lasted for twenty minutes, concluding in a huge multicolored burst of falling stars that lit up the whole horizon. Jim had already started to turn and go back inside the house when he spotted Tad and Julie. They were walking hand in hand along the beach, not far from the water's edge, and they looked sublimely happy with each other. What bothered Jim most about that little scene was that they were coming from the opposite direction, walking back toward the house from the deserted stretch of beach at the other end from where the crowd had gathered to watch the old Italian do his stuff.

Here was another problem he would have to cope with, and without wasting any more time. He'd let this little matter go on far too long; he'd obviously miscalculated badly.

11

"What the hell are we doing here, Victor?" Dorothy Ferrero inquired of her husband soon after they arrived at the party. "We don't play tennis and we don't even know these people."

"You know why, Dottie," Victor said, sipping uneasily from his tall Scotch and soda. "Evan and Jenny wanted to come."

"That surprised me, too."

"They've spent all weekend moving in right next door," Victor explained, "and Jennifer said the Harveys have been terrific neighbors. Even with this party coming up, they and their kids were all over there yesterday helping Evan and Jenny unpack and get settled."

"They're starstruck," Dorothy said. "Do you think they'd **have** been so helpful if they hadn't known it was Evan Gilbert?"

"I don't know."

"I still don't see why we had to come."

Victor didn't answer. He shifted uneasily from one foot to another as he leaned against the wall of the living room and sipped his drink. Parties in general were not his scene, or Dottie's either, but clearly the usual social rules and practices would be subject to modification from now on where Evan and Jenny were concerned, for at least the rest of this summer. The Gilberts had come over for dinner, had mentioned the party, had enthusiastically urged them to attend it with them, and now here they were, trapped in this mass of Colony celebrants and unable or unwilling to talk to anyone but each other. Nevertheless, Victor didn't see how they could have refused.

The quiet, intimate dinner they had planned had turned out to be a real trial, so terribly tense under the surface flow of brilliant gossip with which Evan had kept them entertained. The man was a born performer, but unfortunately Victor and Dorothy had been unable to rise to the occasion. Victor had welcomed Evan's suggestion over coffee that they drop in at the party, if only to get them all out of the house and into an atmosphere where Evan could really shine and not have to carry the burden of the conversation all by himself, just as if nothing were wrong. Poor Dorothy was such a terrible actress; she had barely made it through dinner without bursting into tears or throwing up. They had no right, Victor had fiercely whispered to her in the kitchen, no right to put any pressure on Evan, not now, not after what he'd had to adjust to over these past few days.

"Anyway," Dorothy now said, trying hard to smile, "I guess we had to come, too, huh? I know I blew it. I just can't pretend nothing's wrong, Vic. We shouldn't have had them over alone. I did try to get the Kramers."

"That might have seemed even stranger," Victor said. "What Evan needs most from us right now, Dottie, is as much normality as we can muster, while he's still okay."

"I know, I know," she said, gazing across the room to where Evan Gilbert, tall, relaxed, one arm propped against the end of the bar, was holding spontaneous court to a small group of listeners clearly enchanted by his witty, informed observations. "He *is* a wonder, Victor."

"Always was, ever since I've known him."

Dorothy didn't spot Jennifer in the group around Evan, but guessed she wouldn't have strayed far. "How do you think Jenny's going to hold up?" she suddenly asked. "She was under more of a strain than we were at dinner."

"I don't know."

"She's so much younger than he is."

"Yes. That ought to help. She's going to need all her strength,"

Victor said. "Dottie, can we talk about something else? Let's try to enjoy this party, for Evan's sake, okay?"

Dorothy nodded slowly. "Yeah. I'm going to get some air," she said, heading for the beach. "Coming?"

"Not right now. I'll finish my drink."

After Dorothy had left him, Victor took a big swallow of the Scotch. He allowed the noisy party to swirl mindlessly around him, hoping it would somehow draw him into its vortex, overwhelm him with distracting chatter, but all the time he kept his eyes focused on his ex-roomie. Such a charming, such a truly remarkable man. . . .

"Nice. Very nice," had been Evan's first words to him that terrible Tuesday morning in his office, just after Victor had told him. "I gather you don't think you could be wrong?"

"No, Evan," Victor answered, "no. I'm sorry."

Evan kept his back turned to him and went on gazing out the window toward the misty green hills above Sunset. "I want it straight, Victor," he said quietly. "No fudging or prevaricating."

"What you have is an ependymoma," Victor said in a dull, even voice. "It's a malignancy of the spinal cord. Obviously surgery is impossible. It's absolutely inoperable."

Evan turned now to look at him, and leaned cautiously back against the windowsill. He tried to keep his voice very light, very matter-of-fact. "What can you do," he asked, "besides look glum about it?"

"We can slow it down with X-ray therapy," Victor said. "That's about all."

"Which has some side effects, right?"

Victor nodded.

"Nausea and vomiting, if I'm not mistaken," Evan continued, "and . . . what else?"

"There will probably be some bladder irritation."

Evan forced a smile, pushed himself away from the window, and sank into one of the chairs facing Victor's desk. "A delicious prospect," he said. "And for this all you can promise me is six months?"

"Six to nine months in which you can lead a pretty normal life," Victor said in his coldest professional voice. "I mean, for a man with your varied interests."

107

"Yes? I'm listening, Victor."

"You'll have increasing difficulty getting around," Victor said, "but your mind and the upper part of your body won't be affected for quite a while."

"Swell. Now let's have the worst of it."

Victor didn't answer right away. Perhaps he couldn't. The words, at first, simply wouldn't come, which surprised him, as he had never doubted his ability to get through almost anything in his practice. This wasn't the first sentence of death he'd ever had to pronounce on a patient. Few of them took it as well as Evan was taking it, which should have helped. But it didn't.

"Come on, Victor."

"Eventually," Victor said in a hard, flat voice, "eventually you'll go downhill pretty fast."

"That's the first good piece of news you've given me."

"I'm sorry."

"In fact, I'm feeling a little fragile already," Evan admitted.

Victor didn't answer, but sat frozen to his chair. He'd been chain-smoking, he realized, but what did that matter now? He fumbled still another cigarette out of the pack on his desk and lit it.

"I guess you must know I've been having a lot more trouble than I've let on," Evan continued. "But Jenny knows. Going up and down steps is becoming a real problem. I fell a couple of times. Now I'm extra careful. I get help. I lean on Jenny a lot . . ."

Victor tried to find something to say, but his mind had gone blank. What, after all, was there to say? He exhaled a large cloud of tobacco smoke, turning his head as he did so in order to avoid blowing it directly into his friend's face.

Evan smiled. "Those'll kill you one day, Victor."

"I suppose so. But I'm hooked."

"Vic, thanks," Evan said. "I don't know for what, but thanks anyway. . . ."

Victor waited in silence, hoping, to his horror and despite his best intentions, that Evan Gilbert would get up now and go away.

"The worst of it," Evan observed, "is going to be telling Jenny."

"You want me to be there?"

"No."

"Whatever I can do, Evan . . ."

Gilbert leaned back in his chair and crossed his legs. He looked at himself doing so, realizing, perhaps, what a miracle that simple action would soon seem to him. He laughed at the irony of his own self-consciousness. "I'm something of a poseur, Victor, old boy," he said. "Always have been. This one may be a little tough to carry off."

"I'll do what I can for you," Victor assured him.

"Yes, I assumed you would. Are you surprised?"

"By what, Evan?"

"The assumption."

"Nothing about you surprises me, Evan," Victor said. "You're a phenomenon."

"Yeah." Evan lapsed uncharacteristically into silence for a moment, then suddenly banged a hand down on the arm of his chair. "What the hell am I supposed to be feeling right now, anyway?" he snapped. "I don't feel a goddamn thing!"

"Anger. That would be normal."

"Okay, I'm angry. What else?"

"You'll feel sorry for yourself," Victor said. "You have every right to . . ."

"Sorry for myself? Well . . . Oh, Jesus Christ, Victor . . ."

It was the closest he had come to cracking, Victor realized as he watched his friend struggle to get control of himself. Gilbert shielded his eyes with one hand and tightly clenched the arm of his chair with the other. He was rigid in his seat, immobilized by the effort to maintain control of his emotions. The facade Evan Gilbert had always presented to the world was one of cool, detached amusement, a quality that permeated his books, his lectures, his entire outlook on life. It was an attitude genuine to him, however calculated it may originally have been, but it had become suddenly very difficult to maintain.

"Listen, Evan, I'll do anything I can," Victor told him. "You know I will. Anything. And there's quite a lot I can do."

"Yes," Evan said, not looking at him.

The phone buzzed, a merciful interruption, and Victor picked it up. "Yes?" The nurse had a hysterical patient on the line, but one with whose outbursts Victor had become all too familiar. Sometimes he found himself thinking that half his practice consisted of hypochondriacs. "No, I can't talk to her now," he said, "and I don't want to be interrupted again."

By the time Victor put the receiver down, the worst of Evan's crisis seemed to have passed. The doctor watched with admiration as his friend began, step by step, to reconstitute the front he'd always presented to the world. It obviously wasn't proving easy for him, but he seemed ferociously determined to succeed. Evan Gilbert had made himself an image to live up to, for his own sake most of all.

"A lady in need of an aspirin," Victor growled, by way of marking time, of helping his friend to succeed.

"The only medicine that works," Evan said, managing a laugh.

"Yeah," Victor agreed. "That and having your hand held."

"I don't want to suffer, Victor," Evan said quietly.

"I know that."

"I'm a terrific coward."

"We all are."

"So, obviously, when the time comes," Evan continued smoothly, "I'll . . . I'll find my own way out. You'll have to tell me. You must never lie to me, Vic. You *must* tell me when."

"Have I ever lied to you?"

"Often."

"Evan—"

"In school you were especially mendacious," Evan said, apparently enjoying himself. "In small matters—girls, that sort of thing. I forgive you, Victor."

"You were always stealing the girls I wanted," Victor said. "I didn't lie to you about them. I just kept them away from you."

"Anyway, you won't lie to me now, will you, old pal?" Evan asked. "It's important to me."

"No, I won't lie to you."

"You've got to keep me posted on every single thing, good and bad, that happens to me," Evan explained. "I want to know exactly when the machinery starts falling apart."

"All right."

"Don't worry," Evan assured him, "I won't put you on the spot. But I do want to make a clean exit. You know, a few cheerful reminiscences, a couple of good jokes, and a quick buck-and-wing out. Nothing squalid, Vic, or excessively maudlin. I have high standards."

"You'll have to take things one day at a time," Victor told him. "Don't plan too far ahead of yourself."

"I could hardly do that now," Evan said. "I have a few local lecture dates booked this summer. Will I be able to keep them?"

"I think so. You'll be the judge."

"Yes. And then there's my new book." Evan shrugged, smiled, and stood up, hoisting himself out of the chair by his arms. "All I have is notes. I guess I'd better really get busy."

"You like to work."

"Yes," Evan said, "I always have. Always managed to keep a few balls up in the air at the same time. The wonderful juggling egghead." He started to go, but at the door he turned back, as if, Victor realized, he had to put the whole thing in perspective, tidy up the event, tuck in all the corners, and smooth out all the wrinkles. Only that way would his orderly mind be able to deal with the situation. He was constructing a creative attitude for himself, in much the same way he put together his books, his lectures, his whole swift, flashy progress through life. "Do you remember, in school," he said, "how many times we all used to talk about things like this? About what we'd do and whether there was a life after death and all that heavy late-night buttroom stuff? I used to envy all those people who believed in a god of some kind and that they were all going to heaven, sit around up there strumming harps and all that. And then I got to looking at this big crucifix in church one day and thinking to myself: Wow, I could never believe in a torture symbol like that. I think that's when I knew I was an atheist."

"It's another form of faith, isn't it?" Victor said. "Me, I just don't know. I'd sure like to believe there was some purpose behind all this."

"A god, Victor?" Evan asked, smiling slightly.

"Something, Evan, just something."

"Well, I'll soon find out. And you know what?"

"What?"

"If I turn out to be wrong, if there is something else," Evan said, "why, I guess I'll have a lot of explaining to do. I might even have to admit I'm wrong. But you'll have to grant me one thing, Victor."

"What's that?"

"If there is a god or some higher power watching over us and our affairs," Evan said, keeping it light and charming, "you'll have to admit he's put on a pretty poor show so far."

111

After Evan had gone, Victor remained seated at his desk for what seemed to him a very long time, but might have been no more than fifteen or twenty minutes. He sat as if paralyzed, his mind empty, his soul drained. *Maybe*, he thought, *maybe I shouldn't have become a doctor at all.* He was a good one, he knew that, one of the best. But he'd never been able to adjust to losing a patient, and now he'd have to watch his oldest and closest friend die without being able to do one single thing about it. It wasn't fair. The wrong people were always dying on him; it seemed to make a mockery of his profession. *Sometimes*, Victor thought, *sometimes I really hate what I do.* And he'd never thought he'd ever feel that way, ever. Nothing he had ever learned in medical school, or even in his early years of practice, could have prepared him for that, and it frightened him.

Gail Hessian didn't get to talk to Evan Gilbert until quite late in the evening, long after the fireworks display was over and after about half the guests had dispersed. The fact was, she hadn't immediately recognized him, mostly because she'd always associated the eminent author-scientist with the East Coast and never expected to find him in the Malibu Colony, of all places. When she learned he'd taken a house on the beach for the summer, she was absolutely delighted. Here, after all, was somebody she would be able to interview for her program—and without having to go to bed with him, either. (The man had a very young wife, didn't he?) Gail hadn't given up on Jim Wharton, of course, not this early in the game, but Evan Gilbert interested her far more, and a good segment of a show with him, or perhaps even a whole weekend special, would help to keep Alex West off her back, if, as seemed likely, Wharton wouldn't come through.

After Gail had recognized Gilbert, and received confirmation from her hostess that it was indeed he, she thrust herself into the group around him and introduced herself. "I've read everything you've ever written," she told him quite truthfully. "I think *The Immortality Syndrome* is your best book."

"I quite agree with you," the scientist said. "It was panned by all the right people."

"What are you doing in Malibu?" Gail Hessian asked. "Working on a new book?"

"Yes," Gilbert said. "Sort of a sequel. I hope to finish it this summer."

"Look, Mr. Gilbert, you don't know me," Gail said, "but I have my own TV news show here. I'd love to do an interview."

"Well, perhaps."

"May I call you?"

"Of course."

"I have a place out here for the summer," Gail said. "We could tape the interview right in your own home."

"How convenient." The tall man turned to the serious-looking pretty young woman standing beside him, but a little off to one side, as if ready to wait on him. "Jennifer, darling, why don't you call Miss Hessian—"

"Oh, that's okay," Gail interrupted, "I can call you, as they say out here."

"Either way," Gilbert said, smiling pleasantly. "Jennifer makes all those arrangements."

Gail and Jennifer smiled at each other, but before either of them could say anything, a large middle-aged woman in a purple-and-orange muumuu and white turban, who had been bursting with impatience to get into the conversation, now clasped Gilbert's free hand in both of her own. "I *loved* what you had to say in that book!" she gushed. "Especially about all our longings for immortality and all like that. That's really what's going on. I mean, it was so right. It explained all about the cults and all."

"Well, madam," Gilbert said, allowing her to wring his hand before gently but firmly disengaging himself, "I think we are going to go on trying to get into heaven one way or another. There will always be practical problems, of course, with the travel arrangements, such as how much carry-on luggage we'll be allowed to take with us."

The large woman in the muumuu giggled. "Oh, Dr. Gilbert . . ."

"Dr. Gilbert," one of the other women in the group around him cut in, "I wonder if you know anything about these marvelous new sensory and consciousness-raising techniques we're exploring now?"

"I'm not an expert, I'm afraid."

"Well, I have a friend who's just been through est, and she says . . ."

113

As the woman rattled on, Gail, who had been about to detach herself from the group, suddenly became aware that the scientist seemed to be in some sort of distress. He turned and handed his glass quickly to his wife, excused himself, and walked away.

"I'm sorry," Jennifer Gilbert said to the astonished woman who had been so unexpectedly interrupted, "my husband is very tired. We've been moving into our house all weekend, and he's been working very hard. He's simply exhausted. Please excuse us." And she hurried out of the room after him.

Gail Hessian thought the abruptness of the departure unusual, especially as Evan Gilbert had obviously been making such a successful effort to be charming to everyone, a trait she had imagined was characteristic of him, but it didn't strike her as especially significant. After all, the poor man had obviously been holding court in this corner of the room for hours and must have been bored silly by the sort of inane questions these women had been firing at him. Still, it was a bit odd that he should leave that abruptly. She shrugged it off, however, and turned to go.

What did strike her as very peculiar at that moment was the look on the face of a middle-aged man leaning against the opposite wall, who had also apparently witnessed Evan Gilbert's quick exit. He looked horrified, as if, in fact, he had seen something loathsome or very frightening. On her way out of the party, Gail asked some woman she'd met earlier, named Billie, who he was.

"Him?" the woman said. "Oh, that's Vic Ferrero. He's a doctor, a surgeon. An old friend of Gilbert's, I hear, from way back. Why do you ask?"

"No special reason," Gail Hessian said. "He seemed . . . I don't know, a little funny."

"He hates parties, kiddo," the Billie woman said. "What surprises me is that he's here at all."

"That must be it, then."

"What, honey?"

"He looked absolutely appalled," Gail explained, "as if he'd seen a ghost."

"A nice guy," Billie said, "but an actor he isn't. He must scare his patients to death."

12

Billie Farnsworth came to the party with Jay R. Pomerantz, who had picked her up in a brand-new Lincoln Continental he had leased while his Rolls was being serviced. "It's pretty hard to drive one of these cheap little automobiles," he explained apologetically to her as she got in beside him, "but it takes two weeks to service the damn Rolls, and if you need parts, hell, they hold it for a couple of months. Goddamn, Billie, you sure are a sight!"

And she was. She'd put on a new white pantsuit for the party, and it fitted her to perfection, showing off both her tight, lean figure and her tan. She had also draped two of her handsomest gold chains around her neck, and they snuggled warmly against her skin, visible and alluring through the open collar of her shirt. "Why, thank you kindly, Jay, honey," she said, turning Southern belle for the occasion. "I'm glad y'all like it."

He laughed and gazed admiringly at her out of those strangely mismatched eyes, then turned his attention to the road. He drove over the speed bumps toward the Harvey house with less care, she noticed, than he'd handled the Rolls, but that was understandable. "Goddamn," he said, "there sure are a lot of cars already."

"Yeah. You better park wherever you can," she cautioned him.

He began to nose the big car carefully into a tight space flanking somebody's tennis court. "Say, hon," he asked, turning off the ignition, "you heard anything on our house?"

"We're waiting on one set of owners," she told him, "but they're going to ask for more. But, of course, we figured that."

"Yeah. Look, Billie, I'm getting kind of itchy . . ."

"I know, Jay. But this takes time."

"Meanwhile, I'd sure like to move in. You need a rent check or something? A deposit, maybe?"

"Not if we agree on a sales price," she assured him. "I'll have some news for you by mid-week."

"Good deal, babe," Jay said, now heaving his plump frame out of the car. "But I gotta move. I can't stand the hotel anymore. The service is real lousy. Tomorrow I'm going into the Beverly-Hilton. I'll be there till I hear from you."

"You know your suite number there?"

"Nope," he said, looking around. "Call the switchboard about noon tomorrow. Shit, look at this, Billie. We could have walked."

"Nobody walks in southern California, honey," Billie told him, now taking his arm and guiding him toward the party, the sounds of which echoed in the air around them. "You got to adapt, Jay. Relax, baby, get laid back, as they say around here."

He laughed and took her arm. "That laid part I can sure fancy, Billie," he said. "Don't wander too far away tonight, honey. I got plans for you."

Once inside, however, Jay R. Pomerantz almost immediately abandoned her. Billie didn't mind in the least. It had been her idea to bring Jay to the party, now that it looked as if he would become a Colony resident. She wanted him to meet his future neighbors, but she hadn't expected or desired to be tied down to him all evening. She was genuinely happy that he seemed to find himself so at home in this particular crowd, and she guessed he'd be back to her at some point before the night was over. Meanwhile, Billie allowed herself to drift through the Harveys' crowded rooms, though she stayed away from the rock band, which tended always to give her a headache. What she did best of all at these parties, and where she felt she could make an important contribution, was to yield to whatever strong winds were blowing, floating this way and that like a chip on the surface of a broad stream full of eddies, whirlpools, and sudden shifts of current. It was her technique for getting the true feel of the experience, for savoring it to the full, and she'd always emerge from all such gatherings vastly refreshed and aglow with useful, sometimes fascinating tidbits of information.

The summer Colony parties were Billie's favorites, because there were new faces, new situations, new connections to be made and tested. And the big Colony houses themselves were, of course, such wonderful settings for these celebrations. They specialized in big open family rooms, but with lots of nooks and hideaways for people to snuggle into. The primal-scream rooms had given way to the fad for water therapy, and few were the larger houses without a built-in Jacuzzi and/or sauna. Many were the discoveries such hiding places tended to facilitate. More than once Billie had had occasion to drift into areas where the mere casual opening of a door had revealed wonderful scenes of intimacy or minor carnage that had later kept Colony tongues wagging for weeks.

With all those fences and locked gates, the Colony may have seemed committed to total privacy, but actually the atmosphere was more like living in a big apartment house. People forced by lack of space to cohabit practically on top of one another tended, like New Yorkers, to defend their privacy ferociously, but they were also more tolerant of their neighbors' eccentricities and surprisingly more open to casual contact. It was one of the paradoxes of Colony life that the rules of the place established rigid boundaries and an aura of exclusivity, while the reality, Billie knew, was far more laissez-faire.

Billie had tried to explain all this earlier to Lee Harvey, who had never stopped worrying about the fate of her party. She had refused to believe so many people would come, even though Billie had smilingly reassured her over and over that they would. "God, back in Wisconsin," Lee had wailed to her over the phone just the morning before, "I wouldn't even have dared try this. I don't know any of these people, Billie!"

"Listen, honey," Billie had told her, "in the Colony it's chic not to be chic. We all think it's a very nice gesture, and everybody's going to have a very good time. Just wait and see. And relax, Lee. Your problem is going to be getting rid of your guests, not getting them to show up."

The whole evening started out to be enormously entertaining and satisfying from Billie's point of view. First of all, from talking to Art Bonnell about the outcome of the tournament she realized that he and Laura were having more trouble than she'd imagined. Billie had never seen Art really loaded before, and you didn't have to be clairvoyant to understand that his distress had to have something to do with this guy George Alcorn, who hardly left Laura's side all night and wound up taking her home. Billie also happened to spot Dee Stauffer's quick exit to the beach later in pursuit of the tennis pro, and noted that she came back from her mission after only a few minutes, not looking overly pleased about the outcome. Poor Dee, with all that money and her looks, and she couldn't make anyone, especially herself, even faintly happy. Nothing she tried, and she had tried practically everything, ever seemed to work out for her. And it wasn't because she was a bitch, either; she was desperately available, too available. She was the only woman in Malibu who had never had anything unkind to say about Rich Bentley as a bed partner. That had to tell you something about her, didn't it?

When Rich went off with Charlie Wigham's girl, Billie once again found herself marveling at him. The man did have this easy surface charm, though Billie couldn't for the life of her figure out exactly how he did it. For years now he'd picked off the Malibu wives like a fox in a hen house. Why, he'd whisked this little French tart right out of there as easily as if she'd been waiting for him, but then, Rich Bentley worked very fast. Much too fast, Billie knew. "'Premature' isn't exactly the word for him," Mary Wharton had once drunkenly confided to her. "He's got this little tiny thing down there that looks in action like a worm in heat. All you got to do is look at it and it spits at you." Still, you had to admire the guy, Billie felt. The chase to him was everything, and by that standard he was the undisputed cock of the walk, a most appropriate term for him.

About halfway through the evening, Billie found herself wondering if Rich Bentley had met Gail Hessian. Now, there was a gal who just might be too much for him. She'd obviously charmed Jim Wharton, who certainly must have known who she was and who ordinarily regarded media types as unclean. He was usually about as receptive to their advances, social or professional, as he would have been to lepers, and Billie was astonished to see that Gail Hessian had somehow or other broken through that barrier. Well, she was a good-looking piece, no doubt about that, but a little too lacquered, a little too slick, but then, who could account for any man's taste these days? Billie herself had been after Jim Wharton off and on for nearly two years now, and where had it gotten her? Exactly nowhere, that's where. "Hey, Jim," she had once asked him at somebody's Christmas party, "what have you got against older women?" And all he had done was smile at her and give her a quick hug, the dumb bastard. This Gail Hessian had some mileage on her, too, but she hadn't yet become a classic model, like Billie. *Well, maybe I'm too much woman for him, anyway. He only likes teenyboppers. Poor Jim wouldn't know what to do with a real woman. Look at the mess he's made of his marriage, for Christ's sake.*

The hit of the party, as far as Billie was concerned, was definitely Evan Gilbert. What charm the man had, what poise. Billie spent the better part of an hour just listening to him and watching him hold court. Evan Gilbert could apparently talk about almost anything— science, religion, literature, politics, economics, even sports—and never say a trite or predictable thing. No wonder he'd become a celebrity, the chased-after darling of intellectuals right and left, and the intimate of nearly everybody who counted on the contemporary scene, from Jackie Onassis and George Plimpton to the highest government circles in Washington. One of these days, Billie assured herself, she would get around to reading his books, too. It was a real coup for the Colony to have him here for the summer, a refreshing change from the usual influx of rock stars, Hollywood celebs, and out-of-town rubes like the Harveys.

And his wife seemed so nice, too. Much younger than he, of course, and very quiet, but then, how could any woman married to Evan Gilbert keep up with him conversationally? The man was a formidable talker. It was a wonder he ever found time to write or teach at all, much less carry on the genetic and other scientific researches that had established his academic reputation and won him all those awards, grants, and prizes. Merely by looking at Jennifer Gilbert you could tell right away what sort of person she was—an uncomplicated, serious-minded, idealistic small-town or country girl. She obviously now lived in order to take care of and service this genius who had actually deigned to marry her. Billie knew the type well. A man like Evan Gilbert couldn't be expected to share the limelight with anyone, which must be why his first marriage had broken up so early and he'd been alone for so long, by far the most eligible bachelor on the national scene since Henry Kissinger.

From time to time during the course of the evening, Billie would catch glimpses of Jay, always animatedly involved in one conversation or another. She found herself wondering, as the room began to thin out considerably after midnight, if he'd been serious when he implied he'd make love to her later that night. He sure wasn't much to look at, but all that pure energy had to count for something, she told herself. It might turn out to be a real trip letting this little dynamo bang her. Well, she'd try it, and if he did want her, more out of curiosity, she felt, than any real desire for him. He really wasn't her type at all, but then . . .

Art Bonnell hadn't really wanted to go back inside the house at all after his encounter on the beach with Dee Stauffer. Everything that bitch had said to him had hit him hard, and for the rest of the evening he had hung around the fringes of the party, stalling simply because he had no place to go. At home he imagined Laura might still be up waiting for him, and he couldn't face that right now. On the other hand, if he did go home and find her still out, then the reality of Dee's nasty insinuation would be even harder to bear. What he most wanted that night was oblivion, but even that had been denied to him. No sooner had he sobered up after being sick than he had tried to drink again, but had been unable to. The first swallow of Scotch had almost nauseated him, so, nursing a straight Perrier and lime, he had retreated to the sidelines, as an occasional participant in desultory tennis talk, until, when he could stand no more of it, he excused himself from two D players discussing the fine points of their backhands and eased himself out the back. Only Lee Harvey, coming back from a session on the dance floor with Harry McKay, saw him leave.

As he passed the garage, Art thought he heard a shuffle of feet and a snatch of whispered conversation from the darkness at the top of the outside stairway leading, he imagined, to servants' quarters or a guest apartment, but he ignored it and kept going. When he got to the back gate, he quietly eased himself out, crossed the Colony road, and sat on the low wall overlooking the house's tennis court. A cool breeze off the sea felt fresh and clean against the back of his neck, and overhead, the tops of palms swayed gently beneath a dome of brilliant stars. It was a perfect summer night, he reflected, a scene out of a travel movie or the setting for a romance starring a couple of nice clean actors, like Gregory Peck, say, and Joan Fontaine. He smiled. Maybe he was becoming senile or his brain was turning to mush. After living around L.A. and working with movie people, you began to think and talk like them. Art laughed softly to himself and stretched. It was late, he guessed, and he ought to be going home.

"What's so funny?"

Startled, he turned. Lee Harvey was standing a few feet away from him, but he couldn't see her face clearly in the moonless night. "Lee? What are you doing here?"

"Oh, I saw you sneak out," she said. "You looked so lost or something. Are you all right?"

"Yeah, thanks. I'm feeling a lot better."

"I could use some air, too. Mind if I join you?"

"Of course not. Sit down."

She came and sat beside him, and together they stared out over the court, whose white lines seemed to glow in the darkness. "It's such a pretty night," she said. "I was hoping for a night just like this. We lucked out."

"You strike me as a lucky person."

"Do I? I guess I am. I'm sorry you're having such a rotten time."

"How do you know I'm having a rotten time?"

"Well, aren't you?"

He hesitated before answering. "Yes, I guess I am," he said at last. "Things have been piling up on me a little, and they all just sort of came to a head for me this weekend."

"Just running one of these Colony tournaments would be enough to hand me a nervous breakdown," she observed. "How do you stand it?"

"It goes with the territory, I guess," he told her. "If I don't do it, then somebody else would, and I'd lose points. After all, Lee, I do use several Colony courts to teach on without having to pay for the privilege. I guess my way of paying is to run the tournaments. There are only three or four a year. It's not that bad."

"I'd go bananas. I don't know how you kept your temper when all that squabbling started on our court, and then having to listen to the bitching about everything afterward."

"I don't even hear it, Lee. I can switch it off."

"No, you can't."

"Listen," he said, "I was the club pro down at the South Bay in Laguna for four years. That was a lot worse. In those places you have to be nice to all the members and suck up to the big wheels, or you're out on your can after a year or two. That was really awful. This is a less formal setup here. I don't have to be a nursemaid to all these fragile egos but four or five times a year."

"And always be nice to the rich folks, like Jim Wharton."

"Oh, especially Jim Wharton," Art said, smiling. "Jim's got a lot of clout, in Malibu and everywhere."

"I don't think I like him much."

"I don't ever ask myself whether I do or not," Art said. "I'm making a living here, Lee. I try to get along with everybody."

They sat together in silence for a couple of minutes, but they felt at ease with each other, as if their conversations had already become regular events, pleasant daily routines. Art felt some of the tension drain out of him as he sat beside her. He had begun to like Lee Harvey, he realized, but surely there was nothing wrong or underhanded about that, was there? She was nice and she was easy to talk to, and the night itself seemed to call for it. It had been such a long time, he realized, since he'd been able to talk to anybody this easily and intimately. He felt now a curious, perhaps misplaced sense of gratitude toward her.

"Well, this isn't exactly Forest Hills, is it?" she said as they continued to look out over the court.

"No, it isn't."

"You were very good, Sid tells me. You were the best."

"I could have been, maybe," he said.

"What happened?"

"I was young and dumb. I guess I thought nothing bad could happen to me, that I was immortal or something. I hurt my shoulder two years before I turned pro."

"Oh. How?"

"I tore some ligaments first, but I strapped up and went on playing. When the pain got too bad, I let them inject me, like a cripped horse. I'd gotten to the semis at Wimbledon that year," he explained. "I wanted to play the Nationals. I thought I could win. I wanted to turn pro the next year and go after Pancho for all the marbles. I rushed it a bit."

"You had to quit?"

"I defaulted in the second round at Forest Hills that year," he said. "I went to specialists, I had surgery. I took it easy all winter. I waited until midsummer to come back. At Forest Hills, I ran into Rosewall. I tore myself up again in that match. I went back on the pills and the shots. I kept going. I had my time on the pro circuit, too, but I never quite made it all the way back. That's the story of my life. Think it would make a good movie?"

"Terrific," she said, "and you're the only guy who could star in it."

"Oh, it's not such a tragedy," he said. "I had my good times. Not everyone gets to the top of the mountain. My trouble was, it all came too easily at first. I thought for a while it might go on forever."

"And you were married then?"

He nodded. "Yes. Laura shared some of the good times. She also shared the bad ones. We went through the whole whirling merry-go-round together, and a lot of it was fun. The tennis scene then was fun, a lot more fun than it is now."

"You did it all for love, as the song says?"

He grinned. "Not quite, Lee. I had my eye on the buck, too," he admitted. "Laura was rich folks. Well, not really rich. Her dad was a doctor back in Ohio. He'd died and left her some money. Not a lot, but it helped during the so-called amateur years, when the expense money came in envelopes under the table. We spent all the money, mine and hers, and we lived very well. When I turned pro, the idea was I'd make a killing in a couple of years and quit. It didn't work out. I got caught. I keep thinking I'll get out one day."

"Will you?"

"Maybe. There are a couple of guys I know, they own this big sporting-goods store downtown. They want me to go in with them on a new line, with my name on it and all. I don't know. I don't know anything about the business, and I'd have to raise some capital. I don't know. I'm thinking about it."

"But meanwhile you teach."

"Some days, Lee, I still love it," he said, staring out again over the darkened court. "Some days I get out there and it doesn't matter who I'm teaching or anything. I get that same terrific feeling I used to have, and it all comes back to me, just the way it was. I loved this game, Lee. I grew up in Detroit. My old man was a football player. I got into tennis because I wasn't heavy enough to play football and I couldn't hit a curve ball and I thought golf was for snobs. My dad never got over my passion for tennis, from the first time I set foot on that terrible concrete court in a public playground. I used to play six,

123

seven, eight hours a day. I got a job in a grocery store after school so I could pay for lessons."

"Your father must have been proud of you."

"He thought it was a sissy game. He died when I was sixteen. He never got over my not becoming a real athlete like him." Art laughed. "Poor bastard. The dumb, narrow dreams we dream. How it all gets away from us in the end."

"Yes, I know. But at least you loved it, Art. You have that to hang on to, and a lot of people never have anything like it. You had that love of the game, and it made you the man you are. You must be proud of it."

"I am." He turned slowly to look at her, and they smiled at each other. "My God," he said, "what'll Sid think?"

"Oh, he hasn't even missed me," she said, "but you're right. I'd better get back." She laughed. "I guess Billie will be telling everybody we sneaked off together or something."

"She's a terrible gossip, but she's not vicious," he said. "Anyway, Lee, thanks for the talk and sympathy."

"My pleasure." She reached out a hand to touch him, then turned to go. She took two steps, then came back, put her hands on his shoulders, and kissed him quickly on the cheek. "Good night, Art. Thanks for letting me sit with you. You're a nice man. You deserve the best, whichever way you go in life. Good night."

He did not kiss her back. He watched her go until he heard the gate close behind her and she faded back into the night, leaving in her wake only the cool, soft caress of her scented skin to blend into the night breezes.

"Uh, hi there," this male voice said just as Billie, who hadn't eaten anything since breakfast, found herself leaning over the buffet to see what was left to munch on. "Can I talk to you?"

"Why, sure," Billie said, grabbing a sliver of ham and turning around to find herself facing a sturdily built, intensely serious young man in a pale green leisure suit. Except for his long hair and painfully obvious sartorial attempt not to seem square, he could have been a charter member of the Junior Chamber of Commerce, swinging Malibu division. He had a square-jawed, boyish appearance set off by dimples and innocent-looking large gray eyes under straight, fairly heavy brows. A Dodger rooter, Billie guessed, a closet boy scout. "Who are you?" she asked.

He told her, in stupefying detail. His name was Bertram Felcher, and he and his wife, Edie, a mousy little brunette in a horribly out-of-date mini that, however, showed off a trim little figure, had recently moved to Malibu from somewhere in Orange County. They'd bought this cute little house nestled among the trees back of the highway, along Mariposa Lane, and they were just so thrilled to be there. Bert, it turned out, sold insurance for the Auto Club, and Edie, the little wonder and joyous homemaker, was raising their two adorable kids, a boy and a girl, real cute little tykes. Bert and Edie had heard about the tournament, had played in it, and they were real anxious to meet everybody. They'd been told by a lot of people that Billie Farnsworth knew just about everyone, and so they thought they'd just introduce themselves so Billie would get to know them and they could become friends and all.

"Hey, that's nice," Billie said, tearing off another piece of ham and popping it into her mouth. "Well, you be sure to call me someday and we'll get together."

She made a move to get away from them, but Bert proved to be persistent and apparently oblivious of her complete lack of interest in them. He proceeded to tell Billie that he and Edie were not just ordinary nice folks, but really something quite special; you had to get to know them. They had moved out of Orange County, it turned out, because it was much too square a milieu for them. "We're looking for some nice folks to swing with," he concluded. "Maybe you could suggest somebody."

"What?" Billie asked. "What do you mean, swing? Sex?"

Bert blushed slightly, and Edie giggled modestly. "Yeah," Bert said. "Edie and I have sort of decided that we want to strengthen our marriage and keep it healthy."

"By swinging."

"Yeah. We kind of figured Malibu was the place," he explained. "How about it, Billie? You know some nice couples or singles?"

"Me?"

"Well, sure. I guess you know what it's all about."

"Only in theory," Billie said, the ham suddenly sticking halfway down her throat.

"I'll bet you do know," Bert said. "You just introduce them to us, that's all."

"I can see you're a real sweet person," Edie added.

"Edie's always thought about another woman," Bert continued, "but of course, we've only talked about it. We didn't know anybody in Anaheim. They're very uptight about everything down there. People get offended easy. I mean, if you suggest something really modern and with-it and all."

"Look, Bert," Billie interrupted, "I . . . I think . . ." She gagged and was unable to continue.

"Here," Bert said, suddenly pounding her back.

"Get her some water, Bert," Edie suggested.

"Yeah, good idea."

But by the time Bert returned with a glass of water, Billie, eyes streaming tears, had managed to clear the offending piece of ham from her esophagus. "I'm . . . sorry," she gasped.

"It's really terrible when you get something stuck in your throat like that," Edie sympathized. "It's just terrible."

Billie stared at them. "Uh, listen, guys," she said, "I'm afraid you've got the wrong girl. I—"

"Hey," Bert assured her, grinning broadly, "no offense, Billie. I was just asking, that's all."

"Oh, my, yes," Edie agreed, nodding sweetly. "Bert believes in being out front. Gee, I mean, it's just something we've talked about. It isn't as if we've really done it. . . ."

"Hey, like, Malibu, you know?" Bert said. "It's a whole new trip, Billie. I guess you wouldn't know, being as how it's not your generation and all. Nothing personal."

"No, nothing personal," Billie mumbled. "Look, Bert . . ."

"It's okay," Bert assured her. "Forget it. Just thought you might know. Let's not get heavy. I can see you're really a terrific person and that you understand. What Edie and I want is to build on the foundation we have. We just think that swinging may be what we need, you know?"

"Yes, I understand," Billie said.

"Far-out," Edie said, and leaned over to peck her on the cheek.

"Hey, we'll see you, Billie, okay?"

After they'd gone, Billie began to look around for Jay. She found him in the kitchen talking stock market to a couple of Hughes

Air executives. "Jay," Billie informed him, "I'm going home."

"Sure, Billie, just a minute. Just want to finish a thought I had."

"You go ahead," she said. "I'll walk."

He caught up with her outside the back door. "Hey, honey," he said, taking her arm, "what's the matter? I was just talking business. Nice folks, too. What's happened, honey?"

"Nothing, Jay. I'm just tired and it's late."

"Okay, okay, honey." He patted her on the arm. "Look, I got to finish this conversation I was having. It's important. Met some real nice folks in there, and I want to finish up something I started, okay? I'll call ya tomorrow."

"Okay, Jay."

He went back into the house. Billie stood outside alone in the darkness for a few minutes and listened to the now muffled sound of the rock band playing something soft, for a change, and with an old-fashioned fox-trot rhythm. "Tea for Two," of all songs to be playing in swinging Malibu. *Why do I suddenly feel so old and so out of it? It's not like me,* Billie said to herself, *not like me at all.*

As she walked out toward the Colony road, past the garage, Billie heard a muffled squeal. She looked up. At the head of the stairway leading to what had once been the primal-scream room, a thin sliver of orange light sliced through the gloom. Somebody was up there, Billie realized. The room had no windows, she remembered, and so the intruders, whoever they were, had left the door slightly ajar. Keeping very close to the wall, Billie crept up the stairs, one very careful step at a time, so as not to be heard. When her head reached the level of the landing, she slithered forward like a snake and peered into the room through the slit in the doorway.

Naked and wholly abandoned to the pleasure of the experience, Michelle was lying on the padded floor of the cell, her legs spread wide and both hands pressing hard against the top of Rich Bentley's head as he burrowed into her, facefirst. He was still fully dressed, but with one hand he was grappling frantically to undo his belt. *She'll suffocate him that way, the poor sod,* Billie thought, but then Michelle had at least hit on the only possible technique to keep Rich Bentley from exploding prematurely. *Ah, these clever French girls!* Well, maybe it was going to be an adventurous summer after all, Billie told herself as she carefully eased herself back down.

III

The Early Season

13

"This is a celebration, Laura," George Alcorn said, raising his wineglass to toast her. "Don't look so gloomy."

"I'm not gloomy." She raised her own glass, touched it lightly to his, and sipped from it. The cold white wine, a very good French Chablis, tasted delicious, and she forced herself to smile. "That's a lovely wine. Thank you."

"Well, I thought you'd like it."

"Oh, I do, I do."

"Then what's wrong?"

"Nothing's wrong. I'm happy to be here, George. It's very nice of you to do this."

"I'm a nice guy, basically. If you get to know me."

"I'll drink to that," she said, taking another sip of the wine. "To George Alcorn, my favorite boss and all-American nice guy. Tops in the luncheon league."

He laughed. "Funny," he said, "very funny."

He was a nice guy, she reflected. A little pushy, but nice. It had been obvious to her for some time, of course, that his interest in her went considerably beyond their merely professional relationship, but still he'd never come on too aggressively, for which she could also be grateful. She was good at this job and she enjoyed it. She wanted to be able to remain at Alcorn-Hyland and begin to build this new career, this whole new life for herself. It had become essential to her salvation now, she knew that, absolutely crucial to it. But if George Alcorn had made going to bed with him a condition of continued employment there, obviously she'd have had to leave.

At the office he had never been anything less than correct. They called each other by their first names, but that was because the working atmosphere at the agency was an informal one and kept deliberately so. "We want feedback and creative input from everybody here," George Alcorn had explained to her one day. "We don't want anybody to feel shut out of this operation." Even Mark Hyland, who wore conservative three-piece suits and old-school neckties and lived in Pasadena, liked to joke and kid around. Nor did he mind being called Mark, either, by everyone on staff except the Chicano office boy, who was too awed by his austere Anglo facade to risk this act of lese majesty. Laura had found herself immediately at home in the informal ambience. She and Carlo Rozzi, her immediate superior, had hit it off from the very first day, and he had been her champion with both their bosses. She wanted now to believe that her success really did have nothing to do with George Alcorn's quite obvious interest in her. She wanted to believe that very much.

"You're embarrassed," he said now. "What's wrong? You don't think you deserve your promotion?"

"Is that what it is?"

"Well, isn't it? Not only are you now a permanent staff member of this glorious enterprise, with a huge yearly salary and all the vast array of benefits we so generously provide our pampered employees," he said, "but you actually have a title: assistant production supervisor. I mean, Laura, wow!"

"George," she objected, smiling, "knock it off, will you?"

"Happy to," he cheerfully agreed. "Titles, however, are one commodity we have plenty of. So if you don't like yours, we'll think up another one. Mark and I came up with this theory years ago. Give everybody a big title, with brasses sounding and trumpets blowing and all that, and you won't have to give big raises quite so often. Smart?"

"Brilliant."

"Look at Felipe. He'll never be anything but the office boy. But he can tell his friends he's the mailroom director. Big deal. Puts hair on his chest."

"Which, I gather, he can use."

"Well, he's half-Indian, from the East L.A. barrio." He picked up a menu and handed it to her. "Shall we order?"

"What do you suggest?"

"Anything. It's all good here."

And it was. The restaurant, the name of which she had already forgotten, was small and dark, tucked away in a side street in unfashionable West Hollywood, but it specialized in excellent crepes, fluffy omelets, and crisp, tangy salads. George Alcorn had impeccable taste in food, she knew by now. In the three and a half weeks she'd been with the agency, this was her sixth lunch date with him. He'd always invite her at the last minute, too, usually because some business engagement had fallen through and he found himself unexpectedly free. Or had he deliberately planned it that way, so she'd be caught off-guard, unable to think of an excuse not to have lunch with him? He must have assumed, correctly, that she wouldn't know anyone in Beverly Hills and so would always be available. It struck her that she had become the object of a campaign with him. Did he always woo his women at lunch? she wondered. How quaint.

"You're very quiet today," he told her after they had given the waiter their order. "Maybe I should have picked a more cheerful establishment. I thought this was an occasion."

"It is, George. I'm sorry."

"You can always turn me down," he said. "You don't have to have lunch with me. I won't fire you. Not right away."

She smiled. "You're odd."

"I am?"

"Yes."

"In what way?"

"You ply me with food instead of roses."

"You can't eat roses. They don't taste good."

"You could have tried diamonds."

"I'm too cheap. The lunches, I can write off on expenses. Diamonds are a long-term investment." He stared at her in mock dismay. "I didn't know you were so mercenary."

"Just testing you, George." She raised her glass to him again and drank. "Nice. I like it. And I like your food."

"And me?"

"And I like you."

"Good. Now we're getting somewhere."

They chatted during lunch about the office and her work, which she also liked very much. George Alcorn told her that he'd been able to offer her permanent employment before her six weeks' trial period was up mainly because she had proved herself not only qualified, but creative, imaginative, and dedicated, three wonderful attributes for any employee to have. "You're really much too smart for the job, of course," he said. "Any reasonably bright college girl with some training in commercial art could be doing exactly what you're doing now. But Carlo will throw a screaming fit if I take you away from him."

"Then don't. I love working with Carlo," she answered. "He's every bit as brilliant as you said he was. I'm really learning from him, you know."

"You'll have your own accounts to work on eventually," George said. "You have one asset Carlo doesn't. You can talk to clients and not go into a funk if they don't like what you've done. Carlo is great, but he takes everything so personally. He once flounced out of a crucial meeting with a group from Lavelle, the perfume people, because they didn't like the theme he'd thought up for their Christmas ads last year. We lost the account."

She laughed. "Really? I wish I'd been there."

"There was blood all over the walls" George recalled a bit ruefully. "The Lavelle people were crumbs, and I didn't mind losing them anyway. Their product is mediocre, to say the least. But I have a feeling you could have smoothed things over. You could go far in this business, Laura."

"I'm not an art director, George," she objected, "and I'm nowhere near as talented as Carlo."

"Oh, I know that. Carlo's worth ten Lavelle accounts," he agreed. "But still, you'll have a good career here, if you stick it out."

"I plan to."

She waited until dessert and coffee to ask him what was uppermost in her mind, and then she didn't quite know how to put it so as not to offend him. "George . . ."

"Yeah?"

"All these lunches . . ."

"I deduct them from my taxes."

"That isn't what I meant."

"You want to know why, right?"

"Right."

134

"Your job isn't contingent on saying yes, Laura," he volunteered. "Does that help?"

She nodded, not knowing now what else to say to him.

"Can we be honest with each other?" he asked.

"I certainly hope so," she said.

"I know it's obvious to you that I enjoy your company."

"Yes, I know."

"I guess maybe the only way I can say what I want to say," he explained, "is to tell you something I discovered a long time ago, when I was married."

"Which is?"

"Third parties don't break up marriages, Laura," he said. "Third parties come along very often when marriages are on the rocks."

"And you think mine is?"

"Yes, I think it's in a lot of trouble. I don't know why. If you want to tell me, you can."

"Not today, George. Maybe some other time."

"Anyway, what I really want to tell you is that I'm fond as hell of you," he said. "I know, I know, we're hardly acquainted. But I find you very attractive and I enjoy being with you. If you want to limit us to occasional lunches, okay. I'm not pushy. But I would like to see more of you, and not during business hours."

"I don't think that's possible right now," she told him.

"I figured it probably wasn't." He waited for the waiter to drop the bill on the table, picked it up, reached for a credit card, then finally looked up into her eyes again. "You don't mind if I keep trying, do you?"

"No. As long as you don't mind if I turn you down."

"I'll mind like hell, but I'll understand, okay? And if you think I'm pushing too hard, just tell me to go away."

"Agreed."

"Just don't hold it against me for trying," he concluded. "I really think you're terrific. You're probably much too terrific for me. You already know I'm a lousy husband, but I'm not an ogre either." He smiled now a bit sheepishly. "This is all beginning to sound funny and wrong. I'm sorry. I hope you enjoyed the lunch."

"I did. And I really do like you, George," she said, getting up to lead the way out of the restaurant. "But right now I'd just like to make a go of my job. It's going to help a lot."

"I don't know if that's good or bad for me."

"It has nothing to do with you," she said. "Or Art either. It has everything to do with me and where I am."

"Well, it's the me generation, they tell me."

"I only discovered that very recently, and I'm loving every minute of it."

"Oh, God, I'm so sorry," Lee Harvey said. "I had it on my list of things to do yesterday and I completely forgot. Sid took the boys in town on a shopping spree. They're going away on a river trip for the weekend. To keep them quiet he's also taking them to a movie. But we'll pay you for the time, of course."

"That's okay, Lee, I understand," he said, standing just inside her back door, racket in hand. "How about you? Want to hit some? You might as well, since you're paying for the hour."

"Have you ever seen me play tennis?"

"No, but you could learn."

"Nope, not a chance. Come on in. Want a drink?"

"Why not? It's the end of my working day."

She quickly rustled up ice cubes out of the refrigerator, dumped them noisily into a bucket, then headed out toward the living room. He followed her, dropped his equipment to the floor, and sank gratefully into her sofa, vastly relieved to be unexpectedly freed from the torture of having to teach her children, by far his least rewarding pupils. She settled herself efficiently behind the bar and held up a bottle of Chivas Regal. "This okay?"

"Perfect," he said. "With a little soda, please. If you have it."

"We have everything." She splashed whiskey generously into a tumbler, added a dash of soda, and handed it to him. "Okay?" she asked, heading back to the bar.

"Perfect."

"Gin for me," she said, pouring herself a small one over the rocks. "I'm addicted."

"That stuff is murder," he told her. "It goes through your liver punching holes."

She laughed. "I can't help it. I love the taste." She sank down into a chair opposite him, crossing those long, elegant legs of hers, and raised her glass to him. "Cheers."

He sipped from his drink and eyed her warily. "Nice. Thanks."

"You look bushed."

"I am."

"An especially tough day?"

"They're all tough, Lee, at my age."

"You're not old, Art."

"I'm fifty," he said. "I feel a thousand."

"And I'm sure teaching my two brats doesn't make you feel any younger."

"You said it, I didn't."

She laughed and stretched languidly in her chair. "Oh, boy," she said, "you don't know what a luxury it is to be here alone. I couldn't wait till I got Sid and the boys out of here, and I'm really going to enjoy the weekend. Summers here are pretty hectic."

"You don't like river trips, I gather."

"Never been on one and never will," she said. "Imagine, just sitting there in a stupid raft or a canoe while some prole steers you over the rapids and you get soaking wet, and then the joys of cooking and sleeping out and scratching your mosquito bites. No, thanks, Art, not for me. I don't mind trips—in fact, I like to travel—but I want a comfortable hotel room with plenty of hot water to retreat to at the end of the day."

"I had all the travel I ever wanted and more when I was out on the pro circuit," Art said. "Living out of suitcases was the worst part of it."

"Tell me about it," she said. "I mean, what was it like? Exciting, huh?"

He nodded. "Yes, it really was," he said. "Still, in those days, if you weren't ranked one or two, it wasn't that easy, nothing like the money up for grabs today. I'd have made a fortune."

He hadn't talked about all that and his past in general for so long that he was surprised now to hear himself spilling it again to this woman, talking as easily to her as he had that first time, on the night of her party. Maybe, he reflected, he had just buried his whole past life away and let it sit there, festering inside him like a secret abscess for such a long time that it had begun, without his even being aware of it, to poison the present. Talking about it now seemed to give him relief; he felt tension and hostility and frustration draining out of him, as if he had lanced an infection, leaving himself feeling empty but temporarily at peace. Or was it just the good Scotch she had poured for him? He didn't really know anymore. He didn't care. He sat there, in the gathering twilight, and just talked, as if, perhaps, his very life might depend on it, on his ability to exorcise at least a few of the demons that had been haunting him lately.

"I liked it," he told her at one point. "I really liked it, Lee. I liked barnstorming to all those different towns and every night playing on a different surface in front of a whole different bunch of people. It was hard, but it was fun, too. We used to carry our own court around with us. It was a big tarp that we'd stretch out over whatever surface was available to us. In gyms, parking lots, football fields, whatever we could get to play in. And we turned the people out, too. That first year, I did pretty well. I was in the second rank, with Segura and a couple of other guys, but I won my share and came out okay for the year. The next season, my shoulder started acting up again. I could hardly serve, and my overhead game ceased to exist, so I had to quit halfway through the tour."

"You miss it, don't you?"

"The circuit? No, not really," he said. "It was pretty rough. I'd have gotten tired of it anyway, after a while. The real money was at the very top in those days. The rest of us really had to scramble to make a buck. If you could put together thirty or forty grand, that was terrific."

"Good money for those days, wasn't it?"

He nodded. "Yeah, very good. But we paid our own expenses and worked our asses off."

"So you left the tour the second year. Then what?"

"I went into teaching."

"That must have seemed pretty dull to you."

"Well, I was married by that time," he explained. "Knocking around the country with a racket in your hand is all right, if you're alone. I met Laura during a tournament in Cleveland, you know."

"I didn't know."

"It was a classic affair," he said, smiling. "She was nineteen, the daughter of a small-town sawbones. We met at a party."

"And you were the glamorous jock, the golden boy who was going to take her out of all that."

"You got it. Actually," he continued, "it wasn't quite that romantic. I knocked her up."

"And you've been together ever since?" Lee asked, astonished by this revelation. "That kind of marriage usually doesn't last, does it?"

"Ours did. Listen, Lee, I loved her."

"Is Tad—?" she began.

"No," he said quickly. "We lost the first baby. That was another reason to get out, even if I hadn't been hurt. Tad was born the year after I quit, when we'd settled down."

"Back East?"

"No, in Arizona. A club called the Creekwood, outside of Tucson. I had a pretty nice setup there. We stuck it out for ten years before we moved to California."

She sighed and shook her head, then got up, waving her glass at him. "Ready?"

"Sure, if you are."

She took his glass and went back to the bar for refills, and again he found himself admiring her legs. "Do you ever wear anything but shorts?" he suddenly heard himself ask.

"Not if I can help it. I know a couple of good assets when I see them."

"You've got a great pair of assets, Lee."

"I was wondering if you'd noticed."

"I noticed."

The conversation was becoming a little tricky, they both realized, so they pursued this dangerous topic no further. When Lee returned from the bar to hand him his drink, however, she leaned over and kissed him quickly on the mouth. It was a brief, even fleeting peck, but warm and loving. He made no immediate move to respond, and she returned to her chair facing him. "I'm sorry," she said, looking genuinely distressed. "I just had the urge to kiss you, that's all. I've wanted to ever since we first met."

They stared at each other in silence across an embarrassed little gulf for several minutes that seemed much longer, after which he very carefully put his drink down on the floor and made a move to rise. "I think maybe I'd better go," he said.

"Please don't."

"We could get ourselves into trouble, Lee."

"I know. I still don't want you to go. Please finish your drink."

He hesitated a moment, then leaned over to retrieve his glass. "I need a little more ice," he said.

"I'll get it." She took his glass out of his hand. "Want it freshened a bit?"

"Yes, I guess so."

In silence she fixed his drink, handed it to him, and started to turn away. "Lee . . ." he said.

"What?"

She looked at him now with some alarm, the first time he had ever seen her really unsure of herself. It made him feel suddenly tender and protective toward her. "Listen," he said, "I like you a lot and I think I know how you feel about me. I don't want to play games. I want to face what's happening here without telling you or myself lies about it. Do you understand?"

"Yes. I feel the same way."

"I haven't been a saint, God knows, and I've made a lot of mistakes with my life," he continued. "I don't want to make another one now. Not with you, Lee."

"I didn't plan this," she said. "I didn't lure you here, did I?"

"No, I guess you didn't."

"But I can't help how I feel." She suddenly smiled, but wanly, and then she very nervously brushed a hand over a strand of hair that had tumbled over her forehead. "Methinks the lady doth protest too much," she murmured, then looked up at him. "I did lure you here," she admitted. "I knew you were coming by to pick up the boys and that nobody would be here. I waited for you, okay? I'm sorry. It was wrong, but I couldn't help myself. You can go now, if you like." And she turned her head away from him, so she wouldn't have to see him leave.

"I want you, Lee," he heard himself say, as if some other person had suddenly broken free inside him and was speaking for him. "I want you, too," this other person said.

"Oh, my God," Lee whispered, her eyes filling with tears, "we are in a mess, aren't we?"

He knew it was crazy and wrong, but he didn't much care about that anymore. Over the past few weeks the controls had slipped and his whole carefully structured, precariously balanced daily routine had started to come apart. He was a human slide area, he thought to himself, an incipient ruin, but this woman had made him feel truly human again. He leaned over now, and he kissed her for the first time. Her arms went up around his neck; the kiss was long and tender and very pleasurable, as if the event had all been carefully prepared for and intended from the start.

For a long while not another word was spoken between them. It was easy to undress her without moving her from the chair. She was wearing a man's shirt that he very quickly unbuttoned and slipped off her shoulders; then he went to his knees, opened her belt buckle, and tugged her shorts down and off over her ankles. There was a moment when he stood over her, staring down at her nakedness, surprised by two aspects of her body. Her breasts were very small but had large, soft brown nipples, and her otherwise perfect flat stomach was bisected by a long, thin Cesarean scar. All this he saw and noted before he made his long descent toward her, burying himself upon and within her with such conviction that, right there on the deep rug of her living-room floor, she came twice before he did, thrusting her body up toward him as she climaxed, and each time crying out like a small furry animal in pain.

It was very odd for both of them. Odd not because they had suddenly, without either of them expecting it, made love on the floor of her house, but because neither of them felt in the least guilty about it or that the episode had been in any way sordid. It should have been, they both knew, but it wasn't. Side by side now, and with their arms around each other, they lay on the thick rug by the side windows and let the sun caress them. For a time they were content simply to hold each other. Her head lay against his chest and her arms entwined lightly around his neck. "Are you all right?" she whispered, breaking the long silence at last.

"I think so."

"That was wonderful. It was needed."

"I know. Tell me about it."

"And I don't feel bad about it, either," she continued. "I think I knew we would make love. I wanted to, didn't you?"

"Yes. Yes, I did."

"Let's run away," she whispered. "Just the two of us."

"Sure, why not?"

"Take me away. Please."

"Hey," he said, realizing that she meant it, "where? How?"

"The weekend Sid and the boys go camping," she said. "We could have nearly three whole days, just the two of us."

"I guess we could."

"Please, Art? Please?"

"I'll try, Lee."

"I want to run away with you, even if it's only for three days this time." He didn't answer, so now she raised her head to look at him. "My God, Art, what's wrong?"

"Is there something wrong?"

"You're crying."

And he was, too. He hadn't even realized it. Something cold and dark had broken inside him, and his long-repressed emotions had come surging up from the depths of his soul. The tears were a symptom of life, he knew, not despair. "It's okay," he told her, "it's just been a long time since I felt anything, Lee, anything at all."

"I'll kiss them away."

She kissed him on one cheek, and then he found her mouth again and felt himself go hard against her. Gently, with great care and love this time, he opened her to him again, slid easily into her, and rolled her over on top of him. She buried her face in the hollow between his neck and shoulder and whimpered as they began to make love again, his strong hands cupping her buttocks and thrusting her down to take the whole of him into her. They climaxed together this time, and as they came they embraced and kissed, until at last, with one final shudder of pleasure, she stopped and lay still against him.

"I love you, Arthur," she said. "I know it's insane and all that, but I love you."

He couldn't answer just then, but he held her very tightly. Later, as they began getting dressed, she suddenly flung herself into his arms. "Darling, it's all right, isn't it? Tell me it's all right! Tell me we're going to be all right!"

"I hope so, Lee."

"Please?"

"We'll be all right. We'll be okay. We'll go away somewhere."

"Promise?"

"I promise."

She kissed him again, and then, as the sun began to dip toward the horizon, they slowly, tenderly, teasingly, like a couple of old-established lovers, helped each other put their clothes back on.

142

14

Jim Wharton got to the restaurant five minutes early. After making sure his table was still empty, he went immediately to the men's room and dialed the number of the Malibu Racquet Club. He thought he recognized the voice of the girl who answered. "Is this Jean?" he asked.

"No, it's Terry," the voice said. "Can I help you?"

"Terry? Hi. This is Jim Wharton. What are you doing there?"

"I'm working here now, Mr. Wharton. Just for the summer," the girl explained. "Mike was dumb enough to hire me. What can I do for you? Do you need a court?"

"Listen, is Tad there?"

"Yes, sir. Do you want to talk to him?"

"I don't have time. I've got a lunch and I'm on a public pay phone. Just tell Tad we need him to fill in on Saturday, at my usual time. Mr. Lefkowitz has dropped out." He chuckled. "Poor Dan, I guess we got too rough for him."

"Tad's hitting some on Court Seven, just below. You want me to ask him if he's free?"

"Tell him to get free, if he isn't," Jim said. "We need him." And he hung up without waiting for her answer.

By the time he got back to his favorite corner booth at Tony's,

Mort Lewis had arrived. The attorney general seemed affable enough as he rose to shake hands, but Jim could see he was more than a little nervous and that his eyes were trying to make out the room and its occupants. "Sorry, Mort," Jim said, sliding in beside him. "Had to fix a weekend tennis date. You know, what's more important than tennis?"

Both men laughed, but Jim could see that Mort Lewis still needed reassurance, and clearly it was his duty to provide it. "This place is fine, Mort," he said. "Tony Mancini, the owner, is a very good friend of mine. I always come here when I have business to discuss."

"Don't know it," Lewis answered, his eyes still probing the darker recesses of the small, dimly lit room. "How's the food?"

"The best pasta and veal in town," Jim said. "Actually, I have a vested interest. I helped Tony open this place two years ago. I'm surprised you've never been here."

Jim summoned Tony Mancini from the kitchen. He was a short, dark, dapper little man, who spoke English with a thick New Jersey or Philadelphia street accent, and he was apparently overwhelmed by the presence in his humble eating emporium of so eminent a political and law-enforcement figure as Morton Lewis. There was a good deal of good-natured banter about the attorney general's willingness to prosecute restaurant owners and chefs whose food didn't live up to the press notices, after which Tony Mancini bustled back into the kitchen to oversee personally the preparation of the veal *piccata* both Mort Lewis and his host had ordered. The encounter had consumed a pleasant five minutes and left Mort Lewis more at ease about his surroundings. "A nice little guy," he observed. "I'm glad to know about this restaurant. There aren't that many good places to eat near my office."

"Not only is the food good," Jim said, "but Tony's very discreet. Privacy is a big plus, I find. I only come here when I've got business to discuss. I know I can deal better when the food and drink are up to par."

Mort Lewis laughed, but his eyes were very serious, and they now focused steadily on Jim Wharton's smiling face. The attorney general was an affable-looking man most of the time, and he enjoyed a good joke, but he could also look very stern and unforgiving, especially in photographs advertising his candidacy for public office or in TV debates with opponents. He had never lost an election, and it was easy to understand why, but his forthright, sincere appearance held no awesome mysteries for Jim Wharton, who had sized up the man years before and taken his measure very accurately. As far as Jim Wharton was concerned, Mort Lewis would always be the least of his problems in any matter involving law enforcement. He'd been buying and selling the Mort Lewises on the American political scene for too many years now to even contemplate the possibility that he might have misjudged the man.

While waiting for the food to arrive, Jim quickly explained the problem. "I know it's a difficult spot for you," he said after he'd outlined the situation at El Mirador as he and his Chicago connections saw it. "There's been so much publicity about the place."

"Well-merited, apparently," Lewis said a bit testily. "It's been under investigation for years now."

"We know you inherited that situation," Jim said, "but we've got to try to cool it down, Mort. We can't have your people in there in such force. We've got a big investment in El Mirador."

"Obviously, that aspect should have been considered going in," Lewis said. "A lot of mistakes have been made."

"You're absolutely right," Jim agreed. "It's been a fuck-up from day one. But that doesn't alter the situation much now. We can't risk having El Mirador go under. In addition to the resort itself, we have about six thousand acres of land in development down there. If El Mirador gets shot down on us, what happens to land values and all the projects, all the condominiums? All we're asking, Mort, is your help in trying to cool the thing down. This guy Hester, who's been heading your investigations unit down there, well, we think you might be able to find something else for him to do. He's a little too eager."

"He's my top man," Lewis snapped. "How could I justify a reassignment?"

"Oh, in time, Mort. No rush. Things'll cool down in a few weeks . . ."

Mort Lewis did not immediately commit himself to Jim's point of view. Looking appropriately stern, he proceeded to lecture Jim Wharton on not only the mistakes made in financing and operating El Mirador but also the increasingly open operations of these out-of-state investment interests in California land deals, especially ones involving well-known underworld figures. Jim Wharton and his friends obviously didn't understand the delicacy of Mort Lewis' position. He was the attorney general for the whole state of California, second in importance only to the governor himself. He couldn't take an open hand in killing an ongoing investigation. Jim Wharton would have to explain that to his people back in Chicago.

"They understand your position very well, Mort," Jim answered soothingly. "They don't expect miracles, especially overnight. All they want is some reassurance that their long-term interests will be defended, that's all. That doesn't strike me as unreasonable, Mort."

The attorney general wasn't so sure. "Did you see that story on me in *New West?*" he asked angrily.

"I heard about it."

"All that stuff about there being so many criminal investigations under way when I took office," Mort Lewis continued, "and so few today. Of course, it's all bullshit, Jim, we know that."

"Sure."

"But it's damaging, just the same. It's going to cost me votes. I've got a reelection campaign coming up—"

"In two years," Jim cut in mildly.

"That's sooner than you think, Jim," Lewis pointed out. "People remember."

"Some do, most don't," Jim observed. "Look, Mort, everybody knows *New West* is just a muckraking operation. The people who voted for you don't read it. You're making too much out of this. It's not that serious."

Mort Lewis wasn't convinced. "El Mirador's name gets in the papers all the time. It's notorious, for Christ's sake. I'm not going to sink myself by covering up for hoods in there. It's your problem. Clean it up, Jim. Get it off my back *and* yours."

"We're doing exactly that," Jim said, "but we can't always guarantee our guests down there. If Hester's unit goes in and makes arrests, it may be of people we don't even know. But it looks bad and it *is* bad for us."

Tony now reappeared from the kitchen with a waiter in tow and their lunch. He also hung around long enough to interrupt the business talk for a few minutes, which was a blessing, in a way, Jim reflected. It allotted both Jim and the attorney general some time for hard private thinking before they would again have to confront this increasingly unpleasant little issue. The point was that Jim Wharton

146

had the means at hand, right inside his briefcase, to put a lot of pressure on Morton Lewis. What Jim wasn't sure of was whether Morton Lewis understood that, or whether he'd ultimately have to be shown. Jim Wharton hadn't morally underestimated Morton Lewis, but he might have overestimated his intelligence, a circumstance that could necessitate a naked show of force, the last resort, and one Jim Wharton was always most reluctant to use, as it created lasting bitternesses, festering discontents that sometimes, years later, could cause a great deal of trouble, occasionally real grief.

"Look, Mort," Jim resumed after Tony Mancini had again smilingly retreated from their booth, "there are lots of ways you could help, even now."

"Such as?"

"Paperwork. Move a few people around. Transfer under the guise of promoting. Get everybody to make carbon copies of everything. Get the right people to waste their time writing long reports. Go back into the files to double-check everything." Jim smiled. "I'm not a bureaucrat, Mort, but surely we both know how that process works."

"Pete Hester won't go for it," Mort snapped. "And he'll shoot his mouth off about it if I try to transfer him."

"I thought you said you were the attorney general, Mort. Who's Pete Hester, after all? Are people going to take his word over yours? What office did Pete Hester ever get elected to?"

"He's a good cop, that's all. One of the best."

"Great. Promote him. Bring him into your Sacramento headquarters. You can find things for him to do there, I'm sure."

Mort Lewis did not answer right away, but chewed glumly at his veal *piccata*. Jim Wharton took a sip of Tony's very nice California house wine, then leaned back in his seat with a deep sigh. "Well, Mort," he said, "I'm sure glad you see our point."

Mort Lewis slowly put his fork down, swallowed what he was chewing, then gazed out of his TV-ad-campaign face directly at the lawyer. "I'm sorry," he said, "I don't think I can help on this. At least not right now."

"I was hoping—"

"I can't pull Hester out right now," Mort Lewis continued, "and I don't want him in the home office. I couldn't justify any such move. It would look bad and compromise my office completely, especially after these last two arrests down there. I understand what you're asking for, Jim, and there's certainly merit in your request. I mean, I personally happen to believe that the whole El Mirador thing has been blown up way out of proportion. It's unfortunate. But I'm afraid my hands are tied here, at least for a while."

Jim Wharton was kind and considerate enough to wait until their second cup of espresso before resorting to the contents of his briefcase. No sense playing the game quite as roughly as that, was there? You had to leave the Mort Lewises their self-respect, at least, before taking them by the neck and squeezing hard. There were rules to every game, Jim Wharton knew, and the trick was to master them so completely that the stakes would never be jeopardized by any infraction of them, however minor, however trivial.

Mort Lewis had even managed to glance at his watch, in anticipation of a quick departure back to his downtown chores, before Jim Wharton reached for his briefcase. "Here, Mort," Jim said, opening the case and extracting the thick manila envelope Dudley Kerrigan had turned over to him at their meeting in late June, "you may want to look this over. Keep it. We have others."

The attorney general seemed puzzled, but he shouldn't have been, Jim thought—no, he really shouldn't have been. Jim *had* overestimated his intelligence; he wouldn't make that mistake again. "Mort," he said quietly, "this wasn't my idea, and I'm truly sorry about it." He stood up and shook the startled attorney general's hand. "I really have to run," he said. "I know you'll do what you can, Mort, and I really appreciate your coming here today. Oh, don't worry about the check, it's all been taken care of." And Jim Wharton walked quickly out of the restaurant.

After he'd gone, Mort Lewis made sure he was unobserved, then swiftly tore the manila envelope open. It contained a series of photographs, almost certainly extracted and blown up from a film or videotape sequence. In them, two middle-aged men, one of them definitely Morton Lewis, attorney general for the entire golden state of California, were taking turns performing elaborate acts of sexual bravado on the obviously compliant naked body of a large-breasted, grinning Vegas showgirl. The pictures had been shot from two angles, one from directly above the bed, the other from the side, probably from behind what would have looked to any prospective hotel guest like a large wall mirror. The views left very little to the imagination.

Even more troublesome to Morton Lewis were the four photostats of sizable checks, totaling about twenty thousand dollars, made out to him directly and signed by a man named Edward Baldo, better known to his many friends in real estate, politics, and show biz as Pinky. Morton Lewis had never listed this money as a campaign contribution, which it had been, but he had, thank God, reported it to the IRS as a consultation fee and paid taxes on it. That wasn't the problem. The heart of the matter, Lewis realized, was that his friend Pinky had almost certainly been involved in one way or another with the development and financing of El Mirador. Nor would it be possible now to deny actual knowledge of Pinky's personal involvement with him, even if the checks themselves could be explained. After all, the second reveler in the room with Mort Lewis and the naked girl was unmistakably Pinky Baldo.

Mort Lewis stuffed the pictures back into the envelope, tucked the package under his arm, and left the restaurant. He looked very pale, Tony Mancini noticed, and also very, very angry.

Jim Wharton did not return to his office in Beverly Hills that afternoon but drove straight home to Malibu. The meeting had depressed him profoundly. He had imagined such encounters as elements of his past life he would never have to deal with directly again. Evidently he had not finished paying his dues to the company, and perhaps he never would. When he got home, he went straight up to his room and called the office. "Donna," he said, "I'm home and I won't be back."

"Yes, sir."

"Any calls?"

"Only one I can't handle myself, Mr. Wharton. A lady called Gail Hessian, from *Dateline News*. She said you were expecting her to call. I told her I'd get back to her."

"Don't bother," Jim Wharton said. "I'll probably see her this weekend. She's nothing if not persistent. If she calls again, tell her I'm out and won't be back and you don't know where I am." Jim started to hang up, then paused. "Oh, and Donna?"

"Yes, sir?"

149

"We may be hearing from the attorney general's office either to-day or tomorrow morning. I'll see him again anywhere, anytime. Okay?"

"Yes, sir."

Jim Wharton sat alone in his room that afternoon and stared out to sea for nearly an hour, but the depression did not leave him. *Son of a bitch, I'm nearly fifty-five fucking years old and I'm still a fucking errand boy. . . .*

15

At least half of Charlie Wigham's carefully planned working days were now being spent on the phone talking short- and long-distance to agents, lawyers, and managers of performing talent or to their secretaries. This was because Charlie Wigham had decided to try to finance his production of *Pale Moon Rising* through a process known as packaging. The basic theory behind it, which Charlie had several times in vain tried to explain to Michelle, was simplicity itself. You had to get yourself a star and/or a name director, after which you could take the so-called package—property, star, director, and producer—to where the money was. "It's the only way to go," Charlie had said to Michelle when she incautiously asked him one morning why he spent so much of his time these days talking to perfect strangers and weird people she had never heard of. "I have no choice, baby," he had explained, "now that I've been turned down by the majors."

"Oh, yes, I see that, of course," Michelle had answered, smiling blankly. "But why we never do anything nice anymore, Sharlie? We used to have such fun, darling, but all this is *merde*."

"Yeah," Charlie had said, waving her impatiently out of the room, "but it won't be such shit, babe, when I put this thing together. Wait and see."

The trick, of course, was to convince the people you wanted to include in your package that everyone else was already committed, because the reality was that amost no big-name director or star would commit on his own to a project simply because he liked it. Celebrities, however, loved to cluster together, Charlie knew, on the presumption that it kept them hot, and a bunch of them all wrapped up in the same bundle would almost certainly attract the requisite loot. Most agents and managers these days thought exclusively in terms of packaging, because a really big package, one involving two or three stars as well as a name director and a top screenwriter or two, was the only kind of deal that generated the sort of lucre reminiscent, if only faintly, of the Old Hollywood. Agents, needless to say, chopped their ten percent off the top of the package, but that was okay. They used to carve off little chunks from elements inside the package as well, until the unions screamed double jeopardy, so Charlie felt he really couldn't complain. The important thing was to get the movie made, and Charlie knew that whatever package he could ultimately put together would be nibbled at here and there. The nibbles Charlie would take; the big chunks out of the deal he'd have to resist.

Melvin Schwartz, Charlie's lawyer and friend, was also definitely committed to the concept of a package. Together he and Charlie had written letters and made phone calls all over the place about *Pale Moon Rising*, and scripts had been sent out to many potential packagees, including such established figures as Robert Redford and Al Pacino. They had, of course, overlooked almost no one who was "bankable" from the world of country music and rock. Bob Dylan, Art Garfunkel, Arlo Guthrie, Mick Jagger, the Bee Gees, James Taylor, Tim Bigbee, Glen Campbell, Neil Diamond, John Denver, many, many others—all had been sent scripts of *Pale Moon Rising*.

Even though Mel couldn't see it, Charlie kept bringing up the name of Richard Dreyfuss. "Mel, I just know Dreyfuss is right for this part," Charlie had said to him. "And he's hot. With him we'd get all the money we need, and then some."

"How do you know he can sing?" Mel had asked.

"He doesn't have to sing, Mel," Charlie had explained. "All he's got to do is play the banjo. He played the guitar in *The Goodbye Girl*, didn't he? And sang a little?"

"He didn't sing worth a shit," Mel had objected. "And all he did was strum. He didn't really play."

"Listen, Mel, I'd rather have Richard Dreyfuss strumming than David Soul singing and dancing with a chorus of naked folksingers backing him, got it?"

"I got it, Charlie, I got it."

And so Charlie had also sent a script of *Pale Moon Rising* to Richard Dreyfuss, who was off on location making a picture somewhere. To make sure that Dreyfuss himself got to read the script, Charlie had sent it to him through a very attractive girl named Foxie, whom Charlie had met at a party and who claimed to be a close friend of the actor's. She'd promised Charlie that she'd get Richard Dreyfuss to read the script personally, without its having to go through an agent's or a lawyer's hands.

Two weeks had now passed since Charlie had given the script to Foxie, so he called her up one morning. "Hi, Foxie?"

"Yes," this sleepy female voice mumbled in his ear.

"Foxie, you sound like I woke you up. I'm sorry. It's nearly noon."

"That's okay," Foxie said. "Who is this?"

Charlie told her. "And I'm really sorry about waking you up."

Foxie explained to Charlie that this was her week to be into disco, so she was out late dancing every night and working on her steps.

"That's wonderful," Charlie said. "Listen, what I'm really calling about is my script, the one I gave you two weeks ago to give to Richard Dreyfuss."

"Who?"

"Richard Dreyfuss. You said you knew him and would get my script to him personally."

"Oh, yeah," Foxie said, "the script is here."

"Where's Richard?"

"Who?"

Charlie shut his eyes and leaned forward over his desk, cradling the phone to his ear and keeping his voice low and calm, very calm. "Richard Dreyfuss, the movie star," Charlie explained. "You were going to give my script to Richard to read."

"Oh, yeah. He isn't here," Foxie said. "But he'll be back."

"That's terrifically encouraging to hear," Charlie said. "When?"

"When what?"

153

"When will your friend Richard Dreyfuss be back," Charlie en-nunciated very slowly and clearly, as if addressing a small, dim-wit-ted child, "so that you will then be able to give him the script that I gave you to give to him?"

"I don't know. He's . . . like . . . you know . . . gone . . ."

"Yes, so I gather. Listen, Foxie . . ."

"Yeah?"

"Has anybody read the script?"

"Well, not really," Foxie admitted. "I mean, people who do read come here all the time and all, but, I don't know, I guess nobody's into reading anything this month. There's this big pile of stuff on Eddie's desk . . ."

"Eddie?" Charlie asked. "Who's Eddie?"

"Eddie? You don't know Eddie?"

"No, Foxie, I'm sorry, but I don't know Eddie. Is he your boy-friend?"

"Well, sort of. Not all the time. He lives here."

"I'm glad, I'm really glad," Charlie said. "For both of you. What does Eddie do?"

"He's . . . like . . . you know . . . kinda cooling it and all right now. I mean, this summer. We're all sort of laid back and kinda taking in the scene, you know?"

"Hey, that's great," Charlie said. "Listen, Foxie . . ."

"Yeah?"

"How about you reading the script?"

"Me? What for?"

"Because it's better you should read it than just letting it sit there with all that other stuff on Eddie's desk," Charlie suggested. "I'm sure you've got the time."

"Well, I guess . . ."

"Good," Charlie said. "I'll call you in about two weeks to find out what you think of it."

"That's cool."

"And, Foxie?"

"Yeah?"

"If Richard Dreyfuss should just happen to drop in, you will give him the script, won't you?"

"Oh. Well, yeah, sure," Foxie said. "Hey, Charlie?"

"Yes, Foxie."

"What was the name of that script? I mean, there's all this stuff on Eddie's desk, and I'm not even sure I can find it . . ."

"It's okay, Foxie," Charlie said, just before hanging up on her. "It's called *Pale Moon Rising*. If you can't find it, call me and I'll send you another copy."

"Well, ducks, this is a bit of all right," Alex West said, rubbing himself dry and settling back into his lounge chair. "Pass me the lotion, would you? I can't risk this much sun, with my skin."

"No, you sure can't," Gail Hessian agreed, staring with distaste at her producer's body. It was scrawny, hairless, and so white in this strong mid-July sun that it almost blinded her. As she looked at it, she was trying to figure out how she could ever have found it attractive enough to allow herself to go to bed with it. Her affair with Alex had lasted nearly two years, and she had once found him exciting to be with. Not great in the sack, but certainly stimulating company. Yes, that explained it. Men like Alex were attractive to women on an intellectual level and could talk them into bed, just as Alex had talked her into his. God knows she hadn't wanted him for his great physique. And in darkened rooms, after long evenings of exciting talk, who bothered about bodies? Gail had always favored men with brains over those with mere muscles. By giving herself to Alex, though, she'd undoubtedly overdone it. Out here, attired in those awful baggy English shorts and basking by her pool in this merciless Malibu sunlight, he looked like a worm, something lividly repulsive exposed by the sudden upheaval of a rotting log.

"What are you staring at me for with those great bulging eyes?" he asked as he briskly plastered himself with sun cream. "This graceful form should not be entirely unfamiliar to you."

"Graceful? Alex, you really ought to run or exercise or something," she said. "You look . . . indecent."

"Can't help my complexion, pet. Born with it, you know."

"None of us is born with muscles, either," she snapped, "but most of us do try at least to keep in shape."

"That's because you Californians are addicted to that sort of madness," Alex said, smiling complacently and settling himself more comfortably into his chair. "I have all the muscles I need, two of them. One is located between my ears, the other between my legs. They're both very powerful."

"Really? I hadn't noticed."

"You did once, ducky. I didn't hear any complaints, either," Alex said, looking quite pleased with himself. "Now, come on, darling, let's not be bitchy and start a quarrel. It's much too beautiful a day, and I didn't drive all the way out here to the Malibu from beautiful smog-bound Burbank to be insulted, now, did I?"

"Why do you call it *the* Malibu, Alex?"

"Old California types do. Haven't you noticed?"

"No. Maybe that's because I don't know any old California types. Everyone I know in this area is from somewhere else."

"We did a show once, remember, about the Coastal Commission?"

"Oh, yes."

"Some old geezer petitioning for a zoning change kept referring to his land as being on the Malibu," Alex explained. "I inquired about it. Always like to be accurate and up-to-date, you know. That's what made me a good reporter."

"When was that?"

"When I was an underpaid hack working for news bureaus at home and here, long before I discovered American telly and its lucrative salaries."

"Funny," she said, "I can't imagine you actually covering a story. It does make you more human."

Alex sighed. "Oh, dear, you are in a snit, aren't you? Now, tell old Alex all about it. I did come out here at your behest, you know, and on the off-chance I can help."

She took a deep breath and told him. Not only was she getting nowhere with her novel, but she had begun to think the whole idea was perfectly terrible. She'd just about decided to drop it, unless she could get a ghost writer to collaborate with her. She had discussed the problem at length with her agent and her lawyer, both of whom were against her not doing the book, because they were convinced there would be a lot of money in it and it would surely make a great movie or at least a great mini-series on TV.

"Oh, undoubtedly," Alex interrupted, "if you can keep it clean enough to hold it to an R rating. I'd buy the book myself, just to find out how you did it."

"Fuck off, Alex."

"Sorry, love. Do go on. I'm all ears, really."

So she would do the book after all, but only on the condition that somebody find her this ghost writer. She'd been trying to get hold of Jim Wharton ever since that Forth-of-July party, because he had suggested one for her, but the son of a bitch never returned her calls. Anyway, she was still more or less committed to the book, she wanted Alex to know that, so she would need more time. She couldn't do two nightly news broadcasts and the Sunday specials and her book, all at the same time.

"No, I can see that," Alex said.

"Of course, I have a contract with the network, and you could hold me to it," Gail tactfully reminded him. "If you do, I'll give up the book, Alex. Please help."

"Listen, pet, I've anticipated you and I've already thought it all out," he told her, rubbing his bony knees and beaming at her. "I'm not such a stinker, after all. Give me two specials this summer and I'll let Dotty Datsun anchor the eleven-o'clock show till after Labor Day. She's younger and prettier than you are anyway, and she needs the experience."

"You bastard—"

"That's my offer, take it or leave it. I will not haggle with you."

"Dotty Datsun? Little Lips? She's so dumb she can't even read her lines without flubbing them, much less write them."

"That's my worry, pet."

Gail hesitated. She hated Dotty Datsun, who was obviously being groomed by the station to replace her and in whom she recognized the same ruthless ambitions she had once nurtured herself. But did she have any choice? How else was she to get her book done this summer? She couldn't expect Alex not to replace her with another woman, and it might as well be Dotty Datsun, who was at least every bit as green and awkward on the air as Gail had been when she started out. It was a chance she'd have to take, Gail realized; she'd have to gamble on this book making her a nationwide celebrity. The network wouldn't dare to fire her then, not for all the Dotty Datsuns in the world, or she'd simply go and peddle herself elsewhere for more money and better air time. She'd show them, all of them, these cunning but dumb bastards who couldn't see beyond the ratings and had almost as much integrity and taste as a herd of swine with their noses buried in garbage.

"Don't look angry, Gail," Alex said, sounding almost human. "I am trying to help."

"I guess you are."

157

"Well, of course I am. Now, about your specials . . ."

"Yes?"

"The Malibu is one. The life-style out here. Who lives here, who comes here in the summer, and why. And how it is different from the rest of the L.A. basin. You're on the spot, so that should be easy enough for you. Be sure to interview this chap Gilbert."

"I've been planning to, but his wife keeps putting me off. The other?"

"Hospitals." Gail groaned, but Alex quickly silenced her with a wave of his hand. "Wait. All we want is an update on how they work, on what happens in them during a typical day, all against a background of financing and rising medical costs and so on. But you can build the thing around a single day. Go in there with a camera crew and poke around. You'll have to get legal clearances, of course, but we can handle all that for you."

Gail groaned again. "Alex, for God's sake, that's a back-breaker. I'm supposed to do all this and the five-o'clock news and work on my book?"

"Don't, then."

"Don't what?"

"Work on the book. Let the ghost work on it. Simply tell him what to write. Let others do the work for you. Like me, pet."

"I haven't even found a writer."

"You will. When you do, don't haggle over pennies. Writers, love, are for sale, like everyone else, but the good ones will insist on being paid well."

"You're a terrible cynic, Alex."

He didn't immediately answer, but lay back in the lounge, and basted in salve, spread-eagled himself to the July sun. After a few minutes of heat, Gail stood up to take a dip in the pool and Alex propped himself up on one elbow to watch. "You're aging beautifully," he said, "like a fine Bordeaux. Can we fool around a bit later?"

"Not a chance, you limey worm," she said. "I don't need you anymore, Alex." And she dived into the cool blue chlorinated water, shutting her eyes to its mild sting and blessedly deadening her producer's mock-outraged cry of pain.

It wasn't true, of course. She did still need him, and would go on needing him and having to please him until her book finally set her free. She could become the second Barbara Walters if she played her cards skillfully and didn't push too hard too soon. Meanwhile, if that meant having to jump every time Alex West snapped the network's steely fingers at her, well, she'd jump, through flaming hoops or from bed to bed, if that's what it took. Gail Hessian would be thirty-eight in September, and it scared the hell out of her.

Late that afternoon, Charlie Wigham drove into West Hollywood to confer with his lawyer. Melvin Schwartz's office looked out over the Strip from the eleventh floor of a black-glass tower, and it comforted Charlie to sit there, especially after such a frustrating day capped by that idiotic conversation with Foxie. As the two men talked, Charlie could stare out of Melvin's corner window at the river of cars below snaking their way through the miasma of exhaust fumes that lay banked over the whole city at this hour, a pretty layer of orange soot.

Melvin could tell that his client and friend was discouraged, but he knew better than to try to bolster him with false cheer. The lawyer was short, thin, balding, with quick pale green darting eyes, and had been known to smile occasionally, but never to laugh. He had begun his career as a public defender, had tired of starving while protecting Welfare losers and other petty deadbeats from the larger criminal oppressions of the state's cumbersome judicial system, and had opted for show biz. He was not yet forty, but he and his wife and children now lived in a Bel Air Tudor mansion, on two and a half acres of manicured hillside, and he drove a Mercedes 450 SL that he had paid for in cash. Melvin despised his career, but not his lifestyle. Charlie Wigham was, at the moment, the least successful of his thirty-four clients, but Melvin planned to stick by him. He didn't believe much in *Pale Moon Rising*, but he did believe in Charlie. He'd represented him for five years now, and he knew a good Hollywood hustler when he saw one.

"They don't answer my phone calls, much less the letters I write," Charlie was complaining. "I'm into long dialogues with secretaries and girlfriends."

Melvin nodded. "The problem is, Charlie," he said, "these guys who manage people like Dylan and Garfunkel are very, very rich and their clients are at least five times as rich as they are. What do they need with a movie?"

"Most of the time they don't even send the script back," Charlie continued, "or they send it back unopened. It's discouraging."

"I know. They don't answer me, either."

159

"So what do I do?"

"You keep plugging, Charlie," Melvin said. "And there are other routes we can try."

Charlie went on gazing glumly out of Melvin's window. That very morning, after hanging up on Foxie, he'd called Dan Lefkowitz, whom he knew slightly from the Malibu tennis scene. Dan handled Tim Bigbee and the Hive, currently the hottest country-rock group around, and Charlie had, of course, sent him a script, one of the first to be mailed out. He had heard nothing and figured he might as well call. He'd even managed, by using the tennis connection, to get Dan Lefkowitz himself on the phone. "Charlie Wig-what? Who is this?" Dan had shouted into his ear. Charlie had quickly gone into his pitch, but Dan Lefkowitz had cut him off in mid-paragraph. "Listen," he barked, "listen, we've got fifty scripts sitting right here."

"Does anybody read them?" Charlie had asked.

"No," said Lefkowitz. "Oh, shit, Tim comes in sometimes, and he reads what and when he wants to, that's all."

"Well, Dan, I'd really appreciate it if you—"

"Don't waste your time or mine, Charlie," Dan Lefkowitz had said. "What's your address? I'll have the script mailed back to you."

And that had been that, Charlie explained to Melvin, who was now drumming his fingers lightly against the polished surface of his mahogany desk. "Charlie," he said, "I think we'd better go another way."

"I guess so," Charlie said. "I'm so tired of writing letters and making phone calls I'm ready to jump. The only answer I got was from a guy I didn't contact who asked *me* for a script."

"Who was that?"

"A kid named Lane Ponds."

"Never heard of him."

"I took him the script personally," Charlie revealed. "He's singing at some coffee house in Venice, and Michelle and I went to hear him the other night. The funny thing is, Mel, the kid is perfect. He looks the part and he sings great and he can even play the banjo. He's the only one of these kids I've seen who has any stage presence. He's read the script and loves it."

"So what, Charlie? He's a nobody."

"Yeah, I know. I couldn't raise dollar one on him."

Melvin hesitated, as if turning a possibility over in his head, then suddenly stopped drumming. "Charlie, what about this kid's track record?"

"What do you mean? I told you."

"Has he cut an album yet?"

"One, with some little outfit back in Nashville, and it disappeared in two weeks," Charlie answered. "He told me he's been signed by Continental, but they haven't put an album together yet."

"That's a big outfit, Charlie," Melvin said. "Isn't that your old pal Brian Golding?"

"He's the movie end," Charlie said. "The record division is a guy named Boots O'Hara."

"Never heard of him," Melvin said, "but it isn't going to hurt to talk to him."

"What about?"

"First let me make the appointment for us," Melvin said, reaching for the phone, "then I'll explain it to you."

"You know what this is like, Mel?" Charlie observed glumly. "It's like pointing a gun straight up in the air and hoping you'll hit a fucking duck."

16

"What sort of world, then, are we heading for?" Evan Gilbert asked his small but attentive audience. "Well, we could breed a race of legless mutants with prehensile tails, useful for space travel or Tarzan movies." He waited for the appreciative laughter to subside, smiled, and continued. "We could develop human beings with gills for underwater travel. Or people with two kinds of hands, one for heavy work, the other, let's say, for a little Mozart. Or ear flaps like eyelids to shut out noise, like the sound of your mother-in-law barking." More laughter from the assembled listeners. "Or eyes perched on stalks that could swivel a hundred and eighty degrees to make sure nothing's gaining on you. Science can do almost anything now."

Yes, Dorothy Ferrero thought, except cure the incurable. Science could always achieve the unnecessary, the purely superfluous, never the absolutely essential. That reality had driven better men even than her husband to drink and despair.

"It's conceivable that our descendants will indeed achieve immortality," Evan Gilbert said. "One thing *is* certain: they're sure going to look funny . . ."

The audience, entirely with him now, laughed again. Gilbert beamed; he obviously thrived on such adulation, basked in it like an actor in a curtain call. He reached up to push back a lock of hair, and a page of his lecture notes fluttered to the floor. He reached for it, stumbled, and fell to one knee. Jennifer Gilbert, her face yellow with fear, started to rise out of her front-row seat, but Mickey Kramer beat her to it. He took Gilbert's arm and helped him to his feet. Dorothy, immobilized by an icy ball of pure panic in her stomach, sat rooted to her chair, unable either to move or even to come to Jennifer's aid. She watched the younger woman, now as erect as an iron puppet perched on the edge of its seat, struggle for equanimity and control. From the tiny stage, Evan flashed her a quick, comforting smile, then began to shuffle through his notes. "Thank you," he said to Mickey as he returned to his seat at the end of the first row. Evan then beamed at the room at large. "As you can see, I may be well on the way to becoming a legless mutant myself . . ."

Completely at ease again, the audience laughed. Yes, the man was a marvel, all right, Dorothy told herself. Of the people in this room, only she and Jennifer knew the truth. It had been the Kramers, mostly Judy, who had organized this spontaneous lecture and discussion by Evan to benefit the Malibu Library, sorely in need of funds to stay open a full week, now that the state government had cut back on appropriations in the wake of the passage of Proposition 13. And, of course, Evan had agreed, though Jennifer hadn't wanted him to try. She had confided to Dorothy the week before that her husband was having increasing trouble getting around and could hardly manage any steps at all; she'd have preferred a refusal, even though Evan had pointed out that it would be difficult to justify, since Judy Kramer had given him a choice of three different dates.

Besides, Evan had made it clear again to Jennifer, he was determined to lead as normal a life as possible right up until the moment he couldn't get around at all anymore. He felt he owed that to himself; he was absolutely determined not to give in until forced to. How could Jennifer argue against that? Well, obviously she hadn't been able to, Dorothy realized, so the Kramers had gone ahead with the first open date in the library meeting room. They'd turned out quite a nice crowd on such short notice, too—fifty or sixty people, Dorothy guessed, at a minimum contribution of five bucks a head. Not bad, considering, but then, Evan Gilbert could always draw a crowd anywhere.

"Ladies and gentlemen, it's hard to resist the march of science," Evan Gilbert was saying now. "After all, everyone wants an end to disease and misery in the world, which is the panacea that the scientists now hold out to us and which they use to condone and justify every experiment. The trouble is that, as fallible human beings, we've historically been unable to cope with the potentially marvelous medical and technological advances our scientists have made. We live, in fact, in a world being poisoned and overcrowded by a misuse of those very advances. There's no reason to believe that, once we've been given absolute power over human life and evolution, we'll use it any more wisely and creatively than we've used other so-called miracles in the past. The purpose of power is power, George Orwell told us in 1984, and the future of the human race can also be imagined as a boot stamping forever on a human face . . ."

The room erupted in applause, and Evan began gathering up his papers, even as he grinned and waved at his listeners. Jennifer rushed to his side, and forcing a smile, quickly took his arm, while eight or nine of the audience went up to engage her husband in conversation. Dorothy remained where she was, temporarily unable to make herself get up from her chair. Judy Kramer spotted her, and beaming with delight, sank down beside her. "Wasn't it wonderful?" she said. "It was so nice of Evan to do this. We raised nearly eight hundred dollars."

"That's great, Judy."

"It's such a shame Victor couldn't come."

"He's on call," Dorothy explained. "Anyway, he's heard it all before."

"I can imagine."

Mickey Kramer joined them, and Dorothy got up. "Same old Evan, isn't it?"

"Yes."

Judy gazed sternly at her husband. "And you haven't even read his book. I put it on your desk last week."

Mickey grinned. "Who's had the time?"

"It's just brilliant," Judy said. "He should have been a writer, not a scientist."

"Honey, he's both," Mickey said.

"No, I mean he could have written novels and stuff."

Dorothy liked the Kramers, but they exhausted her. They were such do-gooders, such actively committed community types that they sometimes seemed like parodies of the boosters in the pages of old Sinclair Lewis novels. Oh, not really, she supposed, even as she entertained that thought briefly. The Kramers were nothing if not up-to-date, involved actively in every worthy liberal public cause, from Chavez and the lettuce pickers to sponsoring job programs for the poor, and free medical and legal advice for the indigent. They had lots of time and money to devote to all such causes, because Mickey spent his professional time raping the environment to put up plywood housing developments in hitherto unspoiled areas and chopping up the wilderness into small plots he sold by mail order to unsuspecting city dwellers unable to afford anything more than a tiny piece of undeveloped land somewhere. He drove a Rolls and she did all of her important shopping on Rodeo Drive in Beverly Hills, but nevertheless they had become, in their abundant spare time, prime movers in various Malibu good causes. "You know," Victor had once said to Dorothy after a particularly exhausting ACLU party sponsored by the Kramers, but held in the Ferrero house, "it's hard to disagree with their causes and harder still to dislike Mickey and Judy, but I think it might be important to try."

"Evan's a remarkable man," Mickey now said. "Funny and charming, and yet what he has to say has real substance."

"Like you, Mickey," Dorothy said, "Evan has the Midas touch."

"At his age, he even managed to run Jennifer ragged," Judy observed.

"He doesn't look well, though," Mickey said. "Is there something wrong, Dottie?"

"Not as far as I know," Dorothy lied.

"He's probably just tired," Judy said. "I hear he's working very hard on a new book."

"Yes, I think he is," Dorothy said. "And then, he's been running back and forth to Washington for those hearings on genetics. It's been exhausting."

"Such a wonderful man," Judy said, gazing with shining eyes toward the group around Evan and Jennifer. "I'm so happy that we're friends of his."

"Yes," Dorothy said, glancing at her watch. "Oh, my God, I've got to get out of here."

And she fled into the sunlight, where she wouldn't have to look at Evan Gilbert, already clearly in death's grip.

* * *

166

"Hi, Dad," Terry said, slipping into the booth to sit beside him and giving him a quick peck on the cheek. "I'm glad you showed up."

"What's the big occasion?" Victor asked.

"It's my day off at the club, and I thought it would be nice to have a good lunch with my elderly father," Terry explained. "I haven't seen you, hardly, in weeks."

"And your grammar hasn't improved in the interim, I notice."

"Oh, Dad," she said, grinning in mock exasperation, "don't you ever quit?"

"Never. I have standards. What do they teach you up there in Santa Cruz? Moon talk?"

"Hey, would you explain that to me?"

"Gladly," he said. "I have this theory that California was once settled by a race of mutants from the other side of the moon. They think hardly at all, but they're really into *feeling*, you know? And they communicate in a sort of variation of Newspeak, laid-back division. They're going to take over the country very soon. Do you know what they have instead of brains?"

"You're going to tell me, aren't you?"

"Transistors."

"I'm sure, Dad, that if I really think hard about this, I'll understand it."

"It's crucial, kid. The saucers landed here in the fifties, you know. That's why California is so loaded with fruitcakes."

"What do you mean? Gays? That's only in San Francisco. We have this real macho campus—"

"Beings from another planet," Victor said, holding up a single cautionary finger.

"You're weird, Dad," Terry said, snatching up a menu. "Hey, what's good here?"

"Everything," Victor said. "This is the best genuine phony Italian restaurant in Beverly Hills, with not one spaghetti dish under ten dollars. Eat your fill, kid."

It was good to be with her and to banter with her, Victor realized as he gazed affectionately at his daughter. Not only was the child becoming a beauty, but she had wit and style to boot. It had been a horrendous two weeks for him, with two of his oldest patients dying and a third one being kept alive, barely, in the Mercer ICU unit. No, not a good time at all. *I wish I could detach myself from all of it,* he thought, *just go away somewhere and lie down and forget it, as if it were all happening to someone else, not to my patients and not to me.* Nor was there any relief for him at home these days, with Evan and Jennifer just down the beach in their rented summer house. *Why didn't I become a painter, after all? I had some talent for it, they told me in grammar school. I should have listened. . . .*

"What's the matter, Dad?"

He saw her staring at him with concern. "Huh? Oh, nothing, Terry," he said. "I'm just tired."

"You looked so strange for a moment."

"It's been a rough time, I guess. It gets to me, you know."

"Mom said you were . . . I don't know . . . Anyway, I hope you don't mind my asking about lunch?"

"Mind? Honey, it's the only good thing that's happened to me all week." He squeezed her hand and signaled for the waiter. "Let's eat. I'm starved. And no medical talk, okay? Just tell me about you and how your vacation's shaping up."

Her happy chatter soothed him, and he was able to forget about his professional life, though he knew that by three o'clock he had to be back at the hospital and doing what he could to ease his cases, to say nothing of their distraught relatives, through their terminal agonies. How happy his daughter seemed, how healthily secure in her own untroubled involvement with life, as if immortality were a premise only the young never doubted but assumed as easily as the air they breathed. It made him want to laugh, not at the absurdity of it, but with joy, at the blessed insulation that youth created around itself against all despair and evil. He basked in her self-assurance, warmed himself in it, as if within the glow of a strong shaft of sunlight. He ate better and felt better than he had in weeks, and he realized suddenly how much he needed these children of his. They were his only true and lasting grip on life; he knew it now, more forcefully and clearly than ever before.

"Okay, so I know about your summer," Victor said over coffee and with a quick glance at his watch. "It all sounds good to me. And I like your fall plans, too, especially the idea of taking archaeology next term. Good subject. Opens up the mind, gives you a sense of the past. The past tends to disappear in L.A., because nobody cares about it. Now, what about the rest of your life?"

"What do you mean, Dad—who am I dating?"

"I guess so, if it's somebody important."

She told him then that Tad Bonnell had asked her out, to go to a movie or something, but that she hadn't accepted. "I feel kind of bad about it."

"Why?"

"Because he's been seeing Julie Wharton for so long."

"You're not all that close, are you?"

She shook her head. "No, but still . . . I mean, Tad and I have been seeing each other every day at the club, and we've, we've gotten to talking. I can tell he likes me. But I don't know . . ."

"Listen, a movie isn't going to commit you to each other for life, is it?"

Terry smiled. "Dad . . . I mean, he and Julie have been, you know, like terrifically close and all. I'm not that close to Julie, but I just feel kind of funny about dating Tad."

"He always struck me as a very conceited young man."

"Oh, he's not. He's really shy. I mean, he's a terrific tennis player . . ."

"He ought to be."

"But that's because his father got him into it when he was five or six years old. I mean, Tad likes tennis and he knows what it can do for him, but that's not what he's all about. He's interested in going to medical school, if he can swing it financially."

"Just what the world needs, more quacks." He saw Terry react with surprise to his cynicism, and caught himself in time. "Listen, I wouldn't worry about Julie Wharton," he assured her. "You're all much too young to get married or commit to each other for life, and going to a movie together is hardly an act of treason."

"Well, see, the trouble is, I do care about Tad," she admitted. "It wouldn't be just going to a movie, like with a friend. And Julie would know that."

"Well, she doesn't have to know," Victor said. "Anyway, only you can decide, Terry. In the war between men and women, it's usually the women who make all the decisions."

"Dad!"

"Old-fashioned male chauvinist talk, right?" He glanced at his watch again and signaled for the check. "I've got to go, honey. I'm late."

While they waited for his change to come back, Terry told Victor about the betting now going on at the tennis club. "Mr. Wharton plays there on the weekends," she said, "and Tad's in one of his regular games. They bet a lot of money."

"Tad does?"

"No, the other guys do. Mr. Lefkowitz dropped out of the game, so now Mr. Wharton's gotten Tad to fill in. He doesn't really want to, but he doesn't want to get Mr. Wharton down on him, for his Dad's sake, I guess."

"Jim Wharton's a barracuda," Victor said, scooping up his change and hurrying Terry out of their booth. "You hear all kinds of stories about him."

"Like what?"

"Women, for one thing. And about some sort of shady past he's supposed to have. Just rumors, mostly, but maybe there's some truth to them. Stay away from him, Terry."

"Oh, he gives me the creeps," she said.

"You always get the feeling with that guy that there's a payoff coming somewhere," Victor said. "Tell Tad to get himself out of that game if he can."

During the twenty-minute drive south back toward the hospital, Victor made a resolution to see more of his children. He would set aside specific times, he decided, and barring emergencies, stick to them. Being with either Terry or Michael or both together was the only relief he got these days from the tensions of his practice. He would use their sweet faces as talismans against his . . . what? Despair, was it? What Victor couldn't understand was why recently he'd been having such tough sledding. What was it? Fatigue? Too many recent losses? Evan? Or was the trouble more deeply rooted in himself, in his whole outlook on the course of his life, as well as the profession of medicine? He didn't know. He felt so tired so much of the time, so on edge and distraught, that it drained him of energy. The condition frightened him, because he felt so uninterested in so many of the cares and problems he found himself confronted with daily. It was a dangerous state of mind for a healer, he knew. What was wrong, he had begun to ask himself, what was missing?

When he and Dorothy had first moved out here and bought their house in Malibu, it had seemed like a dream realized. They lived so well, so very well, on the income from his practice, and Dorothy seemed so happy, and the kids so fair, blooming in the cheerful sunshine like flowers transplanted from the weed-choked, rubble-strewn lots of the city. When had this uneasiness, this nervous tic of dissatisfaction begun? When had the first doubts and questions made themselves more than a murmur in his head?

Several times during the past year Victor had tried to talk to Dorothy about these feelings of his, but had sensed immediately her impatience with his self-doubts. So he had never been able to finish exploring his thoughts aloud with her, because her quite obvious reluctance to let him do so had chilled him quickly into silence. Well, he couldn't blame her. On the surface, at least, they certainly had nothing to complain about. His practice was lucrative and growing, their home beautiful and comfortable, equipped with every material possession and labor-saving machine the technology of affluence had been able to devise, their children strong and healthy and intelligent—what was there to bemoan? What guilt-ridden fury gnawed at him, what relic from his past? Didn't Victor realize that in this corner of southern California, in this land of ease and contentment, in this small paradise that sheltered them, the past had no meaning, that it didn't count? *Why can't you just relax and enjoy your life*, Dorothy's eyes had seemed to say to him, *why can't you be satisfied?* He had felt accused and silenced, ashamed of his confused, unfocused discontent.

Was it the unequal contest with suffering and death that lay at the heart of his dilemma? Victor had long since resigned himself, first intellectually and then emotionally, to the basic reality of that struggle. He had understood the rules going in, accepted them and played his role in the farce with skill and dignity. No, perhaps it was something else, something he would dredge out of himself before long; he would have to, he knew, it order to survive. Otherwise it would fester in him, grow, perhaps, into a cancer that would eat him away as surely as Evan's was consuming him now. For that plague of the spirit there was no medical relief at all, only the helpless recognition of a terrible surrender. *I have not come all this way to lose my soul*, he almost said aloud to himself—or had he, indeed, spoken these very words? Shaken, he reached over now and turned the radio on, fiddled with the FM tuner until settled safely within the intricate charms of a late Beethoven trio.

171

He drove on in temporary peace, until, beyond the shabby roof-tops of the run-down residential area south of Culver Boulevard, the glass-and-stone block of the hospital suddenly became visible high above a row of stunted, frayed palms. It seemed a monolith to him, a last citadel against the night. The music became a jangle of incomprehensible, meaningless sound, shattered by the scream of a siren from the ambulance that roared past, lights flashing death and horror to the eye, as he waited for a light to change, his hands on the wheel, his forehead slick with icy sweat.

17

The party at Wilson Mahoney's began on a Friday afternoon and had been going on for three days by the time Rich Bentley showed up. Rich had first heard about the party through the Colony grapevine, and he had immediately estimated that it might turn out to be a good move for him at least to put in an appearance. He had never worked for Wilson Mahoney, but he knew that a lot of important Malibu and Hollywood types had been in and out over the past two days, and Mahoney had apparently welcomed them all.

Rich Bentley hadn't worked for a while, prospects were not exactly glowing, and what did he have to lose by just dropping in? Billie had told him that Mahoney was celebrating a birthday and was also about to decide what his next film would be. The famous director had two scripts under consideration and ready to go into production, both epics of blood and mayhem, in the best gory tradition of the Mahoney oeuvre. "I can't imagine what parts I could play, can you?" Rich had confided to Billie, "but you never know, there might be something."

Mahoney's party had begun as a Friday-night cookout on the beach and had apparently taken off from there. Word of it had spread up and down the coast and into Hollywood and Beverly Hills; it had already made one of the trade gossip columns, and people had begun coming from all over. From time to time guests would disappear to go off and sleep, but others would soon take their place. The affair just kept going, feeding off its own momentum. Billie herself had been in and out of it five or six times, she had confided to Rich, mostly because she always thoroughly enjoyed herself at such celebrity wingdings. The other night, for instance, Jason Robards had showed up in one of his funny hats and warbled a great old number called "April Showers" *a cappella.* Jason knew a lot of old songs, Billie had explained to Rich, and he could really sing them.

Mahoney's funny rented pink house, topped by a spurious Moorish cupola, was really little more than a bungalow wedged in between two of the larger Colony mansions, one of them belonging to Jim Wharton. The first impression Rich derived as he walked into the living room was one of amiable disorder and mild chaos. Mahoney himself, a paunchy, grizzled, spindly-legged, bearded figure under a large sombrero and dressed only in a pair of baggy shorts, presided, beer can in hand, from a corner, where he was telling lewd movie stories to Dee Stauffer and three mildly embarrassed but also obviously delighted Colony housewives. He waved to Rich Bentley as if he'd known him all his life and went right on with his act, much as if Rich were merely a new customer arriving late to a Vegas lounge show. Rich waved back and looked around for a drink and for someone he might know.

He spotted a few familiar faces among the forty or fifty people sprawled about the premises, but he headed for the open kitchen door, where he guessed he'd find liquor and ice. To get there he had to step over and around not only several of the guests but also the boxes, suitcases, and cartons that apparently contained most of the director's personal belongings. Part of the Wilson Mahoney legend was his determinedly nomadic existence, Rich remembered. Mahoney lived much of the time in rented trailers, campers, slightly shabby furnished houses like this one, also in dressing rooms, office suites, and cabins on the back lots of various studios—wherever, in fact, he happened to be making a movie. The boxes, suitcases, and cartons, never fully unpacked, followed him from place to place. "My home is wherever I'm making a picture," he'd confided in a *Playboy* interview some years earlier. "I live where my camera is." Cynics, however, had been heard to say that Wilson Mahoney lived this nomadic life not by choice, but to avoid excessive harassment from several ex-wives and girlfriends with designs on his income and property. In the same *Playboy* piece, Mahoney had divided all women into two categories, "cunts and Good Women." Mahoney had, he said, never lived with a Good Woman himself, but he knew they existed because several of his oldest friends were married to shining examples of the species.

In the kitchen, Rich Bentley found not only the drink, a mild Scotch and soda, that he had begun actively to crave, but also a very sweet-looking little woman whose eyes widened as he walked in. "Hey, I know you!" she squealed, grabbing the arm of the affable young man standing next to her. "You're . . . hey, you're that actor . . ."

"He sure is, honey," the man with her seconded.

"Hey, you're . . . you're . . ."

"Rich Bentley," the actor said, smiling. "Who are you?"

"Oh, wow, we aren't anybody," the woman said.

"Hi," the young man volunteered, sticking his hand out. "I'm Bert Felcher. This here's my wife, Edie. We're new in Malibu."

"Is that so?"

"Oh, yes," Edie said breathlessly, "and we love it here."

"We bought a house on Mariposa—"

"It's so terrific," Edie said. "We're really crazy about it."

"That's awfully nice," Rich told her as he started to turn away. "Well, it's been swell meeting—"

"Hey, Rich, please talk to us a minute," Edie said, taking his arm and gazing pleadingly up at him. "You're the first real movie star we've ever met, you know?"

"Really?"

"Oh, my, yes. And I've just adored you on screen."

"She sure has," Bert agreed enthusiastically. "You really turn her on, Rich."

"Is that so?" the actor inquired. "I don't care much for myself on screen. What have you seen?"

"I just loved *The Mushroom People*," Edie admitted.

"And we used to watch your series, too," Bert contributed. "Edie's always had this thing about you. What was that picture where you tied up all those girls and had sex with them and all? Something about girls who liked girls . . ."

"My only X-rated effort," Rich admitted. "*Amazon Women of Lesbos*. It was a Philippine quickie."

"That's it!" Bert exclaimed. "It really turned us on."

175

"I've always had this fantasy about being tied up," Edie confided, a dreamy smile on her blank little face. "It was so great."

"You sort of inspired us into bondage and all that," Bert said. "It made a big change in our lives."

"Oh, wow"—Edie sighed—"to be tied up by Rich Bentley!"

Rich hesitated, uncertain whether to flee or not. He couldn't tell whether these two strange young people were putting him on or were actually serious, but it was Edie who persuaded him to stay. She put a hand on his chest and looked up at him so sweetly and so trustingly as she said, "You aren't into swinging, are you, Mr. Bentley?"

"Goddammit, Jay," Billie Farnsworth said, over in her corner of the room, "how long are you going to stall me?"

"I'm not stalling you, Billie," Jay Pomerantz answered, gazing happily up at her from his perch on the floor. "I wouldn't stall you, honey."

"What do you call it, then?" Billie asked. "I've had an answer to your counteroffer for a week, and you didn't even phone. What would you call it, Jay?"

"Honey, I told you, I had business to attend to," Jay explained again, smiling through the murky glow of the room. "Business always comes first, babe, you hear? How in the hell do you think I made all this goddamn money in the first place?"

"It sure wasn't by not answering your calls," Billie said. "I've had the lawyers for the estate on the phone all day, every day, and I have to stall them without even knowing where the hell you are. All you ever do out here is get me to take you to parties, for Christ's sake."

Jay reached over to pat her knee reassuringly. "Billie, honey, you just don't know how much money I made this week, but I had to go back to Tulsa for three days to do it."

"And that's another thing," Billie persisted. "I never know where the fuck you are. And take your fat little hand off my knee."

"Jesus, Billie, you are in a mood."

Billie took another savage gulp of her drink, a tall glass of straight gin, and leaned over toward her prospective client. "Jay, baby, from now on it's strictly business. Do you want the house or don't you? We've been sitting here in this room for two hours watching Mahoney and a bunch of Hollywood drunks telling each other lies, and all you do is squat there on the floor and bullshit me. Yes or no, Jay?"

The stocky little financier stared at her unblinkingly out of those strange-looking eyes of his and took his time answering. "Billie, honey," he said at last, "you think it's peanut brittle—eight hundred thousand dollars? I need time to think it over, babe."

"That's what you want me to tell the Careys, Jay? How much time?"

"Another couple of days, okay?"

"Okay," Billie agreed. "You got till Wednesday morning. Yes or no. Take it or leave it. I'll put the house back on the market."

"Fair enough." Jay scrambled to his feet and reached out for her glass. "Let me freshen that for you, honey."

"And where the hell are you staying now?"

"I got me a bungalow at the Beverly Hills Hotel," Jay said. "That's more my kind of place."

"I thought it might be," Billie answered. "All those hookers at the bar and the starlets around the pool. Sure."

"Hey, Billie, honey," Jay said, leaning toward her again and smiling, "I don't pay for a piece, you got that? And I don't go for child actors or starlets neither, you hear? What I am up to, honey, is a good relationship with an older woman."

"Well, you've come to the right place, Jay," Billie said, "because I'm feeling older every minute."

Jay kissed her quickly on the cheek, then waddled off toward the kitchen with their glasses. *The cocky little bastard,* Billie thought to herself as she watched him go, *who the fuck does he think he is? Him and his goddamn money. Hanging me up like this, making a fool of me.* She suddenly decided she would make a grand exit, leave Jay R. Pomerantz to stew in his own fatty juices, but she found herself unable to rise, because the room had become a whirl of smoky lights to a slightly off-beat tune she had never heard before. *Oh, my aching ass, I think I'm drunk. . . .*

"Hey, pretty lady," Wilson Mahoney said to Dee Stauffer, who had been sitting at his feet now for nearly an hour, "show us something."

"Like what, Wilson?" Dee asked sweetly.

"Can't you do anything, woman? Can't you sing or dance?"

"I dance terrific."

"Then show us how you dance. Do that oopsy-daisy thing you used to do. You've been sitting on your ass like a goddamn Malibu princess long enough." Mahoney reached out, grabbed Dee's arm, and yanked her to her feet. Dee laughed gaily, seemingly unaware of the menace in Wilson Mahoney's voice.

A barefoot, wan-looking girl in slacks and a shirt was hovering beside the door leading out to the beach. She seemed undecided now whether to stay or to escape. "Oh, dear," she said in an English accent, "it's becoming ugly again." She had evidently been through a number of similar scenes with Wilson Mahoney before, but would not leave unless he clearly wanted her to. "Wilson," she objected feebly, "do we have to do this?"

The director swung around to glower at her. "Beat it, Twinkie," he said. Twinkie quickly eased herself out the door, and Mahoney turned back to Dee, who was merely standing there now, smiling uncomprehendingly to the room at large. "Dance," Mahoney ordered, sinking back into his chair and beginning to clap his hands rhythmically.

Others joined in, and someone began to sing nasally in Hebrew. Puzzled, Dee looked around her, unsure of what to do. After all, this wasn't the number she was celebrated for. "Dance, woman!" Mahoney shouted.

Despite her flattering self-evaluation, Dee Stauffer was not a good dancer. In her one movie scene, the camera and skilled editing had covered her. In person, she moved awkwardly about in a small circle, not quite in step to the beat and bobbing her head up and down. She kept smiling, though, wondering still what could possibly be expected of her, but confident that this was truly all in fun, just another example of Wilson Mahoney's celebrated penchant for having himself a rowdy good time among friends. And, after all, Dee Stauffer reassured herself, he had told her she was—how had he put it?—"some fine-looking wench."

Somebody in the room now turned up a radio to a loud soul station, and the raucous beat of a repetitious Stevie Wonder hit inundated the room, drowning casual conversation and turning all eyes toward the corner where Dee Stauffer, smiling rigidly, rocked awkwardly back and forth, squealing "oopsy-daisy, oopsy-daisy" and bumping awkwardly. Unfortunately, Wilson Mahoney was in no mood to tolerate her ineptitude. He suddenly heaved himself to his feet, reached out, and tugged at her shirt. "If you can't dance, you dumb cunt," he growled, "at least show us your tits!"

Dee Stauffer shrieked, backed away a step, then swung wildly at him. He ducked, and the force of her unlanded blow sent her lurching toward a window seat, where Mahoney pinned her and began tearing at her blouse. "Your tits," he mumbled, "all God's chillun gotta have tits!"

Before the director could strip her, a tall, husky man with a gray beard and close-cropped hair stepped swiftly into the action. Obviously very strong, he had no difficulty pulling the much smaller man away from his victim and placing himself between them. "Wilson, take it easy," he said quietly. "The lady is upset."

The director stared angrily at the peacemaker but made no move to get at Dee again or to oppose his intrusion. It was easy to see why. Not only did the older man have right and justice on his side, but he could easily have broken Mahoney, drunk or sober, in two. He had the huge, muscled arms of an ex-wrestler or fighter, and there was an undercurrent of menace in the way he stood there facing down any possible challenge to his authority. "Come on, Wilson," he said patiently, "this is a celebration, isn't it? We're all friends here, aren't we?"

Mahoney grunted, then pushed his way out past the onlookers toward the entrance hall and the downstairs bathroom. "Gonna take a piss," he confided by way of explanation. "Too much goddamn beer."

"You bastard!" Dee Stauffer shouted, sitting up and clutching her shirt where Mahoney had torn it open. "You prick!"

"Listen, lady," the big man said, leaning down to console her, "he's just drunk. He's been partying for three days, and he doesn't know what he's doing."

Dee got up and brushed past him toward the beach doors. "I'll sue the son of a bitch! Who the fuck does he think he is?" She stormed out, nearly flattening the tall English girl now returning from her quick stroll along the water's edge. "and you too, you silly English twat!"

"Oh, dear," Twinkie observed, watching the older woman stride angrily away across the sand toward her own house, "oh, dear, I knew this would happen. Wilson's such a swine, really . . ."

Inside, by the open kitchen door, Edie Felcher was staring wide-eyed into the room. "Oh, wow," she exclaimed, "who is that?"

"That, my dear, was Dee Stauffer," Rich Bentley informed her, his right hand resting lightly against the small of her back and rubbing it gently. "Dee Stauffer is a Colony hazard, more annoying and dangerous than a bad case of piles."

"No, not her," Edie squeaked. "I meant him." She gazed admiringly toward the big man, who was now in earnest conversation with a group of revelers around the fireplace. "He's terrific, just like John Wayne!"

"Oh, I think that's Morgan Longworth," Rich said. "He's Wilson's A.D., been with him for years."

"A.D.? What's that?"

"Anno Domini, my dear."

"Huh? What do you mean?"

"Assistant director," Rich explained. "He's sort of Mahoney's bodyguard and keeper."

"Boy, I could go for that hunk of man!" Edie said. "I wonder if he's with anybody? That English girl, maybe?"

"I haven't the foggiest," Rich said.

"The things you say, Rich!"

Bored by the woman's simplemindedness, Rich excused himself and returned to the living room. Twenty minutes later, on his way to the downstairs bathroom, he spotted the Felchers in earnest conversation with Morgan Longworth and two of Mahoney's older gofers, burly middle-aged men in jeans and Western shirts, open at the neck to display sizable slices of hairy chest. "Swinging, kid?" Morgan's voice boomed off the walls. "What's that? Sort of like a gangbang?"

By midnight the party had thinned out some in the living room, but a group of activists had gathered in the kitchen, where the director, Morgan Longworth, and several other guests in various stages of disrepair were conducting a knife-throwing contest against the back door. Rich Bentley, still intent on eventually bringing himself to Mahoney's attention, had wandered in looking for a drink and had unexpectedly found himself enlisted in the competition. Morgan Longworth, who had been keeping score, had spotted him by the sink and handed him the knife, a wicked-looking bowie with a horn handle and a gleaming, lethal blade. Rich looked a bit puzzled at the honor so unexpectedly thrust upon him. "What do I do now?" he asked, weighing the weapon uneasily in the palm of his hand.

"You throw it, dummy," Mahoney ordered. "Over there." And he waved toward the target someone had clumsily outlined in red marker pen on the door.

Rich wasn't certain he ought to try, since he had never been much good either at games or at this kind of mindless carousing, but he had no desire to anger Mahoney, whose temper was famous and especially mercurial when affected by alcohol or cocaine. Morgan, whose sheer size troubled him, was another negative factor in the situation. Smiling weakly, Rich now grabbed the handle, cocked his arm, and let fly. The knife turned over several times on its wobbly course, clattered against the wall, and fell to the floor. "Jesus Christ," Mahoney growled, "he throws like a fucking fairy."

"Sorry," Rich said.

"Here," Morgan told him, picking the knife up and handing it back to him, "try again. Only, hold it by the blade, at the tip. That way it should turn over only once, if it's balanced right."

"Oh, I see," Rich said. "But why—?"

"Throw the fucking knife, faggot," Mahoney snarled, hitching up his shorts and leaning back against the icebox with folded arms.

"Take it easy, Wilson," Morgan said. "He's doing his best." He took the knife from Rich and aimed it at the target. "Here, Rich, let me show you how." He let fly, and the weapon impaled itself squarely in the center of the target. Everyone in the room applauded. Morgan retrieved the knife and handed it back to Rich. "Here," he said. "Try it again."

The actor tried to imitate exactly what Morgan had done, but when he cocked his arm back, the knife slipped out of his sweaty grasp and fell to the floor. It embedded itself in the linoleum, barely missing the bare toes of Mahoney's English chippy, the ubiquitous Twinkie, who had just entered the kitchen to catch up on the action. "Oh, my God!" Rich exclaimed, going pale.

"What the devil!" Twinkie shrieked, slamming empty glasses into the sink as she jumped for safety. "Are you all mad?"

"Faggot," Mahoney mumbled, turning his bleary eyes upward in mock despair.

Morgan Longworth smiled. "Too bad, Rich," he said, placing a consoling hand on the actor's shoulder. "This isn't really your game, is it?"

"No, I'm afraid not," Rich said, leaning over to retrieve the knife.

As he did so, the house suddenly shivered, then seemed to lurch sideways, causing a great rattling of dishes and glasses and sending the actor stumbling headfirst into Twinkie, who shrieked; Rich fell to his knees.

"Christ, what was that?" the girl cried.

"A quake," Morgan said. "That was a pretty good one."

"Oh, fuck, that was nothing," Mahoney growled. "We have them here all the time. Nothing's happened. Let's get on with the game."

"I don't know, Wilson," Morgan warned him. "There may be two or three more of those. Maybe we'd better get outside."

Rich scrambled to his feet just as the house shook a second time, though not quite as severely as the first. "A three-point-eight on the Richter scale," he estimated calmly. "Nothing to worry about. The epicenter must be way out to sea. It's the second one this year."

"Hey, how about that?" the director exclaimed, beaming with pleasure at the idea. "By morning we could get a tidal wave here!"

"Oh, my God!" Twinkie said, turning white. "I'm getting out of this place!"

"Stay right where you are!" Mahoney roared. "No one abandons *this* house! On with the game!"

"Hey, Wilson, how about a pool on the magnitude?" Morgan asked. "Rich here says three-point-eight. I say four-point-two. We put in ten bucks apiece. What do you say, Wilson?"

The director laughed. "Three-point-two," he said. "It was nothing."

"I'll get in on that," Jay Pomerantz said, suddenly appearing, drink in hand, in the doorway. "I say four even."

"You're all mad, absolutely bonkers," Twinkie said. "Oh, well, might as well die here as anywhere." With a nervous little laugh she snatched up a half-finished glass of wine and pirouetted back into the living room, where only four or five of the remaining couple of dozen guests had even noted the tremors. None of them seemed in the least alarmed, even though the first shock had spilled two glasses off a bookshelf and the hanging plants were still swaying gently to and fro like huge pendulums.

The first shock had awakened Billie, who had dozed off in her corner of the room. She sat up, dazed, and looked around. The second tremor sent her scrambling to her feet. Though still quite drunk, she had immediately remembered her crystal, all of which she had just washed that morning and left on open shelves above the kitchen sink and counter to dry. With a hoarse cry she tottered to her feet and lurched out into the night through the open doors leading to the beach.

The cool night air hit her abruptly and helped her to sober up a bit. She plunged on through the soft sand toward her house, while all around her lights began going on here and there as various Colony residents appeared outdoors. The first person Billie almost bumped into was Dorothy Ferrero, who had run outside, holding her sleepy son by the hand. She looked frightened. "Victor says it's nothing," she confided to Billie, "but these things always scare me. I can't help it. I'm not going back in until I'm sure it's over."

"All we'd get now, honey, is an aftershock," Billie reassured her. "You can go back to bed."

Dorothy smiled wanly. "I know I'm being a fool," she said. "I couldn't even get Victor up, he's so tired."

Billie kept going, wondering why in hell she had chosen to come home along the beach rather than by the Colony road, but now she had no choice. Panting, she finally scrambled inside her house, turned on the lights, and ran into the kitchen. To her vast relief, none of the good stuff had fallen. Two Waterford goblets had toppled from the highest shelf and shattered against the sink, but all her best pieces were safe. Just to make sure, Billie now shoved them all as far back from the shelf edges as she could, then sank, exhausted, into a chair. Her head was spinning and she told herself she needed another drink now, but the last thing she remembered was her relief at finding her expensive stuff safe. Mouth open, she snored quietly in her chair.

Out on the beach, Dorothy watched her neighbors, chatting and laughing, go back inside their houses. Michael tugged sleepily at her arm, and she let him go back to bed. The beach seemed very peaceful now, in the pale light of a half-moon, and the ocean washed the sand in its unceasing, rhythmic cadence. Dorothy looked up along the line of Colony houses and thought she could see lights on the second floor of the Gilbert house. How had Evan reacted? she wondered. Had he been awakened and lured out onto the balcony outside his bedroom to witness the Colony's reaction to the event? She imagined him now still out there, his tall, angular frame poised calmly above the scramblings of his neighbors down below. He would have derived some comfort, she knew, from this reminder of the common mortality, of the terrible fragility of the human condition on even this most fortunate of terrains. Knowing Evan as she did, Dorothy imagined she could hear his light, mocking laughter as an echo in the soft caress of the night breezes off the turbulent black surface of the sea.

18

When Billie Farnsworth woke up the morning after Wilson Mahoney's party, she had no idea at first where she was. She was also
very disturbed by the fact that she immediately felt so disoriented.
Perhaps it was because she had been lying on her back and her eyes
were staring at the ceiling, a plain cream-colored expanse of plaster
she felt certain she had never seen before. She then made the mistake of sitting up too abruptly, and nearly passed out. Not only did
she have an agonizing headache, but her stomach seemed to be
entirely on its own and engaged in turning a series of sickening
cartwheels inside her body. At the very instant she realized she was
actually in her own bed in her very own room, she also knew she was
going to be very, very ill. Naked, she forced herself quickly into the
bathroom, where she knelt over the toilet bowl, lowered her head,
and heaved.

Ten minutes later, feeling slightly more human and wrapped in a
large bath towel, she came to the bathroom doorway to peer anx-
iously back into her room. A strong morning sun beat hard enough
against the drawn venetian blinds to enable her to confirm a vague
suspicion that she had begun to entertain: she suspected she was not
alone. And, in fact, a round, bulky form, snoring loudly, lay huddled
under the sheets. Billie did not have to ask herself who it was. She

groaned, and the body in the bed stirred, snorted, coughed once, then resumed its noisy breathing. "Oh, God," Billie muttered; then, overcome again by nausea, she retreated for a second bout at the bowl. By the time she had once again recovered control of herself and returned to the bedroom, the body under the blankets had propped itself up on one elbow. "Why, hi there," Jay R. Pomerantz said brightly. "How're you doing?"

Billie ignored him. She tottered to her closet, grabbed her light blue warm-up suit from its hook by the door, fished out a pair of sneakers, and fled to the living room. Luckily, Jay R. Pomerantz made no move to follow her. Billie pulled on her clothes, swallowed a glass of milk in the kitchen, and staggered out onto the beach, where the sun hit her like a blow in the face. She forced herself to break into a painful jog, first toward the waterline, where the sand was firmer, then, in an uneven crablike shuffle, up along the flowing curve of the tideline to the northwest. Her head pounding, her eyes feeling like marbles embedded in cement, she ran, determined at any cost to unpoison herself and to salvage the rest of this otherwise lost day. What she did not want to face quite yet or think about at all was the presence in her bed of her elusive, prevaricating financier. Obviously she had slept with him, but had they actually made love? Billie could not for the life of her remember.

She ran hard, pausing twice to turn her head toward the water to heave again, in vain, then slowing down to a walk as she neared the last of the big Colony houses. From a recumbent position a few yards away, an oiled, tanned female torso thrust itself up out of the sand to confront her. "Hey, Billie," Dee Stauffer called out, "I didn't know you were a runner!"

"I didn't either," Billie answered glumly. "This is more in the nature of a rescue operation."

"Boy, you look terrible."

"I disappeared into a gallon of gin last night," Billie admitted, sinking down beside her. "I ran home after the quake hit, and then . . . Hey, you got any fruit juice or cold milk in there?" She indicated the large thermos sticking out of Dee's basket at the foot of the blanket.

"Tab. Will that do?"

"Thanks, but no thanks. I can't drink that stuff even when I'm not sick. I'll wait till I get home."

"Did Jay take you home last night? I saw you come with him."

"Well, honey," Billie admitted, "I'm not sure."

"You heard about what that shit Mahoney tried to do to me, didn't you?"

"I saw it, I think," Billie said. "The noise woke me up. What happened?"

Dee told her version of the story. "That shit," she concluded, "and I don't even like his movies." She laughed raucously. "But I got even with that prick. I sicced the cops on him."

Billie's eyes opened wide. "You did? What for?"

"I complained about the noise first," Dee said, "and then I told them I thought there were drugs."

"Holy cow! Did they come?"

"You bet your ass they did!" Dee exclaimed. "I ran back to make sure, and I saw a lot of what happened. Rich filled me in later. It's the talk of the Colony this morning."

"Well, what did happen?"

Dee giggled and hugged herself with pleasure. "The deputies rang first, but nobody heard them, so they came in anyway. One of Mahoney's friends, a stuntman or somebody, thought they were intruders and decked the first guy through the door. They'd had a bunch of teenagers pestering them earlier. So the cops arrested Mahoney and two others. They took them down to the station, booked them, and then released them. There'll be a trial, they say."

"What charges?"

"Assault on a police officer, for one."

"Oh, Mahoney's lawyers will beat that rap."

"Yeah," Billie continued gleefully, "but they also searched the house and came up with amphetamines. And then, in the upstairs bedroom, in that little cupola the house has, they found a regular orgy going on."

"You're kidding? Really?"

"Yeah, that young couple, the Felchers, the English girl, and two men. One of them was that big brute, Morgan. Mahoney got mad as hell. He's thrown the girl out and fired both the guys."

"Morgan's been with him twenty years," Billie said. "He won't fire him permanently. He's Mahoney's enforcer."

"Wilson's such a phony," Dee said. "Under all that macho bullshit of his there's this fragile little Hollywood ego. If his girlfriend hadn't been involved, he wouldn't have given a damn. Hell, he'd have probably jumped into the middle of it. Anyway, it was pure carnage, and I loved every second of it."

"It was a horrible evening," Billie said. "I didn't want to go there again."

"The worst," Dee agreed. "And those Felchers, aren't they weird?"

"You said it. Have they asked you to *swing* yet?"

"Nope," Dee said. "I wish they or somebody would. I'd like to try it."

"You're kidding."

"No, I'm not. What else is going on around here this summer? Rich Bentley?"

Billie laughed, but stopped immediately because it made her head throb.

"Hey, stick around," Dee said, "I'll go in and get you some juice, okay?"

"Yeah," Billie said, flopping over on her back and gasping on the sand like a stranded porpoise.

"What was going on next door?" Gail Hessian asked. "I heard there was quite a brawl."

"That's exactly what it was," Jim Wharton said, handing Gail the glass of Chablis she had requested. "Wilson Mahoney's rented that place for the summer. It's been a pain in the ass ever since we moved in here. The owner goes away and rents it during the summer, always to some noisy Hollywood slob like Mahoney. I've been trying to buy the place so I could tear it down, but the guy won't sell. He's old Malibu. The house has been in his family for forty years, ever since it was built, and he can only afford to live here now by renting it out in the summer."

"What's he do?"

"He's a retired architect, I think."

"Why don't you make him an offer he can't refuse?" Gail asked, keeping her tone light and airy.

Wharton regarded her thoughtfully for a few seconds, then shrugged and sat down. "He wants too much," he explained. "I guess we can put up with it two months a year."

"Why don't you complain?"

"We have. Mary called the sheriff's station last night, but somebody beat us to it."

"Yes, I heard about that," Gail said. "I almost got a crew out here to film it."

"Thank Christ you didn't."

"Don't you ever go away for the summer yourself?"

Wharton shook his head. "No. I've got too much to do. Besides, I play a lot of tennis, as you know, and what do I need a vacation for? Living here is a vacation all year round."

"And your wife?"

"Mary doesn't care. She and Julie love Malibu."

"I would, too, if I lived here," Gail said, strolling over to the picture window facing the ocean. Wharton's house sat on a slight rise only a few feet above its much smaller neighbors, but that gave it enough of an advantage so that from the beach side one had an uninterrupted view of the coastline. "It's really pretty. Did you build this yourself?"

"Yeah, five years ago. We used to live back in the Crosscreek area, but then we acquired this lot and built to suit ourselves."

"Did you have problems with the Coastal Commission?"

Jim smiled. "There are ways to handle that."

"Well, it's spectacular." She turned away and gazed back into the huge room, with its heavy stuffed furniture, thick Oriental rugs, and hunting trophies. Either Jim Wharton had shot a lot of game in his life, or maybe, she thought, he'd bought himself this part of his past, too. The warm, golden light of the midmorning sun softened the contours of the lawyer's big-boned features, made him seem more kindly and benign than she knew he was. He sat calmly, waiting for her to complete her appraisal, but without real interest. She found herself beginning to wonder again why he had summoned her here, after a week or more of not returning her calls. No one else from her world, as far as she knew, had ever been invited to Jim Wharton's home. "By the way," she asked, moving now toward a small love seat facing his armchair, "to what do I owe this honor?"

"Didn't you want to see me?"

"Sure. I did and I do." She sat down and sipped her wine. "Mainly, I've been pursuing you to get the name of that writer—"

"I've got it right here." He reached into his shirt pocket, produced a printed card, and handed it to her. "Heard of him?"

189

"No."

"Well, he's good. He's written three of the better bios of old Hollywood types. He'll want fifty percent of the advance and a cut of the rest. You're free to negotiate that."

"*I* won't. My agent will."

"Sure, but agents are always trying to better deals. Tell yours not to haggle. I think the guy'll settle for a third."

"You've dealt with him yourself, I gather?"

"Something like that."

"For one of your clients?"

"As you know, Gail, I never discuss my business affairs."

"But I keep trying."

"Don't. It's really a waste of time."

"Well," Gail said, pocketing the slip of paper and finishing her wine, "thanks again. But you could have given me the name by phone. You didn't have to see me."

"I don't like the phone much. And I did want to see you."

"Oh? Why?"

"Let's not play games with each other, Gail. I think you're still snooping around for a story. Am I right?"

"Wrong. I've given up on you, Jim. I'm working on other stories. One is on Malibu itself."

"You won't mention my name in it."

"Why not?"

"Because I don't want you to."

"Jim, you live here. You know all the celebrities. You've become kind of a local celebrity yourself. Whether you want to be or not, you're part of the Malibu scene. What are you so afraid of, anyway?"

"I enjoy my privacy."

"Which, of course, makes you even more intriguing to people like me. Don't you care what they say about you?"

"No."

"Do you know?"

"Why don't you tell me, Gail."

"I'd never use any of this, of course."

"Go on."

"Well, the word is, you came out here originally from Chicago as a syndicate lawyer, dealing mainly with labor problems. Am I warm?"

He smiled faintly. "No comment."

"Ah, that's your famous Chinese smile," she said. "Okay, you settled a lot of problems for your people here and in Nevada, but I'm talking about ten or twelve years ago now, when the casinos and a lot of the restaurants around town were being unionized. Then you went Hollywood, Jim."

"I did?"

"Yes, and in a big way. Through your union connections you're supposed to have invested a lot of money in at least two major production companies and negotiated contracts with the networks and at least one major studio. Want me to name them?"

"Don't bother."

"The more recent stuff concerns money skimmed out of Nevada casinos and invested in various real-estate ventures," she continued, actively enjoying herself by this time. "Any truth to all or any of the above?" she asked brightly.

"I have no idea what you're talking about, Gail," he answered, still smiling. "It's all news to me. Of course, if I were to read that kind of shit about myself or see it on screen anywhere, I'd sue for everything I could get, and it would be plenty. I can always use the money. Any other hot items, Gail?"

She flung her hands up in mock despair. "I'm afraid I've given it my best shot, Jim."

"No, you haven't."

"What do you mean?"

He reached into his pocket again. "I have a little something for you." He handed her a small but beautifully wrapped parcel from Tiffany's.

"What . . . ?"

"Go ahead, open it. It's for you."

She tore away the outside wrapping, opened the pale blue box and found herself staring at a handsomely sleek gold pen with her initials imprinted on the case. "Jim, what is this? I can't accept this."

"Sure you can," he told her. "It's just a little gift."

"It's beautiful."

"Even TV news ladies have to make notes from time to time."

"But, Jim . . ."

"Forget it. I wanted to buy it for you."

She got up and kissed him, aiming for his cheek, but he reached up, took her by the neck, and made her kiss him on the mouth. His tongue thrust savagely into her. "Hey," she gasped, backing away, "what is this?"

"It's okay," he said. "Everybody's out. They won't be back for a couple of hours."

"But *here?* I mean, it's a little sudden."

"Cut the bullshit, Gail," he said, standing up and taking her by the hand.

She began to speak again, but he casually reached out, opened her blouse, and felt her breasts. She gasped but did not back away. "I thought so," he said. "We understand each other, don't we?" It was not a question he expected answered.

She allowed herself to be led upstairs into a guest room. He shut the door behind them and turned toward her. She made a move to embrace him, but he fended her off. "Stand still," he said in a hard, flat voice. "I'll do everything." He began swiftly, methodically, and with cold, efficient precision to strip her. Naked, she tried again to put her arms around him, but he seized her wrists, pinned them behind her back, leaned down, and bit her nipples until she nearly cried out in pain. When he had finished, he flung her on the bed and loomed over her. "I know what you need, sweetheart," he whispered. "Now, listen very carefully and do exactly as I tell you. Lie down on your back, open your legs, and pull them back toward you as far as they'll go. I want you totally open and waiting for me."

She began to tremble, but something in his tone of voice, in the total possessive contempt with which he now regarded her, thrilled her. She felt helpless, degraded, like a piece of meat, but the very realization made her suddenly wild with excitement. As he stood there waiting to see if she would obey him, she flung her head back so she wouldn't have to look at him and slowly did what he had demanded of her, until she gaped open and helpless to his gaze. Only then did he begin to remove his own clothes with casual, unhurried deliberateness.

She felt herself shake as he eventually took her, without tenderness or the slightest concern for her comfort or enjoyment. No one had ever treated her like this, as if she were a street hooker, and she couldn't understand how he could have dared, though she had to admit to herself, then and afterward, that no one in her whole life had ever given her such total sexual satisfaction before. It amazed her, even as she responded to him; she couldn't understand it at all. And it frightened her more than a little.

"I guess I'd better get back," Billie said, pushing herself to her feet. "If I stay down too long, I could grow roots."

"Good-bye, Billie," Dee said. "You remember what I told you, now."

"How could I forget? I think you've gone nuts, too."

"Oh, Billie, get laid back," Dee told her. "Don't be such a square."

Billie walked back to her house, beginning now at last to feel a little better. A hot sun beat down on the narrow Colony beach, where a representative sampling of some of the finest and most expensive flesh in the world was on display. A handful of noisy Colony kids was in the surf, which seemed dirtier than usual, Billie thought, fouled by thick clumps of floating kelp. Billie never went in the water here, because she had long ago convinced herself that all the sewage in the area seeped down from under the Colony septic tanks directly into the ocean and flowed into it from the creek. She had been assured by experts that this wasn't so and that the creek sewage had been treated to make it safe enough to drink, but to Billie the Malibu surf always looked dirty, and she did not trust experts, but only the evidence of her own senses.

That aspect of her character was at the root of her uneasiness at the moment. What *had* she and Jay R. Pomerantz accomplished last night? she found herself wondering, disturbed not so much by the possibility that she might have made love to him as by the total absence of any recollection of the event. Her senses had clearly failed her, and that worried her a lot.

When she walked into her house, Jay R. Pomerantz, luxuriously outfitted in one of her bathrobes, was frying eggs and making toast in her kitchen. Coffee was percolating on a back burner, and the room reeked of unwanted domesticity. Billie flung herself into a chair and looked grimly at her houseguest. "You look very cute," she said.

"Glad you think so, honey," Jay chirped, beaming at her. "Want some coffee?" Without waiting for an answer, he poured her a mug, then turned his attention back to the frying pan. "Want some eggs and bacon? Toast?"

"No."

He flipped the eggs over and began buttering the toast. "Got any jam or honey?"

"In the icebox. Jay?"

"Yeah, babe?"

"What happened last night?"

"You passed out. I found you here when I came to see if you were okay."

"Oh."

"Then you came around pretty good there for a while."

"I did?"

"Oh, yeah. You don't remember?"

She didn't answer, and he laughed. He slipped the fried eggs into a dish, smeared strawberry preserves over his toast, poured himself a cup of black coffee, and sat down across from her. "You were terrific," he said.

"I was?"

"You betcha. You're one of the great lays of history, babe. But I knew you would be. Boy, you were hot."

Billie's heart sank to her ankles. "Shit," she said.

"No, it's not," Jay assured her. "You were real good, honey. You mind if I come around for seconds?"

"Stop talking like that. You make me sound like a lunch counter."

Jay laughed. "You're all woman, Billie. You're quite a gal, yes, ma'am."

He wolfed down his breakfast and slurped coffee over himself and her clean robe. "You eat like a pig," she said.

"I'm mighty hungry, woman. Getting laid by the likes of you sure gives a man an appetite."

Glumly she swallowed some coffee and averted her gaze so she wouldn't have to witness his carnivorous assault on his breakfast. When he finished, he banged his hands down on the table. "Well, now," he said, "when can I move in?"

"Are you kidding?"

"No, ma'am, I'm not. You said I could."

"Forget it. I was drunk."

"Listen, honey, for eight hundred of my big ones, you all can sure bend a little."

Her jaw sagged slightly open, but she quickly recovered. "Oh. I thought you meant move in here."

He guffawed with delight. "Here? Oh, God! Jesus, Billie, you're a great lay, like I said, but there ain't a piece of ass in the world worth that kind of money."

"The last I recall, Jay, you were going to give me an answer in a couple of days."

"Boy, you sure were drunk, lady. We talked about half an hour after that."

"Oh. Where? Here?"

"There and here, honey. I told you I'd pay the eight hundred big ones, but that I wanted to do it my own way and that would take a little time."

"How much time?"

"Three, four weeks, maybe."

"Why was that?"

"Boy, you got to lay off gin, Billie. It wipes your ass out."

"You're right, obviously. Tell it to me again, Jay, so I'll understand it."

He did. It seems that after he'd come back from Mahoney's kitchen with a fresh drink, they'd talked again about the negotiations for the Carey house and Jay had explained his peculiar situation to her. He was involved in a deal with the Getty—yes, *that* Getty—oil company in developing a huge new offshore drilling operation in the Gulf of Mexico, and that was tying up all of Jay's available capital at the moment. To buy the Carey place he'd have to sell some bonds he'd been holding, and that would take a few weeks, as the deal would have to be handled through his accountant's office in Tulsa and his brokers in New York. It was a tricky, complicated little maneuver that would take a little time, because Jay, like all big financiers, had to operate behind a facade of holding companies and corporate entities to protect himself from the tax people. Surely Billie and her clients could see that? He was offering now to buy the house without any further haggling, but only on the condition Billie would let him move in even before escrow. Jay was dog-tired of living in hotel rooms and didn't want to let the whole summer slip away before he could get into his own home. That wasn't so unreasonable, was it?

"And I agreed to that?" Billie asked.

"You sure did, honey."

"Was that before or after?"

"Oh, before, before, babe," Jay answered with a proprietary slap on her thigh. "Hell, after we got going in there, who the hell was gonna talk real estate?"

"I must have passed out," Billie said glumly.

"Later, honey. Right after."

"After what?"

"Well, you was doing a lot of whoopin' and hollerin'—"

"Don't tell me," she said. "I'd rather not know."

"Why, sure, Billie. So, listen . . . we got a deal, right?"

"I'll have to phone the Careys' lawyers . . ."

"Well, now, you tell 'em, honey. They gotta deal this way or we can all just forget it. I'll look around for something else, hear?"

"I hear."

Later, after Jay R. Pomerantz had showered, dressed, and driven off in his rented Buick, the latest and least grand in his string of interim cars, Billie went to the phone. She felt reasonably sure she could convince the Carey lawyers to agree to the deal; after all, the house was empty. But what bothered her a lot was the feeling that somehow, somewhere along the way here, from her drunken outburst of the night before at Mahoney's party to her horrid awakening early that morning, she had missed out on something important to her. Never in her whole life had Billie been to bed with a man, been told that she'd been wonderful, but failed to remember one single moment of such a presumably pleasurable experience. Also, she was having a lot of trouble convincing herself that she'd wanted to go to bed with Jay R. Pomerantz in the first place. Something about the man had begun to make her more than faintly uneasy.

19

"Arthur, did you read this story?" Lee called out.

"What story?"

"On the front page. They had an earthquake in Los Angeles."

He came to the bathroom door, with lather still on his face. "No kidding? How bad?"

"A four-point-six on the Richter scale," Lee read aloud, "whatever that means. It was centered somewhere out in the Pacific, off Mexico. There were two big tremors during the night."

"Four-point-six is a pretty nice jolt," Art commented. "They must have felt it out in Malibu."

"Thank God I wasn't there," she said. "I'd have panicked. I've never been in an earthquake."

He smiled. "Oh, we have them all the time," he assured her. "A few years ago, we had one that knocked a lot of my trophies off the wall and broke glasses. Laura got mad as hell."

"I think I remember reading about that one."

"It was a nationwide media event, like our big brushfires and the ten-day winter rains with accompanying mud slides," he said. "Oh, living in Malibu is an adventure."

"Ever had a tidal wave?" Lee asked nervously.

"Not yet, but sooner or later we'll probably get one. That'll take care of the Colony," he added cheerfully.

"That's comforting."

"The risks are one of the major attractions of Malibu," he said. "My friends from the East always ask me how I can live in such a place. Laura's mother, who's still in Cleveland, thinks California is a jungle full of savages. This from a woman who has three locks on every door, a burglar alarm, has been mugged once on the street and had her car stolen twice, once out of her garage." He laughed. "I'll take Mother Nature."

"There are plenty of crooks in L.A.," Lee said. "They don't all live back East."

"True enough. Still, Malibu has less violent crime than most places. It's too far to drive just to rob and kill people," Art explained, "when the pickings are just as good in Brentwood and Beverly Hills."

"And since we're speaking of making the earth move," she said, "come back to bed."

"In a minute. Boy, you're insatiable, lady."

He went back in the bathroom and finished shaving, slapped lotion on his cheeks, and emerged to find Lee lying on her side facing him, her head propped up against her pillows. He came and sat beside her and leaned over to kiss her. Her mouth opened hungrily to him. "Take off that silly robe," she said, "and get back in bed."

He complied and slid in beside her under the single sheet. Her body felt warm and soft within his embrace, and for a while he simply held her close to him. "Your skin is like silk," he said. "I love to touch you."

She wriggled contentedly within his arms and thrust a long leg between his own, shoving her thigh up into his crotch. They had already made love that morning, but to his amazement he felt himself growing hard again. She was already damp before he touched her, so he quickly rolled over and gently thrust into her again. With a whimper of pleasure she opened wide and linked her hands behind his neck, rose to receive him fully, and in no more than a dozen long, drawn-out strokes made him come again, even though he had been more concerned with giving her pleasure this time than in coming himself. He looked down at her in wonder. "I didn't think I could," he said.

"Why not?"

"Three times in a morning, and after last night?" he observed. "Lady, I'm a fifty-year-old dropout."

"Not in bed, you aren't. You're a terrific lover, lover."

"I'll bet you say that to all your men."

"No, just you."

"Well, you inspire me. Not to poetry and great works," he said, "but to pure lust."

"I'm so glad."

He eased his weight off his elbows and rolled away from her. "Want some more coffee?"

"Yep. What time is it?"

"Nearly noon. We'd better get cracking."

"Coffee first, then tourism."

"Right. You're the tour guide. Wherever you go, I follow."

"Which is as it should be."

He poured the last of the coffee from their room-service breakfast tray into her cup. She sat up against the pillows, allowing the sheet to slide away, and cradled the cup with both hands as she sipped from it. He studied her with pleasure, from the strong, square shoulders above the small, large-nippled breasts to her long, flat stomach, bisected by the Cesarean scar, and the wiry tuft of her pubic hair, nestled between her firm, deeply tanned thighs. "Stop staring at me," she said. "You'll see all my scars."

"I only see one."

"Oh, I have them all over," she said. "I was always getting cut up as a kid. I was a tomboy and fell out of trees and broke things."

"I love your scars. They become you."

"I hate them. Why do you think I keep so tan? I do this all year round, so I don't have to look at them. They look awful when I'm white. At home, I lie under the lamp at least an hour a day."

"If you moved to Malibu," he said, "you wouldn't have to do that."

"No."

"Anyway, I think your scars are terrific."

"So are yours." She reached out and traced with her index finger the curving loop over his shoulder, where, years before, they had cut to scrape away calcium deposits and to ease the pain that had ended his career.

"You're a tease," he protested.

"You bet I am." She put her cup down and kissed him. "Hey, we'd better get going."

"I'm ready," he said. "All I've got to do is put on my pants and a shirt. You're the one who's delaying us."

"Some tour guide I am," she said, jumping out of bed and hurrying off to the bathroom. "I'll be out in ten minutes. Call for the car."

While waiting for her, he walked over to the window, parted the curtains, and looked out. From the tenth story of their downtown hotel room he could look out over rooftops and up to the steep hills above. A clear blue sky sheltered the city in its embrace, even though a strong breeze was blowing out of the north; all the flags he could see were flapping in the same direction. Art had always loved San Francisco, though it had been five years now since he had visited the place. When he and Laura had first moved to Laguna, they had promised each other to sneak away occasionally for two or three days at a time by themselves up here, but for some reason they had managed to do it only a half-dozen times in all those years, and not at all recently. Something had always come up—a tournament, one of Tad's school functions, a lack of money, lately just inertia. Lee's suggestion that they spend their weekend together here had been a marvelous one, though it had taken him a day to figure out how to get away.

It was a lucky thing he'd remembered his old friend Gene Layton and dreamed up the idea of a veterans' tournament at Gene's club in Sausalito. One call to Layton had set the whole thing up, and Laura had bought it. The way things were between them these days, it figured she wouldn't want to come, and in any case, he'd gone off in the past by himself occasionally to play in small local tournaments here and there, mainly to keep his hand in and his game reasonably sharp. Gene Layton had been out on the tour during Art's last year, though when Art was on his game, Gene had never been able to beat him. That last time, when Art had had to default and drop out of the tour, it had happened in a match with Gene, which Art had, as usual, been winning. It was nice of old Gene to help out, Art thought, but then, boys would always be boys; they'd always stick together in the unequal war between the sexes. Gene had always liked Laura, but he was basically Art's friend, not hers.

He and Lee were going to drive out that way this morning, but not to visit with old Gene. They were going to keep going up the coast to see the redwoods, find a good place to picnic, and come back in the late afternoon, early enough to have a drink and a good dinner before heading for the airport. It was their last day together, but it was not going to be a sad one, they had promised each other, because obviously, the way it had gone, the affair did not qualify as a casual one. This was a beginning, not an ending, they'd told each other. "I love you, Art," Lee had said to him again last night. "I love you and I love being with you. Do you love me?"

"Yes, I think I do," he said.

"You *think* you do?"

And so he'd smiled, then laughed. "Jesus, we get cautious, don't we?" he told her. "It's having goofed up a little too often." And he'd kissed her very gently. "Okay, you win. Yes, I love you, Lee. You're the best thing that's happened to me in a hell of a long time."

Lee approached every day as an adventure, with the enthusiasm of a child, and it had proved infectious. They ran about the beautiful city holding hands, they kissed in taxis, they touched each other on cable cars, they flung themselves into every experience like a couple of schoolchildren on holiday. Lee related everything to the senses, he realized, as if by denying herself anything she risked missing out on an important, perhaps crucial aspect of life. In restaurants she reached out to pick tidbits off his plate, she sipped or nibbled on everything ordered that was different from hers, because she was anxious to have it all, even fleetingly, even vicariously, if necessary. "You know what?" she'd said to him over salad at Jack's the night before, "I love previews. If I can't see the whole movie, or even if I don't want to, I'll love the preview. That way I'll always know if I missed out on something good or not."

"That's what this weekend is to you?"

"What?" She'd seemed startled by the image.

"You know, a preview, a sample?"

"You bet, but of a big coming attraction. Eat your salad. I want to get back to the hotel and ravish you."

"You're clearly a sex maniac."

"You know I am, mister." She'd laughed and then reached over to pluck a palm heart off his plate. "That's what I should have had."

"Eat your endive and shut up," he ordered. "This is costing us a fortune."

In bed she'd do anything and try anything. Nothing about the act of love embarrassed her or put her off. She had once been shy, she told him, but in her mid-twenties, after the birth of Peter, she'd begun to expand her horizons. There had been an affair with a doctor. Later, after the second child, there had been another one with a married salesman for Sid's company. Both, especially the second one, could have been sordid, but hadn't been, and she had profited by them. The doctor had opened her up sexually, made her unafraid, as well as unashamed, of her body. The salesman had been very sweet and desperately in love with her, but hadn't found the courage to leave his wife and three children for her. She had loved him a lot and had suffered a long time over it, but in the end, as she looked back on it now, she saw that it had been hopeless from the start. The man had been terribly good-looking and very gentle, very nice with her, but it had been sort of a delayed adolescent crush on her part, fantasy time. "He was so sweet, and kind of helpless," she said, "He touched some nerve in me, I guess. I wanted to be a mother to him, but then I realized I had children of my own by that time and it was all completely unrealistic."

"And what about Sid?" he asked.

"What about him?"

"Are you happy with him?"

"What do you think?"

"I don't know. That's why I'm asking."

For the first time since he'd met her she had seemed genuinely ill-at-ease, unaware of how she felt or what she wanted. "I guess I must have loved him once," she finally answered. "I don't know. The whole thing seems so remote to me now. I was pretty young when we met. Sid's ten years older than I am. I was attracted by his self-confidence, by his drive. Sid's a terrific worker and very smart about money."

"I'll bet."

"I knew he was going to be a success at whatever he did. That can be exciting for a woman."

"Do you love him, Lee?"

She shook her head. "No. I'm . . . used to him. And he's always taken good care of me and the boys. That matters. Sid's very generous. For a long time—and even now—we'd see so little of each

202

other. When Sid was setting up the business, I'd hardly see him for weeks at a stretch. Even when he came home, he'd be on the phone half the time. Anthony once drew a picture of him at school as a man with a phone growing out of his head where his ear should be."

"So you were restless and bored and got involved with other men."

"You don't make it sound very nice."

"I'm sorry. I didn't mean to be crude."

"That's what Sid was and is, crude," she explained. "His way of making love was to bang me fast and hard, as kind of an afterthought to his working day. Slam-bam, thank you, ma'am, for the use of the hall! Crude enough for you?"

"Yeah. Let's not talk about Sid right now."

"You brought his name up."

"Guilty as charged. Jealousy."

"Of Sid?" She'd laughed and leaned across the table to kiss him. "You're my lover, my all," she whispered. "No need to be jealous, darling. I'm the one who should be jealous. Laura's a beautiful woman."

"Maybe, just maybe, we could get them together, that is, if it doesn't work out for Laura with her boss. By the way, does Sid know anything? Has he ever?"

She shook her head. "Oh, God, no! With his ego, he couldn't imagine me with anyone else. Besides, I know he plays around on his business trips. There was a steady girl up in Canada, I think. But then, that's par for the course, isn't it?"

"I guess so."

"Sid's nothing if not predictable. And you know what?"

"What?"

"We won't mention his name again this weekend, all right?"

"All right."

"This is our time together, Arthur, and I want every minute of it to be with you and no one else. Do you understand?"

"Yes. And I love you, Lee, and I bless the day I met you."

The male voice at the other end of the line sounded very young and rather breathless. "Hello?" Laura said. "Is this the Ridgeway Tennis Club?"

"Yeah," the young voice replied. "You want a court?"

"No, I'm trying to find my husband," Laura said. "His name is Arthur Bonnell. I think he's playing there this weekend."

"Oh. Okay. Just a minute, please. I'll ask somebody."

After a couple of minutes a mature woman's voice came on the wire. "Hello, who is this, please?"

"My name's Laura Bonnell," Laura said. "I'm looking for my husband. I think he's playing in your tournament this weekend. I just wanted to tell him the house is okay and we're okay. We had a quake here last night."

"Oh, yes, I heard about it."

"You could give him the message, if you would. Just tell him I called and everything's all right. Arthur might be out on the court right now."

"I'm afraid I don't know him. Is he a friend of Mr. Layton's?"

"Yes."

"Well, Gene's giving a lesson right now, but I'll tell him you called."

"A lesson? Isn't there a tournament there this weekend?"

"A tournament here? No, I'm afraid not. Not as far as I know."

"Are you sure?"

"Oh, positive. I'm filling in for the girl who usually books the courts here for the members. She's out sick today, and I came in to help out. Actually, I'm her mother. I think Gene would have told me if there were a tournament. Do you want to talk to him? I could have him call you back."

"No, that won't be necessary."

"I'll tell him you called. How do you spell your name?"

"Never mind," Laura said. "Skip it." And she hung up.

Funny, she thought later as she sat on her terrace and looked out over the beach, *funny, but I really don't care. And I'm not surprised, either.* She didn't ask herself why she was crying. She just sat in her chair out in the sunlight, sipped her glass of white wine, and cried, but for some reason it didn't hurt all that much. It really didn't. . . .

IV

The Last Week in July

20

It was the last Monday in July before Boots O'Hara, director of audiovisual development at Continental, could find the time to receive Charlie Wigham and Melvin Schwartz, whose secretary had been devoting a considerable portion of each working day for nearly two weeks to setting up an appointment for them. O'Hara was evidently a man of many projects, with heavy demands being made on his valuable time. When Charlie and Mel did finally get in to see him, however, they found themselves confronted not by a harassed show-biz type surrounded by jangling telephones, which was what they had both expected and geared themselves for, but a tall clean-cut, bland-looking young man who came on like an IBM or Xerox executive, complete with Ivy League suit and attaché case. He seemed, however, to have mastered the jargon of his profession, and he gave a clear impression, beneath the surface smoothness, of being very much in charge of his world. Conversation with him would require a concentrated effort and some self-discipline, Charlie quickly realized, because Boots O'Hara's style was to speak softly, and the talk had to be conducted through the hard rock that at that moment was being piped in through the walls. Mel seemed ill-at-ease in this milieu, but Charlie decided to ignore him and to bear down hard on Boots, who, after all, seemed affable enough, even civilized.

Charlie knew better than to waste O'Hara's time. He opened by explaining to him that he wanted to star Lane Ponds in his movie and that he needed a couple of million dollars. "The kid is perfect for the part."

"Not interested," O'Hara said.

"Why not?"

"Because we don't know anything about movies at this end and we don't want to know anything. For that kind of money we can make fifty albums."

Mel bounced to his feet. "Nice talking to you," he said.

"But if you want to use Ponds," O'Hara continued, "we can see some value in that."

Mel sat down again.

Charlie went into his pitch. "And you've got the kid under contract," he concluded. "He could use the promotion. Other country and rock stars have made it in pictures. Like Arlo Guthrie, remember? He was unknown to the general public before *Alice's Restaurant*."

"That was a long time ago."

"Sure it was," Charlie agreed, "but it worked for him, and it can work again."

"Well, we'd certainly like to encourage you to use Ponds," O'Hara said.

"How much would it be worth to you to have Lane Ponds star in a movie?" Charlie asked.

Boots O'Hara thought it over carefully. "Fifty or sixty thou," he said at last.

Mel again got up to go.

"Wait a minute, Mel," Charlie said. "The hardest dollar to raise is the first one." He waved Mel back into his chair and turned to O'Hara again. "You see," he explained, "with a check for something like seventy-five thousand dollars in my hand, I can get to anyone with tangible proof of Continental's interest in the project."

"Yes, sure," O'Hara said.

"Now, I'm also ready to guarantee that the check will not be cashed until the film actually goes into production," Charlie continued. "What can you lose?"

"Nothing," O'Hara said. "When can we read the script?"

Charlie looked stunned. "Wait a minute—"

"I thought you said you didn't know anything about movies," Mel interrupted.

"That's right," O'Hara agreed, "but we still want to read the script."

"Fine," Charlie said, getting up to go and shaking O'Hara's hand. "I'll send one over today by messenger."

"That was beautiful," Mel told Charlie as they headed for the elevators. "Here's a guy who, by his own admission, doesn't know shit about making movies and doesn't want to know anything about it, but for his lousy seventy-five G's he's a script expert."

"You're right, Mel," Charlie said, "but what choice do we have? We'll send him the script. It's a step."

"I'm glad you see it that way, Charlie," Mel said.

"How do you see it, Mel?"

"I see it as a rejection," the lawyer explained. "Asking to read the script is his way out. All he's got to do now is say it's not right for his artist or what they have in mind for him."

"You may be right."

"Of course I'm right."

"We'll play the string out, Melvin."

"Sure. That's show biz, Charlie."

As the two men emerged into the reception area by the elevators, Laura Bonnell looked up from her seat and saw them. "Hi, Charlie," she said. "What are you doing here?"

The producer stopped to greet her and introduced her to his lawyer. "I could ask you the same thing."

"I'm working now, you know."

"So I heard," Charlie said. "In the record business?"

"No, for an ad agency, Alcorn-Hyland."

"Oh, yeah."

"We're thinking of buying space for a client on record jackets. It's a whole new thing."

"Who are you seeing?"

"A Mr. O'Hara. He has to okay the idea first."

"We just came from his office."

"He didn't seem enthusiastic over the phone, but we're willing to spend some money, and that interests him." She patted the bulky portfolio beside her chair. "We have a nice campaign plotted."

"Sounds good. Anyway, you'll love O'Hara," Charlie said. "You goyim will get along famously."

"Are you Jewish, Charlie?"

"You hang around Mel here long enough, you become Jewish."

Mel glanced impatiently at his watch. "Charlie . . ." he began, edging toward the elevators.

"Yeah, we're kind of in a rush," Charlie said. " 'Bye, Laura. Say hello to Art. Tell him I'll call him this weekend. I need a couple of lessons, if I ever get the time. My backhand has ceased to exist."

"I'll tell him, Charlie."

"Mr. O'Hara will be a few minutes," the cool blonde behind the reception desk informed Laura after Charlie and Mel had left. "He's on a call to New York."

"That's fine," Laura said. "Thank you."

It was funny about Malibu people, Laura reflected, how they always seemed surprised to see each other around town, as if they were travelers here from some distant, more favored land, tourists meeting by chance on hegiras through alien cultures. She hardly knew Charlie Wigham, had never spoken to him more than a few minutes at a time, usually at parties, but because they both lived in Malibu they shared a common bond; they were members in good standing of a society of the blessed, the sweet sharers of a delight unknown to the tribes that flourished in the Hollywood hills, the Valley, among the run-down stately mansions of Pasadena, in Beverly Hills and Bel Air and Brentwood, in Orange County, even in other, nearly equally exotic locales such as Laguna, or up in the hills above the more expensive canyons. Malibu was a true subculture, Laura had decided; it was to L.A. in general as Greenwich Village was to New York, or Princeton to the whole state of New Jersey. *We are the golden people*, she had told herself. *Or was that how George had phrased it?* She shut her eyes and sighed.

"I'm sorry," the receptionist said. "I'm sure it will only be a few more minutes now."

"That's quite all right."

She shouldn't have given in to him so soon; she knew that. It had been a mistake. But her defenses had been down and he had been so charming. She had loved the rustic-looking little inn he had taken her to for lunch the week before, halfway up Beverly Glen. That the place just happened to be only a block away from his condominium had made both of them laugh, because it had been such a nakedly plotted move on his part. But the comedic aspects had also effectively disarmed her. Laughing still, she had allowed him to lead her to his hideaway, a simply but elegantly furnished duplex on a hillside above a development of small Mediterranean-style villas nestled among groves of eucalyptus, sycamores, pines, and oaks. There she had allowed him to take her on the broad, firm playground of his king-sized mattress, an arena where, she imagined, he had gamboled with dozens of others. The whole apartment, she had noticed at once, had the air of a bachelor encampment, not the more settled one of a divorced father living alone, maintaining rooms for children to occupy on occasional visits. But though she had distrusted his ardor and the studied professionalism of his lovemaking, she had to admit that he had been solicitous of her pleasure and, more important, both gentle and kind. To her amazement, she had enjoyed it, too. A dam inside her had broken, and she had responded fiercely to him and climaxed with him, her own cry of pleasure heard by her as if from a great distance. When it was all over, she had sat up and turned away from him. "Now that you've had me," she said, "you can chalk me up on your scorecard and forget about me."

"Why do you talk like that?" he answered, obviously irritated by her cynicism. "Why do you put yourself down all the time?"

"I guess I realize I'm not the first to be here."

"Of course you aren't. I'm not a monk, you know. What right do you have to want to wipe out my past?"

"None, I know that."

"Or to make me feel guilty about it?"

"Okay, I'm sorry."

"Do I ask you if you still sleep with Art?"

"No. But since you ask, the answer's no. Not for weeks now."

"It wouldn't matter," he said. "We're adults, supposedly. We do what we want because we want to do it, and we'll accept the consequences, won't we?"

"Will we?"

"Laura, I've already made it clear to you that you're not a casual lay to me."

"This was certainly casual enough, wasn't it? Do we go back to the office now separately or together?"

"Actually," he said, "I'm not going back, which is why we both brought our own cars. Why don't you stay?"

"Because I can't," she told him. "Carlo and I have a three-o'clock meeting with the Holbourn people. But you can stay, George. Call in the afternoon shift."

He sat up and swung his legs over the side of the bed. "Damn it,

Laura, why are you doing this?" he said. "Didn't you like making love to me?"

"Yes."

"Then why are you dumping on it now?"

"Because . . ."

"Because what? Why are you making yourself and me feel so cheap?"

"I guess I'm not used to playing around."

"And that's what this is?"

She shrugged. "I don't know."

"Why don't you look at me," he asked, "so we can talk about this?"

So she had finally turned to face him, and he could see that she was struggling with her emotions, that she was on the edge of breaking down. "Hey," he said, "it's all right . . ."

But she had refused to let him comfort her. "I guess . . . I guess I just can't handle this, George," she said. "I can't fake it."

"Fake what? What do you mean?" He took her hand and she allowed him to hold it. "I'm listening. Honest."

"My husband can do this," she explained, "I can't. He's played around for years, and he's doing it now. But I'm not like that, George. I'm still married to him. And I feel married. And coming here with you today makes me feel . . . well, cheap, as you put it. I can't help it. I'm sorry. I'm sorry I took it out on you."

"But I've been trying to tell you, sweetheart, that I care about you," he said. "Doesn't that make any difference?"

"I thought it would, but I guess it doesn't."

"Why doesn't it? You wanted to make love to me, didn't you? I didn't coerce you, did I?"

"No."

"Then what is it?"

"I guess it's just me," she said, withdrawing her hand. "I'm in a difficult position, don't you see that? You *must* see it."

"At the office? Maybe, but—"

"More important," she continued, "I don't know whether it's real to me or not. By real, George, I mean whether I'm responding to you or to the whole turmoil my life is in. The fact that I enjoy myself in bed with you and that I also like being with you doesn't make all that much difference right now. All this is doing is putting more pressure on me. This job has been my salvation this summer. It gets me out of the house and away from Malibu and that whole summer scene out there. And it's giving me time to find out about things—about myself, what I want out of the rest of my life, about this lousy mess Art and I are in. Don't you understand, George? Can't you try?"

He sighed and got up. "Okay," he said, "so now what?"

"I'm just asking for a little time, that's all. I've got to get it settled in my own head."

"Okay." He'd leaned over then and kissed her on the cheek and squeezed her shoulder. "Okay," he whispered, "I do understand. Now what?"

"Now I'd better get back to the office."

They had finished dressing in silence. At the door, he'd taken her in his arms and held her for a moment, before she had freed herself and run away. At the foot of the driveway she had looked up, and he was at the window watching her go. He waved, and she waved back, got into her car, and drove away. . . .

Two days after their meeting with Boots O'Hara, the record executive called Melvin Schwartz to tell him that Continental would not be investing in the possibility of an involvement by their future star, Lane Ponds, in Charlie Wigham's forthcoming production of *Pale Moon Rising*. It was put to Mel just that formally, and he passed the rejection on to Charlie. "Just like that," was Charlie's comment on the phone.

"It wasn't quite that simple," Mel explained. "I had to listen to a lecture from Mr. O'Hara, delivered over the pounding from a soul group being piped right into his desk, about how come *Pale Moon Rising* could never be made into a successful motion picture."

"What the fuck does he know about it?" Charlie asked.

"Not much," Mel said, "but evidently more than we do."

21

The Wharton court was hidden from the Colony road by a chain-link fence overgrown by ivy, and it was sheltered on the other three sides by the overhanging boughs of tall trees. The light on the playing surface, even at midday, was dappled by shadows, which was why the court was rarely used, except during tournaments, when the D players were condemned to it, or for teaching. Art had access to it, but also used it only when no other courts were available to him. On this particular day, he had had to call Jim to get on it early enough, as the Kramers were having their court resurfaced, two other courts Art used were occupied, and Sid Harvey was playing singles with Harry McKay on his. Art had two lessons to teach from eight to ten, after which he was free until early afternoon, when he had a date with the Harvey boys on their court, followed by three hours of other lessons.

The morning had gone fairly well, Art thought. He'd especially enjoyed the second session, because young Danny Frankel, Burt's fifteen-year-old son, had talent and was a joy to teach. He was already playing in junior tournaments in the area and doing quite well; he had real promise, as well as a good temperament for the game. He also made Art work hard and at least kept him interested, which was a lot more than could be said for most of his pupils. Very often Art would let Danny win a game or two, just to feed his confidence, and it was fun to see the boy develop from week to week. Art took nearly as much pleasure coaching and working with Danny as he had with Tad at his age, which was saying something.

As Danny walked off the court and began getting his stuff together, Jim Wharton, to Art's surprise, strolled in through the gate. "Hello, Danny," the lawyer said, "how's it going?"

The boy shook his head and grinned. "Oh, I'm serving so bad," he said. "It just screws me up sometimes."

"He takes his eyes off the ball," Art explained with a grin. "You know how it is, don't you, Jim?"

"You bet. When my serve goes off, my whole game goes."

"Me, too," Danny said. "Well, tomorrow, Mr. Bonnell?"

"Yeah," Art said. "Two o'clock, on the Harvey court. Okay?"

"Yeah."

"Think about what I told you."

"Yes, sir. Good-bye, Mr. Wharton."

"See you, Danny."

The boy ran out, his rackets tucked under his arm. Jim closed the gate behind him and turned to Art. "Got a moment or two, or do you have to run?"

"I'm through till this afternoon," Art said, sinking into a courtside canvas chair and mopping his neck with a towel. "What's up, Jim?"

The lawyer sat down on a bench facing the pro and stretched. "I've got to go into town this morning, but I thought I'd shoot the breeze with you for a minute. It's about the kids. I hope you don't mind."

"Tad and Julie?"

"Yeah."

"Of course I don't mind."

"I'm probably out of line or making too much of it, Art," the lawyer said, "but I'm worried."

"What about?"

"The two of them. They're seeing an awful lot of each other."

"I guess they are. Is that bad, Jim?"

"It's not bad. It's just that Julie's very young to be . . . you know, seeing so much of anyone."

"Have you talked to her?"

"No," the lawyer answered. "She's pretty stuck on Tad. I don't think she'd listen to me."

"I'm not sure what I can do about it, Jim."

"Well, you could sort of casually discuss it with Tad."

"And he could tell me to mind my own business," the pro said. "Tad's twenty years old."

"That's the point, Art," Jim insisted. "He's in college, and she's just out of high school. She's just a kid. And in the fall, I want her to go East. She's been admitted to Swarthmore."

"And she doesn't want to go?"

"She's wavering, I guess. I'm afraid to put too much pressure on her."

"I see."

"And I don't like the idea they're going to bed together, either," the lawyer said. "I know it's done these days, but I just don't like it."

"Jesus Christ, Jim, what the hell can I do about that?" Art asked, astonished by this conversation. "They're old enough, aren't they?"

"Look, I'm just telling you how I feel," the lawyer insisted. "I want Julie to get a good education and have enough time to find out what she wants to do with her life. She's so infatuated with your boy she can't think straight. I'm worried about it. I want the best for her. Tad's a good kid, I know that. That's not it. It's Julie I'm thinking about. I'd feel the same way about anybody she'd be involved with right now."

"I guess I know what you mean," Art said.

"Anyway, Art, I'd appreciate it very much if you'd talk to him," Jim said. "I don't want Julie's head turned around, and I don't want her hurt. Still, if she's going to be hurt, I'd rather it were now, when we can deal with it, than later, when we could be in a real mess."

"Well, Jim," Art said with a sigh, "I think you're really making too much of it."

"Maybe."

"But I'll talk to Tad. You want him to stop seeing her? I don't think I can guarantee that. They both have minds of their own."

"Do what you can. See, the bottom line here is that I don't think Tad is as stuck on Julie as she is on him. That's what worries me, Art. And if he isn't, I want this thing to cool down, so Julie doesn't get mangled. Okay?"

"Yeah. Okay, Jim. I'll talk to Tad."

"Good." The lawyer bounced briskly to his feet, and they shook hands. "You're a good man, Art. Anytime I can do anything for you . . ."

"Yeah. Sure."

For quite a long time after the lawyer had driven away, Art remained seated in his chair. He was more than a little annoyed by the implications behind Jim's concern, but he tried to rationalize them to himself. It was only natural the man should have been worried, wasn't it? Julie was his only daughter, and it was her welfare that concerned him. It had nothing to do with the fact that Tad was the son of a bust-out-, has-been pro, or had it? Art stood up and began to pack up his teaching gear. Jim was right, after all, he reasoned. It would do no harm to talk to Tad when he got a chance. And at least now Art had some credit he could draw on with Jim Wharton. It just might do him some good, when and if he decided at last to take real charge of his life. Isn't that what Lee would expect of him and want? A man in charge of his own life? Yes, it was, he knew that. And now, very soon, maybe he'd be able to act on it, he told himself. Yes, very soon.

As Art stepped out the gate and headed for his car, Lee's Mercedes suddenly turned the corner and nosed down the Colony road toward her house. She saw him and beeped the car horn at him. He waited for her, and she eased the convertible over the traffic bumps until she drew up beside him. Peter and Anthony were sitting in the back, sandwiched between bags of groceries. "Hi," Lee said, smiling brightly. "How are you, Arthur?"

"Just fine, Lee. Been shopping, I see."

"Ugh. Once a week. I try to get it all done in one swoop," she explained, "but with these two bottomless pits to feed . . ."

"Hey, Mom," Peter asked, "can we go swimming now?"

"Sure. But by the lifeguard station, okay?"

"Aw, that's the dumb part of the beach," Anthony protested. "The waves are too small there, and there's all this seaweed in the water . . ."

"There or nowhere," Lee said. "Get going, you guys. I want to talk to Mr. Bonnell. I'll bring the groceries in."

The boys scrambled quickly out of the back seat and ran down the road toward their house. "They're turning into beach freaks, I gather," Art said.

"Yeah. Next week I suppose they'll want surfboards. I'm going to have a hell of a time getting them readjusted to Appleton in January," she said, then smiled ruefully up at him, as if this small but painful reminder of the future might have been better left unsaid. "I miss you. Please kiss me," she whispered.

"Out here?" he said, looking uncomfortable. "Jesus, somebody'll see us."

"I don't care." She suddenly opened the car door and dropped a box of tissues on the road. "Oh, dear!" she exclaimed.

When he bent over to pick it up for her, she leaned down to him. Shielded by the open car door and on the beach side by the body of the car itself, they were able to kiss passionately with a reasonably good chance of not being spotted. "That was nice," she said, as their heads bobbed into public view again. "I needed that. It's been two whole days."

"You bet. Anything worth having is worth taking chances for, right?"

"Right."

"Tell me you love me."

"I love you," he said, "and don't look at me that way because I'm in my shorts and I'll be arrested for indecent bulging in a minute."

She laughed. "Arthur, I think about you all the time," she said. "When, my darling, when am I going to see you?"

"Tomorrow," he said. "I was going to call you as soon as I got home. I got us a room at the Beverly-Wilshire under the name of Quinn. Can you make it?"

She nodded. "I'll have to be home by six," she said.

"We'll order lunch in the room," he said. "That way we can't be seen together and we won't waste any time."

"I feel positively conspiratorial," she said, with obvious delight. "Can we afford all this luxury?"

"Why not? Let's go first class all the way."

"It's such fun," she said. "And I'm going to ravish you!"

"Get out of here, Lee," he told her, grinning. "You're turning me into the only X-rated pro in town." He leaned over, shielding himself behind his teaching gear, and lurched sideways toward his car.

As he did so Billie Farnsworth turned the corner and drove past, shooting him a startled look. "It's all right, Billie," Art shouted after her. "it's only a cramp!"

"You look like a crab!" Billie shouted back.

Lee laughed. "You're crazy," she said.

"It's better than my imitation of a unicorn."

"You also do a great old goat," she said. "Goodbye, you mad fool." Still smiling, she waved and drove away.

Yes, two whole days now without her, he thought, as he dumped his equipment into the trunk of his car. *But tomorrow we'll be together for six hours at least. No, I'm not going to look ahead, I'm not. One day at a time for us now, that's all, just one day at a time . . .*

When Jim Wharton got home late that afternoon Mary was in the living room waiting for him. A half-empty shaker of vodka martinis sat on the end table by her chair, and he could tell at a glance that she was well on the way to one of her solitary drunks. She was dressed in faded blue terry-cloth pants, open-toed pumps, and silk shirt, and her long copper-colored hair, streaked with gray, tumbled to her shoulders. It was odd, Jim thought, pausing in the entrance from his hallway, but in this soft summer twilight, from a distance you could still easily mistake her for the beautiful woman she had once been. It wasn't until you looked closely at her in a full light that you grasped the extent of the wreckage. Though only in her late forties, Mary Wharton had begun to come apart during the past year. Her body looked bloated now, her breasts sagged, and her face, under its heavy layers of makeup, looked ravaged by more than time. He'd ignored the accelerated pace of her decay, but it struck him now that it was threatening to become dangerous to him. He had not yet decided what to do about it, but he knew something would have to be done, and soon now.

"Mary?"

She raised her glass and mockingly toasted him. "Cheers, Big Jim."

"What are you doing?"

"The sun is setting. It's drinkie time down south."

"Where's Julie?"

"Who gives a shit?"

"I do."

"Well, I don't, Big Jim." She drained her glass and set it carefully down beside her. "She's supposed to be at the movies. She's probably shacked up somewhere with that tennis player."

Jim flushed angrily, set his briefcase down, and stepped into the room. "Shut up! Don't talk that way about her!"

"Why not? It's the truth, isn't it? Have a drink, Big Jim."

He went to the bar, poured himself a light Scotch, and turned to look at her. "You disgust me," he said.

She smiled. "So what else is new? Hey, who'd you fuck today?"

"Mary, I'm warning you . . ." He loomed over her, leaning down to bring the full weight of his anger to bear. "I'll have you committed."

"No, you won't. Killed, maybe, yes. Committed, no," she said. "I know quite a lot about you."

He sat facing her. "Mary, why are you doing this to yourself?"

"I like to drink," she said, pouring the remains of the shaker into her glass. "It relaxes me, Big Jim."

"Stop calling me that."

"You were the best-hung stud in Chicago. Everybody said so. Boy, I sure found out."

"You're a drunk."

"Tell me about it," she said, raising her glass in another mock toast and sipping greedily from it. "Tell me something I don't know. Surprise me."

He started to say something, then thought better of it. What was the use? They hadn't been anything to each other for so long now that it made all communication, except of the most routine kind, impossible. But he hadn't counted on her becoming a total lush, nor on the growing menace of her mouth, with its repertory of threatening hints, its outbursts of savage, uncontrolled hatred. She could not turn Julie against him, that much he felt sure of, but she was becoming dangerous, a sideshow freak some enterprising enemy might find a way to use. If Mary couldn't any longer control herself . . .

"Listen, Big Jim," she said, "I want you to know something. You want to hear what I have to say?"

"Is it about Julie and Tad? No. I'll take care of that."

"It's not about Julie and Tad. It's about us. It's about me."

"I'm listening, Mary."

She giggled. "I went to a lawyer today."

221

"You what?"

"He's a good lawyer, Jim."

"We've been all through this before," he said patiently. "You can't have a divorce, Mary. You won't get a cent. I'll fight you for years, and I've got the evidence on you to do it with. You won't get a dime, and I don't care what the courts decide or how many injunctions you get. There isn't any way at all you can get to me, sweetheart. Not a chance. And you know it, don't you?"

"Oh, sure," she agreed, nodding heavily. "And you know what? I don't give a shit about that, either."

"Mary, why are you . . . ?" he began in a cold, hard voice, but then abruptly switched tactics; it had worked before. "Listen, Mary, what can a lawyer do? Haven't you got everything? What else do you need? Tell me and I'll get it for you. You want more money? You want to take a trip? I'll give you more money, take any trip you want. Get out, enjoy yourself. What is it you need, Mary?"

"What do I need?" she echoed. "Me? Nothing. From you, nothing."

"Then what's all this about?"

"You, Jim. It's about you."

"Me?"

"Yeah, you."

He stood up. "This is a pain in the ass," he said. "Hey, why don't you go upstairs and pass out? I don't like Julie to see you this way."

She looked up at him with an expression of exaggerated cunning on her ruined features. "You wouldn't. The one thing you'd never do, Jim, is face the truth about anything, or have Julie face it, your precious Julie."

"What the hell do you mean?"

"*I* told the truth, Jim," she said. "It's all on tape, you see. I dictated it into a machine and made this nice little cassette. I gave this cassette to this very nice lawyer I met. He's keeping it for me. Jim. Just in case. You see? Smart, huh?"

He looked down at her with disgust and total contempt. Look what she had come to, this golden girl he had married and made rich, look what she had turned into. Sad, it was sad, he told himself. "Who'll believe you, you dumb cunt?" he said quietly. "You think I'm such a dope I'd have let you find out anything? Mary, go to bed. Sleep it off. We'll talk about this again when you're sober."

She laughed, a great hoarse cry of delight, and flung her empty martini glass into the air. "Oh, boy," she said, "I'd give anything, anything to see you nailed!"

He lost control for a moment. He reached down, grabbed her by the shoulders, and hoisted her to her feet. She shrank away from him and flung her arms up to protect her face, but he swung hard and his open right hand caught her on the cheekbone and knocked her down. She fell on her side against the carpet and lay there dazed and unwilling to move. He stood over her, undecided but fighting an insane urge to kick her; then he leaned down to find out if he had hurt her.

"Daddy!"

He turned his head. Julie was standing a few feet away, an expression of horror on her pretty face. Behind her, young Tad Bonnell loomed out of the shadowed hallway.

"Honey, it's all right," Jim said. "She had a fall, but she's all right."

"But what is it . . . ?"

"She's been drinking, sweetheart, what else? Tad, give me a hand, will you, boy? I want to get her upstairs."

The two men lifted her carefully, and then Tad took the woman into his arms. "It's okay, Mr. Wharton, I've got her," he said.

"This way," Jim said, heading for the staircase. "Julie, get some ice, will you?"

Crying, Julie headed for the kitchen. Luckily she did not see her mother's face, because at that moment Mary Wharton, inert in Tad Bonnell's arms, grinned and stuck her tongue out at her husband. "Fuck you, Big Jim," she whispered hoarsely. "You can't even put the women away anymore. You've lost your clout."

"It's okay, Tad," Jim told the boy after they'd left the woman laughing on her bed, "she's an alcoholic. I'm sorry. I just don't know what to do about it. It's hell on Julie as well as on me."

"Hey, it's okay, I understand."

"I knew you would. Thanks."

They intercepted Julie on the stairs; she was carrying a bowl full of ice cubes and a face towel. "Hey, honey, I'll take those," Jim Wharton said. "She'll be all right. Don't you worry now."

Julie smiled through her tears and kissed her father's cheek. "Poor Daddy," she said. "I wish Mom would get some help."

"We'll get her some, honey," Jim said, hugging his daughter, "if I have to carry her there myself. You'll see."

He smiled at Tad. "Hey, Tad, stick around a minute, I want to ask you something." He clapped the boy on the shoulder and steered him carefully back toward the living room. "I have a little proposition for you."

Art Bonnell was alone in the house that evening when Tad finally got home. Laura had called from her office to say she would be late, due to a crisis of some sort, an art meeting or something that had begun in midafternoon and might go on till eight or nine, and Art was fixing himself a hamburger, after which he intended to plunk himself down in front of the TV set to watch the ball game. The Dodgers were up in San Francisco again, and Montefusco, whose conceited, abrasive verbal style had always amused Art, was slated to pitch for the Giants. It had been a long afternoon, with an uninterrupted string of lessons from two till six, and Art ached all over. He had showered, eased himself into his second margarita, and was finally feeling better, mellowed and less muscle-sore, when his son walked in. "Hey, want a hamburger?" Art called out. "I'll fix you one."

"No, thanks."

The boy brushed quickly past him, went into his own room, and closed the door. It didn't hit Art right away that the kid might be upset about something, but after twenty minutes had passed and Art had heard nothing from him, he finished wolfing his sandwich and knocked on his son's door. "You okay?" he called out.

"Sure. Come in."

Tad was lying, still fully dressed, on his bed; he was propped against the pillows, his hands clasped behind his head, as if he'd been thinking hard about something. He looked up at his father, but he didn't immediately volunteer any information. "What's up?" Art asked. "You sick? Anything wrong?"

"No."

"I make terrific hamburgers."

"Not hungry, Dad," the boy said. "I overdosed on popcorn."

"How was the movie?"

"All right."

"What'd you see?"

224

"*Norma Rae*. It was good. Kind of old-fashioned, but I really dug it."

"You take Julie?"

"Yeah."

"So how is she?"

"She's okay."

"Boy, you sure are full of chatter, kid. Lots going on, huh?"

Tad grinned and sat up. "I dropped Julie off, you know? Her old man was there. He and Mrs. Wharton had been fighting or something. Anyway, I helped get her to bed."

"Mrs. Wharton?"

"Yeah."

"She was drinking?"

"Boy, she's become a real lush, Dad."

"So I hear. Julie upset?"

"You bet." Tad stood up and stretched. "Maybe I will eat something."

"Ball game's on in ten minutes. Want to watch?"

"Baseball is the pits."

"You used to think it was great. Remember, I used to take you to Dodger home games?"

"Hey, that was a long time ago, Dad. I was a kid."

"Oh, yeah. Seems like two or three months ago."

"I switched off on the Dodgers when they got Lasorda and made Steve Garvey a saint. I was rooting for the Yankees in the Series."

"God, that's like rooting for Exxon."

"Well, I liked Alston and that old team. I just can't get with this group. I mean, they're so sanctimonious and all."

They went out to the kitchen, and Art fished a beer out of the icebox while Tad began to spoon down a large container of cottage cheese. "My favorite junk food," he called it. "Lots of substance and no fat. Gotta stay in shape."

"Yeah, that's a big problem at your age."

They passed a pleasant fifteen minutes or so, during which Tad explained exactly what it was he had liked and also not liked about *Norma Rae*, a movie Julie simply hadn't dug at all, after which Art headed for the set and began lining up his chair. He hadn't yet settled down, though Montefusco was throwing the last of his warm-up pitches, when Tad joined him, sinking to the floor beside him.

225

"Get a chair," Art said. "This is going to be a good game. The Dodgers are pitching Welch, and the Giants are hot."

"Naw," the boy answered. "Dad, I want to ask you about Mr. Wharton."

"What about him?"

"Well, you know, he's had me playing in his regular foursome in place of that guy Leftkowitz, who dropped out."

"Yeah?" Art leaned forward to adjust the color on his set. "You aren't betting, are you?"

"Oh, no," Tad said. "They play fifty dollars a corner now. I don't think anybody likes it much, but Mr. Wharton always gets his way."

"Usually, yeah."

"Anyway, we round-robin," the boy explained. "Whoever gets me has to carry my share of the bet. But that's okay, because we usually win. I mean, whoever I play with."

"That figures. So?"

"So when I play with Mr. Wharton, he tips me five or ten bucks."

"Is that bad? I play tennis for money, too."

"Yeah, Dad, but . . . I don't know, this is different," Tad said. "Mr. Wharton tips me like he owns me, and I don't like it."

"I know what you mean. Don't play, then."

"Well, that's what I wanted to talk to you about. I mean, I sure don't need the money that bad, and I'd like to get out of it. Only, I know you use his court sometimes and he's this big wheel and all . . . and . . ."

"And what?"

"Oh, you know what I mean, Dad. I mean, he kind of runs everything."

Montefusco threw his first pitch, a strike, past Davey Lopes, but Art now looked away from the screen at his son; he was surprised as well as touched by the boy's concern for him. "Listen, Tad," he said, "you do what you want about Jim Wharton. Don't worry about me. He spoke to me today about you, by the way."

"He did?"

"Yeah, about you and Julie."

"What did he say?"

"He thinks you're too serious about each other. You know he worships that kid, don't you? She's the biggest thing in his life."

"Yeah," the boy said, looking uncomfortable. "Yeah, I know."

226

"Something wrong there?"

"No, not really." Tad looked down at his bare feet and rubbed his ankles. "You know I took out Terry Ferrero last week, don't you?"

"No."

"Anyway, I kind of like her. I mean, I'd like to take her out again. It's nothing about Julie. It's just that Terry and I really talk about things, about everything. She's got a terrific brain and good ideas about everything. Julie's nice and real sweet and all, but I don't know . . . And now Mr. Wharton's asked me to play in town with him next week. It's all sort of coming down on me."

"Does Julie know you took Terry out?"

"No."

Tad looked so unhappy that his father suddenly clapped him on the shoulder. "Hey, Tad, you're not married or engaged or anything. Take out anybody you want. What's the big deal?"

Tad sighed. "Nothing, I guess. It's just me. I feel funny about it. I mean, Julie and I, we did get kind of heavy there for a while. And I think she's sort of serious about me and all. And now this thing with her dad, well, it's too much pressure on me, I guess."

"Look, all Jim cares about is that Julie doesn't get hurt," Art explained. "He wants her to go to college back East."

"I know. Julie told me."

"He'd rather you broke up now than later. He doesn't think you're good enough for her."

"What? You're kidding!"

"No. It's no reflection on you, Tad. It's on me and where I am. But it wouldn't make any difference. Nobody's good enough for Julie."

"Boy, no wonder I felt all this tension. How am I going to get out of all this?"

"Well, you can start seeing less of Julie," Art suggested. "Take out Terry, if you want. Let Julie find out about it. But don't make a big thing of it. She'll be hurt, but she'll probably get mad, and that'll help her get over it. As for the playing with Jim for money, just tell him you can't make it. You don't have to invent any excuses."

"I can't get out of this next one," the boy said. "He's set up this match with that guy Lefkowitz at somebody's court in Bel Air," Tad explained. "We're actually going to play two out of three, for a thousand dollars. Actually, it was Mr. Lefkowitz who called him. He wants revenge or something."

Art snapped off the sound on the TV set just as Montefusco got set to pitch to Cey, with Garvey on first and two out, and shifted in his seat to focus one eye on his son. "A grand? You and Wharton against Lefkowitz and who?"

"Some pro named Stevens. I guess he must be good."

"You bet he's good," Art said. "He's a teaching pro, one of the best. He's worked with a lot of the stars. He's just about the best money player at his level I ever saw."

"He's that good, huh?"

"In a tournament, playing singles, he'd be lucky to get two games a set off you," Art explained, "but in old men's doubles, with money on the line, I don't know. Old Bill Stevens has every shot in the book, and he can think of more ways to win a match than anyone since Bobby Riggs. You and Wharton might be in trouble."

"Mr. Wharton sure wants to win," the boy said. "He's promised me half the pot."

Art sank back into his chair and tried to think it out. "I don't like it," he said at last. "Jim Wharton doesn't like to lose anything. He'll blame you if he doesn't win."

"I'm kind of committed, Dad. To this one match, anyway."

"When are you playing?"

"Weekend after next," the boy said. "Mr. Wharton wants to challenge some couples around here for practice first. You know the Buckleys? They're number one on the A ladder at the club. We're going to play them. Not for money, just the practice."

Art didn't answer right away. He watched Montefusco retire the side by getting Cey to fly deep to center, and then he got up to get himself a beer. When he came back, his son had stretched out on the floor and lay with his head back, staring at nothing in particular. "Listen, Tad," Art said, sinking back into his seat, "I think I'd better say something to Wharton. I have to see him anyway about a deal."

"I'll play the one match, Dad, and then get out of the others, okay?"

"I don't know. I want to think about it."

"Have you ever played Stevens?"

"Sure, I know him. He was the kind of player who'd lose in the third round of a major tournament, but he's aged like fine wine. He's a real smart doubles player."

"You better coach me, then. I think I need some work on my

backhand, and I'm hitting short on the second serve. You got any time?"

"We'll find some."

"What are you going to talk to Mr. Wharton about?"

"A business proposition."

"Maybe you better forget about this other thing."

"I don't like the smell of it, Tad. He's using you. Especially after all this crap about you and Julie." Art turned up the sound now just in time to hear the roar of the Candlestick Park crowd huddled in its sweaters up north. Welch had walked the batter on four pitches. Art suspected it was going to be a long, tough evening for Dodger rooters.

22

"The real difficulty, I suppose," Evan Gilbert said, "is that you medical types are being asked every day to make decisions you're not really equipped to make. It's like expecting a trained orangutang to sit down and write *Hamlet*."

Why had the conversation turned to medicine and the ethics of dying? Victor wondered. Who had started this discussion, anyway? Probably the Kramers. It figured. They read too many goddamn newspapers and magazines, Victor thought. Until then the dinner party had gone so well, a typical Kramer affair, with excellent food, fine wines, and a lot of brisk talk about inconsequential subjects. Victor had gotten up to go to the bathroom, then picked up his phone messages from the answering service, called the hospital about two of his patients on the critical list, and returned twenty minutes later to find everyone gathered in the living room and Evan holding forth on the one subject neither he nor Dorothy wanted to talk about.

The Kramers, of course, knew nothing about the true state of affairs and both had plunged into the subject feetfirst, with, Victor felt sure, their customary misplaced enthusiasm for causes. Evan had taken up a dominant position by the fireplace, glass of brandy in hand, and he seemed to be enjoying himself. Victor did not find the topic congenial, to say the least. He avoided looking at either Dorothy or Jennifer, who, as usual, had faded into the background somewhere behind her brilliant husband. Dorothy had volunteered to serve the espresso, since the Kramers, side by side on the sofa, were basking in what they hoped would be the continued flow of Evan's witty conversation. The scene angered Victor a little, because Evan was being so infuriatingly flip and superior, as if the matter of his dying had become a comical secret he and three other people in the room shared at the expense of their hosts.

"Listen," Victor said, pouring himself a brandy and sitting down across from his wife, "I just got off the phone with the hospital and the last thing I want to talk about tonight is medicine."

"Hear, hear," Dorothy said, falsely cheerful, as she handed Judy Kramer a cup. "Sugar?"

"No, thanks."

"Oh, come on," Mickey said, "this is interesting. I was just talking about the Clark case, that boy down in Gardena who's been plugged in to a machine for three months now, just because the family are religious fanatics, some cult about life being sacred or something. Anyway, that's how we got into this. We're just talking."

"What sort of decisions did you mean?" Judy asked Evan. "Medical ones? That doesn't make much sense, Evan."

"No, I meant ethical and moral ones, over issues of life and death," Evan explained. "Not only doctors, but scientists in general have been given that power, and we shouldn't have it."

"Why not?"

"Because, Judy, we're not qualified to judge."

"Who is, if you aren't?"

"Well, in the good old days, the priesthood," Evan said. "But that was before the boys forgot they were supposed to be in charge of our souls and began dabbling in real estate and putting on bingo nights."

"What are you saying, Evan?" Mickey asked. "That we all have to make our own decisions in these matters?"

"Something like that," Evan answered. "We sure as hell can't leave it to the politicians."

"Do you really think most people can handle ethical and moral questions?"

Evan laughed. "Scratch a liberal and you'll always find a member of the royal family," he said. "Spoken like a true elitist, Mickey. Sure

I think they can. They have to every day, don't they? I mean, who's bringing the kids up?"

Dorothy set her coffeecup down with a decisive little click, as if anxious somehow to terminate the dialogue. "That's what I'd like to know," she said, making light of it. "I mean, who *is* bringing the kids up?"

Evan continued to focus on Mickey, as though he felt it was important right now to thrash this issue out—but for whose benefit, neither Dorothy nor Victor could be certain. "We have to respect the individual's wishes," he said quite seriously now. "We have to stop meddling and experimenting on people as if they were rabbits. We have to accept the *fact* of death and allow everyone to act accordingly and on his own behalf."

"You've got a point," Victor said, "but I'm not sure how valid it is. Doctors have to go against their patients' wishes all the time. Among other things, they're protecting themselves."

"From what?" Jennifer suddenly asked.

Victor saw how pale she was, how tense, but neither of the Kramers noticed. "From malpractice suits," he said. "We've had a number of terminal patients in the past couple of years who clearly should have been allowed to go but were kept breathing on machines for months simply because no one wanted to accept the responsibility of having to make a decision. In several cases there were large estates involved, and possible conflicting interests. A modern morality tale, if you like."

Mickey nodded thoughtfully, absorbed in the legal considerations. "I suppose the success of a lot of these suits," he said, "is based on the obviously mistaken assumption that doctors ought to be infallible, like the pope."

"As far as I know, I'm the only one who is," Victor said with a dim smile.

"I don't know what I'd do," Jennifer murmured in a voice so low only Dorothy caught it. "I really don't know."

"Victor, you're as big a bumbler as the rest of us," Evan said. "We muck everything up. Science and medicine have only one thing absolutely in common: we're engaged in a huge conspiracy to hide our own ineptitude. Look at what we've done to improve—ha-ha—the quality of life in general. But people want to believe the experts are infallible, so we assure them we are."

Dorothy looked at Jennifer, who seemed to be miles away now, her eyes clouded by the immediate future. She was such a beautiful woman, Dorothy thought, and so young. She had married this famous man, whom she worshipped and wanted to serve, and life had handed her its usual ironic twist of fate. What would she do? Dorothy wondered. How would she cope? Could Evan count on her now?

"Victor, you know I'm right," Evan continued. "And just as with the ancient priesthood, appearance is everything, you know. That's one reason you guys have to live as well as you do—drive fancy cars, buy the little lady fur coats and jewels, take expensive trips. Would anyone pay attention to the pope if he actually practiced the Christian vows of poverty and abstinence? How many paying patients would you have, Victor, if you lived in a walk-up apartment on the wrong side of town and drove a five-year-old car?"

"Ah, but we've done all that," Dorothy said. "What's the matter with living well?"

"I don't think I could convince anyone I could even take out their tonsils," Victor agreed with Evan.

"You see?" Evan crowed. "And that's known as putting on the emperor's clothes."

"I think the public is scared of the truth about most things," Jennifer said quietly. "The truth is frightening."

"Sure," Mickey said. "What they really want is what they get on TV in prime time."

"Such crap," Judy said.

"The only thing I ever watch on TV is game shows," Dorothy chirped. "I love all that naked greed on display."

"But where do you think they get those *clothes*?" Jennifer said with a kind of desperate gaiety. "All leisure suits and leather."

"I know, but don't you just love it anyway? It's a lot more fun than *Masterpiece Theater*."

"I can't believe this!" Judy exclaimed. "Don't you even care about what Evan's been saying?"

"Oh, we care, Judy," Dorothy said. "It's just that maybe we ought to talk about something else."

"But why?" Judy insisted. "This is so interesting. And it's a problem affecting all of us, really."

"Sorry," Dorothy said. "No jokes from now on." She wanted to get up and run out of the room, but forced herself to resist the impulse.

She hid her hands in her lap and clenched them tightly, her face a pallid blank in the soft orange glow of the room.

"Jenny," Victor said quietly, "it's not true."

"What isn't?"

"About the public not wanting to know. I think that's changing. I notice it with my patients."

"Seriously," Mickey observed, "listening to you people talk, it occurs to me we're going to have to pass some laws concerning these points."

"Absolutely essential," Evan agreed. "We're letting the scientists and doctors do whatever they want. That's what my book is about."

Victor sloshed the brandy around in his glass, then looked up at his old friend. "I'm not sure you can legislate any of this stuff," he said. "Maybe in your field, Evan. Not in mine."

"Why not?"

"Because every case is different."

"We'll have to pass some laws," Mickey insisted. "Evan's right. Science is running amok."

"Some states have euthanasia laws, don't they?" Judy commented. "Others are considering various kinds of right-to-die legislation. That's one problem we are beginning to deal with, right?"

"Yes, and I'm against it," Victor said.

"But why?"

"Because I don't think you can legislate the right to kill anybody," Victor said, keeping his gaze focused on the Kramers and away from Evan, who stood very still now and uncharacteristically silent by his post, one arm learning on the mantel.

"Why can't you?" Mickey argued. "I should think you could make a pretty good case for it. Set up some sort of death committee consisting of, you know, people from different areas of society."

"It wouldn't work," Victor said, "and it's risky."

"But somebody has to make a decision, don't they?" Judy asked.

"Yes," Victor said, "but only the person on the spot can make it. There simply isn't time to go through committees or the courts. The person on the spot is almost always the doctor. He's the one who has to act."

"He's got to be able to act within the law," Mickey objected.

Victor avoided not only Evan's eyes now but also those of his wife. He shook his head stubbornly and bore in on the Kramers.

235

"The more the law is involved, Mickey," he averred, "the less able we find ourselves to cope with events. The only society that lives entirely by the law is a military one."

Dorothy stared at her husband. She knew, of course, that Victor was talking about himself and Evan. *My God, he's going to kill him! He's talking about us!* "Victor?" she heard herself ask very softly.

Her husband's head turned slowly toward her. "What, Dottie?"

"I'd like to go home now."

Victor started to rise. "Yes, it's late."

"Wait a minute, wait a minute!" Mickey pleaded. "It's early!"

"Victor, you're not implying you doctors should have carte blanche, are you?" Judy asked. "I find that incredible!"

"What I meant was, the law is the lowest common denominator of social behavior," Victor explained.

"It's the only foundation we have," Mickey said.

"Granted, but that's all it is. You have to go out beyond the perimeter of the law, push it a little farther each time," Victor said. "We *have* to push beyond it. The only way things ever get done in life is by people who break the law."

Judy laughed now and clapped her hands. "Victor, you're a flaming revolutionary!"

Dorothy was on her feet now, but Victor waved her back into her seat. "In a minute, Dottie," he said. "I want to finish. It's important."

"I'd like to hear him out," Evan said, in what amounted for him to a whisper, but which they all clearly heard.

"I know the law has to change," Victor resumed doggedly, "but it's not enough. Not for a guy who every day has to face an infinite variety of choices. Like me."

Jennifer slowly shook her head. "I understand what you're saying, Victor," she observed, "but I couldn't do it. I don't think I could."

"Everybody has to make his own decision about it," Victor answered. "There are no pat answers."

"I . . . I've always felt that no one had the right to take a life, any life," Jennifer continued. "I've always felt that way, ever since I was a kid. I can't help it."

Dorothy felt herself staring at her, but could not stop. "And you still feel that way now?" she asked.

Jennifer nodded. "Yes."

"Jenny and I have discussed this whole question quite often,"

Evan said briskly. "I don't agree with her, but we respect each other's point of view."

"I see," Dorothy said. "I didn't know."

"Look, Jenny," Victor resumed, "every good doctor kills, most often by mistake," he said. "Don't look so surprised, Mickey. Doctors aren't the only ones screwing up. You business tycoons make colossal blunders every day, and some of them cost human lives, and in the hundreds and thousands."

"Yes," Evan agreed enthusiastically, "and the lawyers and the judges send a lot of innocent people to jail. Our ineptitude at life is part of the human condition."

Mickey laughed. "Hey, I heard a terrific joke," he said. "A doctor, a lawyer, and a scientist fall out of a plane together and their chutes fail to open. Who hits the ground first?"

Judy groaned. "Oh, Mickey!"

"Give up?"

"Okay, Mickey," Dorothy said, "we give up, we give up."

"I'm breathless with anticipation," Evan said. "Absolutely agog."

"The answer is, 'Who gives a shit?'" Mickey concluded triumphantly.

The call from Jennifer Gilbert came in close to noon, three days after the dinner party at the Kramers'. Victor, however, had not yet arrived at his office. He had been in surgery most of the morning, vainly trying to remove a malignant tumor the size of a small orange from the brain of a twenty-two-year-old girl who had worked as a secretary for an insurance company in the Valley and who had been complaining about severe headaches for over a year before going in to see her doctor. She was now lying in the intensive-care unit at UCLA, where she was giving an excellent imitation, Victor thought, of a bandaged carrot.

He had spent nearly an hour trying very tactfully and gently to explain to her distraught parents that they ought not to insist on keeping her breathing, since the tubes plugged in to their daughter might keep her going for weeks or even months, even though, by most advanced medical standards, she could be considered dead. Victor had not insisted, but he had made it clear, he thought, what the prognosis was. Evidently it had not impressed the parents, both of whom belonged to some California religious cult, the Church of the Mind Triumphant or something like that, which Victor had never heard of, and he had left them weeping and holding on to each other in an empty doctor's office he had commandeered for the occasion. He would probably have spent more time with them, but his office interrupted with the message from Jennifer. Dorothy had also called. Victor quite literally ran to his car.

But why was he hurrying? What was the rush? Evan had fallen in his bedroom that morning. He had found himself unable to rise, and Jennifer had had him taken to the Malibu Emergency Medical Center, where he now awaited Victor's arrival. Jennifer was with him, and Victor had spoken to her and Dorothy on the phone, as well as with the attending physician, a young doctor whom Victor had never met but who seemed competent enough. Evan was not in pain; he just couldn't make his legs move. He was resting comfortably, more comfortably than either Jennifer or Dorothy, who were both badly shaken by this sudden development.

Dorothy had sounded especially upset on the phone. "Victor," she had asked, "so soon?"

"I don't know, Dottie," he'd answered. "I've got to see him first. But it doesn't sound good."

"But you said he might have nine or ten months."

"I was wrong. Dottie, it's impossible to predict this kind of illness. He could have had a year or more. He's unlucky. How's Jenny holding up?"

"It's been rough."

"I'm on my way."

"Where are you now?"

"In Westwood."

"Please hurry."

Victor picked up the San Diego Freeway heading south, then the Santa Monica heading west to the end. He slowed down as the freeway petered out under the tunnel that disgorged him onto the Pacific Coast Highway. How well he knew this route by now, he reflected, how often he had driven it over the past twelve years. Luckily, at noon on a weekday the road was relatively free of traffic and he was able to make fairly good time heading up the coast, though he kept his basic speed, even in the open stretches, down to about fifty. The coastal highway, with its traffic lights, frequent curves, bumps, hidden driveways, and occasional falling rocks, was among the most dangerous in the whole L.A. basin. Victor, unendowed with the insane overconfidence of native southern Californians, all of whom considered themselves born to drive, defended himself by refusing to take chances. When he and Dottie had decided to live in Malibu, they had preached to each other the necessity of surviving the lethal hazards of this road, on which people died and were maimed as routinely as if it had been constructed for that very purpose.

Beyond the Topanga traffic light, more than halfway home, Victor began to wonder what exactly he would do about Evan. Had he really faced the implications of what would now be in store for all of them? Why hadn't he yet discussed the matter with Jennifer? Why had he left it to her and Evan? How much did Dorothy know? Too much, Victor suspected. Well, now they would all have to face the possible alternatives together.

Victor turned off the highway onto Crosscreek Road and headed for the medical center, a small, square block of glass and stone standing at the corner of an open lot just beyond the shopping center. He found himself wondering now what exactly Evan and Jennifer had decided to do. His friend had always been a great one, even back in school, for abstract discussions of great moral questions. Evan had spent his life, in fact, debating the issues in books and on the lecture circuit. It had been left to Victor and the other plodders to cope, not with issues, but with nasty facts and brutal realities. Evan Gilbert, in the grip of his lethal malady, was a reality that would have to be dealt with now, in the same blundering, imperfect, agonizing manner typical of every major human endeavor, whether motivated by the highest or meanest of purposes. Victor had fought the war with death for too many years to believe in much of anything but luck and the small victories one could hope to achieve with time.

The first person he saw as he stepped into the lobby of the building was Dorothy. She had been sitting there waiting for him, and the expression on her face told him all he needed to know about Evan Gilbert's condition. Victor smiled at her, but it was not one of his better efforts.

23

"It's nice of you to drop in, Art," Jim Wharton said. "You need to use the court?"

"No, Jim," Art answered. "I had a couple of things I wanted to talk to you about. I'm sorry to screw up your Saturday, but this is about the only time I can get you, and I've got a free morning myself. No more lessons till two."

Jim Wharton glanced at his watch. "Well, I've got half an hour before your boy and I are due up at the club. Let's go out this way. Want a drink or a cup of coffee or something?"

"No, thanks," Art said. "I've just had breakfast."

They skirted the house, which seemed curiously dark and empty for so late on a bright, sunny morning, and walked around to the back patio, where Jim pulled out an uncomfortable cast-iron chair for Art and sat down opposite him on a bench, with his back to the ocean. The lawyer seemed somehow diminished by the outdoors this morning, less formidable and physically overwhelming than usual. Art sat upright, propping his lean frame against the back of his chair, and smiled. "God, Jim," he said, staring out over the shining strip of sand to the choppy waves foaming against the shoreline, "I wonder what the poor folks are doing this morning?"

Jim grinned at him. "Probably trying to figure out how they're going to get this all away from us," he said. "How are things going?"

"They could be worse."

"We haven't seen much of you or Laura this summer."

"I've been busy as hell, and Laura's working in town."

"Is that so? Come to think of it, I guess I did know that. She enjoying it?"

"Yeah, I guess so. She was getting kind of restless around the house."

"You're not using my court much anymore, I notice."

"A couple of times a week, Jim. Is that still okay?"

"Of course. That was the whole idea. I don't use it much myself. I really prefer playing up at the club. Better courts, and you can always pick up a game. What's on your mind, Art?"

"Well, it has something to do with tennis. A couple of things, in fact."

"Shoot."

"Jim, I've had this idea for a while now. I want to put out a line of sports stuff, my own line," Art explained. "I think I'm about ready to move on it."

"Sounds right."

"I'm tired of teaching and I've got to make a move now, if I'm ever going to do it. My name still means something in tennis, I think. I've talked to some guys I know who'll go in with me. We'll manufacture all our own stuff, with a distinctive style and of the highest quality. Nothing cheap, no cutting of corners, strictly top of the line. Like the Tacchini stuff or that Fila brand of clothes. The Italians do a nice job."

"They make nice shirts," Jim said. "You talking about clothes or equipment, Art?"

"Both."

"Just a tennis line?"

"No, broader than that," Art explained. "Obviously, with my name, it's logical to begin with tennis, but we'll get heavily into skiing and other winter sports as well."

"What do you know about the business, Art?"

"Not much," the tennis pro admitted, "but I'm learning. And I've got a couple of partners who do know a lot about it. They have a big sporting-goods store downtown, Meadows. You know it?"

"Sure," Jim said, nodding. "I used to have an account there."

The longer Art talked about the scheme, the more plausible it seemed to him, even though he had raised the subject with considerable trepidation. After all, as Jim Wharton had suggested, what did Art know about the business, any business? Nothing, really. But the opportunity had presented itself, when Phil and Dave Meadows had approached him six months ago, and he knew they'd still be there, if he could raise a third of the capital needed and go in with them; he had the name and they had the expertise. He'd taught tennis to both Phil and Dave years ago, during another Malibu summer, and they'd both been fans of his for years. Fans and businessmen, and the two elements could be made to mix for him, Art thought. Anyway, it represented a chance for him to break out of this rat's maze he was in, to build something a little more solid for himself. He hadn't really thrashed it all out in his own mind, but his ongoing relationship with Lee Harvey depended, he knew, on his taking some sort of positive action, though he hadn't come prepared to discuss that aspect of his scheme with Jim Wharton this morning. What Art wanted from Wharton was his support, and he was prepared to give him a piece of the action for it, too, though clearly Jim didn't need it. Still, business was business. Art had the name and the desire, Jim Wharton the legal expertise and the money. Especially the money.

"How much do you think you'd need, Art?" Jim asked.

"For my third, twenty-five thousand," Art said. "We're drawing up a prospectus we can let you see. We're capitalized at two hundred and fifty thousand, most of which we'll get from a bank. Phil and Dave can raise that on their own. They have the store and they're pretty well established."

"And you've got your name," Jim said.

"For what it's worth," Art conceded with a faint smile.

Wharton rubbed the palms of his big, heavily knuckled hands over his knees. "Well, Art, I'll think about it," he said. "It's an area I don't know much about."

"I can raise seven or eight thousand on my own," Art elaborated. "I need another fifteen or so, and somebody on my side who knows about contracts."

Jim rose to his feet and stretched. "When can I see a prospectus?"

"By midweek, I should think. If you're interested, you and I can go in as partners in my third."

"Fair enough," Jim said, "but I want to think it over, Art. It's not my kind of thing, really. And I do know it's a touchy proposition, a field with a lot of competition and built-in risks on the manufacturing end. You can have big union problems. Maybe you should stick to hitting little rubber balls with fuzz on them, Art."

"I'm getting a little old for that."

"Well, your boy's going to be real good in another couple of years, if he sticks at it." Jim Wharton clapped him on the shoulder and headed for the house. "With the kind of money he can make on the pro circuit these days, he can support you in your old age."

"That's not the point," Art said, getting slowly to his feet. "I've got to make a move for myself, Jim."

"Yeah, I can see that," Wharton said. "Listen, we'll talk again next week. Send me that prospectus or drop it off one day. See you, Art. Nice talking to you. Can you find your way out?"

"Yeah."

The lawyer disappeared into the house. Art remained alone on the patio, feeling as if he'd been suddenly backhanded across the mouth. He didn't like the feel or the taste of it. He turned now to look out at the beach again. The sun beat down on the back of his neck, and he instinctively put up his hand to shield himself from it. *Holy shit,* he thought to himself, *I've got nothing to do with the rest of my life but suck up to the Jim Whartons of this world. Win or lose on this deal, I lose. No wonder Laura can't stand the sight of me or of herself in my life anymore. What would Lee think? And I didn't even have the balls to talk to him about Tad and the gambling.*

He turned and walked slowly back to his car; then, instead of going home, he drove south along the highway to the Crazy Horse, where he planned to have a few beers, enough at least to clear the sour taste out of his mouth.

Gail Hessian might have begun to enjoy her summer by now, if only Alex hadn't kept bugging her all the time about progress on the specials. He kept popping into her office and leering at her over her desk and dropping nasty little hints about time flying and all the rest of it. It wasn't as if she hadn't been trying. It wasn't her fault that Evan Gilbert had suddenly canceled her interview with him and that her attempts to set up another time for it had met with polite but firm procrastination. She hadn't even been able to get the scien-

244

tist himself on the phone, only that frozen bitch of a wife, who simply wouldn't commit herself. Either Mr. Gilbert was working very hard or hadn't been feeling well lately or something; it was always something. Gail, in fact, had just about given up on Evan Gilbert, but then, whom else could she build the segment around? Gilbert had been a perfect choice after Jim Wharton had, predictably, taken himself out of the picture. Just for once, Gail wanted to film a special about a place like Malibu without having to structure it around Hollywood types, all of them available, of course, but too easy and too familiar. Why did every story about Los Angeles have to end up being really about Hollywood? She could always fall back on the technique, but she was determined to do something different, something a little better. But if not Evan Gilbert, then who? That was the crucial question.

"Darling," Alex said, smirking infuriatingly at her around the edge of her half-open door, "if you can't persuade Mr. Gilbert either, how about some rock group? I understand Malibu is infested with them this season. Have you ever heard of an excrescence called Tim Bigbee and the Hive? They should be good for a grunt or two, live, on film."

Gail groaned. "Go away, Alex."

"Or Linda and Jerry? Do you suppose they do actually get together? I imagine they meditate. He'd consider it a wasteful excess in a time of limits and self-discipline. Don't you think this is a boring decade we live in?"

"Alex, fuck off," Gail said. "I'm trying to think."

At least the hospital special would be easy. The people at Mercer had seemed interested and cooperative, and it was geographically the closest major medical institution to Malibu, which meant that if she filmed there in September, she wouldn't have to do much extra driving; she'd be able to time it so she could go in there with her crew as part of her regular commuting pattern. She had the Malibu apartment through September and could extend the lease month by month, she'd found out, if she wanted to. And now that work on her book had actually started, it made sense to maintain the present arrangement. Shawn Williams, her hired ghost writer, lived in Pacific Palisades, only fifteen minutes away from her.

"The first thing to do," Shawn Williams had said to her at their first session, "is to get it all down on tape. That should take us three or four days, a week at most. After that, I'll have the tapes transcribed and we can go over them and make any additions or deletions you want. Then I'll rough out an outline, twenty or twenty-five pages or so, and we'll begin to write. I never work from a chapter-by-chapter breakdown. It inhibits me. We need room to breathe, don't we?"

It had sounded very good to her. Williams was clearly a pro, who was used to working on a tight schedule; he had no ego problems and a highly practical approach to his craft and the task at hand. "You talk and I write," he had explained to her at their first meeting. "Your publisher wants this book in seven weeks, which means that I have to turn out between ten and fifteen typed manuscript pages a day, after all the preliminary stuff is out of the way. We haven't time for second-guessing and heavy rewriting and all that. You'll go over what I write chapter by chapter, make notes, observations, whatever you want, and I'll interpolate everything into the copy before it goes to the typist, okay? That way we don't waste any time—the publisher's, yours, or mine."

"Well," Gail had told him, smiling a little sheepishly, "I guess so. Only, I feel a little funny. I mean, your name isn't going to be on this, because my publisher wants it that way, but you're doing most of the real work."

Shawn Williams had sighed, folded his arms, and looked at her with what she'd interpreted as mild irritation, as if he'd been suddenly and unexpectedly asked to explain the unseemly facts of life to a particularly dense adolescent on the brink of puberty. "Look, Gail," he'd said, "I didn't make the ground rules, but they're part of our deal, and I'm perfectly happy with them. In fact, I'd have insisted on two things myself—anonymity and a free hand in the writing. It's the only way I can work. I can't write your novel in seven weeks if you're peering over my shoulder all the time and correcting me line by line or worrying about your possibly beautiful prose style. They want your book in seven weeks? Fine, they'll get it. Only, you have to step aside and let me do it."

"You make me feel like some kind of dummy, Shawn, that's all."

"Try to get over it," he'd said. "Everybody in America thinks he's got a book in him and could write it if he only had the time. Well, everybody in America is wrong. I can write books. I can't do what you do, and you can't do what I do, not now anyway. We've got to work this way. Trust me."

"It doesn't bother you?"

"What?"

"I mean, the ethics . . ."

"Ethics? What ethics? We're talking about money. I can't feed my five children on ethics. And anyway, there are no ethics, in the book business or any other business. There are contracts and practices, that's all. Let's get to work."

And so there he sat now, this very minute, in his little office out back, over his garage, this serious little man with the thinning blond hair and thick rimless eyeglasses and nimble fingers, typing away at sixty words a minute, writing her novel for her. For fifty percent of the advance and forty percent of the paperback and foreign rights and twenty percent of everything else. *Her* novel. *Her* story. *Anchor Woman*, by Gail Hessian, author. She could shut her eyes and easily envision the volume, fat and elegant-looking, pyramided in the windows of her favorite bookstore, Hunter's, in Beverly Hills. She'd have to autograph a lot of copies, she knew that, and do the whole interview circuit, but she'd be good at it. She'd make herself and Shawn Williams a bundle. And it was her story, after all, not his. What stories did Shawn Williams have to tell? *Anchor Woman* was by Gail Hessian, novelist. Who was Shawn Williams, anyway? Who had ever heard of him? Nothing, a nobody, a ghost. . . .

The phone rang and made her jump. She picked up the receiver, unprepared for the voice at the other end of the line. "I didn't know whether you'd ever call me again," she said.

Jim Wharton didn't waste time on the amenities, but gave her the address of a small apartment house on South Roxbury, in Beverly Hills. "The name on the door is Smith—"

"That's original."

"—initial D," he said. "Ring one long, two short. What time can you make it?"

"Well, I'm working . . ."

"Yeah, I expected to find you at home today," he said. "You surprise me."

"Do I, now?"

"You'll be there?"

"I guess . . ."

He laughed. "I thought maybe you would be. I have some things I want to try with you," he said, "a little unfinished business. Four o'clock sharp. Don't be late."

After hanging up, she sat very still for a few minutes. She remembered very clearly now, and in excruciating detail, exactly how it had been that first time, when he'd taken her like a whore in his own home. He'd known then, hadn't he? He'd sensed at once how it had been for her. She had since put it out of her mind, but he hadn't. He wanted her again. And she would go to him and let him take her again, any way he wanted to. Yes, she knew that now as well as he did. She thought she would come to hate Jim Wharton, as much as she had begun to fear him, but she also ached for him, in a strange and frightening way, an entirely new way.

As she sat there, alone in her small office in Burbank on this bright, sunny Saturday morning, she began to tremble, but more from excitement than fear.

"Where have you been?" Laura asked as her husband walked more than a little unsteadily into the kitchen. "Everybody's been trying to reach you."

"Like who?"

"Like all your afternoon pupils."

"Fuck 'em."

"That's charming. And your friend Lee Harvey called twice."

The sun looked huge as it dipped toward the horizon and bathed their seaward windows in golden light, but inside the house itself it had begun to grow dark. Laura flipped on the kitchen light, and the effect threw her husband's ravaged face into startling relief. "My God, you're drunk."

"Not quite," he corrected her, "but well on the way." He opened the icebox door and peered inside. "We out of beer?"

She didn't answer him, but retreated into the living room, where she sat down with her back to the spectacular view of sunset and ocean and waited, arms calmly folded across her stomach, for him to appear. She heard him rummage messily about, then the sound of the refrigerator door shutting. She did not move.

After another couple of minutes he came as far as the doorway and squinted myopically into the room, an open beer bottle dangling from one hand. He could see the outline of her sitting there, but with the light at her back, he couldn't make out her features. "Laura?"

"Yes."

"I just couldn't hack it today."

"What do you want me to tell your pupils?"

"Tell them I'm drunk." He laughed.

"No, I don't think I'll do that," she said. "I could tell them you were in bed with Lee Harvey, maybe, except that she called here twice, so perhaps you have someone else now. Do you?"

"Christ. Who told you?"

"Or I can say your car broke down on the freeway and you couldn't get to a phone," she continued. "Nobody will believe it, but they'll accept it, maybe."

"They should. You're getting pretty good at excuses from your office," he said. "Tell them I'm in an art meeting with a client who gives good head."

"You're disgusting," she answered, rising quickly and heading for the bedroom.

"Better still," he called out after her, "give 'em the old W. C. Fields! Give 'em a noncommittal answer! Tell them to go fuck themselves!"

She left the room and he sank to the floor, his back against the wall and his gaze dimly focused toward the corner where his pictures and his trophies gleamed dully in the chiaroscuro of early evening. He swallowed some beer, belched, and listened without much interest to the muted sound of her falsely cheerful voice lying for him on the phone. After a few minutes of that, silence at last. But why didn't she come back? What the hell was she doing in there? He started to push himself to his feet, but thought better of it. The effort didn't seem worth it, especially as he still had a swallow or two of beer left. He killed the bottle and suddenly flung it across the room. It shattered against the opposite wall, directly under his array of silly trophies. He laughed again and wondered if he were about to become hysterical.

Laura reappeared. She looked pale, but rather sweet and very young as she stood there staring down at him. He remembered her

249

suddenly as he had first seen her, so long ago, running like a fawn across the lawn of that small-town country club, her brown legs twinkling in the sunlight, all those years ago. "I'm going," she said.

"What?"

"I said I'm going."

"What for?"

"If you don't know, Arthur, I have nothing else to say to you."

"I don't get it."

"Maybe you're not listening," she said. "You don't hear anything I say. I could have put up, maybe, with another of your summer romances, but this one no. Or perhaps I've run out of tolerance. I don't care, really, who you go to bed with now. I've always looked the other way during your casual lays. Anyway, not anymore."

"Hey, wait a minute, Laura—"

"No, I'm not going to wait a minute, Arthur," she said. "Now or ever again for you. I called you in San Francisco after the quake."

"You did?"

"Yes. There was no tournament. I should have known, of course. Yes, I should have known," she continued. "But now you go away for whole weekends. Lee Harvey? God, Arthur, it's sad. You're sad. I don't think I'm even angry at you, not really. I feel sorry for you, that's all."

He started to get up, but he was having more trouble than he'd anticipated. "Laura, listen . . ."

She stepped past him toward the door. "Good-bye, Arthur."

"Where the hell are you going?"

"I don't know. A motel, I guess. I'll call you tomorrow."

"What about Tad?"

"You can explain. It won't be a surprise to him. If you ever spent any time talking to him, you'd know that."

"Dammit . . ."

He never should have mixed the whiskey with the tequila, he realized. That had been his crucial mistake. He wanted somehow, for some reason he didn't understand, not to let her go, but he couldn't stop her. Holding her overnight bag in one hand, she breezed quickly past him. He heard the click-clack of her heels in the hallway, then the sound of the front door closing. By the time he finally got to his feet, the hum of her car engine had faded in the distance.

Smiling foolishly, Art leaned against the wall, unable to figure out what he should do next. He couldn't quite make himself believe that she had actually left him, though surely he could not pretend to be surprised that she knew about Lee. *My God, I've got to call Lee.* What the hell did Laura mean about going to a motel, he wondered, what could she mean? She'd go to Alcorn, of course. Wouldn't she? He laughed stupidly, gave up trying to rise, and sank again to the floor, where he eventually rolled over on his back and went to sleep. He was still there, mouth open and snoring loudly, when Tad came home shortly before midnight.

24

"I still think this is crazy," Billie Farnsworth said as Dee Stauffer gunned the big Lincoln Continental sedan around the tight curves of Malibu Canyon Road, heading for the Valley. It was the last day of July, a Monday, and the smog was bad; it came seeping through the mountain gorges toward the sea, and even with the air conditioning turned on in the car, Billie could feel her eyes begin to sting.

"What's crazy about it?" Dee asked.

"I'll tell you," Billie said. "I'm an old broad and you're middle-aged. Orgy clubs are for teenagers."

"Teenagers don't need them," Dee shot back. "Besides, this is not an orgy club."

"What is it, then?"

"It's a social club in which swinging is the main attraction."

"You sound like a brochure for a health spa. What's the difference?"

"Lots of difference. Mostly, it's a one-on-one deal. And like I told you, you don't have to participate if you don't want to."

"I think it's nuts."

"Why? What else is happening this summer?"

She had a point there, Billie had to admit to herself. Despite her fondest hopes for an active Malibu season, nothing had as yet really worked out. Jay had disappeared back to Tulsa or somewhere, then had spent the whole weekend moving into his new house. Anyway, it wasn't up to her to call him, Billie reasoned. She had more pride than that. As for Dee, she'd had a lot to say recently about what a lousy summer it was turning out to be. Mahoney's party had certainly turned into an almost unmitigated disaster for nearly everybody, including those weird Felchers. And Billie was tired of the Malibu party scene. Always the same people, the same conversations. Where were all the unattended males, for Christ's sake? Even Rich Bentley seemed to have taken himself out of the action recently.

Billie glanced over at Dee. Look at her, she thought, look at that absurd wig and the space glasses. "What the hell are you all dolled up like that for? What good is a wig at an orgy?" she asked.

"Don't be dumb, Billie," Dee said. "I can't afford to be recognized, you know."

By whom? Billie wanted to ask, but didn't. Nor did she tell her friend how absurd she looked in her black Medusa headgear and the goggles that made her look like a praying mantis. Billie smiled and looked back at the road. "Holy shit!" she screamed.

Dee hit the brakes, then sent the big car swerving out onto a narrow dirt shoulder guarded only by a slender stone wall from a precipitous drop down the canyon slope to the creek hundreds of feet below. Dee just missed grazing the wall, then swung the car back onto the asphalt as the tires screeched and the body of the clumsy machine lurched heavily on its carriage. She also, for some reason, came down hard on the horn, perhaps as a scream of protest, but it had no effect whatever on the open dune buggy full of teenagers that had suddenly come swinging wildly around a curve in the middle of the road and nearly caused a head-on collision. By the time Dee had recovered full control of her car, the offending buggy had long since disappeared. "Goddamn fucking kids!" Dee shouted. "They nearly killed us!"

"I hate this road," Billie said. "I hate all California roads. I'm going to die on one, I know I am."

The incident had sobered both of them, but now, as Dee shot out from under the tunnel and onto the last stretch of slightly less dangerous road between Malibu and the Ventura Freeway, Billie began again trying to figure out exactly what she was doing there, on her way to join a club for swingers. She could, however, understand Dee, who would do anything at least once, wanting to give it a whirl. "The whole goddamn sexual revolution has passed us by, Billie," Dee had proclaimed two days ago on the beach. "We watched all the kids and young folks have a good time while we were still married. Now I'm going to find out what it's all about. The pricks I meet swinging can't be worse than the ones I've been meeting socially in Malibu recently. And this way you can at least see what you're getting and make some choices, if you know what I mean."

Billie knew exactly what Dee meant, and that's what troubled her. Dee had explained it all to her and told her what the whole plan was, but somehow Billie still didn't feel comfortable with the idea. Dee had had to do a lot of proselytizing to convince her even to go along as an observer, which was exactly what Billie intended to be. What the hell, she was fifty-two fucking years old and beginning to feel like a mummy.

It wasn't simply a question, Dee had assured her later, of getting laid frequently, with a great variety of partners and a minimum of effort. Not at all. That was the way they went about it in New York, at clubs like Plato's Retreat, which they'd all recently read about. In California, swinging was a whole way of life and had been for years now. No one was available indiscriminately to anyone else. That kind of thing was totally at odds with the basic principles of swinging. Swinging did not mean having to jeopardize a secure and meaningful relationship with a permanent partner. The primary purpose of swinging, as Dee understood it, was to bring people closer together; that was its real justification.

Even at her most serious, Dee hadn't really managed to impress Billie, who had always assumed that swinging was nothing more than a somewhat sleazy, disorganized affair arising out of boredom and the overall decline of Western civilization. Billie hadn't realized it had a firm moral basis or that it was highly organized. Her only previous brush with the practice had been her recent meeting with the Felchers, who seemed to be devotees, but apparently there were several hundred thousand swingers in the L.A. area alone, and millions more across the country. They joined organized clubs, frequented certain bars, subscribed to their own newspapers and magazines that served primarily to reassure them, if nothing else, that they were part of a great nationwide moral crusade. Billie wondered whether any of these organizations passed out bumper stickers or lapel buttons, so that swingers, like the early Christians or a gaggle of conventioneers, would be able to instantly recognize each other in a crowd. "See, that's got to be one of the advantages of swinging over just dating," Dee had said.

"What?" Billie had inquired.

"I mean, this is a chance to relate to people who we might otherwise never have met."

"That's bullshit."

And Dee had grinned at her and propped herself up on one elbow to stare wickedly at her. "You bet your ass," she'd said. "I'm just telling you what they say. I just want to do some classy fucking."

"That's better," Billie had told her. "That sounds more like you. Just don't try to sell it to me as a moral imperative."

"I don't even know what that means, Billie," Dee had answered. "I want to try it, but I'm scared to go alone. Come with me. If it's horrible, we can split and we can help each other out."

And so here they were now, speeding along the Ventura Freeway, heading for the San Fernando Valley office of the Club Nirvana, an organization Dee had selected out of the dozens with ads in various underground and swingers' newspapers. It was one way, maybe not the best, to kill a slow Monday, Billie reflected.

After leaving the freeway, they drove for miles into the Valley along a series of straight, dusty boulevards to the address Dee had clipped out of the paper. It turned out to be a small, empty-looking office building on the corner of a block peppered with food stands, small shops, and vacant lots.

The office itself consisted of a ground-floor two-room suite furnished in functional pseudo-Danish, and the walls were festooned with crudely drawn charcoal nudes of young ladies with huge bosoms. A tired-looking woman in her mid-thirties was working a mimeograph machine in the outer room, but a young man who introduced himself as Eddie immediately appeared to usher them into an inner office. "Come on in," he said cheerfully, "this is where the fun begins."

Eddie had a moon face, thinning blond hair, and a pasty complexion. He chatted with them briefly about their reasons for wanting to join the club. "Usually, we admit couples only," he said, "but recently we've decided to admit singles, too. We have many more men who want to get in than women, you know, but we only admit an equal number of each sex. Getting two of you gals at one time is a real coup." He smiled brightly.

Neither Dee nor Billie commented on this observation, so Eddie produced a long mimeograph form and began firing questions at them. He wanted to know what Dee and Billie did for a living, if anything, what their backgrounds were, what social organizations they belonged to, what sports they played, what cultural and artistic activities delighted them, what their favorite hobbies were, and whether they belonged to any far-out religious or political institutions. As the questions succeeded one another and were dutifully answered, Billie almost forgot why they had come. She could easily have imagined herself applying for some sort of minor government post or admission into a not very exclusive neighborhood fraternal organization. "Well, that's about it," Eddie finally concluded. "In organizing our parties we try to bring people together who have mutual interests. We have to be a little careful. We don't want any weirdos. By the way, do you have any hang-ups we ought to know about? Is there anything physical, for instance, that turns you off?"

"Well, I'm not attracted to hunchbacks or people with club feet," Dee said. "And I can do without dwarfs."

Eddie laughed. "We don't take pigs into Nirvana," he said. "All of our members are perfectly presentable. It's just that some people have a thing about beards or blacks, say. We try to avoid uncomfortable situations, that's all."

Before asking them to pay their initiation fees and monthly dues, which amounted to fifty dollars apiece, Eddie proceeded to enlighten them concerning the club rules. No pornography. No pictures, either stills or movies, were to be taken or shown. No narcotics or illegal substances of any kind were to be consumed or smoked. No sadism. No masochism. No flagrant homosexuality. He glanced up at them. "You both—that is, between women . . ."

"We're not gay," Dee snapped. "We're just friends."

"I was about to say," Eddie continued smoothly, "that homosexuality between guys is out absolutely, but between gals it's okay if it's part of the overall big picture. I mean, if it arises out of group involvement."

"A sexist orgy, I see," Billie said.

"It's fine, but women don't turn us on," Dee explained.

Eddie resumed his catalog of don'ts. No falling-down drunkenness.

No extemporaneous guests or participants who didn't know basically what was on the evening's agenda. No coercion or forcefulness of any kind. No crudeness or rudeness to fellow members. "You'll also be asked to host your own function within two months of joining," he concluded. "And remember—you're always free to leave a party or a function anytime, but you have to leave with the person you came with."

Dee paid in cash for both of them, after which they received pink membership cards listing their first names only and proclaiming that they were now members in good standing of Nirvana. "See, we're like an extended family," Eddie said, beaming, as he rose to usher them out. "You'll learn to love us, not just swing with us. Call on Thursday for instructions concerning next Saturday's get-together."

Dee and Billie emerged into the sunshine and headed for the car. Billie felt depressed, but was surprised to note that Dee actually seemed mildly elated. "What's wrong with you?" Billie asked.

"I think it's going to be fun," Dee chirped, patting her wig.

"Yeah?" Billie said. "I feel like I've just been admitted into a bowling club in East Orange, New Jersey. Are you sure we came to the right place?"

"Oh, Billie," Dee said impatiently, "why don't you just relax and look on the bright side, for a change?"

"Listen, Dee," Billie told her, "this is *your* idea. I'm just along for the ride."

V

August Dog Days

25

It really had been a stroke of luck, Charlie told himself on his way over to the party, the only really hopeful development from his whole summer-long involvement with the rock-music scene. Having heard from Billie Farnsworth weeks ago that Tim Bigbee and the Hive had rented premises for the season back in the Crosscreek area, Charlie had, as a matter of course, sent the group a script. After his frustrating conversation with Dan Lefkowitz, the group's agent, however, Charlie had simply put any hope of hearing from Bigbee and his musicians out of his mind. So he had been doubly startled by the two-A.M. phone call the night before informing him that Tim Bigbee himself had actually read the script of *Pale Moon Rising* and loved it. "That's wonderful," Charlie had mumbled into the receiver. "Hey, who is this?"

The caller had not identified himself, but merely suggested to Charlie that he drop in the following evening. There would be a party, and Charlie would meet Tim and presumably have a chance to talk turkey with him. Charlie had inquired a second time after the identity of the caller, but he'd been rewarded only with a laconic, "Forget it, man, just show up, all right?" After which, the man (although it could have been a girl, Charlie realized later, impossible to tell, really) hung up. Charlie had been unable to get back to sleep, and now here he was standing in front of the big sprawling house tucked back into a fold of the hills below the Serra Retreat and waiting for someone to open the door. So many guests had already arrived that Charlie had been forced to park a half-mile or more away and walk, but, he told himself, sometime during the course of the night he and Tim would surely get together, unless, of course, Charlie was the victim of a hoax or a cruel practical joke by one of his so-called friends. Charlie tried not to think about that possibility, but to concentrate on getting to Tim himself, or whoever had called him the previous night.

The door opened to reveal a long-haired golden waif in a red caftan. "Hi," she said, taking his hand and pulling him inside.

"Hello," Charlie said. "I'm Charlie Wigham. Tim invited me."

"Oh, sure."

Without a hint of recognition or another word, the waif led him down a dimly lit hallway and into a big dark room full of people and left him there, fading away into the recesses of the house like a shred of mist. Feeling terribly awkward and ill-at-ease, Charlie looked around.

The party had obviously been going on for hours, or maybe weeks, and the whole scene made Charlie uneasy, as out-of-place in such surroundings as a Rotarian in an opium den. Nobody around him paid him the slightest attention, but perhaps that was because they were still all sitting or reclining and he was clearly out of reach. Gingerly he lowered himself toward the floor, where he found a cushion, sat on it, and tried to pick out a discernible motif or two from the soft, confused hum of the room. *Where the hell was Bigbee?* All sorts of odd people dressed in funny-looking clothes and smoking funny-smelling stuff seemed to be sprawled all around him. From somewhere in the darkness a hand thrust a glass of wine into his lap, where he clutched it firmly, not daring to sip from it. He had to keep the old head clear, he knew that much at least, and Christ only knew what they'd put into his drink.

Beside him, on either side, two couples lay twined around each other, limbs interlocked in serpentine contentment. "Hi," Charlie kept saying, nodding and smiling idiotically, but in vain. He sat cross-legged for minutes, hours perhaps, ever nodding, ever smiling, stiff with anticipation of acute discomfort and awaiting a clue, some sign from somewhere.

It came eventually, in the form of the waif, back again to sort him out of the pit and take him coolly by the hand into another room, where, in a circle of blinding light, Tim Bigbee *himself* and three troglodytes in fringed Robin Hood jerkins were leaning over a table shooting pool. The waif faded away, and Charlie waited, hovering at the edge of the light like a suppliant at the throne of the Sun King.

"Hey, Tim," one of the troglodytes said, "this must be Charlie. Hey, Charlie, that's Tim."

"Hi," Charlie said, his eager smile slowly freezing into a grimace as Tim neglected to acknowledge his existence. "Hi," Charlie said a little louder, "I'm Charlie Wigham. The movie? *Pale Moon Rising?* Remember?"

Somebody giggled in a corner and the troglodytes stirred restlessly, pool cues in hand. Who was this boor? How had this mutant penetrated such a sanctum of the inner consciousness? Tim Bigbee, however, did not move; clearly he had chosen to pardon the offense. He merely leaned over the table and contemplated the position of the balls and the geometric possibilities open to him. Click, and the shot caromed off one ball, hit another, and sent it spinning into a side pocket. "Nice shot," Charlie said, too far out of it to know the extent of the sins he was committing against good form. *Oh, fuck it,* he told himself, *I'll have to be me, I'll have to do it my way.* "Tim, it's nice to be here."

Still the tyrant did not speak. He spent what seemed to Charlie like the next ten hours lining up his second shot; then, as capriciously as any emperor at last deigning to acknowledge the lowest of his subjects, he looked up and peered across the circle of light toward the end of the table where Charlie, isolated in his boorishness, stood alone. "That's a heavy script, man," the emperor said. And click went the ball again, this time toward the sanctuary of a corner pocket.

"I'm glad you liked it," Charlie answered, smiling hideously.

Tim Bigbee played out his string, spoke no more until at last he stepped back and allowed one of his retainers to participate. "I *really* liked that script," the emperor said, leaning now against the wall.

"Terrific!" Charlie cried. "I'd like to talk to you about it."

"Yeah, in a minute," the emperor commanded. "I'm really into this right now."

"Oh, sure," Charlie said, gracious in understanding, as always. "Sure. Take your time. I guess we got all night."

"No," Bigbee said, "no, not all night. But the time, you dig?"

"Oh, yeah," Charlie agreed. "Oh, of course. Yeah. Sure."

After at least another hour, during which Charlie watched Tim Bigbee shoot pool in this circle of light, isolated temporarily from the blurred intermingling of his tribe, they moved back into the main room. Bigbee, hunched over, broad-shouldered, his long greasy-looking black locks spread over his shoulders in the accepted court style, pushed his way over and through the recumbent bodies of his attendants, eventually sank to the floor in the secluded corner reserved exclusively for him. Charlie, with a plate of what looked like potato salad that another waif had suddenly, inexplicably thrust into his lap, descended with him and maneuvered himself as close to him as he could. "I'm really glad you liked the script," he said. "Is there anything you want changed?"

"No, man, don't change anything," Tim said. "It's a great script."

"How'd you happen to read it?" Charlie asked.

"I'm interested in what people think of me," Tim explained. "I can tell what people think of me by the kind of things they send me to read. You dig?"

Charlie wasted no time, but went into his pitch. "Look, Tim, I'd like to make a deal," he concluded. "With you committed to this picture, we can go into production tomorrow."

Tim nodded, but there were problems. He had this other picture to do first, with the Hive and his own company. "Like, you know, we're a family."

"When, Tim?"

"April," said Tim. "May, June. You dig?"

"But that's next spring," Charlie exclaimed. "That's nearly a year from now. We have plenty of time."

But Timmy and the Hive also had an album to cut that would take him through September, also several concert dates around that time.

"We can shoot in October and November," Charlie said.

"Well, that's when I got to go back to my farm, because I got to build my barn," Tim said.

"You got to build your barn?"

"Well, yeah. I got to build the barn before the winter sets in or the animals'll get cold."

Charlie could tell right away, by the tone of Tim Bigbee's voice, that it would have been useless for Charlie to suggest that he'd gladly hire a man to build Tim's barn for him. I mean, sun kings and emperors didn't build their own barns, did they? No, they hired serfs to build them, while all the emperor's retainers, their agents and producers and managers, put lucrative packages together for them; they just sang their songs and counted the money as it rolled in, great tidal waves of loot, borne ashore on currents of myrrh and frankincense and percentages of grosses, all the golden points in the money spread. What was the matter with this clown?

"Look, I really dig this script," Tim Bigbee said, "but you know, like, it's complicated. Have you talked to Dan?"

"Dan?"

"Dan Lefkowitz, my agent. I sent him a copy yesterday, after I read it."

Charlie decided he wouldn't tell Tim Bigbee that he and his agent had already had one go-around on *Pale Moon Rising*. "Oh, sure, sure," he said instead, nodding so hard that something on his plate slid off and spread a warm sticky pool beneath one paralyzed buttock, "yeah, Dan Lefkowitz, that's right."

"Yeah, well," Tim said, "like I say, I really, *really* like your script, man. It's great. Whatever, you know, hey, don't change a word, dig?"

Charlie sensed death in the room. Where was the eye contact, where was the enthusiasm? Talking to this freak was like talking to Marlon Brando, who is never an easy guy to talk to, but from Marlon Brando you put up with it because—well, because it's Marlon Brando. But Tim Bigbee? The Sun King of folk rock? The emperor of the charts? *I mean, what the fuck am I doing here?*

When the room got darker still and smokier, the incense in the air heavy enough to push aside by hand, when the evening faded at last into a languor so total that even Charlie felt the marrow beginning to leak out of his bones, he somehow pushed himself to his knees, and like a man running through a bed of molasses, staggered out into the air, remembering in flight the blank stare of the golden-haired waif, still smiling, still fading like soft smoke into the recesses of the palace, lost forever in self-induced dreams.

Because Charlie had always thought of himself as a pro, he had no choice but to play out the last hand. He waited until late afternoon of the following day before trying to get in touch with Dan Lefkowitz. After more than an hour, and only by repeatedly invoking Tim

265

Bigbee's name, he was able finally to bring the agent in person to the phone. "Tim suggested I call you," Charlie explained. "I've been trying to get through to you for over an hour."

"Yeah," the cold, dry voice said at the other end of the line. "Yeah, Timmy and I talked about it this morning."

"Then I guess he told you he really likes the script."

"You know, Wickman," Dan Lefkowitz said, "I co-produced Timmy's first picture, *Dandelion Song*."

Ah, he wants in, Charlie thought. *I've got a chance*. "I'm sure we can work something out," he said.

"I never read the script," Dan Lefkowitz said, "but my secretary read it. She didn't like it much."

"Dan, I'm not really into discussing this project with your secretary," Charlie answered. "The point is, your client likes it. I like your client, and I'd like to make a movie with him."

"You know, Wickman, Tim's not really an actor," the agent said. "He's a performer, a great one. But he's not an actor."

"I've seen him twice in *Dandelion Song* and I think he can cut it," Charlie said. "And my name is Wigham."

Dan Lefkowitz then asked who was directing the picture, and Charlie told him that he had several very good people in mind whose names would not necessarily mean very much to Dan, even though they were well-known and respected in the industry. "My own personal choice would be Lester Markham, who wrote the script, worked for me in TV, and has a couple of small features to his credit," said Charlie.

"You're right, Wiggerman," Dan Lefkowitz said, "the name doesn't mean very much to me."

"When can I hear from you?" Charlie asked.

"I'll get back to you in a few days," Dan Lefkowitz promised.

Charlie was sitting disconsolately on the edge of the bed beside the phone when Michelle, looking adorable in her infinitesimal bikini, came in from the beach. She asked Charlie how it had gone with Dan Lefkowitz. "Not too well," Charlie told her.

"Oh, that is too bad, darling," Michelle said. "By the way, I have met the most interesting man on the beach this morning. He is a director in the movies. His name is Mahoney. You know him, Sharlie?"

Charlie seemed not to have heard her, let alone grasped the possi-

266

ble implications of such an encounter. "The son of a bitch," he said. "If I had Tim Bigbee, the whole deal would fall into place in a minute."

"He has asked me to visit him," Michelle continued, removing her bra and turning to admire her body in the full-length mirror beside the bed. "Do you think I should, Sharlie?"

"He's not going to call back," Charlie said. "No. His secretary doesn't like the script."

Michelle turned to look at him as if she had never really seen him before. It was probably at that very moment, Charlie was to tell himself later, that she decided to leave him and move in with Mahoney, who at least was not boring.

26

"Jennifer's got this great faith in Mother Nature," Evan Gilbert said. "I razz her about it all the time. Mother Nature deals out so many goodies of her own—famine, disease, earthquakes, floods, and fires. But she says we scientists are worse, and maybe she's right. We're busily inventing a god and asking everyone to accept our version of him simply on our say-so. Another pure act of faith. It's an exquisite irony, isn't it?"

Victor didn't answer, because he knew he didn't have to. His friend and patient was talking now to cover himself, to construct, in effect, an intellectual platform where he could make a stand.

"I love the idea that perhaps two thousand years from now our descendants, if we have any, will look back upon us as we now look back at the early Christians," Evan continued. "Already we're building the new catacombs, where we'll be able to hide out, not from the Romans this time but from our own technological blunders."

Victor hoped desperately that Evan would succeed, because otherwise what was happening to him would become unbearable. He wanted Evan to have what little was left of his life, and Evan knew it. They were building the platform together, really. Victor nodded and smiled understandingly as Evan talked; he fed him straight lines and encouragement, but mainly he just listened.

From where they sat together in the large master bedroom over-looking the beach, they could look out over a wide sweep of sand and sea, dotted on this warm, clear day by the suntanned bodies of swimmers, joggers, volleyball players, surfers, just plain basking sun worshipers—all the people enjoying in their own way simple pursuits now beyond Evan's most ambitious reach. Though not yet in severe pain, the scientist could no longer get about unaided. A pair of light metal crutches stood against the wall in one corner behind a shiny new wheelchair. Evan himself, already looking drawn and pale, reclined on a wicker settee, turned so that he could have a good view of the lost world of movement below. From downstairs the low, serene chatter of women in the kitchen punctuated their dialogue.

"Did you read about that Swedish doctor a couple of years ago?" Evan suddenly asked.

Victor shook his head. "No, I don't think so."

"I forget his name," Evan said. "Anyway, this doctor in Stockholm began weighing his terminal patients on a very sensitive scale, and he began to note that when they died, there was a sudden small but quite measurable weight loss. In every case it came to exactly twenty-one grams, about three-quarters of an ounce. Curious, wouldn't you say? A confirmation that the soul has fled the body? A scientific proof of its existence? I like the idea, don't you? Science, always good for a laugh."

"Yeah," Victor agreed, not laughing.

"Well . . ." Evan swung his legs out of bed and gestured impatiently toward the crutches. "Potty time."

Victor retrieved the crutches, helped Evan to his feet, and watched his friend drag his helpless legs toward the bathroom. "I'm going down for some coffee," he said. "Do you want anything?"

"No, thanks."

"I'll be back."

"Good. I might need you to change my diaper or to wipe my bottom."

"I'm terrific at that," Victor said. "I can't cure the common cold, but at ass-wiping, as well as -kissing, I'm supreme."

He went downstairs and found Jennifer, looking cool and elegant in slacks and a silk blouse, cooking tiny pancakes. Lee Harvey, in a spanking new tennis outfit featuring very tight shorts, was sitting at the kitchen table sipping coffee. "I'll have some," Victor said. "Hello, Lee."

"Hi, Victor."

"Some what?" Jennifter asked. "Buttermilk pancakes? Is that okay? I thought Dorothy said you were on a diet."

"That's why I want some," Victor explained. "She's starving me to death."

"You don't look fat," Lee said.

"I'm not. Dottie believes in preventive dieting, as well as medicine."

"A cruel woman," Lee observed.

"Amen." Victor sat down across from Lee, lit a cigarette, and smiled.

"How's Evan doing?" Lee asked.

"He's fine."

"Well, that's good," Lee said with slightly forced gaiety. "I just came by, really, to see if there was anything I could do, Jen. Evan feeling better?"

Victor did not answer, but Jennifer flipped the pancakes over, turned a serene face toward her neighbor, and said, "No, Lee, he isn't. Evan's very sick. You're the only other Colony person who knows now, besides Victor and Dorothy, and we'd appreciate it very much if you and Sid would please not say anything to anyone about it. It's very important to us. Evan wants to be able to go on working."

Lee Harvey looked stricken. "Oh, my God, Jen," she said, "I knew it was bad, but I had no idea . . ."

"And another thing," Jennifer said, "I don't want to talk about it, at least not now. Do you understand?"

"Oh, sure. Of course."

Victor thought Jennifer looked very beautiful at that moment, and he found himself admiring her composure and her strength. She would need much of both in the weeks ahead, he knew, and he was grateful for her existence in his dying friend's life. He found himself wondering, too, about Dottie. How would she react when the time came? Could he count on her now? He honestly didn't know, and it frightened him a little.

* * *

271

"Hi," Lee Harvey said, coming up to the grassy knoll where Art Bonnell sat under the shade of an oak, tossing bits of grass and twigs into the sluggish waters of the creek. She leaned over and kissed him. "I'm sorry I'm late. I had to get Sid and the boys off to Magic Mountain. It took some doing."

"But you did it."

"Yes. And now we have at least three whole hours to ourselves. Come on." She held out her hand and he got up. "I couldn't take another minute in that motel room on a gorgeous day like this," she said, "not even with you."

"Pretty horrible, isn't it?"

She shuddered. "Ugh. There's something about a row of naked wire hangers in an empty closet . . ." Hand in hand now, they began to walk up along the creek.

"How about the decor in general?" Art asked.

"Early-American nausea," she said. "When are you getting out of there?"

"Just as soon as I can," he answered. "I saw a couple of places this morning, but they wanted too much money. It's Malibu in midsummer, you know. I'll be lucky to find something. I might have to move into Santa Monica, at least until Labor Day."

"Why can't Laura move?" Lee suggested. "She'd be closer to her job. And anyway, she left you."

"A technicality," he said. "We left each other. Women usually get the home and hearth, even today. Also, I'd feel a little funny having you visit me there. Couldn't, in fact, with Tad around. Anyway, don't worry, I'll find something."

She squeezed his arm tightly and they stopped walking long enough to kiss again. "I'll come to you anywhere," she said, "even that surfers' hangout you're in now."

"*But* . . ." he began, grinning.

And she laughed. "*But* is right!" she said. "There are limits, Arthur, my love."

They walked on in silence along a narrow trail flanking the creek, now little more than a series of stagnating pools after three bone-dry months. The water, so clear and silvery in winter during the rains, when it tumbled over rocks toward the sea, now looked green and thick with algae. The last good place to have their picnic would be the big pool about a half-mile farther upstream, around the last big bend but still well below the dam. There Lee planned to stretch a blanket out on the shore and serve the picnic lunch she'd bought earlier that morning. The idea for the picnic had been hers, since she'd imagined Art might be as depressed by the prospect of being enclosed within the four dingy walls of his motel room as she was at having to meet him there. The trysts in hotel suites had become too expensive now that he was no longer living at home. Though they would not be able to make love today, at least they'd have some time together, she reasoned, in more congenial surroundings. The last two times they had made love in his room, they had both felt cheap and low, as if their affair had become the standard sordid scene of the erring wife and her stud knocking off an afternoon quickie while hubby was still at the office and the kids at school or camp. Dreary, depressing.

As they had hoped, the big pool was deserted. It was probable, Art knew, that other hikers, as well as horseback riders, might show up, but for now, at least, it was all theirs. Malibu locals rarely strayed up this way, so the chances of their being spotted by anyone they knew were very slim. They were both willing to take the risk by this time. Lee spread the blanket out, stripped down to her bathing suit, then fished about in the basket for the tall thermos full of cool lemonade she had made herself right after breakfast.

"Want some lemonade?" she asked.

"Yeah."

She poured him a cup, and they lay down, propped up on their elbows facing each other. "To us," Lee said, toasting him.

They drank in silence; then, still holding his cup in one hand, he leaned over and they kissed, a long passionate kiss that made her drop her cup, spilling the remains of her lemonade on the blanket. It didn't matter. Her arms went around him and they clung to each other, as he gently stroked her hair, her neck, the long lean sweep of her bare back. She shuddered and pressed into him. "Hey," he whispered, "we'll be arrested."

"I don't care. I love you."

"I love you, Lee," he said. "I wish there were something grand and beautiful I could do for you."

"I'll think of something," she answered, smiling up at him now as

273

she sank back against the blanket. "Oh, God," she suddenly exclaimed, "the lemonade!" She had rolled over on the wet part of the cloth.

"Here, let's shake it out and roll it over," he suggested.

"You do that while I take a dive into the water. Is it clean enough?"

"Should be," he said. "I wouldn't get my face wet."

She stepped into the pool, which looked fairly clean, and deep enough at this level to be free of algae, then eased herself into it and floated out, keeping her head dry. By the time he had fixed the blanket and rearranged the food and opened the chilled white wine, she was drying herself off. "Want some wine now?" he called out.

"You bet," she said, and rejoined him.

After they had eaten the sandwiches and finished the wine, they lay down on their backs in the shade of the trees and listened to the insects and the birds and the slow gurgle of the creek. For a long time they didn't even talk, but simply touched and basked lazily in their happiness with each other. Two groups of chattering hikers skirted their position, but otherwise they remained undisturbed. Sometime toward the middle of the afternoon, Lee rolled over, gently kissed him, and said, "I've got to go. I'm sorry."

"I know."

"They ought to be getting back around now."

"Don't explain. I understand."

"I love you, Arthur."

"I love you."

She smiled. "We have a limited vocabulary."

"There are only so many ways you can say it. Besides, I'm only an aging jock."

They stood up and packed up the remains of their picnic and walked along the trail in silence. Just before they parted, they embraced, and Art looked down at her shining face. "Tomorrow?" he asked.

She looked troubled. "Oh, damn," she said, "I just remembered."

"What?"

"We have a dinner party in town. Some business acquaintances of Sid's."

"But that's in the evening."

"I know, but it may be a problem."

"Want me to call you in the morning?"

"Yes. Around eleven, all right?"

"Okay. I'm through teaching at four."

"Okay, but let me call you, then. Will you be back at the motel?"

"I'll make sure I am, okay?"

"Yes."

She kissed him again, but in a hurry this time, and moved quickly toward her car. He waited until she had gone, then walked the remaining hundred yards to his own car, which he'd parked beyond hers, at the end of Mariposa Lane, where the road disappeared into the creek bed. She had left in a hurry, he noted, and he had to admit, as he drove away, that the sudden haste of her departure annoyed him a little. But that was crazy, he reasoned. Why should he be bothered by her social and family obligations? They had nothing to do with him, and it was only natural she'd still have to function as a wife and mother to her family, wasn't it? So what was bugging him? He couldn't quite put his finger on it, but he decided not to think about it. He would concentrate on her, the way he felt about her and the way he imagined she felt about him. It almost worked, but not quite.

"Victor, you've been so quiet all evening," Dorothy said to her husband that night over dessert. "Did something happen?"

"No," he said, "nothing special."

"Hey, Dad, can I go now?" Michael asked from his perch at the end of the table.

"You didn't finish," Dorothy told him.

"Aw, Mom, I'm not hungry. Honest."

"That's because you eat all that junk food all day long. Why don't you wait till dinner? What's the sense my cooking for you at all?"

"I got hungry, Mom," the boy explained. "I forgot to eat anything at lunch."

"So you loaded up at Hickory Burger at five o'clock, right?"

Michael grinned. "They make the *best* hamburgers, Mom."

"And what else did you have?" Victor asked.

"A chocolate shake," the boy answered. "They make them so thick there you eat them with a spoon, honest."

"This sounds like a damn TV commercial," Victor said.

Dorothy shrugged helplessly as Michael bounded away from the table and disappeared into the den, from where in a few seconds could be heard the dulcet baritone of somebody selling autombiles. "Shut the door, Michael!" Dorothy called out.

"Terrific," Victor said. "We're raising a boy to become a moon person."

"He's just a kid, Victor."

"By the time I was his age I'd read a thousand books," Victor observed. "Does Michael ever read anything?"

"The sports section. And in school, of course."

"The kind of school in which they don't even correct his spelling and grammar because that might inhibit his creativity," Victor said. "I can imagine the books. 'This is Jane. This is Dick. This is Jane and Dick's house. This is Gorko, their pet Japanese color TV set.'"

"Oh, Victor, give him a chance," Dorothy objected. "He's fourteen years old. The fact you read a lot when you were a kid doesn't mean much. You didn't have television when you were growing up. Terry reads a lot, after all."

"Yes, she always has," Victor conceded. "It surprised me, and it still does. She must have gotten it from us by osmosis."

"I think you're too hard on Michael."

"I don't blame him," Victor said. "With the kind of education he's getting in these California public schools, it's a miracle he can spell his own name."

"We've talked about private schools," Dorothy argued. "We found out they're not much better. We decided not to send him East to a boarding school. So what do you suggest, a parochial school?"

"Oh, hell," Victor said, pushing himself away from the table and heading for the bar in the living room, "I don't know, Dottie. I don't know much of anything anymore. I don't have any answers."

She followed him and waited until he'd poured himself a stiff brandy and soda, then sat down beside him on the sofa, from where they could look out on the beach and watch the moon-flecked waves shower against the rocks. "Victor, what's really bothering you?" she asked. "It's Evan, isn't it?"

"It's everything. It's been another one of those weeks."

"You need a vacation."

"I need something," he admitted. "I can't seem to connect to anything anymore. Maybe I'm going through the male menopause."

"I was wondering," Dorothy said, smiling. "We haven't exactly been insatiable in bed recently."

"Very nicely put," Victor said with a laugh. "Oh, God, I don't know. I'm so tired all the time. I'm tired of rich old ladies who aren't really sick but want their hands held. I'm tired of most of my other patients, too. I'm tired of the state of California and the insurance companies and the government with their endless forms to fill out. I'm tired of banks and prices and cars and the air I breathe. Most of all, I'm fed up with the routine of failure, no matter how much money it means."

"We've been there before, Victor," his wife said quietly. "You always said you had doubts about becoming a surgeon, that maybe you weren't tough enough."

"I'm not. I know that now. I think I might have been happier teaching somewhere."

"It's not being tough that counts," she said. "You care, Vic. That's what's wrong with you. When you lose any patient, you suffer. I've seen you go through this a hundred times. It's always the same. Only now it's Evan you're losing. You know that's it, don't you?"

"I've lost four people in the last ten days," Victor said. "The oldest one was forty-one. I've got two in IC, and one of them, that girl at UCLA, might as well be dead. She's a living, breathing turnip, kept alive by the miracles of science."

"Now you sound like Evan."

"Yeah," Victor agreed, nodding. "Just like Evan. He was right all along."

He got up and went back to the bar for a refill, but this time he remained there, bouncing nervously on the balls of his feet and cradling the brandy glass with his hands to warm it. Dorothy swung about in her seat to look at him. "Victor," she said, "I do know what you're going through. I *do* know. Can't you ever believe that?"

"Most of the time."

"Then what is it? Anything else?"

"No, not really." Could he tell her, he wondered, that lately he'd begun to question in his mind and soul not only the practice of medicine in general, but his specific role within it? Was it for this, he had asked himself a dozen times recently, was it for this sybaritic life on the California gold coast that he'd spent all those years learning how to cut people open and rearrange their structural deficiencies? What was he, really? An overpaid glorified mechanic? Another of the technological miracle workers the industrial state had produced to ease people through life as if it were a successful TV series instead of the struggle merely to survive that was the reality for most of the world's inhabitants? He felt himself trapped within some sort of widespread conspiracy, perhaps one designed at any cost to avoid ugliness. What was the purpose of American middle-class life these days, if not to imitate with meticulous, depressing efficiency the false images emanating daily from millions of TV screens? Life in America is not life, Victor had already told himself, it's show biz.

"It *is* Evan this time," Dorothy said. "It is, isn't it?"

"Maybe," he admitted, "but not entirely. Just seeing what's happening to him has sort of focused a lot of feelings I've been having for a while, I guess."

"You do need a vacation," Dorothy said. "We both do. If we could just go away somewhere, even for a week or so . . ."

"Impossible right now, Dottie," he told her. "Evan's going downhill so fast."

She looked alarmed. "It's that bad?"

"Yes." Victor sighed and took another gulp of brandy. "I thought the malignancy would respond better to treatment. Secondly, Evan doesn't seem to have much resistance. And the radiation therapy is debilitating to him physically."

She started to ask him the crucial question, but couldn't find the words to phrase it, so she simply stared helplessly at him.

"The best thing that could happen to him, Dottie, is that he goes quickly," Victor said. "So you see why we can't go away now?"

She nodded. "And after?"

"After?" he echoed her vaguely. "After, well, it's more than a vacation we have to consider, Dottie. It's surely more than that."

"But can we . . . will we get away somewhere, just the two of us?" she pleaded. "I need it as much as you do, Vic."

"I know," he said. "It's not us, Dottie, you understand?"

She nodded. "I think so."

"It's a lot of things, but it's not us," he tried to explain. "I tend to underrate you, I guess," he added with a wry smile. "Or maybe I take too much for granted. I love you, sweetheart."

She walked over to him and kissed him lightly, and for a few minutes they stood together silently holding one another.

27

Laura loved everything about her working routine. She loved parking her car in the open lot behind the building, in the space designated specifically for her, and then walking from the lot into the premises through the back entrance. She loved the cool, efficient feeling of the small air-conditioned lobby at that hour and the hum of the self-service elevator as it lumbered upward, carrying her and others who worked in the building to the day's tasks. She loved the inevitable cheerful hello from Marian, the agency's plump, middle-aged receptionist, and the smiling, casual greetings from her colleagues when they encountered her in the halls or stopped by her desk. She loved the smells of the office, from the fresh, artificial mountain breezes of the executive rooms and the faintly sweet-sour aromas of the art department and photo lab to the inky tangs of the mailroom, where Felipe—hairless, gold-toothed, "El Macho Grande"—presided cheerfully over In-Out baskets, trash containers, the coffee maker, the refrigerator, and, dominating the very center of the room, its central nervous system, the ubiquitous Xerox machine.

Most of all, Laura enjoyed Carlo, with his flashing smile, softly accented voice, bright eyes, and auras of expensive colognes and hair dressings. Tightly sculptured into his perfectly tailored custommade Italian suits, exuding soft-core chic, Carlo reminded her of a tame leopard she had once petted; he was swift, sure, smart, and temperamentally unreliable. He kept her, and all of them, alert, slightly fearful, and above all, interested. She would have worked for him for nothing, but that, of course, she would never have admitted to anyone, especially George or Mark Hyland. She had learned so much from Carlo in these few weeks that she felt now on top of everything connected to her job; if she ever left Alcorn-Hyland she knew she'd be able to find a job anywhere, though never as gratifying a one as with this young Italian, with his flair for the right image, the best color, the most instantly striking and eye-catching designs.

George Alcorn had hinted at one of their lunches together, not long after Laura had come to work at the agency, that he and Mark would probably make Carlo a full partner in another year or so. A smart move on their part, Laura had sensed immediately, or Carlo could be lured away from them, at disastrous cost. Advertising was a fragile, cutthroat business, up one day and down the next, dependent on the whims of clients and the market.

It was hard to imagine now, Laura had been telling herself, a life before she had found this job. She could hardly remember or account for how she had passed her days out there in Malibu, fiddling through this and that, while that poor bastard of a husband of hers pounded fuzzy rubber balls back and forth across other people's private arenas. What a waste, what silliness. For Laura now, there was this job, this routine that was not a routine, this daily challenge that engaged her attention and talents to their utmost. How had she stood it with Art as long as she had? And Tad? She could not account for her passivity and listlessness all these years. Was this what women's liberation was all about? *My God,* Laura said to herself this particular morning, *I've damn near missed out on my life! It's me, it's what I want! I'm my own, my very own person.* . . .

She was deep in a conference with Carlo over the layout of an inside-cover magazine ad, in which the color and basic design seemed off to him, when George Alcorn came up behind them. "It looks good," he said, unaware of their concern. "When's this one running?"

"*Mai!*" Carlo said, scornfully flicking away the proof with a careless backhand shove. "Never, George! It is pitiful, a disgrace!" He turned to Laura. "Laura, *mia cara,* send this back to the printer and call Lulli, the artist. We will design a new image!"

280

"But, Carlo," she protested, "we have to close this by Thursday morning."

"I do not care a fig," Carlo said, snapping his fingers. "Either the picture is correct or we do not run it. Get me Lulli, and we will discuss this *in private!*" With a challenging glance at George, Carlo bolted away from the art table and disappeared into his office, slamming the door behind him.

"Oh, dear," Laura said, smiling wanly at her boss, "everything is a crisis. He's upset now because he doesn't think we gave him enough time on this one."

George sighed. "I know," he answered, "and it's my fault. But Carlo doesn't have to deal with old Frank Ransom, the VIP over at Keller's. I couldn't even get an okay on a concept until two weeks ago."

"I know. I was there, remember?"

"Oh, sure, I forgot."

"Well, let me track down Lulli. If I can get him here this morning, he and Carlo may be able to do a quick fix."

"Right," George said as Laura headed for her desk and the phone. "Listen, Laura, I want to talk to you."

"Now?"

"When you've got a moment," he said. "I'll be in my office."

"Okay."

She phoned Lulli, who luckily was still in bed, and told him to come in by eleven if he could. She made two more calls for herself and Carlo, checked some proofs awaiting her final approval, then, unable to think of any other delaying tactic, finally went to see George Alcorn.

He was on the phone, but quickly broke off the conversation when he saw her standing in his open doorway, and motioned her in. "Please close the door," he said. "This is private."

"I was afraid it would be," Laura said as she lowered herself into a chair across from him.

He looked at her in silence for a few seconds, as if unsure where to begin, then leaned back and smiled tentatively. "Have I done something wrong?" he asked.

"No, George."

"Are you mad at me?"

"Of course not."

"Then why are you ducking me?"

"I'm not."

"Come on, Laura," he said. "You won't have lunch with me. You rush out of here when you're done as if somebody put a firecracker on your tail. You manage always to avoid me if you can. What's going on? I didn't know we had agreed not to talk to each other. Are you angry?"

"It has nothing to do with you, George."

"Oh," He looked a trifle pained. "You and Art . . . uhm . . . are you . . . ? Damn, I don't know how to phrase this."

"Are we getting back together, is that what you want to know?"

He nodded. "Yeah." Before she could answer, he held up a cautionary hand. "Look, it's okay," he said. "I have no *right*, I know that. I mean, no right to talk about this."

"It's fine, George, really. I guess I do want to talk about it."

"Oh? Then . . . what?"

"The answer to your question about Art and me is no, George," she said. "We are not reconciling."

"Oh. I thought, maybe . . ."

"I know. It's only natural."

"Then it *is* me."

"No, it has nothing to do with you right now, George," she tried to explain. "It's me, that's all."

He looked at her helplessly for a moment, then started to speak. "I think—"

"Wait," she said. "Let me see if I can explain it, okay?"

"Okay."

"It's . . . well, it's . . ." She, too, was suddenly having a hard time, she realized. Was it because she herself hadn't quite figured it all out? Was that the reason? She felt herself suddenly to be on a treadmill, running hard and getting exactly nowhere. "The truth is, Art and I are split," she said. "He moved out. That is, I moved out first last weekend, then he left the house on Monday and I came home. Art's taking an apartment somewhere. I suppose . . . well, I suppose we'll stay split. There isn't much left for us together."

"I see. But why . . . I mean, if he moved out . . ."

Laura smiled wanly. "Look, George, try to understand," she pleaded. "All I've got right now is this job. I love it here. I love working for you and Carlo. About everything else, well, I'm maybe just a little bit dead inside right now. I don't need complications. I need more time, George."

"I understand."

"No, I don't think you do, but I think you're trying to, and I'm grateful for that."

"And I guess I'm happy you're not sore or anything."

"You know I'm not," she assured him. "It's not easy to watch twenty-years crumble into nothing. I'm still not ready for anything or anyone else. The work here is a blessing. Time will have to take care of the rest."

"Sure, Laura. You're right."

"Can I go now, George? I really am swamped this morning, and Lulli's coming in by eleven."

"Oh, sure, sure," he said with fake heartiness. "Go to it." She stood up to go. "Only . . ."

"What?"

"It's all right if I sort of check up on you from time to time?"

"Of course." She opened the door and turned to go.

"And one other thing," he said.

"Yes?"

"If I can be any help . . . I mean it, sincerely. No strings."

She glanced back at him and blew him a quick kiss. "That's the nicest offer I've had recently," she told him. "Thanks. I'll be all right. Really."

Five minutes later, back at her desk, she had so buried herself in her work that she didn't have to think again about her marriage, her son, or George Alcorn, until late that night, before sleep came at last on the soft wings of Valium. What a blessing work was, she remembered thinking dreamily, what a relief from the burdens of past failures and present unhappiness. Work for an upper, and a couple of pills as a downer, and the days would pass, one after the other, like the great hands on the unseen clock that silently ticks our mistakes, despairs, and old wounds into oblivion.

"So *this* is where you are," Lee Harvey said as Art opened the door. "Don't you have a telephone?"

"Not yet. They're putting one in tomorrow."

"It's lucky I bumped into Tad. Can I come in?"

"Of course."

She walked past him into his one-room studio flat, took a quick disapproving look around at his bare walls, then stepped out onto the small terrace overlooking the beach. The apartment was about five hundred yards south of the Malibu pier, and the terrace jutted out over the water. "Well, at least you have a view," she said, popping back inside. "The rest of it is pure Holiday Inn. What do you pay for this?"

"Eight hundred a month," he told her. "I took a year's lease."

"Good God!"

She was right, he had to admit, but then, he'd been lucky to get anything in Malibu at the height of the summer season. This place, a corner flat on the top floor of the Malibu Riviera Apartments, had become available because the TV actress who had rented it, ostensibly for the season at fifteen hundred a month, had skipped out the week before, leaving in her wake a shower of unpaid bills. Art had rented some furniture, which was at least serviceable, and the bed was comfortable.

"It's large enough," Lee said, bouncing on it and smiling up at him. She extended her long brown legs for him to admire, and rubbed her knees. "Want to try it out?"

"I've got a lesson in twenty minutes," he told her.

"I'll come back, then. What time?"

"I'm through at five today."

"That's a little late. How about tomorrow?"

"I'll be free at three."

"I'll come by around four," she said. "That'll give you time to wash up and get ready. I'm going to be extremely naughty." She bounced up off the bed and kissed him. "Missed me?"

"What do you think?"

"I missed you," she said. "Got anything to drink?"

"There's a bottle of Scotch in the kitchen. Or would you rather have coffee?"

"Maybe that's a better idea. After all, it's only ten-thirty."

"Yeah, and I've got pupils."

"I'm sorry I didn't call you back yesterday," she said, following him into the tiny kitchen, where he set a pan of water to boil and fished out a jar of instant coffee and two mugs. "Oh, God, instant?"

"That's it. You take sugar?"

"One lump, or half a teaspoon. Got any cream?"

284

"Milk." He opened the icebox door and pulled out a carton. "What do you think this is, the Ritz?"

"I've never been to the Ritz, even the one in Boston."

"Me neither."

They took their coffee out to the terrace and sat down opposite each other in rickety wicker chairs with torn pillows. "Well," she said, toasting him with mock solemnity, "cheers."

He did not answer her, but took his first sip in silence. "How's Sid?" he asked.

"Like always."

"That's good."

"The boys doing better?"

"Not really. Neither of them will ever be much good."

"I know that."

"I guess I'm into telling the truth today. I assume you want the truth?"

"Of course," she said, smiling. "I always want the truth, Arthur. You can lie to Sid, but not me. Sid never wants to hear the truth. Sid hears only what he wants to hear."

"You're throwing your money away."

"Not mine, Sid's. He's got a lot of it, so let him throw it away if he wants to."

"It's okay with me," Art said. "I get paid."

"Yes, and this way I can keep an eye on you." She stood up, leaned over, and kissed him again. "You're angry, aren't you?"

"What do you think?"

"You are angry. Oh, Art, I'm so sorry," she said. "Please don't be. Honest, I couldn't call you, I just couldn't. We had a houseful of guests, and I was busy as hell in the kitchen."

"You didn't call me back the day before, either," he said. "Or the day before that."

"But I told you why. And then last night Sid made me go with him. I didn't want to," she explained. "I thought I could get out of it, but he insisted and insisted, and we had a real scene. He said he'd bought the damn tickets weeks ago and I was damn well going to go with him because I was the one who'd wanted to in the first place. Sid hates opera. Have you ever been to the Hollywood Bowl?"

"Once, a long time ago."

"Anyway, I couldn't get out of it, don't you see?"

"How was it?"

"I loved it. I think Caballé is probably the greatest soprano in the world."

"I'm glad you had a good time."

"I'd rather have been with you, you know that." She tried to kiss him again. "Darling, please."

He let her kiss him, but sat in place like a stone. "Somebody will see us," he said.

"I don't care."

"Yes, you do. What if Sid finds out?"

"Let him. This morning I couldn't care less." She laughed. "You see? I'm prepared to live dangerously."

"Maybe not dangerously enough," he said. He glanced at his watch and stood up. "I've got to go."

"Mustn't keep your pupils waiting?"

"Right."

"Darling, I'm sorry. Please . . ."

"Lee, the next time you say you're going to call me, call," he said. "It's bad enough to sit around a motel room for two hours every day waiting to hear from you, but then you think all you have to do is bounce in here and say you're sorry and everything's okay."

"Darling, I did try to call you."

"When?"

"This morning, just as soon as I could get out of the house to a pay phone, but you'd already moved out," she explained. "And you didn't even leave an address. How was I supposed to find you?"

"If you'd called when you said you would, you wouldn't have had the problem," he told her. "And all yesterday, when again I didn't hear from you . . ."

"I told you why."

"Okay, Lee, it's okay," he said, "only, I got the strong feeling I wasn't number one anymore. It's the same feeling I got when I was playing tennis. I still have a lot of very misplaced pride."

"Art, I know I'm spoiled," she said. "I know I'm not such a wonderful person, but what did I do, really, that was so terrible? I do love you. And I need you. Don't you know that?"

"I don't know," he said. "I'm not sure."

"Will you please let me do the worrying and try to believe in me, just a little?" she asked, putting her arms around him and holding him close, so that this time he did, at least, kiss her back.

"Lee, I have to go," he said more kindly, looking her in the eyes. "Please let me, or I'll make love to you right here, out in the open where everyone can see it, and then what would Sid say?"

She laughed. "The hell with Sid. I love you."

She ran away from him and out the door, and he waited till he could no longer hear the clatter of her clogs on the stairs before he began to dress for his lessons. By the time he had picked up his rackets and headed for the car, he had begun to feel better. Maybe she was right, he told himself, maybe he had expected too much of her. *I don't know anymore. I've lost my confidence. I'd better be careful, or I'm going to kick this one apart, too, just like my marriage.*

28

In midafternoon, Tony Mancini's restaurant was nearly empty, but Jim Wharton had no trouble spotting the attorney general, who was sitting in a corner booth behind the bar; his pale, high-browed face seemed to leap out of the shadows as Jim approached the table. "Jim, I'm glad you could come," the attorney general said, jumping to his feet and vigorously pumping Wharton's hand up and down. "I know it's short notice."

"That's okay, Mort," Jim said, sliding into the seat across from him. "What's up?"

"Well, I think we may have a real mess on our hands," Mort Lewis said. "Want a drink?"

"Why not?" Jim answered. "They make a great margarita here." And he signaled Tony, who was behind the bar and knew exactly what Jim drank at that hour of the day.

"I tried to get hold of you last night from Sacramento, when this thing started to develop," Lewis said. "Then I thought I'd better come down here and get together with you."

"What's the problem?"

"Hester won't play ball."

"Oh?"

"Look at this," Lewis said, producing a front-page newspaper clipping from Sacramento for Wharton to read.

Jim scanned it quickly. "Who's this guy Johnson?"

"The paper's top investigative reporter," Lewis explained. "Obviously, he got next to Hester or somebody in his office."

Mort Lewis was right, Jim saw at once. They were in trouble. Johnson's story was essentially an analysis of the activities of the attorney general's Organized Crime and Criminal Intelligence Branch since Mort Lewis had taken office. The year before the election, Johnson pointed out, there had been twenty-eight organized-crime prosecutions and twelve convictions; in the two and a half years since the election, there had been none. The story went on to castigate Lewis for his failure to investigate and prosecute. According to Johnson's source, described as a high-ranking investigative police officer operating in the San Diego area, "we're getting no guidelines from Sacramento or anywhere, and we might as well close up shop if we're not going to be allowed to accomplish anything."

Pete Hester's name appeared later in the story, as a dedicated cop who had recently been notified he was being transferred to make police training films, this at a time when arrests had been made in the ongoing investigation of irregularities at Rancho El Mirador. "To stop any investigation," the anonymous source was quoted as saying, "all you have to do is move people around, shove a lot of paperwork at everybody, and bring in some guy at the top who is gung-ho on making carbon copies of everything." Rancho El Mirador, the story also observed, had been under scrutiny for years, ever since it had opened, in fact, and recently it had been learned that unnamed sources in Chicago or Detroit had lent sizable sums of money, perhaps as much as fifty thousand dollars, to the attorney general's political campaign. Whether these sources were also involved in the financing and operation of Rancho El Mirador was another of the lines of inquiry being pursued by Hester's small local task force. For him to be transferred at such a time seemed to the reporter a curious coincidence demanding some sort of statement of policy and clarification from the attorney general's office. "My impression is that somebody very high up in this administration doesn't want some people to be spied on," concluded Johnson's informant. "There are big wheels here. They don't like being investigated at all."

Jim finished reading the clipping and gave it back to Lewis. "You're right," he said, "we have a problem. What are you planning to do about it?"

"I don't know, Jim," Lewis said. "Obviously, I've got to answer this charge. The story broke this morning. By tonight it will be on the news, and I'm sure the L.A. *Times* will also pick it up. I'm going to have to make a statement."

"Yeah."

"Look, Jim, your people have got to understand," Lewis insisted. "I can't stop this cold."

"You've already transferred Hester," Jim pointed out. "Don't change that. Go on the offensive."

"How, for Christ's sake?"

"The usual way," Jim explained. "You know how it's done. You attack Hester for wasting time arresting punks who just happen to be staying at El Mirador, while allowing the real investigation to languish. The point here is that you are developing an important line of inquiry that is being jeopardized by overeager local officers who can't see the forest for the trees."

Mort Lewis nodded thoughtfully. "That makes sense," he agreed. "I'd already worked something out along those lines."

"You tell the press that Mr. Pete Hester, the obvious source of this inflammatory article, is a fine officer, with a splendid record, who has, however, outlived his usefulness in certain areas and it's time to bring in younger men and more skilled investigators from your own staff," Jim concluded. "You stick to your guns, Mort. You're the man the people of California elected to this office, not Pete Hester. But be sure to butter Hester up. Do it right, and you can bury him in it."

"And what about the rest of it?"

"What about it?"

"The loans."

"Ignore it. Or, better, you claim angrily that the charges are false. You filed proper campaign disclosures and listed everything. Your integrity, Mort, is beyond question."

"It is that."

"Good, then what have you got to worry about? Will the governor back you?"

"He'll hedge, as he always does. The bastard's running for president."

"Well, you don't need him."

"What I can't figure out is where the information on the possible source of the loans came from," Lewis said. "The guy must be guessing."

"Sure he is," Jim agreed. "It's easy. For years there's been talk of El Mirador and where that money came from. All a nosy reporter has to do is put two and two together and he writes it up. But remember, there's no way they can prove anything. Let the sons of bitches say what they want. You have nothing to hide, Mort."

"No," the attorney general agreed, nodding gloomily. "If you . . ." He looked up at Jim and waited, with drawn features, for some reassurance.

"I'll take care of my end, Mort," Jim Wharton said. "You go about your business. Handle this the way we've discussed it, and we'll ride it out."

"I'm not sure we can shut Hester up permanently."

"We don't have to," Jim said. "He's taken his best shot."

"Yeah?"

"Sure, and it isn't going to be good enough. When's he up for retirement?"

"Two years to go."

"Keep the bastard shuffling papers, Mort, or playing musical desks, and you may speed it up some. If I know Hester, he's just another ambitious prick. He'll get winded pretty fast and head for the sidelines or go somewhere else when it doesn't work his way. You'll be well rid of him."

"I sure hope you're right, Jim," Lewis said, shaking his head. "And I sure hope your people don't lose their grip on reality. We could be in the middle of a real shit storm."

Jim Wharton happened to agree with this estimate of the situation, but he kept that opinion to himself. Later that afternoon, upon returning to his office, the lawyer put through a call to Chicago that, he knew, would bring Dudley Kerrigan, or some other emissary from the company, back to Los Angeles on the first available plane.

"I'm a bit worried about you, love," Alex West said, hovering like a bird of prey in her open doorway. "You don't look well at all. Are you ill?"

"No," Gail told him. "I'm not getting a hell of a lot of sleep, that's all."

"And why not?"

"The logistics of this operation are beginning to get to me," she explained. "I'm living in Malibu and commuting to the studio and rushing around trying to put both these specials together for you and handling my regular show in between. It's too much, Alex."

He nodded thoughtfully. "So I guessed. And then, of course, there's the novel."

"Yes, that, too."

"How's that coming?"

"Fine, fine. Not that you give a shit."

Alex continued to regard her pensively, and it began to make her nervous. "There's something else, isn't there?" he asked.

"No."

"You're not in love, are you?"

"No, Alex. Look, go away, will you, like a good little producer?" she said. "I have a hundred calls to make."

But he did not go away. "The thing is, pet," he said, "you're beginning to look rather like Bette Davis on screen these days. There *is* a limit to what makeup can do, and we can't embalm you. What I was going to suggest, so that we don't unduly alarm our viewers, is that you try going to bed alone for the next few nights. That or put ice on the pouches under your eyes. You look leprous. Of course, we could try hanging a bell around your throat and calling out 'Unclean, unclean!' as you come on the air."

Something in her snapped. She picked up a heavy glass paper-weight he had given her the year before, probably as a small token of his contempt, and flung it at him. He moved his head to one side only slightly, but the object missed him by a wide margin and thudded heavily against the wall, where it left a nasty little indentation in the plaster.

"Oh, dear," he said. "You are touchy these days. Before you throw anything else, pet, I did want to tell you we're dropping the Malibu special for now, unless you can get the key interview with Gilbert. If you can't, then you can concentrate on the hospital. It might take some pressure off you, all right, love?" And he quickly retreated, closing the door on her as he left.

It was so typical of the little worm, she reflected, to bring her good news in such a negative form; it was so like him. By narrowing her options in the matter of the Malibu special down to securing the interview with Evan Gilbert, Alex had, in effect, taken a lot of pressure off her. She could now give that one last try, even if she had to barge in on Gilbert unannounced, and then devote all of her energies to the hospital documentary, which she'd already arranged to shoot in mid-September, even though she was still awaiting a final clearance and go-ahead from the Albert Mercer governing board. Why couldn't Alex simply have put it to her that way, instead of cutting her down by hitting her hardest where she was most vulnerable these days.

She should have been pleased, too, Gail told herself. That very morning she'd called Shawn Williams to congratulate him on the first fifty pages of *Anchor Woman*, which she'd read eagerly the night before. He was doing a terrific job for her; every line of it could have been written by her, so closely had Williams been able to imitate her speech patterns. Not only did the material sound like her, it was in some cases simply a brilliantly edited version of what she had put on tape. Shawn Williams was clearly a pro; she'd made a great find there, all right. *And wait until that bastard Alex reads it! He'll shit in his pants. . . .*

She got up and walked over to the wall mirror above her filing cabinets. The face that stared back at her frightened her. *My God, Alex is right! I look like a hag! What the fuck is wrong with me?*

Shaken, she retreated to her chair and sat down, hugging herself. It felt suddenly very cold in the room. Had they turned up the air conditioning? She didn't think so. What was it, then? What was wrong with her? She knew, if she could only face it, but it was hard to do. Very hard. Even as she held herself and began slowly to rock back and forth in her chair, she knew. When she could no longer evade the knowledge, she made herself stop rocking and slowly peeled away the long sleeves of her silk blouse so that she could look at her wrists.

The ugly red wounds, where she had fought and strained against the binding cords, had begun to grow scabs, but it would be weeks before all traces of that afternoon in Jim Wharton's hideaway faded. Her ankles, hidden by her slacks, displayed similar, though less severe marks. The bruises and welts on her torso and thighs had begun to turn yellow with age, but still looked hideous. She would not be able to go out in the sun for another week or so without attracting curiosity. But that was not the worst of it. What Gail was having a very difficult time adjusting to was the memory of how she had received those wounds and marks.

She had screamed, or tried to, through her gag, but even as she had writhed in pain and terror to the coldly calculated, meticulously conceived violence of his attack, she had experienced a depth of sexual pleasure she had never tasted before or even dreamed about. What he had done to her, she realized with horror, was tap into a well of desire that she had never known existed and that contradicted every rational thought and feeling she had ever had. She hated Jim Wharton for having done this to her, as well as for what she now believed him to be, but she also knew with absolute certainty that if and when he ever called for her again, she would go to him and submit to whatever else he wanted of her.

It was not because of what he had done to her physically that Gail now hated him, but because of what he had revealed to her about herself. He had forced her to stare into an abyss and confront what she saw there. She would have been happy to hear that morning, or anytime, that Jim Wharton was dead, but she knew, no matter what, that her own life, after what they had done together, could now never be the same again. She had traveled beyond a hidden, carefully guarded secret door into uncharted territory and for the rest of her life she would have to live on its edge.

It was becoming a week of confrontations, Jim Wharton told himself as he sat down in Larry Feldenstein's office the following morning. The room was on the second story of a small professional building on Pacific Coast Highway in Malibu; from where Larry Feldenstein sat, you could see across the highway and through a gap between two houses across the way to the water. Larry Feldenstein was young, balding, with fleshy features and mild brown eyes. He had a fairly successful civil practice, Jim knew, but as a lawyer he was still very small potatoes. Jim anticipated no real trouble from him. "Larry, I'm glad you could see me," Jim said affably. "I've been meaning to stop by for a few days, but I've been busy as hell."

"Sure, Jim. What can I do for you?"

"That tape cassette my wife entrusted to you a few days ago," Jim explained. "I'd like to have it back."

Larry looked surprised. "Did Mary tell you I had it?"

Jim smiled. "It wasn't hard to figure out," he said. "You're Mary's favorite mixed-doubles partner."

Larry groaned. "Oh, Lord," he said, "I knew tennis would get me into trouble one day."

"No trouble, Larry. I just would like to have the tape."

"I want you to know, Jim, that I had nothing to do with it," Larry explained. "Mary just insisted I keep it for her. I have no idea what's in it."

"Nothing that crucial, Larry, believe me," Jim said. "But I would like to have it back. It's not Mary's tape, it's mine."

"I see," Larry said, turning very serious, "but I don't think I can do that, Jim."

"Oh? Why not?"

"Because Mary came to me and asked me to keep it for her."

"And I'm asking you to give it back, Larry."

"I'm kind of in a spot, aren't I? I mean, Mary could be considered my client in this matter."

"But the tape belongs to me," Jim insisted.

"I understand what you're saying, Jim," Larry countered, "but I have nothing to go on here but her word against yours."

Jim sighed. "Was she drinking when she came to see you?"

Larry nodded. "I think she'd had a few drinks," he admitted, "though I can't be positive."

"Larry, she's an alcoholic," Jim said. "It's becoming very bad, and she's irrational at times. It may become necessary to commit her."

"I'm very sorry to hear that, Jim, really."

"So you see, that's why I had to come to you," Jim continued. "Mary doesn't know what she's doing half the time."

"I'm in a tough spot here," Larry said. "Surely you can understand that? I mean, it could be considered a question of professional ethics."

"In what way?"

"I'd be violating a client's trust."

"Oh, come on, Larry," Jim said, "you know as well as I do that we all cut corners occasionally. You can't do everything by the book."

Larry Feldenstein looked genuinely distressed, and hesitated before answering. "I'd have to discuss it with Mary," he said at last.

Jim laughed. "That's funny," he said, "and you know it."

"I'm sorry, Jim."

"I'm sorry, too," Wharton said, and put both hands on the arms of his chair as if to heave himself to his feet, but then, as Larry also started to rise, Jim allowed himself a small observation, almost as an afterthought. "Look, Larry, I did have one other matter to discuss," he began. "Might as well smash all the birds with one big rock. It's about your house."

"What about it?"

"The second-story addition you made last fall and the extension of the patio onto the beach," Jim continued.

Larry Feldenstein shifted nervously in his seat and stared at Jim with wide-eyed alertness. "Yeah?"

"I've done some checking in the county records," Jim elaborated, "and I found nothing to indicate you cleared the construction and alterations with anyone, including the Coastal Commission. You know as well as I do, Larry, that anyone with waterfront property has to obtain the proper permits these days."

"It would have taken months," Larry protested.

"I know," Jim agreed, "and there was no guarantee you'd have been given a go-ahead, at least not without providing a public right-of-way to the beach through your property. I mean, I understand why you simply went ahead and did the work, Larry. I sympathize, because we're all more or less in the same boat. We don't want the public on our property, but the law sees it a bit differently, as you know. Even up where you are, north of Trancas, it's a bad situation, with the goddamn state buying up all that land up there and threatening to build parking lots."

"Listen . . . My God, Jim," Larry Feldenstein said, "it could cost me a fortune—"

Jim held up one hand and smiled amicably at the much younger man. "Larry, I don't want to make waves," he said. "I'm just making a point about how you can't always play everything by the rules in life."

Larry Feldenstein nodded silent agreement, paused for a few seconds, as if to weigh what could only have seemed the simplest of alternatives, then rose to his feet. "If you'll excuse me, Jim, I'd like to send Rosemary to the bank," he said. "Can you wait ten or fifteen minutes?"

"Sure, no hurry," Jim said affably.

"Would you like a cup of coffee?"

"Why not?"

"How do you take it?"

"With a little cream, but no sugar, please."

The young lawyer bustled into the next room, and a few minutes

297

later his secretary, a tall pale blonde in a smart-looking pantsuit, walked briskly past his open door and down the outside stairway toward the parking lot. Larry came back holding two plastic cups full of coffee and handed one to Jim, who took a sip and nodded his appreciation.

For the next few minutes, until Rosemary returned from the Malibu branch of the Bank of America with a small wrapped box that she dropped nonchalantly on the corner of her boss's desk, the two men talked about nothing but tennis and how the world's two top players, Connors and Borg, compared with the greats of yesteryear. When Jim Wharton got tired of treading conversational water at a level that didn't match what he considered essential to civilized discourse among equals, he abruptly stood up, stuck out his right hand, shook Larry's firmly, and picked up the parcel. "Thanks very much, Larry," he said, heading for the door. "Don't worry about your house. It was just a hunch I had, and nobody else knows a thing about it. Also, there will be no need to mention this matter to my wife. I suggest that a blank cassette will serve her purposes equally well and cover you, in case you signed a receipt or anything."

Larry Feldenstein said nothing, but then, he knew anything he might have to say now could only be superfluous, perhaps even slightly embarrassing. He waited for the sound of Jim Wharton's heavy footsteps to fade away down the stairs before he felt safe enough to resume his normal working routine. At noon he sent Rosemary out to buy a tape cassette.

29

"He wants me to kill him," Jennifer Gilbert said.

Victor did not answer. He continued to rummage about in his medical bag until he found the prescription pad, then groped clumsily in his pockets for a pen. Unable to find one of the ball-points he usually carried, he looked up at her. "Got a pen?"

Jennifer rose from her chair, walked over to the desk against the far wall, and found a pen, which she now wordlessly brought him. He took it from her with a mumbled thank-you and began to write. Jennifer sat down again, poised on the edge of her seat, as if ready for flight. "Did you hear me, Victor?"

"Yes," he said, continuing to write.

"I can't do it," she said.

Victor finished scribbling, tore off the slip of paper, and put it on the coffee table in front of him. "Here," he told her, "this should make him more comfortable. "We'll have to increase the dose as necessary. When the Demerol stops working, we'll go to morphine. I'd like to delay that as long as I can."

"Victor, did you hear what I said? Really?"

"Yes, Jenny, I heard you." He looked beyond her toward the beach, where a solitary jogger loped past, then back at her drawn, pale face. "Give him the shot every six hours," he said. "Eventually we may have to go to every four hours."

"Victor . . ."

"Jenny, you look like hell," he said. "I suggest we get a practical nurse in here, at least part-time. I can give you the number of an agency."

"No, it's all right," she protested. "I can manage. Victor . . ."

"Stop being so damn heroic, Jenny," he snapped. "It's a pain in the ass."

She flinched as if he had struck her. "But I can—"

"No," he interrupted. "You can't see what you're doing to yourself, but I can. I know what you're going through, but do you want him to know it? He can still read and write. He can talk. He can think. And for now we can control the pain. Let's give him as much time as we can, Jenny."

She looked confused. "These nurses—what. . . ?"

"You take your chances," he explained. "Some of them are poor, so you get rid of them and ask for someone else. You can still go on taking care of him, Jenny, but at least whoever you get will take some of the physical part of it off your back. Evan needs a wife now, not just a nurse."

She started again to protest, then seemed to be thinking his suggestion over. "And you think I should . . ."

"Of course. Call up my office, and they'll give you the number to call. Be sure you explain to the agency exactly what kind of man Evan is, so at least they won't send you some kind of religious fanatic."

"The worst of it," Jenny began to explain, "the worst part . . ."

"The physical humiliation, I know," Victor said. "I should think you'd both prefer to have some stranger take that part of it off your hands."

"He's never said anything," Jenny whispered. "We just get through it. It has to be done."

"This is only the beginning, Jenny. It's going to get worse, a lot worse. You need help."

"All right," she agreed, "all right." Still awaiting an answer to her earlier question, she gazed at him helplessly, but he seemed to want to ignore what she had said. He snapped his bag shut and stood up.

"Victor," she called out to him, "for God's sake help me!"

An enormous paralyzing weariness settled over him. "I can't tell you what to do, Jenny," he heard himself say, as if from a great distance, from beyond some wall he had erected within himself for just such emergencies. "It's not my decision . . ."

"He told me a week ago he'd kill himself," she said, "when the time came. I didn't say anything then, because it still seemed a ways off to me. But I'm not going to do it for him. I can't."

"Has he asked you to?"

"He has a gun. He says the drugs might not work, and he doesn't want to involve you."

"Where is it?"

"I have it."

"You took it away from him?"

She indicated the desk. "It's over there, where he always kept it," she explained. "But he can't get to it now."

Victor nodded and tried to force himself to move, but could not.

"I never thought . . . we never thought . . ." she continued. "I mean, that he'd be unable to . . . It all happened so fast. He was still getting around some until a few days ago . . ."

Victor didn't answer, but perhaps she no longer expected him to. She seemed to be attempting to justify her position, as much for herself as for anyone else.

"I can't walk in and hand him the gun," she said. "I don't believe in that. I don't think anyone has the right to kill, for any reason. Do you understand?"

"A lot of people feel like you, Jenny," Victor finally answered. "You have a right to your beliefs."

"But I can't stand to see him this way," she protested. "He's already so . . . so helpless!"

Victor turned again to look out the picture window at the ocean and the sky. Every game in life, he knew, made up its own rules as it went along, as if life were a cruel farce improvised for any occasion by bands of untrained lunatics. None of it made any sense to Victor anymore; the farce had reached a level of surrealism quite beyond his present ability to understand it, much less deal with it.

"Victor, I was nothing when I married Evan," this woman was now saying to him. "Do you know that?"

"Yes," he said, not really knowing it at all, "yes."

"I grew up in a small town in the Bible Belt and worked in the library there, and I didn't know anything until I met Evan," she continued. "He blew into my life like one of those tornadoes we used to get every spring. He changed everything for me. He helped me to make something of myself, to be somebody. And I loved him for it, Victor. I love him now, and I'd do anything for him, almost anything. But I guess we never quite shake off the way we were raised, do we?"

"I don't know," Victor said. "I grew up in a big-city slum. I shook that off pretty fast."

"Victor, my folks believed in the Bible," Jennifer explained. "That's all they believed in. In my town, when somebody got sick, most people wouldn't even send for a doctor. They'd pray."

"My people prayed, too," Victor said. "Every Sunday, in church."

"My mother died without ever seeing a doctor," Jennifer said. "What I inherited from my folks, I guess, is this belief I've got in the sanctity of life, all life."

"I understand, Jenny," Victor said in a dull, flat voice he himself hardly recognized. "I know."

"Do you? Evan and I have talked about it a lot. I think I've had some influence on him, on what he's been saying in his books and lectures."

"I'm sure you have." Should he ask her, Victor wondered, what she imagined books and lectures could mean to a man dying horribly of spinal cancer? Should he ask her that? Not now, not now, he told himself.

"Maybe I'm no better than my folks, I don't know," Jennifer said. "They wouldn't do anything to stop death, and I can't make myself do anything to help anyone die. I don't want Evan to suffer, that's all."

Victor could not make himself answer her, because he knew no answer could make any sense, either to him or to her. He understood that she did not want her husband to suffer, but the desire, like the circumstances it arose from, was insane, as removed from reality as the gibberings of a monkey. He rubbed a hand wearily over his face and sighed.

"I'm sorry. I had to tell you," she said. "Evan hasn't said anything to you?"

"Yes, he has."

"Oh."

"I promised I'd help him," Victor admitted, "when the time came. He'd have to tell me, or if he couldn't, I'd have to try to decide."

She seemed shocked. Perhaps she was crazy, Victor reflected. "You'd do that?" she asked.

"I won't give him the gun, no," Victor explained. "I'd prefer to do what doctors usually do in these cases. Call it 'benign neglect.' We do it all the time."

"That's different."

"Is it?"

"It's not . . . I mean . . ."

"I let a lot of my patients go, Jenny," he said. "I also help quite a few of them to go. I have a very high percentage of terminal cases in my practice. And I don't believe in miracles."

"I used to," she said. "I wish I could now."

Victor sighed. "One of the few things I do believe in is the right to die," he told her. "It's not a legal right. It's not in the Constitution." She put her head down and began to cry, but he stopped her by going quickly to her and taking both her hands in his. He realized he was going to have to make her see, help her to make sense out of this craziness, even if he himself could no longer do so. "Jenny, we can't even define death anymore," he said. "Is a person alive simply because his heart is kept beating by a machine? Or because he can still feel pain, even though he can't move or do anything for himself, even think? You define the difference between life and death to me, Jenny, and I'll listen to what you have to say. Maybe you'll hit on a better formula than the one we've been using."

"Me?" she protested feebly. "But I don't know anything . . ."

"Who does? I'm serious, Jenny," he said. "We're humane enough to put suffering animals out of their misery, but not ourselves. I've got to go now." He squeezed her hands, kissed her, and walked out of the room. As he let himself out, he glanced back at her. She was still in tears, still sitting on the edge of her chair, as if at any moment the world might tilt and send her spinning forever into space.

30

Laura had packed the rest of his belongings into five cartons, one of which had been left open and contained his tennis trophies; several of them stuck out above the open lid, a golden racket-holding arm raised on high toward nothing, bits of immortal moments jumbled together, devoid of any meaning. She had piled all the boxes, probably with Tad's help, on top of one another in the living room, near the hallway, so he'd have ready access to them without having to come into the main part of the house if he didn't want to. She herself wasn't ready for any sort of confrontation scene, she had told him over the phone, but if he had anything to ask her or tell her, she'd be there. "No, Laura," he'd said to her that morning when he called, "I don't have much to say now, either. I'll just pick up my stuff."

But now that he was actually there, inside his own front door and knowing that she was somewhere inside, he had an urge to see her, and chose not to resist it. First he loaded the boxes into the trunk and backseat of his car, then walked into the house looking for her.

She was out on the deck alone, sipping coffee and stretched out in the sun in her shorts and a halter. For the first time in months he saw her as a good-looking, sexually attractive female. Except for the sprinkle of gray in her dark, curly hair, she could have been taken for a much younger woman. Her body was firm and she had, of course, those finely boned long legs and arms that he remembered so well from the first time he had ever seen her, such a long time ago now.

She saw him eyeing her from behind the glass partition, so she reached out to pry the doors open and smiled tentatively at him. "Hi," she said. "Did you find everything?"

"Yeah, thanks. It's already in the car."

"Oh. Good. Want some coffee?"

"No, thanks. I guess maybe I'd better go."

"Yes."

He hesitated, but she seemed to have dismissed him from her mind. He watched her take a sip of the coffee and turn her face, half-hidden by oversized sun goggles, to the glare off the water. "Laura, you're all right?"

"Yes, Arthur, I'm all right." She turned her head to gaze at him with mild curiosity. "Are you all right?"

"I think so. I'm a little numb."

"Me, too."

"Maybe . . . I don't know, maybe later we can talk?"

"Yes, I suppose we'll have to."

"Don't you want to?"

"I don't know, Arthur. I know we'll have to eventually. We'll have to settle . . . a lot of things."

"You want a divorce?"

"Yes, I do."

"But you don't want to discuss it right now."

"No, I don't." She removed her goggles and looked up at him. "Arthur, I tried for a long time to talk to you," she said. "You never wanted to. How's Lee?"

"She's fine."

"Good," Laura said, snapping the goggles back over her nose.

"Why ask about her? Did I ask about Alcorn?" he said.

"Arthur, please. No confrontations. Not today. It's been a bad time."

"For me, too."

She did not reply, but waited instead for him to leave. He tried to make himself go, but couldn't. "Where's Tad?" he asked instead.

"Jim Wharton came by to pick him up," she answered. "They were going into town to play a match."

"Oh, yeah. The big bet."

"What big bet?"

"Wharton likes to play for money," Art explained. "He set up a match between himself and Tad against a guy named Dan Lefkowitz and Bill Stevens. You remember Stevens?"

"No, I don't."

"He's a teaching pro around Beverly Hills," Art said. "He likes to hustle."

"I don't want Tad involved in that kind of thing."

"Neither do I."

"I suppose that's why he didn't tell me about it."

"They're playing for a thousand dollars."

Laura looked alarmed. "You're joking. Tad?"

"He's not involved, except as a player. If he and Wharton win, which they do most of the time, Jim tips him a few bucks."

"I think that stinks. Why do you let him do that?"

"He's a big boy now, Laura," Art said. "He can do what he wants."

"Why don't you talk to Wharton?"

"I started to."

"And couldn't?"

"Something like that. Another matter came up first, and I didn't get to it. But I will."

"I hate Tad being involved in all that. It's ugly."

"I know. You're afraid, I guess, he'll become like me."

"No chance of that," she said. "He wants more out of life."

"That was kind."

"I'm sorry. I didn't mean that."

"Yes, you did," he said, "but it's okay, honest. Listen, I'll go now."

"Yes. And you'll talk to Tad, won't you? And Wharton?"

"I'll try."

"Do more than that, Arthur. You owe it to him."

"I owe it to him? What do I owe him, Laura?"

Her face flushed slightly, but otherwise she gave no sign of being annoyed or upset in any way. "He needs a father."

"And I haven't been one?"

"Not recently. Not for several years, in fact."

"You're right," he said, "I don't think we can discuss anything right now."

"No. Please go, Art. We'll talk when we can do it without irritating or hurting each other, all right?"

"All right." He turned, walked out of the house, and quietly closed the door behind him. The last memory he had of that morning was of the barren nook around the bar where, in place of his vanished photographs and mementos of past glories, only nail holes and empty shelves testified to his once having been there. Otherwise the house could have been that of a total stranger to him and he fled from it now with relief.

At forty-love in game two of the first set, as he came in behind his serve, Bill Stevens' sneaker caught on the surface of Bud Lavin's court in Bel Air, and he fell. He cried out and rolled over on his back, clutching his left ankle with both hands.

"Get up," Dan Lefkowitz snarled. "You're all right!"

But Stevens was not all right. He had almost certainly torn ligaments, and Tad ran down toward Lavin's house, a quarter of a mile away, for an ice bag. "Christ," the pro said. "How the hell am I going to teach now? I'll be in a cast for weeks."

"Oh, Dan here will take care of you, won't you, Dan?" Wharton said cheerfully.

"Yeah," the agent said. "Yeah, I'll take care of it."

"I could claim the dough by default, couldn't I, Dan?" Jim asked. "Just about the easiest grand I ever made."

The agent looked up at him in horror. "What?"

"But I won't," Wharton continued. "Just get yourself another partner and we'll set the match up again. Anytime at all, Dan."

"We'd have beaten your ass, and you know it," Dan protested.

Stevens groaned and continued to hold his injured ankle. "I don't know," he said. "The kid's really good, Dan. He's very quick, especially at net. We'd have had to play really well."

"You see, Dan?" Jim asked with a hard, flat laugh. "You see?"

"Someday, Wharton," the agent said, "someday your fucking luck is going to run out. I hope I'm there to see it, that's all."

"You always were a gracious loser, Dan," Jim said. "You show a lot of class, for an agent."

Half an hour later, as they drove away from Lavin's place, Tad noticed that something in Jim Wharton's attitude toward him had changed. He guessed it had nothing to do with the aborted match, but might have everything to do with Julie. The older man **had** spoken to him only briefly on the drive in and then had concentrated exclusively on the match they were about to play. Wharton had wanted to win it very badly, Tad knew, and the strategy he had devised had seemed basically sound. The plan had been to hit very hard at Lefkowitz, in an attempt to make the agent angry. "If he gets mad," Wharton had confided, "we'll win it easy. His temper has always been his big weakness."

Now, however, Wharton had nothing to say about what had happened; he had simply lapsed into a sullen silence, his eyes fixed on the road.

Tad decided to try to clear the air. "Mr. Wharton," he began, "I want to explain about me and Julie—"

"There's nothing to explain, kid," Wharton interrupted. "She's very hurt, that's all."

"Honest, I'm awful sorry about that," the boy affirmed. "I guess it meant more to her than to me, and I let it kind of get away from me. I mean, I should have said something earlier, I guess. I . . ."

"Look, Tad, let's not discuss it, okay?" Wharton said. "Not today."

"I understand, sir. I'm sorry."

"It's okay," Wharton said, but there was no approval in the tone of his voice. *These fucking kids,* the lawyer thought as he eased the car along Sunset Boulevard toward the coast, *they hit and run like petty hoods. He didn't have to do it this way. This lousy kid fucks my daughter and then he thinks he can drop her like a dirty sock. She cried for two days. I'll teach this kid something. Not today, not tomorrow even. Not as long as I need him. But I'll find a way, sometime. Julie will get over it, but this kid won't, not if I have to break both his arms.*

Phil and Dave Meadows were thirty-four-year-old twins, but they made every effort not to look alike. Phil was clean-shaven and kept his thick brush of curly brown hair cut very short; he wore conservative three-piece business suits and was never seen in public without a necktie. Dave wore his hair long, usually tied back into a ponytail, sported a full beard, and dressed in baggy slacks, open-necked shirts, and sports jackets. Nevertheless, the brothers, both bachelors, were very close, thought much alike, and gazed shrewdly at the world through exactly similar pairs of piercing blue eyes. Art knew they were smart, ambitious businessmen who gave value for value received, but were unsentimental about money. He liked them both and had enjoyed helping to make them into strong B players. He knew, however, that in their business venture he'd have to deal with them on an equal basis or not at all. If he couldn't uphold his end of the deal, they wouldn't take him seriously and he'd lose his best chance yet to make a new life for himself. Maybe his last chance.

Art waited to broach the subject with them until they had finished their first singles set, won rather easily by Dave this particular Sunday morning at Phil's private court in Brentwood. "You're pushing your backhand," Art informed Phil as the latter sank with a groan onto the bench beside him. "You're not turning your body enough."

"I was out late last night," Phil explained. "I think I left all my turns on the dance floor."

Dave grinned at his brother and waved his racket at him. "Come on, you coward," he said, "let's play another one, and no fair coaching, Art."

Phil shook his head. "Not me. I've had it."

"Art? Feel like indulging me?"

"You got an extra racket?"

"Use mine," Phil said. "You could beat him using a Ping-Pong paddle."

"I came to talk business, not play tennis."

"Hit with me for ten minutes and then we'll talk," Dave pleaded.

"You're on."

They rallied briskly, while Phil retreated to the house and came back, just as they were finished up, with a pitcher of cold fresh orange juice. The three of them sat down, and Art explained his position. "I can't raise my end," he said. "I can raise part of it."

"How much, Art?" Phil asked.

"At the moment, maybe ten or twelve thousand," Art said, allowing himself to be optimistic. "Some of it I have to borrow."

Dave nodded, glanced quickly at his brother, then began gently toweling himself off. "Well," he began, measuring his words carefully, "we'd like to get into this venture with you, Art. Phil and I have talked about it a couple of times recently, and we figured the front money might be a problem for you."

"Maybe we can restructure the deal," Phil added.

"Phil and I could cut you in for a quarter," Dave explained, "then work out some percentages based on what you *can* contribute—volume, profits, and so on."

"We could also put you on a small drawing account while you learn about the business and spend some time with us in the store," Phil suggested. "This would help make up some of the money you'd lose by not teaching."

"There'd be promotional tours, maybe some exhibition matches, but for a while you'd be on a tight budget, Art."

"And this would be a full-time operation. It would need your concentrated attention and commitment."

"Can you afford that?"

"Do you *want* it bad enough, Art?"

"You guys work together like a good doubles team," Art observed with a laugh.

"We always talk like this," Phil explained.

"We're really one schizoid personality," Dave added, "and we hate ourself a lot!"

Art laughed again. "Okay, the answer to all your questions is yes," he said. "I want it and I'll give it everything I've got."

"We know you will, Art," Dave said.

"We want you with us, and we want your name on the whole line," Phil elaborated. "You can be the Joe DiMaggio of the sporting-goods racket. You've got the looks, Art, and a good personality for it."

"Laura and I are split," Art said.

"So we heard," Dave answered.

"We're sorry about it," Phil added.

"It happens to everybody, I guess," Art said. "Anyway, Laura's working and Tad will be in college. Somehow I'll make out. And maybe I can come up with more than ten or twelve thousand. I might have fifteen."

"Whatever you can raise, Art," Phil said, "We'll work something out."

"When can you let us know?"

"In two weeks, three at most. Okay?"

"Okay," Dave said. "Want to hit some more?"

"You're too easy," Art told him, "and I'm not getting paid for it. By the way, does my being in business with you guys mean I have to play tennis with you? That will up my percentage, won't it?"

311

"Mercenary bastard, aren't you? Phil?"

His brother groaned. "Oh, God, one more, and that's it."

"I gotta catch you now, while I can," Dave said. "You beat me the last three times. I gotta catch you in this hung-over condition and fatten my average."

"Some brother and alter ego I got here," Phil protested.

"Remember to turn your body, Phil, and stroke from under the ball and follow through," Art told him. "I'm supposed to be a good teacher, and you're making me look bad."

When Art left, the brothers were halfway through their second set, and Phil was already doing better. They waved good-bye, and Art went out to his car to head back toward Malibu. *Fifteen thousand bucks?* he asked himself. *Now where in hell am I going to get that kind of loot?* And he thought again about Jim Wharton.

31

The Arbiter West mansion was located in the Hollywood hills. It was a large two-story structure and the only one in the neighborhood with all the blinds drawn. The windows reflected a flickering pink glow, and cars jammed the empty lots beside the house and across the street. Dee parked in the first available space, about halfway up the block, a maneuver that gave Billie enough time to entertain serious second thoughts. "Do you really think we ought to go in there?" she asked. "I don't think I can go through with this again."

But Dee had her mind made up. "You promised," she reminded Billie. "So the Nirvana party was full of creeps. We can always leave, just like we did before. Just think of it as another party. Anyway, with or without you, I'm going in." Dee had the key to the place, which meant that Billie would have had to sit it out in the car, so there was nothing for it now but to go through with it.

As they headed for the front door, Billie tried to reassure herself. After all, the pleasant-looking young man who had interviewed them for this club had seemed nice enough. In fact, he had been so serious and high-minded about what he apparently considered his mission in life that Billie had had to remind herself several times about the real purpose of their visit.

Arbiter West had a mansion of its own, at which the weekly

get-togethers were conducted, Val had informed them, and the club rules reflected it. In addition to all the dos and don'ts the Nirvana had listed, Arbiter West requested its members to respect the living room, dining room, and kitchen areas as "sanctuaries." "Swinging takes place in the bedrooms," Val had explained. There were also rules about group nudity ("never required and should not be promoted"), dress ("it is important that you look nice"), hygiene ("cleanliness is an obvious aesthetic requirement for successful swinging"), voyeurism ("peeksies are okay, but unabashed voyeurism is a no-no"), interloping ("it is inexcusable to butt in on a couple who are relating successfully"), deviate stuff ("sadism, animals, and other extreme forms of sex do not really fit into the big picture at Arbiter West"), games ("there are never any official games or other forms of random selection of partners"), smoking ("excessive smoking leads to air pollution in the living room"), and open-door policy ("always use the door chain when you open the door to someone who doesn't have a key").

In addition, before taking their money and handing Dee a key to the mansion, Val had delivered a small combination lecture and pep talk on the relationship of Arbiter West to square society. "Our American society equates possessiveness with virtue," he had said. "As a people we are motivated primarily by incentives related to ownership and profit. Swinging is one way of rebelling against what's phony and corrupt in our system. Our system is based on greed. Swinging is based on love. And yet there's no conflict, because swinging doesn't endanger the system. By joining Arbiter West you've opted for the best of both worlds."

Billie hadn't been able to make much sense of this speech, but she gathered it had been intended to fill her with enthusiasm, a sense of mission, and patriotic self-awareness. Dee, however, had seemed puzzled. "That Val," she had said as they'd driven away, "he's too much. He's kind of a nut, wouldn't you say?"

Billie's first impression, as they let themselves into the house, was that they had intruded on a not very interesting cocktail party. The small kitchen was full of guests pouring themselves drinks, and the living room, whose furniture consisted of one couch, a king-sized double bed, two armchairs, and cushions propped against the walls, contained about thirty people talking quietly to one another in small groups and couples. A closer look, however, revealed some startling differences. At least half of the guests were barefoot, while some of

314

the women were hardly dressed at all. One girl, attired only in a see-through mini-shift, was doing a slow wiggle all by herself in the center of the room to a rock beat from a portable stereo propped up in the fireplace.

The second thing that struck Billie rather forcibly was the age and general appearance of the guests, all of whom were, like themselves, on a first-name-only basis. From their earlier experience with Nirvana, Billie had expected a lower-middle-class scene of not very attractive people in their late thirties and forties. The Arbiter West members, however, were mostly in their twenties or early thirties, with a sprinkling of older but good-looking types, and were, on the whole, a nice-looking bunch. Some of the men looked like responsible young business executives, and a few of the women were actually beautiful.

Val, dressed only in a smoking jacket that barely covered his pelvic area, padded barefoot around the room introducing people to one another. Billie and Dee sat down in a corner and got into a conversation with a couple of airline pilots and their wives, attractive girls dressed in slacks and loose shirts. The whole scene reminded Billie of shipboard social life, where intimacy is achieved simply on the basis of being on a voyage from which no one can escape until it's over. Nothing she and the pilots had to say to one another qualified as more than chitchat, but it was as if they had been talking this way for years. Dee got bored and wandered off toward the kitchen, and later one of the wives got up and sat down across the room with some other group. Billie wasn't aware at first of much else going on, but eventually she noticed that from time to time the room would thin out as couples disappeared into the rest of the house.

After a while Billie felt brave enough to go into the kitchen after a drink and found a chunky blonde stripped to the waist posed against the wall while two men played a psychedelic-light machine over her bare skin. Nobody seemed to be paying much attention. Billie found ice cubes, salvaged the quart of Scotch she and Dee had brought for themselves, and poured herself a stiff belt. After her second swallow, she noticed for the first time that the walls of the house were decorated primarily with nude photographs, some of an openly pornographic nature, but hardly anyone glanced at them. Glass in hand, Billie returned to the living room to mingle, a tactic she considered safer than strolling about on her own. Dee seemed to have vanished.

Over the next couple of hours Billie must have talked to at least

315

twenty people, and she found out a good deal about the Arbiter West members. Most, as she had suspected, were thoroughly middle class. Among the men she ran into a lawyer, a doctor, a child psychologist, a producer of commercials for TV, several aerospace engineers, the pilots, a salesman of men's clothing, a diamond dealer, and several real-estate agents. Almost all of the women were housewives, and most had small children. It was also Billie's impression that most of those at the party had been swinging for only a few months or less. She tried to sound Val out on the subject. "Well, that's right," he said. "Usually it's the guy who wants to swing first and persuades his gal to try it. After they get into it, though, it's the women who really cut loose. Some of them turn into real exhibitionists. It isn't often we get women in here alone, like you and Dee, but it's happening more and more. It's nice. Are you having fun?"

"Oh, you bet," Billie said. "But I'm taking it slow."

Val smiled brightly at her. "Well, we're all here to share the experience. Don't feel you're under any pressure."

"Oh, no, I don't," Billie assured him.

Billie had just retreated again into a corner when Dee reappeared. Her wig was slightly askew and she looked disheveled. A rugged-looking type in slacks and sandals trailed nonchalantly after her. "Hey, Billie," Dee said with a giggle, "I want you to meet Buddy. He's too much!" Billie shook hands with Buddy and chatted with him for a couple of minutes, but he suddenly made a beeline for a young brunette he'd spotted across the room. Dee watched him go and shrugged. "He told me he loved me," she said, patted her wig, and went off toward the kitchen again.

The hand Charlie Wigham had been waiting for didn't come along until the last round of the evening. Predictably enough, Rich Bentley dealt it to him and then stayed in to become the prime mover in the betting. Charlie allowed himself to sit back, looking dubious and worried, apparently on the edge of folding, but with the prospect of a sandbagging dancing up there behind his eyes. Mel Schwartz, who had the best chance to beat him out of the pot, knew Charlie's style too well to be fooled by him and would drop out on the next card, unless he caught his third six, but the others might go along. Maybe not Mikey Kramer, who was a smart, tough player. Bentley, who was down over five hundred for the night, would stay in, however, and so would Gail Hessian, the only woman in the game. She obviously didn't know much about five-card stud and was working on a flush. And maybe Harry McKay, their host, would also stick; he only had a pair of threes, but for some reason he'd been drinking heavily all evening and his judgment was becoming suspect.

The hand turned out to be a dandy. Even after Charlie drew his third ace, Bentley figured he was bluffing and tried to ride out his two pairs, kings high. Gail Hessian missed out on her flush, and Harry drew a third three and got nailed. Charlie raked in a seven-hundred-dollar pot, then looked up to catch Mel grinning at him. "Jesus, Charlie," Mickey Kramer said, "I wish you'd go back to work so some of the rest of us could win a big pot once in a while."

"If you sons of bitches would finance my picture," Charlie said, "I'd leave you alone. I'd rather not have to make a living this way."

"Hey, Charlie, don't you know we all want you to make the movie?" Mel said. "Me more than anybody?"

"Fat lot of good it's doing me," Charlie snarled.

Ellen McKay, Harry's wife, looking demurely attractive in a long terry-cloth robe, appeared in the kitchen doorway. "Any more coffee or a drink for anyone?" she asked.

"No, thanks," Rich said, smiling at her and waving. "Awfully good cheese, Ellen."

"Glad you like it, Rich," Harry said. "Anything else you've got your eye on?"

"Last hand?" Mel asked.

"Yeah," Harry growled, reaching for the cards. "My deal. Draw, jacks or better to open." He shuffled the pack, then waited for Gail, on his left, to cut it. "Ante up, everybody."

"I can't understand it," she said. "I was sure I'd draw a club. I had this feeling."

"The odds were against you," Charlie explained. "There were four other clubs showing, and it was costing you too much to stay in. You should have folded."

"I thought I could play this game," Gail said. "I guess I can't. But this is becoming an expensive education."

"I've had terrible cards all night," Rich Bentley said. "Absolutely appalling."

Harry looked up at him as he started to deal. "It isn't the cards, Rich," he said.

"No?"

"No. You're a dumb poker player, one of the dumbest I've ever seen," Harry said.

"I like the action," the actor explained.

"Then it'll cost you, won't it?"

"I'm always ready to pay," Rich said with a charming smile. "It's one of my major talents."

"By the way," Gail suddenly inquired, "whatever happened to Evan Gilbert?"

"What do you mean, what happened to him?" Mickey asked.

"Wasn't he supposed to be around all summer? I can't even get him on the phone. Is he still here?"

"Judy and I haven't seen him for a while, and I hear he's pretty sick," Mickey said. "That's what Judy says, anyway. Vic Ferrero's over there a lot. Why don't you ask him?"

"I will. I want to interview Gilbert if I can."

"Well, nobody's seen him," Mickey said. "Judy asked Dorothy the other day, but she didn't know anything. Or wouldn't admit it."

"Did anybody ask Billie?" Charlie wanted to know. "If she doesn't know, nobody knows."

"She hasn't been around that much either," Mickey said. "She and Dee have been going into town a lot."

"Shit," Harry exclaimed, gazing with disgust at his cards. "I pass."

Mickey Kramer opened the bidding, Mel and Charlie dropped out, and the others only called. Mickey wound up winning a small pot with three eights and emerged from the evening as the only other winner besides Charlie. Mel broke even, but Gail, Harry, and Rich were all big losers. No one seemed to mind much, except, perhaps, Harry, but he had been a sullen host all evening. It was Ellen who bid their guests good night and saw them safely out. Outside, in the road, after the others had dispersed, Mickey Kramer walked Charlie to his car. "Listen, about this movie," he began. "How are things going?"

Charlie was surprised. "I thought you didn't invest in movies."

Some years before, Mickey had been mildly singed in a movie deal and had slammed a door in his head. He was a businessman, he had explained to his friends, and the movies were monkey business. "It's true," he told Charlie now, "I don't. But how is it going?"

Charlie told him. "And I can't understand it," he said. "I've got a good property and a good track record, and I can't get off first base."

"So how much money do you need?"

Charlie told him. "But I can trim it if I have to."

"Why do you need that much, Charlie?"

"You really want to hear?"

"Yeah."

So, standing out there at night in the road between the silent Colony houses, Charlie broke the budget down for Mickey Kramer. But every time he mentioned a salary, a fee, or an advance, Mickey wanted to know if the payment couldn't be deferred. "If the picture isn't made," he explained, "none of these guys get anything. I want to know what the picture costs in terms of film, equipment, all that. These other guys can wait."

"That's a lousy way to make a movie, Mickey," Charlie told him.

"Why?"

"Because some deferred costs come to more in the end," Charlie explained, "and besides, people work better if they're getting paid."

"That's all right," Mickey said, "we can overcome all those problems."

"What are you saying to me, Mickey?" Charlie asked. "Are you going to write me a check?"

"I just might."

"Mickey, don't jerk me off," Charlie pleaded. "We're Malibu neighbors, we play tennis together, and I've been through a lot this summer. I'm very vulnerable."

"Look, I'm serious," Mickey said.

"Okay, I'll let you know in six weeks."

"What's with the six weeks? Don't you want my money?"

"I've got two or three other irons in the fire," Charlie said. "And I'd rather make the picture my way."

"Why?"

"For the reasons I just told you," Charlie said. "And also, quite frankly, because it enables me to bail out a little bit financially. It gives me some front money—"

"Ah hah!" Mickey exclaimed, jabbing a finger at him. "You movie guys are all alike! You go around crying about starving for your art, but when somebody comes along willing to finance your picture, you're trying to get some money out of him. Charlie, you've got to face a fact of life here. Either you're an entrepreneur like me or you're a salaried guy all your life. You can't have it both ways."

Charlie thought that one over a moment. "Okay, Mickey," he said very deliberately, "you've got a deal. I'll waive my fee and we'll defer what we can, within reason."

"Give me a copy of your budget," Mickey said, "and I'll get back to you as soon as I can."

They shook hands, and Charlie got into his car and drove out of the Colony. As he turned right, heading for the gate, Wilson Mahoney drove past him in his maroon Mercedes convertible. Michelle was sitting beside the director in the front seat. She actually had the gall to wave to Charlie as she went past, but Charlie didn't care; he hardly saw her. After all, Mickey Kramer had the money and the connections to other money to get *Pale Moon Rising* before the cameras. This was the biggest poker game Charlie had ever played in, by far.

It must have been sometime after two A.M., just as Billie had begun to speculate about finding Dee and getting out of there, that she felt a hand on her shoulder and looked up to find herself staring at a familiar face. "Hey, Billie, how are you doing?" Bert Felcher asked. "I didn't know you'd gotten into swinging!"

"Well, I'm not really . . . I mean, I just kind of . . . sort of . . . drifted into . . . I mean, I . . . Oh, shit," Billie stammered.

"Hey, it's cool," Bert Felcher said. "I understand."

"No, Bert, I don't think you do."

"So are you here alone?"

"No, I came with Dee. You know, the Mouseketeer."

"Far-out. I don't think I've met her, have I?"

"I guess not."

Billie had been about to ask where Edie was when she saw her. Dressed only in what looked like gauze, she was wandering off hand in hand toward the bedrooms with a stranger.

"I'd like to meet her," Bert Felcher persisted, his gaze now scanning the room. "I've never balled a Mouseketeer. This is great, isn't it? We sort of expected to find a club like this in Malibu, but we had to come to Glendale to join this one. Isn't that amazing?" Before Billie could answer him, he excused himself and headed off toward the group that included the airline pilots and their wives.

Billie hurried back to the kitchen for a refill, her nerves all but shattered by this incident. It had never occurred to her that she'd actually ever meet anyone she knew at an orgy. Her kind of people simply didn't behave this way. Of course, Edie and Bertram Felcher were not her kind of people, but they did live in Malibu and it shocked Billie down to her insteps. *I guess I'm too square for this,* she told herself, *or maybe just too old.*

Dee's Medusa wig had been left over their Scotch bottle. Billie flung it aside and poured herself a big drink. When she turned around, she found herself confronted by a lean, rather attractive-looking man in a jumpsuit and sneakers. He was leaning against the icebox, smiling at her. "Don't you swing?" he asked.

"Me? Well, that depends."

"I thought maybe you were just some kind of voyeur," he said.

"What's wrong with looking?"

"It's not as much fun as doing," he said. "Let me show you." He took her hand and led her out into the hallway.

Something in Billie gave way. She had certainly not intended to participate, but the offer had caught her at a very low psychological ebb. What other offers had she had recently that were any better? She hadn't even seen Jay, who had whisked out of town again for a week and left only a message that Billie was not to put his first check through until after he got back and she heard from him. She hadn't. The guy was shaping up as a complete phony. She had peeked into the house that morning and been startled to discover that it was empty of furniture.

And as for the rest of her highly anticipated Malibu summer action, well, it had simply not materialized. And so, without having planned it or expected it, and having felt old and inadequate for most of the evening, Billie now allowed herself to be taken. *What the hell, at least it proves I'm not quite dead yet,* she thought, *not totally out of it.*

They climbed a stairway to the second floor. The one upstairs bedroom was large and crowded with loving couples. There was a single empty mattress in one corner, and they headed for it. With sinking heart, Billie stripped and lay down. Her nameless lover looked her over as he wriggled out of his jumpsuit and casually began to massage himself into an erect state. "Boy," he said, "you have a terrific shape."

For an old broad, Billie wanted to add, but didn't. Before she could say or do anything, he descended upon her. Billie shut her eyes and allowed herself to be made love to. She could not, however, relax enough to enjoy it. When it was over, in a matter of a few minutes, she sat up. "I'm sorry," she said. "I can't get used to doing this in a room with a lot of other people."

"It's okay," he told her. "I was the same way at first. It takes getting used to."

"Are you here alone?"

"Oh, no," he answered cheerfully. "That's my wife over there." He pointed to a mattress where a dim female shape bounced up and down on somebody's lap. "She has a real good time."

"Look, a real orgy scene I could understand," Billie said on their way downstairs, "but everyone pretending nobody else is in the room with them—well, that's too strange for me."

"Forget it," her lover said. "I understand."

Thoroughly depressed again, Billie looked around for Dee, but couldn't find her. Finally, an hour or so later, she reappeared, looking dazed. "Are you through?" Billie asked her.

"Wow," Dee said, "these people are too much. I was just the middle part of a sandwich."

"I didn't think that was in the rulebook."

"Are you kidding?" Dee said. "You must have been in the wrong room. In mine we had a regular pyramid going for a while."

"I was in the square room," Billie confessed. "It reminded me of a monkey cage."

"The only bad thing that happened," Dee said, "was some creep named Bert who tried to get in on our scene, and one of the guys punched him out. Except for that, I had a super time. Malibu is nowhere compared to this."

Obviously I'm out of step with my time, Billie thought as she settled herself comfortably against the back of her seat for the drive home. *Maybe because I'm basically a private person. I just can't get with this group-self-awareness crap and self-indulgence, no matter how hard I try. Evolution has passed me by out here, and I'm as out-of-date as the dodo. Maybe the whole country is out-of-date, and only southern California, in its headlong rush into the future, is really fit to lead us. Thank God I don't really think that. Well, another first. I actually fucked some guy and never asked him his name.*

Billie laughed, but wouldn't tell Dee what she thought was so funny. Dee would never understand.

At four A.M. Rich Bentley was awakened by the sound of someone pounding at his back door. He rolled out of bed, turned on the hall lights, and went out to see what was happening. When he opened the door, he found himself confronted by the drunken figure of Harry McKay. "Harry?"

"Come out here, you prick," Harry mumbled, grabbing Rich Bentley by the lapels of his robe and dragging him out onto the sand.

"Wait a minute, Harry!" Rich Bentley shouted. "What the hell's the matter with you?"

"You fuck my wife—"

"No, I didn't!" Rich protested. "Honest to God, Harry, I haven't touched her!"

Harry McKay was not in a listening frame of mind. He swung wildly and hit the actor just below the ear. The force of the blow fractured Rich Bentley's jaw in two places and also broke Harry's hand. The incident effectively ended any possible hope Rich Bentley might have entertained of seducing Ellen McKay. It also cast a pall over the entire summer social season. He was left to try to salvage what he could of the event by contacting his lawyer, Larry Feldenstein, from his bed at Albert Mercer Memorial Hospital the very next day.

"You want to prefer charges?" Larry asked.

"No, I want to sue," the actor said.

"What's the matter with your voice?"

"My jaws are wired shut, Larry."

"Oh. Well, we'll do both," Larry Feldenstein told him. "You're sure he had no cause?"

"I took his wife to lunch a couple of times. She was lonely and bored. She wanted to talk."

"We'll settle out of court, if we can," the lawyer said. "Harry's got plenty of money, and he doesn't need this kind of publicity, where some actor knocks off his wife."

"Larry, old man, you don't understand."

"Yes, I do, Rich," the lawyer assured him. "Whether you actually seduced Ellen McKay or not, everyone, especially in Malibu, will assume you did. I understand all too well."

32

"I try to pretend that half of my body has simply ceased to exist," Evan Gilbert said. "It's dead, gone. I try to live with what is left."

The furniture in the scientist's bedroom had been rearranged so that from where he lay he could easily keep an eye on the beach comings and goings below, as well as on the ocean and the now familiar thin orange line of smog along the horizon. At the moment, Evan was sitting up, propped against a bank of foam-rubber pillows and surrounded by a scattering of books and papers. He was obviously in some discomfort, and already the onrush of the disease had taken its toll; he looked gaunt and gray, and there were deep dark hollows under his eyes, but his spirit seemed unbroken. He was smiling at Victor, who was rummaging about in his medical bag. "The absentminded cancer quack," Evan said.

"I couldn't even find my goddamn glasses today," Victor muttered. "Do you have a thermometer?"

"Jenny does. In the bathroom. You know we fired that nurse, don't you?"

"So I heard."

"She was impossible. Kept quoting from what I took to be the collected works of Dr. Panglosss."

"One of America's favorite philosophers."

"Sounded a lot like Jimmy Carter, actually."

"We'll try to find you somebody else."

"Jenny wants to go it alone for now."

"So I gather." Victor looked up. "How bad is it? The pain."

"Comes and goes."

"I can increase the medication."

"Not yet, Victor," the scientist said. "That stuff you pump into me makes me woozy. I can understand the charms of addiction now, but I want to be able to function for a while yet."

Victor admired the surface tone of Evan's observations, but he could sense the undercurrent of fear in every line. He concentrated again on trying to find what Evan called his "magic charms" within the jumbled confusion of his kit.

"I haven't disappointed you, have I, Victor?" Evan asked.

"In what way?"

"I seem to be a little ahead of schedule," Evan said. "I was supposed to have a good six to nine months, as I recall. But evidently, in the highest traditions of medical bungling, you were a bit optimistic, weren't you?"

"*Mea culpa, mea culpa,*" Victor mumbled as he headed for the bed to take Evan's pulse, then remembered the missing thermometer and went into the bathroom.

"How can you stand it?" Evan called after him.

"What?" Victor asked, reappearing with the thermometer Jenny had left in the medicine cabinet.

"Me."

"What about you?"

"I'm beginning to stink like a rotting corpse," Evan said. "I can see it in Jenny's face every time she comes near me, no matter how hard she tries."

"I've smelled worse," Victor said, sitting on the edge of the bed and placing his stethoscope against Evan's chest.

"Breathe deeply."

"Christ, Victor, I can breathe."

Victor ignored him, listened to his breathing, then put away the stethoscope.

"What nonsense. You want to look at my tongue, too?"

"No, I can tell it's as sharp as ever," Victor said. He shook the thermometer, but Evan took his hand and stopped him.

"Cut it out, Victor," the scientist told him. "What would you do about it, anyway? The only bad part of this is what you can't help me with."

"What's that Evan?"

"It's not dying that's hard, Vic," Evan said. "I got myself ready to do that. I can face that. What I wasn't prepared for was the incredible growing isolation of being sick like this. It's an effort now for Jenny to be around me. I don't want to ask my friends to come by. All I have is the telephone and the mails. Are you afraid, too, Vic?"

Victor looked startled. "Afraid? Of what?"

"Of dying. What else?" Evan paused, as if to collect his thoughts. "My friends call and write and we talk about everything except that I'm dying," he said, "that in a matter of weeks, a month or two, I won't even be able to carry on a conversation. Are you afraid of me, too, Victor?"

"Of course not."

"You deal with this kind of thing every day, but you're no different, really, from anyone else," Evan continued. "You come in and out, you take my pulse, you give me drugs—what the hell does it all mean? If I didn't have my books, my work, I'd have put myself out of this misery weeks ago."

"I'm . . . helpless, Evan," Victor confessed. "I keep busy around you because . . . because there really isn't much I can do. No magic charms this time, as you call them. . . ."

"I know."

Evan turned his gaze away from him and looked out on the beach, with its sprinkling of tanned healthy bodies. Victor abandoned his charade of trying to seem purposeful and efficient, as if anything he could do counted at all. He sat down at the foot of Evan's bed. "Mind if I smoke?" he asked.

"Of course not," Evan answered, smiling. "Why should I be the only one here to die of cancer?"

"How's Jenny holding up?"

"Fine, considering. I hope we can find someone else to help her. It's got to be hell for her. She keeps me as presentable as she can."

"It helps her, perhaps," Victor observed. "She needs to keep busy, too, Evan. And she's very young."

"Yes, she'll be able to build another life for herself," Evan said. "I don't have a hell of a lot of money, but some. A couple of ex-wives who prudently and thoughtfully remarried, no kids. I didn't make *those* kinds of messes. I'm not keeping you from your rounds, am I?" he asked.

"No, no. I got home early today. Nobody to carve up," Victor answered.

The time passed easily for them as they chatted of this and that. Even the presence of so much health and life on public view below seemed to comfort Evan rather than mock him. He sucked in the sights with his eyes, as if only from such a source could he derive the strength to keep on living against the hopeless odds he faced. "You know what I was thinking just now?" he asked Victor toward the end of the visit as the light began to fade outside and the beach people gradually cleared the sands to head for home.

"What?"

"I was thinking about Sigmund Freud, of all people," Evan said.

"What about him?"

"You know, he took eleven years to die," Evan said. "At the end the pain was so bad he couldn't write or even read. But the hardest part was that he stank so badly that his own dog, who adored him, wouldn't come near him."

Victor had no answer for that one. He and Evan looked at each other, and Victor merely reached out his hand and clasped that of his friend. They sat there in this way for several minutes in silence. Evan had reached that moment toward the end of his life when words hadn't really failed him; they had simply proved inadequate.

"Hi," Gail Hessian said when Dorothy answered the door. "Are you Mrs. Ferrero?"

"Yes."

"I was looking for your husband. I'm Gail Hessian, *Dateline News.*"

"I recognize you."

"The thing is," Gail explained, "I've been trying to contact Evan Gilbert for an interview he promised me some time ago, but I can't seem to get an answer out of Mrs. Gilbert, and I never get him on the phone. I was told you and your husband are close friends of theirs, and I thought maybe I could get to him through you."

"I don't think Evan's giving any interviews right now. He's been ill."

"He must have been pretty sick," Gail said. "It's been a long time."

"Yes, it has. Look, Miss Hessian, I don't really think I can help you."

"I see. Well, what about your husband? Isn't he Mr. Gilbert's doctor? Perhaps I could get a statement from him."

"I don't think so, but you can try. He's not home right now."

"Okay, I'll call later, if I may." Gail turned to go. "By the way, how sick is he?"

"I don't know, Miss Hessian. Maybe he just doesn't want to talk to you. Not you especially, just anybody."

Gail smiled. "That doesn't sound much like Evan Gilbert, does it?"

"I wouldn't know. I was just guessing."

Gail found herself wondering later about this brief conversation. All these people around Evan Gilbert seemed to her to be withdrawn, unnecessarily mysterious even, as if shielding the man from the outside world. Why? Gail Hessian had begun to sense a story. Maybe, instead of dropping the Malibu project entirely, she ought to talk Alex into assigning her to a segment on Evan Gilbert alone. Maybe the man was really very sick, even dying. Gail sniffed an old-fashioned scoop, and she decided to try to get to the bottom of it. It wasn't like Evan Gilbert, this media manipulator and celebrity, to drop completely out of sight, in the Malibu Colony, of all places; in fact, it was entirely uncharacteristic of the man. It was probably no big deal, but it might fill up a minute and a half of exclusive air time, and that kind of minor coup was what kept network news editors and producers happy, something Gail knew a lot about.

VI

September Songs

33

The last big party of the summer was given on Labor Day by Jay R. Pomerantz, back again from his mysterious forays into Oklahoma and seemingly permanently installed now in the old Carey house. He was more anxious and excited than ever, he told Billie, over launching what was going to be an entirely new life for him. Once again, however, and for the third time now, he had had to ask Billie to delay putting his first check through, and that *had* alarmed her, but he had sounded so plausible, as well as basically incomprehensible, about his extremely complicated financial transactions that she had given in. "I know, I know, honey, you're right," he had shouted at her over the phone, "but the trouble with you people here is you don't know nothin' about big money. Hell and damnation, woman, you think it's easy being a goddamn billionaire and not having even a lousy eight hundred thousand in cash to buy me a little old house? If it wasn't for the damn tax people, we'd have wrapped this up weeks ago."

Somehow, by the time Jay had finished explaining it all to her and assuring her it was essentially a question of structuring the deal so that the U.S. Treasury could be safely circumvented, she had decided to let him have his way. What the hell, she had told herself, even if he did turn out to be a fraud, she was in so deep on this one she was going to look bad anyway, and who else had made an offer for the Carey house recently?

Jay wanted to celebrate, he explained to Billie. Apparently the oil-development deal in the Gulf of Mexico or somewhere with the Getty people was turning out to a true bonanza and he wouldn't have to be going back to Tulsa quite as much in the future. He really wanted now to get to know a lot of nice folks in Malibu and start putting together some local "business propositions."

"What kind of propositions, Jay?" Billie had asked him.

"I'm open to suggestions, honey," he'd told her. "Yes, sir, I sure am."

"Like what?"

"Like just about anything, even the movies," he'd said. "I want to have some fun, and I think there's a lot I could do out here for myself and some real smart live wires like me."

Naturally, Jay had called on Billie to get people to come to his party, and had also asked her what he could do about furniture. "What do you mean, what you should do?" she had countered.

"I ain't got any," he'd revealed. "I've been in and out of town so much, honey, I haven't had the time. I got me a bed, and that's about all."

"Call a rental company, then. You can't expect people to sit on the floor, Jay."

"Aw, hell, you give 'em enough free booze," he'd said, with a laugh, "they'll lie down on nails!"

The morning of the party, Billie called Charlie Wigham and asked him if he was still trying to finance his picture. When Charlie said yes, Billie told him about Jay R. Pomerantz. "He may be all hot air, Charlie," she said, "but I gather you've got nothing to lose."

"Nothing but more time."

"Send the script over to him. He's looking for what he calls propositions."

"Hollywood is teeming with propositions," Charlie said. "Right now I'm waiting on Mickey Kramer. But thanks, Billie."

Charlie carried the script over by hand. His arrival at the house coincided with that of the furniture-rental company and the caterers, so Charlie simply thrust the script at Jay, who seemed very pleased to get it and promised Charlie he'd read it right away, that very afternoon, in fact, before the guests started arriving. Charlie couldn't imagine how he'd find the time. Still, Billie was right—what did he have to lose?

The attrition of the summer on Charlie's judgment and pride had been devastating. In fact, they had been nibbled away until there was very little left of either. Otherwise how to account for the latest fiasco, his involvement with an outfit called Stairway Investments?

This company, supposedly a group of independent investors, had been dug up by Melvin Schwartz' process server, a twenty-one-year-old kid named Ellsworth Hoad, whose main job was to run around town handing people unwelcome papers at ten dollars a shot. Somewhere or other, perhaps while spraying subpoenas around the city, he had dug up Stairway Investments. When Mel first heard about it, he had tried to dissuade Charlie from attending the meeting Hoad had arranged. "Ellie's a nice kid, but he doesn't know anything," Mel had told Charlie. "Ellie knows streets." But Charlie had not let himself be put off. He had gone to the meeting without Mel, who had a date in court, and all he remembered clearly about it now was that one man with a badly shaved chin had done most of the talking, while a second one, a gorilla in a shiny blue serge suit, had remained silently in the background, his chair tilted against the wall. When Charlie had sat down to figure the deal out later with Mel, they discovered they had been left with seven and a half percent of the movie. "Well, that's that," Mel had commented.

"Shit, we'll do it!" Charlie had exclaimed.

Mel had regarded him with pity. "Charlie, what is the matter with you?" he'd asked him. "Where's your pride? Just because the animal in you wants to make this movie, you don't have to strip yourself of everything."

"But, Mel, they'll put up—"

Mel had quickly interrupted him. "Listen, Charlie," he'd said, holding up a deprecating hand, "if you take this deal with these goons, you are no longer my client. I can't represent anyone who goes off his rocker because he can't accept the possibility of not being able to get what he wants. Some things just aren't worth it, Charlie. We'll make the picture any reasonable way, but not by giving up everything we've worked all this time for. What's the matter with you?"

* * *

335

Jay's party turned out to be an unusual one, to say the least. The financier's guests, most of them either recruited by Billie Farnsworth or simply Colony residents and hangers-on who had dropped in because they had nothing better to do, sat on folding chairs, danced to recorded country-western music, ate cold cuts and potato salad, and were offered whiskey, vodka, beer, soft drinks, and a cheap California Chablis. Dee Stauffer showed up, stayed five minutes, and departed in a minor pique. "This is the tackiest affair I've ever been to," she announced, making an exit of it.

Nevertheless, well over a hundred people came and managed to have a pretty good time. Perhaps this was because it happened to be an off-year for Labor Day festivities; Jay's party was the only major one of the weekend. "I guess everybody's about had it with summer," Billie explained to Judy Kramer, who had come alone because Mickey had had to go out of town suddenly to look at some unspoiled land he planned to develop up around Eureka. "I guess it's always this way by Labor Day. We all just wish everybody would go home so life can get back to normal."

Even the tennis scene had cooled. For the first time since anyone could remember, there had been no Labor Day tournament. This was because Art Bonnell, who had been expected to run it, as usual, had backed out at the last minute. He was apparently having personal problems and just didn't have the time or the desire to immerse himself in the annual courtside follies of the racket-wielding set. It was too bad, Billie felt, because tennis was a Malibu Colony tradition and the tournaments had always been such great catalysts for juicy crises, major confrontations, and therefore sources of marvelous gossip to carry everyone through the quieter off-season months.

The party's chief adornment turned out to be Jay R. Pomerantz himself. Dressed in magenta slacks, Gucci loafers, a crushed-velvet dark blue sports shirt, and a pink cashmere cardigan that flapped around him like a cloak, he circulated among his guests like a man possessed. Sweating profusely, he talked nonstop about money to anyone and everyone. He talked about what he'd paid for his house and about how much he was planning to spend to fix it up. He talked about his oil wells and his bank loans and his international wheeling and dealing in stocks, bonds, and commodities. Most interesting of all, he persisted in hinting that he and he alone had been entrusted with investing the nearly four hundred million dollars realized from a recent sale of Getty oil leases in the Persian Gulf. For tax reasons this money had to be invested soon, he made clear, and did anyone there have some good ideas? Jay R. Pomerantz was open to solid propositions of any kind.

"He's incredible," Lee Harvey said to her husband about halfway through the night. "Do you think he's for real?"

"I don't know," Sid Harvey said. "Back home, I'd have him pegged as a bullshit artist, but out here? I don't know. Still, I don't trust guys who talk all the time about what they say they've got going for them. It's like guys who talk a lot about how much they're getting laid. You know they're not getting any."

"That's what I love about you, Sidney," Lee commented. "You have such a delicate way of putting things."

"We used to call a spade a spade back where I come from," Sidney said. "But that was before the civil-rights movement."

Later, in a secluded nook, Billie finally got the whole story out of Jay R. Pomerantz. It sounded like a pulp romance to her. In fact, it convinced her that she had been dealing with a man whose grasp on reality was, at best, tenuous. Almost in tears from the excess of bourbon he'd been downing, Jay told Billie that he had been a foundling. At the age of eleven or so, he had run away and hitchhiked to Tulsa. There, while sleeping on a bus-stop bench, he had been awakened by a strange old man, who had spotted him from the backseat of a limousine proceeding down the road. He had taken the boy in and raised him as his own son, then, after educating him in the business, sent him out into the world to make his fortune.

That strange old benefactor had been none other than J. Paul Getty, Jay confided. The old man, disappointed in his own children, all of whom had either turned out badly or proved to be inadequate businessmen, had placed all his hopes in Jay, who had not disappointed him but had soon established himself as a successful oil wildcatter and speculator, along the lines of J. Paul Getty himself. Thus, at the age of twenty-five, with his first million safely in the bank, young J.R., as the old man used to call him, had been taken into the tycoon's confidence and entrusted with secretly investing hundreds of millions of the old man's profits in various tax-shelter deals. "Of course, honey, I made a lot of money on my own," Jay told Billie. "But I've got this heavy burden to bear now, which is the legacy the old man left me. Hell, I can triple anybody's money in six

337

weeks out here, if I could find the right situation." He also confided to Billie that he stood to inherit a hundred million dollars of his own when he got married. "The old man loved me like a son, Billie," he said. "He wanted me to settle down and raise a real family. That's because he never really had one of his own, you know. He had a lot of wives and a lot of women, but, you know, nothin' ever really worked out for him. They were all after his money, and he knew it. He was a smart old fart, no doubt about it."

"Married, Jay?" Billie said. "Now, a good old boy like you wouldn't want a dumb young thing, would you? You would want a mature, responsible woman to share your life and the hundred million, now, wouldn't you, Jay, sweetheart!"

And Jay threw his arms around her with a big laugh. "Oh, God, Billie, you're a caution, you are!"

"Actually, Jay, caution has never been one of my big virtues," she said, "or I wouldn't have messed around with you."

Charlie showed up at the party very late, by which time most of the guests had gone and Jay R. Pomerantz was very drunk. He did, however, come up to Charlie and hug him. "Boy," he bellowed at him, "you got yourself a deal! That script is a wonder! I wish I had ten like 'em, we'd build a whole goddamn studio right out here in Malibu!"

"You really like it?" Charlie asked, astounded.

"I don't know much about show business, Charlie," Jay said, "but I sure as hell know what I like. You and I, fella, are going to make a little old movie together!"

"That's wonderful," Charlie said, disengaging himself with difficulty from the financier's bearlike grip. "When can we get together? I've got a budget breakdown of above- and below-the-line costs you could look at, and I want to tell you where we are in terms of production plans so far."

"Hell, anytime you say, boy," Jay bellowed. "How about tomorrow afternoon, around five o'clock?"

"That's fine with me."

"Good, good, Charlie," Jay said. "I'll expect you here, then. You got a great one there, Charlie. And it's just the beginning. *Pale Sun Riding*, that's a hell of a title!"

Charlie didn't bother to correct him, but, luckily for his peace of mind, he didn't hear about Jay's account of his childhood background from Billie until long after the party was over. Several days after, in fact.

When Charlie showed up at Jay's house the next afternoon, the place was empty. No one came to the door and no car was parked in the garage. Charlie walked around the back and peered inside. The debris from the previous night's party littered the floor, but the furniture had already been taken away and the rooms had a desolate, abandoned look. Charlie thought that perhaps Jay had been delayed in town or somewhere, so he sat on the beach behind the house and waited. When Jay hadn't shown up by six o'clock, Charlie drove home and called his answering service. No messages. He called Billie, but she was out. At last Charlie telephoned the Colony guardhouse and got Wally, one of the staff on duty, on the line. "Wally, this is Charlie Wigham," he said. "Do you know Mr. Pomerantz?"

Wally chuckled. "Oh, yeah, I know Mr. Pomerantz, all right."

"Wally, that's a very strange reading," Charlie said. "Have you seen him around lately?"

"Not since about two o'clock," said Wally, "when the FBI and the Santa Monica police was out here arresting him."

"Arresting him? What did he do?"

"I'm not sure," Wally said, "but it must have been something pretty good."

Even then Charlie clung to his belief in Jay R. Pomerantz. Feeling sure that there had been some terrible misunderstanding, he telephoned Melvin Schwartz and set him to tracking down the whereabouts of his financier. A couple of hours later Mel called back. "Hey, do you have a *bumika*," he said. "He's in for grand theft auto and for cashing a whole bunch of bum checks."

Jay R. Pomerantz' real name, it developed, was Harry Leonard, and he had only recently emerged from a long holiday in San Quentin. His only regret about the whole Malibu caper, as he expressed it to Mel through a grille at the county jail, was that he really hadn't had enough time to get his act off the ground; six months more and he'd have been able to put together some very legitimate deals for all those nice rich people out in Malibu. "How'd they get him?" Charlie asked glumly.

"Oh, they've been chasing him all over town for weeks now," Mel explained, "but he was also changing hotels and cars just before the crunch came. By the time he moved in out there, he had eight hotels and six car-rental companies looking for him. He's pretty good at using other people's credit cards, too, and better still at talking his way through life. But I guess you know that by now. They finally caught up to him because he made one small mistake. He bounced an eight-dollar check at a Malibu gas station last week, and the attendant there remembered his current license plate and turned him in."

Charlie felt rotten, but he couldn't resist a smile. "So are the mighty fallen," he observed, "by flea bites."

"Charlie," Mel pleaded, "will you please listen to me? Will you please stick to the legit route?"

"What is the legit route, Mel?" Charlie asked. "This guy is no more of a thief than half the so-called legit people we've been dealing with. And I got to hand it to him, he had a little razzle-dazzle about him. Maybe he's right. Six more months and he could have become the head of a studio."

Later, when Charlie told Billie Farnsworth what he'd found out, she wasn't at all surprised. "I should have known, but I looked the other way," she said. "The guy was down to a Chevy Nova last week. He must have been running out of car agencies."

Billie added up her losses on Jay R. Pomerantz and concluded they hadn't come to that much. If the Carey heirs wanted to place their property in some other agent's hands, that would be all right with her. She'd about had it with them, anyway, and that very morning she'd sold a Tudor cottage back in the Crosscreek area for seven hundred thousand, so the summer hadn't been a total loss, especially with all the high seasonal rental commissions. Jay had at least been comedy relief, but Billie would never know now whether Jay had been any good in bed or not. She had to make herself believe he couldn't have been a whiz or she'd have remembered something about it, drunk or not.

34

"Jim, this whole situation is coming apart," Dudley Kerrigan said. "Matters appear to be deteriorating rather than improving. Can't anything be done to make this guy Hester shut up?"

"Nothing drastic," Jim Wharton answered. "We appear to be dealing with a tough guy who's got a real bug up his ass about the raw deal he's been getting."

"And, as we understand it, Lewis seems to be doing very little about it."

"He's doing what he *can*, Kerrigan."

"It's not enough."

"He's in a bind," Wharton said. "If we crucify the son of a bitch, how is that going to improve the El Mirador situation?"

Kerrigan chose not to answer the query directly. His pale, cold eyes stared beyond Jim's shoulder to the window looking out on the thick traffic clogging the Beverly Hills streets below. "It is absolutely imperative," he said, "that we get the pressure off El Mirador. With that reporter down there now and obviously being briefed by this guy Hester, we're getting more and more bad publicity. Are you aware that business is off in the hotel by over twenty percent? So far, the condominiums haven't been affected and the land-development deals are on schedule, but we've got a domino factor to consider.

With the newspapers printing all this stuff about Mafia this and that, we scare the banks, we scare a lot of respectable investors. Do you see what I'm driving at, Jim?"

"Of course. I'd like to remind you again, Kerrigan, that I was the first guy to point out the problems with El Mirador from day one," Jim elaborated. "I'm not going to be the scapegoat for this fuck-up, Kerrigan, and you better carry that message back with you."

The Chicago emissary gazed calmly at the lawyer. "Nobody's blaming you, Jim," he said. "We're trying to find a way to get on top of this one."

"Then don't tell me, Kerrigan, that I'm in a spot here."

"You're not, Jim, unless we all are."

"I'm recommending simply that we'll have to hold on and ride this out," Jim said. "We've got to play a waiting game."

"I'm not sure that will sit very well with the company."

"What are the alternatives?" Jim asked.

"You could find a way, through Lewis, to get Hester out of our hair."

"Impossible right now," Jim explained. "Lewis has to make it look like he's doing everything he can, but without putting Hester back on the job. He loses credibility if he does that. If he dumps Hester completely, he's all but confirming the guy's charges. Now we've got a reporter down there sniffing around, and he sure as hell will seize on anything Lewis might do along the lines you suggest. If we put too much pressure on the guy, or use what we've got on him, he pulls us down with him. We have no choice, Kerrigan, but to sit tight."

"We're not impressed with Lewis," the emissary said. "We don't think we can count on him."

"We're stuck with him for now, and that's it."

Kerrigan pursed his lips and drummed his long, delicate fingers rapidly on the arms of his chair. He seemed to be seriously mulling over what Jim had just told him, but he gave little evidence of having been convinced. "And that's the best you can do for us, Jim?" he asked at last.

"It's not the best, Kerrigan," Jim snapped. "It's the *only* thing any of us can do. We ride it out, that's all. We've got one big factor working for us."

"And what's that?"

"These news stories fill up the papers one day and they're gone the next," Jim explained. "We keep quiet. We make no statements. We encourage Mort Lewis to do his job, and he butters this guy Hester up while at the same time explaining that Hester has no idea what the real, full scope of the investigation might be and that he's jeopardizing it by going public with it this way. Lewis is no problem. The guy is in our pocket. As for the reporter, he'll write what he wants, but he's got nothing more to write, and there's nothing, Kerrigan, quite as dead as yesterday's news headline. Why do I have to spell this out for you? There was a time when the company understood and let me run it my way. That's what I'm paid to do, isn't it?"

"We're very appreciative of everything you've done, Jim, surely you know that?"

"I suppose I do," Jim said. "Now, you've got to explain it to Chicago. If you can't explain it, Kerrigan, then I'm coming up there, and I'll explain it for you."

"No need to do that, Jim," the younger man said, suddenly rising to his feet. "I'll be home tonight, and by dinnertime I think the company will have a better understanding of your position. I want to thank you, Jim, for the good briefing."

After Kerrigan had left, Jim Wharton sat alone in his office for five minutes. He should have been at least satisfied that he had gotten the message across, but something about the way the meeting had gone nagged at him. He finally realized what it was, and it made him not so much nervous as slightly restless. Perhaps he should have gone to the company himself, rather than call for this messenger boy. What had bothered Jim Wharton, and it continued to trouble him off and on for the rest of the day, was the sudden crisp exit Kerrigan had made, as if the man's mind had clicked into place and locked on some fixed position. Kerrigan could not have that much power, Jim reasoned, but a young executive, ambitious and smart, would know how to report negative news so as to favor himself rather than the person he'd heard it from. In some ancient countries, Jim now recalled, the messenger who brought bad tidings did not survive to perform that role again.

He glanced at his watch, wondered about possibly going out to lunch, then felt the urge for the woman he'd not seen now for over two weeks. He smiled and reached for the phone.

* * *

"I've got to go," Lee Harvey said, sliding out of bed. "I'm late."

Art sat up, watched her scramble into her clothes, and began to chuckle. She ignored him at first and rushed into the bathroom, where she did what she could about her hair and added a touch of makeup. When she emerged five minutes later to find him still grinning at her, it angered her a little. "What's the matter with you?" she asked. "This isn't funny."

"Are you sure?"

"I'm already half an hour late, and you know how Sid is."

"Yes. He doesn't like to be kept waiting," Art said. "I suspect you have a pact on that score. It's probably the foundation of your marriage."

"I told you," she said, "it's Anthony's birthday. We're due in town with the boys at seven for dinner and we have tickets for *Annie* at the Shubert."

"Yeah, I know."

"I told Sid I had a dental appointment in Pacific Palisades," she explained, "and that I'd be home by five-thirty. It's nearly six now. Ten more minutes and Sid'll call the dentist's office to find out if I've left."

"And if he does that," Art continued for her, "he'll be confronted by a breaking of the pact. Disaster."

"What do you mean by that?"

"Oh, only that I imagine your casual summer affairs have never gotten you in trouble before, and you're going to keep it that way," he said. "The basis of your marriage, Lee, is that Sid will always look the other way, as long as you play within the well-defined boundaries he's laid down for you. Am I right?"

She stared at him, a flush of anger darkening her face. "That's a rotten thing to say."

"Is it?"

"You bet it is. That stuff about casual summer affairs. Is that what this is to you? Do you think I enjoy having to sneak our time together?"

"I don't know," he answered. "I do know we haven't been having much fun lately."

"Why are you doing this now," she asked, "when you know I'm in a rush?"

"Well, you asked me what I thought was so funny."

344

"I don't think this is funny at all."

"Because you don't see it from my point of view, Lee."

"No, I guess I don't."

"What's funny is that in most affairs of this kind it's the woman who sits around waiting for the man to call," he explained. "Usually he's the one with the responsibilities at home, in the form of a wife and kids. We've simply reversed the usual formula. We're right in tune with the times."

She sat down on the edge of the bed and tried to reach out to him. "Darling, please. We have just ten more days, and . . ."

"And then you go," he said, submitting to her gentle caress without responding.

"But I told you, we'll find a way," she insisted. "Sid's talking about moving out here."

"That's next year."

"Yes, but we can get together till then. We've talked about all that. Oh, sweetheart, why are you doing this to me now?"

"Listen," he said, "you'd better go. You don't want to make Sid angry."

She tried to kiss him this time, but he responded without enthusiasm, not even bothering to lift his head off the pillow. "Damn you," she murmured, taking his head in her hands and looking into his eyes, "don't you know I love you?"

"In your fashion, as the old Cole Porter song goes," he said.

Angry now, she stood up and backed away. "You shit!"

"Listen, Lee," he said, "you'll have the memory of your wonderful Malibu summer to carry you through the long, cold Wisconsin winter. That's something, isn't it?"

"You bastard," she said, "dumping on me now, just because your macho pride can't take it. You bastard . . ." She snatched up her bag and ran out of the apartment, neglecting to close the door behind her.

Tad Bonnell saw Lee Harvey run down the outside stairs and across the open lot to her car. He waited until she had driven away before going up to see his father, whom he found, dressed only in boxer shorts, emerging from the kitchen with a bottle of beer in his hand. Tad closed the door behind him and looked at him coldly. "You having a good time, Dad?"

"Not very," Art said. "What's the matter with you?"

345

"Nothing." Tad dropped the packet of mail he'd brought on the coffee table. "I brought you these."

"Thanks. How are you? And what's new?"

"Nothing. Only, Mom wants you to call her. She has to talk to you."

"Okay. Sit down. Want a beer?" He sat on the edge of his bed.

"No, thanks. I've got to go. I have a date with Terry."

"Oh, that's the big one now, eh?"

"We're seeing each other. Mom wants to know when you're going to have a phone. She's tired of taking your messages."

"Tough," Art said. "There's been some kind of mess. The starlet who had this place before me ran out on about five hundred dollars' worth of calls."

"What's that got to do with you?"

"Nothing, but by the time I got it all straightened out with the robots and the computers at the phone company, I'd missed one date," Art explained. "Then, the next two times I wasn't here when they came. I tried to explain to them that the old man has to work to support his expensive kid and I can't sit around blowing away four or five hours of lessons waiting for them to connect me to their wires. Anyway, they're supposed to come again Monday, and I should be set by next week. You sore about something?"

"No, Dad."

"Then what's eating you?"

Tad shrugged. "Nothing."

"Oh, come on, Tad, I know you a little better than that by now. Out with it."

"It's your life, Dad, that's all."

Art looked up at his son and smiled. "You know what? You sound like your mother. Whose life did you think it was?"

"Look, Dad, I don't want to get into this with you."

"Why not? I'm getting a little tired of all this disapproval. All I've done with my life is pay my bills so your mother could sit out here on the beach and you could get a fancy education," Art said. "I'm sorry I don't seem to be able to live up to everybody else's idea of what sort of person I ought to be. I'm just a tennis bum, Tad, who happens to have worked his ass off so you could grow up to disapprove of me."

346

The boy's face looked drawn, but the heat of anger flushed his cheeks. "I don't see why you're doing this, that's all!"

"Doing what?"

"Living like this."

"How am I supposed to live? How much money do you think I make? Your mother's got the house, or aren't you living there anymore?"

"It isn't only living," the boy said. "I mean, other things. Like Mrs. Harvey. And there have been others, haven't there?"

"Sure. Every lonely Malibu housewife wants a tennis pro at least once in her humdrum life."

The boy turned to go. "No wonder Mom left you," he said.

His son's disapproval made Art furious, so that suddenly he was out of control and knew it.

"What the fuck do you know about it?" he said. "What do you know about anything? Who gave you the right to make any moral judgments? And who do you think pays your goddamn bills?"

Tad whirled on him. "I don't want your money!"

"No? You mean you might actually go to work for a living? Or is your mother going to support you in high Malibu style?"

Tad wrenched the door open, but before he could escape, he allowed himself one parting shot. "At least Mom is trying," he said. "What are you doing?"

In a cold fury now, helpless to stop himself, Art pursued the boy into the hall. "Nothing," he called out after him. "Not a goddamn thing! But I don't have to worry, because among your mother's other great achievements is going to bed with her boss, in the highest tradition of American office romance!"

Tad turned back again and took a step in toward his father. His face was contorted with rage, and tears rolled down his cheeks, but his fists were clenched. "You bastard!"

"I'm not, but maybe you are. Have you asked your mother?"

Tad swung at him, but Art easily sidestepped the blow and pushed the boy away from him. "Beat it, Tad," he said. "You hit me and I'll deck you."

"I never want to see you again," the boy said. "I don't want your money, either."

"So what'll you do, Tad? Become a bum like me? Go ahead.

You're good, kid, but I was the best, and look where I am. Go ahead. Fuck it all up. I feel sorry for you, because I thought at least you had some brains."

The boy ran from him. Long after he'd gone, Art stood there, paralyzed by grief. Then he went back inside his apartment, sat on the edge of his bed, and cried. He had not cried in years, but it was not for himself that he wept. There are only so many losses anyone can sustain without suffering, and Art had crossed the blurred line from disappointment into grief; he felt like a wanderer in a maze from which only chance could now rescue him.

Okay, one thing I do know: I was the best, he told himself later, under a welcome cascade of hot water from the shower. *And if I'm going to go down the tubes, it's going to be like a champion, and not the bum my son thinks I've become.*

Jim Wharton was sitting fully dressed in the room's only armchair when Gail Hessian let herself into the apartment. He smiled pleasantly at her as she walked in, saw him, and hesitated at the door, her arms crossed at waist level and her eyes alive with excitement and fear. She was bare-legged, naked beneath the short skirt and silk blouse he had asked her to put on, and her ankles still bore the now faint traces of their previous encounter. "Hello, Gail," he said kindly, "come in."

She remained in the doorway. "Jim, please, not like last time," she said. "I've got a job. I can't—"

He casually waved her objection aside. "It's all right," he told her. "I never like to repeat myself. It's been a long time since I've had anyone like you, though. We'll experiment as we go along. Come here."

Trembling, she forced herself to walk up to him, but he stopped her before she came within reach. He did not move from his chair. "Strip," he said, the smile now fading from his face.

She stepped out of her sandals, unbuttoned her blouse and flung it behind her, then slid her skirt down to her ankles and stepped out of it. Naked now, she stood before him, her skin tightened to his appraising stare.

He nodded. "Good. I like that. You follow instructions very well."

She knew the rules of their game; she could not speak now unless he instructed her to, but all he wanted, apparently, at least for the moment, was to look. To every command she turned this way and that, opened herself everywhere to him, then stood still again, silently awaiting his pleasure.

"You like this, don't you, Gail?"

"Yes."

"All right, now listen very carefully," he said. "Today we're into fantasy, not pain. You'll enjoy yourself, won't you?"

"Yes."

"Good. Now, come here and do exactly what I tell you. Will you do that?"

"Yes."

"And you'll do it until I tell you to stop."

"Yes."

"And when I tell you to stop, you will wash yourself, get dressed, and leave in silence. You won't speak a word, and you'll go quickly. Is that clear?"

"Yes."

"Good. Now, here's what I want. You'll sit down right here, on this chair, facing me."

"Yes."

"And you'll open yourself and touch yourself. Understand?"

"Yes."

"Like that, exactly like that."

"Yes," she gasped.

"And this is very important, Gail," he said. "You must look at me. Your eyes must never look away from mine. Do you understand?"

"Yes."

"All right now, begin . . ."

"Oh, no," he said, smiling. "That was much too easy, Gail, and you put your head down, you looked away. Again now, until we get it just right. Look at me, Gail . . ."

It was nearly seven o'clock that night when Art Bonnell finally got Dan Lefkowitz on the phone. The agent was still in his office, but Art had failed on three previous attempts to talk to him, and Dan had not returned his calls. He finally consented to come on the line because Art's persistence must have impressed him.

"Yeah, who is this?" the agent asked.

"My name's Bonnell, Art Bonnell," the pro said for the fourth time that afternoon. "I explained to your secretary. I'm a tennis pro. I teach sometimes on Jim Wharton's court in Malibu, and you've seen me around the Racquet Club."

"Oh, you must be the kid's father."

"Right. I'm in a phone booth," Art said, "and I've got plenty of change, so don't hang up."

"Okay, what can I do for you?"

"No, you've got it wrong, Mr. Lefkowitz," Art said. "It's what *I* can do for you."

"Look, I got an active deal going, and—"

"I heard about the accident to Bill Stevens."

"So what?"

"So you still want to play Jim Wharton for money?"

"Maybe."

"All right, that's what I can do for you," Art explained. "Set up the match again. I'll play with you."

There was a moment's silence at the other end of the line. "I don't get it," the agent said.

"Let me tell you what I have in mind," Art said. "You take me as your partner. We play two out of three sets, any court you guys pick."

"You and me against Wharton and your kid?" the agent asked. "What do you think I am, the patsy of all time?"

"I haven't finished," Art said. "I'm willing to lay eight thousand of my own money on the line."

"What? What is this, some kind of joke?"

"No joke, Mr. Lefkowitz. I need the money. You can bet whatever you want. Wharton's out on a limb with you. He'll bet whatever you say."

"What makes you think he will? Even if you're on the level, why should Wharton trust you and your kid any more than I do?"

"My kid and I are not on great terms at the moment," Art explained. "That's all you need to know. I'm willing to bet every goddamn cent I have on the match. You and me against them. You want to fix Wharton for good? Here's your chance. If you haven't got the stomach for it, forget it." Art started to hang up.

"Wait a minute!" the agent snapped. "Just a minute!"

Art waited. After a few seconds he heard the agent begin to laugh. "Eight grand?" Lefkowitz said. "You've got to be nuts."

"What do you want to bet?" Art asked.

"I'll throw in for two."

"That makes ten. Are you on?"

"Yeah."

"Okay, you call Wharton and you convince him. Don't tell him the money is mine, or he'll think Tad and I are cutting him up. It's your ten grand, understand?"

"Okay, but suppose he won't go for it?"

"He'll go for it," Art said, "because he won't let you make him back down."

"That figures. I hope you know what you're doing, Bonnell."

"Don't worry about it," Art said. "I know what I'm doing."

The two men sitting in the blue Oldsmobile parked halfway down the block from the apartment house had been waiting nearly an hour. The man behind the wheel was tall, balding, with a pale moon face and light gray eyes. The man in the passenger seat was short, but heavily built, with big hands and feet, cropped black hair, and eyes hidden by sunglasses. The short man had been sleeping, so it was the driver who saw Gail Hessian emerge from the building. Head down and walking quickly, she came out the front door, turned left, got into her car, and drove away.

"The girl just left," the driver said.

The short man opened his eyes and sat up straight. "You sure it was her?"

"Yeah, it was her."

"The TV-news broad?"

"Yeah, it was her, all right."

The two men relaxed again in their seats and waited, both wide-awake now.

Twenty minutes later, Jim Wharton appeared. He looked up and down the block, but at that hour he failed to spot the two men in the blue Oldsmobile, who had slumped low in their seats when they saw him. Jim Wharton now walked to the end of the block, again checked his surroundings, then at last got into his own car and drove away.

"That does it, right?" the driver asked the other man in the blue Olds.

"Yeah," the short one said. "Let's go."

Jim Wharton had driven away toward Malibu, but these two men headed up toward Wilshire, then turned east toward downtown Los Angeles or some point in between. If Jim Wharton had happened to notice them, he would not have recognized either of them. They knew him and Gail only from photographs they had studied.

35

"I should come right now," Jennifer Gilbert said. "He'd want me to be there."

"No, he wouldn't, Jenny, not right this minute," Victor assured her. "We've already discussed it."

"Even these last few days, when things got so bad, he'd always want me with him," she said.

"That's natural, Jenny, And you've done what you could, but enough is enough," he said. "I want you to get a couple of hour's rest, at least. You've been up all night."

"But he could . . . he could. . . ."

"No, it won't happen that fast, Jenny," Victor explained. "Right now he's going through the worst part. By the time you get to the hospital, he'll still be sedated, but, I hope, a little more comfortable. You'll be able to see him."

"But he won't know me, and—"

"Yes he will. There will be times when he won't, but at some point he'll know you, you'll be able to talk to him. But you've got to get some sleep, Jenny. Take the pills and go and lie down. I'll be at the hospital, but I'll have Dorothy call you, I promise."

Still uncertain, despite his assurances, she picked up the pills and headed for the kitchen, but then turned back. "Victor, you don't blame me, do you?"

"For what?"

"These past ten days, when Evan got so bad, all I did was think about it," she said. "But I told you I couldn't do it. You remember?"

"I do. And no one would blame you, Jenny," he said. "But surely Evan understands. Did he ever reproach you?"

She shook her head and began to cry. Perhaps, he thought later, he should have comforted her more then, but he couldn't make himself do it. After all, he'd been up all night as well. "Look, Jenny," he said instead, "Evan's the only one who counts now. We have to think of him. If you rush down to the hospital now, you won't do him or yourself a bit of good. You'll collapse down there and I'll have another patient to deal with. Besides, he won't know you now anyway. That last shot I gave him was very strong."

Without another word she went into the kitchen, poured herself a glass of water, and took the pills Victor had given her. She came back into the living room long enough to kiss him on the cheek, then went upstairs to sleep.

She was once a beautiful woman, Victor thought as he let himself out of the house and into the mocking brightness of a perfect, balmy mid-September day, *and she's only twenty-eight years old. Evan's dying is aging all of us a year every day. But she'll be a beautiful woman again.*

Lights flashing, the ambulance turned into the emergency entrance of the Albert Mercer Memorial Hospital and parked close to the door. The driver got out and helped the attendant in back to unload the wheeled stretcher containing the semicomatose, wasted body of Evan Gilbert. Moving carefully, but with deliberate speed, they pushed him inside toward the nurses' station, where a matronly-looking gray-haired woman presided at the admissions counter. She looked up as they reached her. "Yes?"

"Dr. Ferrero's patient," the driver said.

"Oh, yes. It's all been taken care of. Take him to the third floor. They're expecting you."

The driver seemed surprised. "Third floor?"

The nurse again checked her instructions. "That's what it says here. Go on up. I'll phone ahead."

354

The driver, who had obviously expected the patient to be wheeled directly either into emergency itself or into one of the intensive-care units, merely shrugged. The body on the stretcher was not his ultimate responsibility, after all. He nodded to his helper and they pushed the gurney through the swinging doors leading down a corridor to the elevator shafts.

Evan Gilbert lay flat on his back, not moving, and his dull, glazed eyes stared unseeingly at the ceiling.

Dorothy Ferrero sat on the edge of her seat in the living room listening to her husband talking into the wall phone in the kitchen. She had a drink in her hand and another one she had mixed for him on the coffee table beside her. The sun had begun its long dive toward the sea outside their window, and the room was bathed in broad golden shafts of light. Dorothy did not sip from her drink, but waited tensely, both hands clasped around her glass.

"Yes. . . . Yes, that's right," Victor's voice could be heard saying. "Never mind that, nurse, I'm on my way. I should be there within the hour, depending on traffic. . . . Yes, thank you."

Dorothy heard him hang up. When he appeared in the entrance to the room, she handed him his drink. "Evan?"

"No," he said. "I have one patient who's not going to make it through the night. I have to go in."

"And Evan?"

"You're to call Jennifer at six," he answered obliquely. "She wants to go down and be with him tonight."

"You haven't answered my question, Victor."

"Evan is not going to die tonight," he said. "I wish he would, but he's not going to. His kidneys are infected and failing, and he has massive stones. He could live a week or two, three at most."

"But the IC unit—"

"He's not in intensive care," Victor explained. "He's in a private room. I'm doing nothing in that line to save him, Dottie."

"What if he doesn't go in a week or ten days, then what?"

"I'm taking this one day at a time, Dottie. That's all I can tell you."

He took a big swallow of his drink, stretched himself, and leaned forward to kiss her. "Victor, you can't," she said.

"Can't what?"

355

"If he doesn't go fast," she said. "It's not just you I'm thinking about. It's me. It's all of us."

"I told you, Dottie, that I'm taking this one day at a time, but I've been prepared for it for weeks now," he explained. "I promised Evan."

"You had no right to. Do you realize what's at stake?"

"Maybe better than you, Dottie," he said. "Evan's situation is no different from that of any of my other patients. Anyway, I don't want to talk about it right now."

"We've got to talk about it. Why do you have to take all the responsibility?"

"Who else is going to?"

"Evan could have. So could Jennifer."

"Evan would have, but by the time he wanted to, he couldn't. It happens all the time, sweetheart, you know this. You can't predict absolutely what's going to happen in these cases. It can be weeks, it can be years. In Evan's case, it should be soon. It must be."

"And Jennifer? If it isn't, what about Jennifer?"

"Don't knock Jenny," he argued. "She's had a hell of a time."

"Yes, playing Florence Nightingale the whole summer," Dorothy said bitterly. "But now, of course, she steps aside, and suddenly it's your decision."

"I don't think you're being fair," Victor said.

"And if something has to be done, you take all the risk."

"I promised Evan I'd help him, that's all," he said. "If I knew he wanted to die and couldn't, or if, in my judgment, he was suffering too much and it was too prolonged."

"That's goddamn noble of you!"

He swung on her and took both her hands in his, trying to get the message across to her, at no matter what cost to himself. Didn't she know he was dying inside now, right here in front of her? Couldn't she see he no longer cared about the living and the dead, but only about the pain, spiritual as well as physical? Why couldn't she see that and understand? he wondered. "I couldn't treat half my cases if I felt any differently about this," he said. "I know it's not part of my Hippocratic oath, but it's one I made to myself a long time ago, Dottie, and you know it. I'm not going to make an exception for Evan, who is our friend. Do you want him to suffer needlessly for maybe weeks more?"

"What I'm trying to tell you, Victor, is that this is different," she said. "Evan's not just your patient and not just a friend of ours. He's a celebrity. You could go to jail."

"He's dying," Victor answered. "He's dying and I'm going to take care of him the best way I know how. That's all I'm thinking about, Dottie. What are you thinking about, sweetheart? All this?" And he encompassed the whole room in one broad sweep of his arm. "The golden life? Is that what matters to you?"

"The golden life?" she echoed him. "That's what you think of me? That all I care about is this?"

"Okay, I didn't mean it quite that way," he said, realizing how deeply he had hurt her.

"Yes, you did," she said "I know you did. My God, Victor, I don't give a damn about all this. I don't care where we live. But we do have a life together, and that matters. Not the luxuries, not the Colony. None of that. I'm talking about a career and a life together, a whole lifetime, Victor. There's also Terry and Michael. They matter, too."

"I know they do."

"Then how can you just slough the whole thing off?"

"That's what you think I'm doing?"

"You worry about Evan, fine. You worry about Jennifer, fine. But you don't worry about us."

"What do you think has kept me going all this time?" he suddenly almost shouted at her. "What do you think this whole thing is about, anyway?"

"I don't know. Why don't you tell me, Victor? You've been wanting to tell me something all summer, and I thought at first it had to do with Evan. And now I know it doesn't, not entirely. You've been like a wild man sometimes. Why don't you tell me?"

"You'd know, if you opened your eyes."

"You think I would?"

"Yes. That's why I'm so impatient with you sometimes. You don't see because you don't want to see."

"If you've kept things from me, it was your choice," she said. "I never wanted you to. For God's sake, Vic, what is it? I honestly don't know what you're talking about."

He turned and walked away from her toward the picture window. She thought he might try to escape again, as he had so often before

357

during the summer, to one of his long solitary tramps up and down the beach, but this time he stopped and merely considered the view for a minute or two. "I'm tired of it," he said. "I'm very tired. Evan's dying is just one more case, I know, but it's the one that breaks me. It's my last one, Dottie."

"You don't *have* to tell me, if you don't want to," she said, suddenly and unexpectedly made fearful by his subdued tone, so unlike him at any time. She feared for him more than for herself. He sounded so tired, so defeated, and that was very unlike him. "Victor? What is it? Do you really want to tell me?"

"I don't know. I think I have to," he said, turning now to face her. The light from the window threw his features into shadow but outlined the shape of his head in a pale yellow glow, as if the scene had been set by a skillful director or some genius of a cinematographer. How ironic real life can be, Dottie thought as she waited in silence for him to speak, and how farcical, too.

"Do you know what some of the nurses call me around the hospital?" he finally asked in a very calm, dead voice.

"No."

"The executioner," he said.

"Oh, Victor."

"You know, I didn't start out to be one when I went to medical school."

She wanted to run to him, but for some reason couldn't make herself do so. So that was it. They lived in a house built on blood and death. Yes, that was it, all right. And Victor had told the truth; she hadn't wanted to see it. No, she hadn't wanted to face that at all, though she'd really known all along that he couldn't go on playing God forever. Who could? And now what would they do?

Feeling defeated, she walked away from him and out onto the patio. A strong breeze was blowing in, scuffing the surface of the dark blue water into choppy caps of foam, and a flight of pelicans skimmed the shore. To the south a solitary surfer straddled his board, waiting, as ever for the perfect wave, while to the north, along the line of the horizon, a cluster of brightly colored sails indicated the progress of a race. Despite the sun, she felt chilly and hugged herself. She did not hear him come up behind her.

"Do you know what Evan said to me last night, while we were waiting for the ambulance to come?" he asked. "'I don't want to see the morning.'" She did not answer. "Do you know what he's been going through, Dottie? He could live another two or three weeks like this. I know you blame Jennifer. . . ."

"No, I don't blame her," Dorothy said. "I'll hate her, if anything happens, but I don't blame her."

He put his arms around her from behind and hugged her as he placed his cheek against hers. "Listen, somebody once told me there must be an easier way to make a living," he said. "If there is and I find out about it, I'm going to get very depressed."

He went on holding her for several minutes, but she did not move or answer him. Finally he broke away, squeezed her shoulder briefly, and went back into the house. She did not follow him or hear him drive away. After she had finished her drink, she remained outside, alone on their patio, until the light began to fade. At six-fifteen she telephoned Jennifer, but she'd already left for the hospital.

Janet Morgan, the young nurse on duty at that end of the floor, made one last check of the room, then leaned down over the bed where the patient lay twitching restlessly but otherwise quiet. "Mr. Gilbert?" she asked. He didn't answer, though his lips seemed to be trying to form words, and soon, after she had made one last check of the I.V. bag, she left, closing the door quietly behind her.

36

News of the match had apparently circulated through Malibu, because by the time Art Bonnell showed up at the Racquet Club, a small crowd of about forty had gathered to watch. Among the spectators Art spotted Billie and Dee; the Kramers; Rich Bentley, dressed in lounging pajamas and with his jaw still wired shut; Charlie Wigham and a couple of his friends from town; and, of course, the Harveys. Lee had on her usual pair of tight white shorts showing off her wonderful legs, and she sat behind Sid, who was hunched forward in his seat, his teeth clamped on a cigar. She waved tentatively at Art, but he ignored her; his mind was fixed on the event at hand. He had hoped, for some wild reason, to see Laura there, but she apparently hadn't come. *Too bad, he thought. I could have shown her something, an aspect of me she had once admired and since forgotten. Too bad.*

Originally the match was to have been played at Bud Lavin's place in Bel Air, but it wasn't available on this particular Sunday, so Jim Wharton had reserved the club's center court. Dan Lefkowitz, of course, had objected, since he felt that the club was, in effect, Wharton's home base and would give him and Tad an advantage. But when the lawyer had agreed to allow Bill Stevens to umpire, Dan had yielded. Besides, Art had told Dan it didn't matter what court they played on. "I can beat these guys anywhere they want to play," he'd assured the agent.

"And Tad?"

"Tad has a nice game," Art had conceded, "but I'm going to teach him a few things he doesn't know yet about this sport."

Mike Kenmore was astonished by the turnout for the match, especially for a Sunday midafternoon, but he had no idea it was being played for money. He knew it was a grudge match of some kind, but he assumed it was all basically in fun, and he was delighted by the brisk business the club was doing in beer, wine, and soft drinks. Terry Ferrero, suddenly cast in the role of courtside waitress, served the spectators, most of whom sat on chairs above the court or crowded onto the patio area at the clubhouse end.

Art Bonnell had arrived late, and his appearance alarmed Dan Lefkowitz, who had been rallying nervously with Wharton and Tad for nearly ten minutes. The pro hadn't shaved, and he was dressed in soiled white slacks and an old long-sleeved tennis sweater torn open at the elbows. He ignored Dan's savage look and gazed calmly over the crowd as he set his rackets down by the umpire's high chair. "Where's Bill?" he asked.

"He's in the clubhouse," Dan said. "Why?"

"I came here to play," Art said. "Let's get going."

"Don't you want to warm up?" the agent asked.

"What for? I'm ready."

Art walked up to Wharton. "Let's play," he said.

"Anytime you say." He caught Terry's eye. "Tell Bill Stevens we're set to go here."

Art avoided his son's sullen stare and addressed himself again to the lawyer. "Is Stevens holding the money?" he asked.

"What do you care who holds the money?"

"I'm in for a cut of this action," Art said. "I want to know Bill Stevens is holding the bet."

Wharton nodded. "He's got it."

"Good," Art said. "You don't think I'd waste my time playing you for nothing, Wharton?"

The lawyer's face flushed a dark red. "Watch yourself, Bonnell."

Art smiled at him. "Let's play tennis," he said as Bill Stevens now came hobbling out of the clubhouse and took his seat above the court.

A hush spread over the crowd as Art spun his racket and Wharton won the serve. "Ladies and gentlemen, this is a challenge match, best two out of three sets," Bill Stevens announced. "In case of a six-all tie, a seven-point tiebreak will be played. Mr. Wharton has won the serve. We ask you for tournament conditions, which means quiet and no moving around, please, except when the teams change sides. I will call all lines, and my decisions will be final. Players ready?"

"One minute, please," Art said, taking his partner aside. "You nervous, Dan?"

"Me?" the agent answered. "I wouldn't be if I knew what you were up to. But not even hitting a ball—"

"I know what I'm doing," Art said, keeping his voice low. "Now, listen to me. The only problem here is your return of service, okay? Here's what I want you to do. You lob every service return."

"What? But that's nutty. I can—"

"You want to win this or not?"

The agent again started to protest Art's strategy, then changed his mind. He looked at the pro with some skepticism. "Okay, I lob, and then what?"

"I've seen you play, Dan, and I know you can lob," Art told him. "You lob every return and every other chance you get. I'll take care of the rest. You got that?"

"It's nuts."

"Never mind," Art said. "I've got more riding on this than you do. Just lob and keep it as deep as you can. Let's go, now."

As Art took his place at defensive net, standing in the middle of the court just inside the backhand service line, he glanced again up into the stands, and this time he spotted Laura. She was sitting alone at the end of the last row of chairs, and she sat hunched forward, her elbows resting on her knees. She was wearing very dark glasses and her face was expressionless. Art smiled at her but got no reaction. He couldn't blame her; he had been very hard on her at their last meeting, two days earlier. At least, that's how it must have seemed to her.

"I think the whole thing is silly," she said. "Just because you and Tad had a fight."

"That's not the reason," he answered. "Come in. Sit down. You want a drink?"

"No." She had entered his apartment but remained standing just inside his front door and refused his hospitality. "Arthur, I want you to cancel this match."

"I can't."

"Why not?"

"There are reasons, that's all."

"I've tried to talk to Tad, but he won't listen. He insists on playing you."

"I figured he would."

"He has some crazy idea about beating you. Not just beating you, Arthur, but as if he wants to hurt you as badly as you hurt him."

"I know. We hurt each other. I feel like hell about it."

"Then cancel this match. It'll only make things worse."

"I told you I can't do that."

"Why? So Tad can beat you? Do you think that will help? Is that it?"

"No, Laura. It won't help. I'm not throwing the match. I'm going to try as hard as I can to win."

"To beat your own son in public, and for money?"

"I guess that's the way it must look to you."

"What else am I to think?"

"You'll have to make up your own mind about it. I'm sorry."

She stared angrily at him, as if seeing him for the very first time as a narrow-minded, selfish man, certainly not the man she'd married, but the one he had obviously become in her eyes. "I want you to know that what you're doing stinks," she said in an even, very controlled voice. "Not only haven't you stopped Tad from playing for money with Wharton and his friends, but now you're part of it. I've always despised this aspect of the game, like all those years when you took money under the table for playing in tournaments."

"How else were we to live?" he asked. "It was accepted practice."

"I hated it. And I hate this, and I hate you for what you're doing now," she continued. "It's mean and cheap."

"Okay, I'm mean and cheap. Sure you don't want a drink?"

"I hope to God you lose, Arthur. Though, either way, you lose."

"I'm going to win."

"Are you? Congratulations," she said sarcastically as she turned to leave.

"Laura," he said, "I couldn't stop this match if I wanted to. Not without losing a lot more than you can imagine. And I'm not talking about the money. Basically, the money is secondary."

"I don't believe you."

"I can't expect you to," he said. "I can't tell you everything. Not now. All I ask is that you suspend judgment, that's all."

"I'm sorry for you, Arthur. He's your son, too. And he loves you."

He could think of nothing to say to that, so he simply let her go. Later, maybe, she'd know all of it, and he hoped she'd understand. If not, then he'd have to learn to live with her hatred and, worse, contempt.

Tad served first and held easily. Both Dan and Art lobbed their returns, and Tad smashed three of them for winners, while Wharton also put his only chance away. In the second game, Art, serving softly, was easily broken. The lobbing strategy failed to pay off in the third game, which Wharton took at love. Then Dan, unnerved, double-faulted twice, and in less than twenty minutes he and Art stood at love–four. In the fifth game, Tad held his service, but had to struggle. Wharton missed two overheads, and Tad hit one long, but eventually, after one deuce, the boy ran the score to five–love.

As they switched sides again, Wharton laughed at Dan. "That's a great strategy you got there." He chortled. "Whose idea was it, Dan? Yours?"

The agent didn't answer, but grimly took his place at net. Art picked up the balls, strolled to the backline, and served. This time he hit his shots with authority, followed them into net, and held, to win their first game. The crowd, puzzled and restless till now, applauded. Scowling, Dan prepared to receive Wharton's serve. "Can we play now?" he snarled.

Art looked at him and smiled. "Just keep doing what I told you," he said in a low, calm voice. "If you don't, we may lose."

But again the strategy failed to work. Wharton missed two more of his smashes, and Art cut off two others for winning volleys, but Tad, playing flawlessly, hit four good overheads and twice outdueled the agent at net. "First set to Wharton, six–one," Bill Stevens intoned from his high chair.

"This is awful," Dee Stauffer said as she and three other people in the audience rose to leave. "I thought Art could really play."

"I wish I hadn't come," Lee Harvey said.

Sid turned to look at her. "Why?"

"Because I don't like this. It's embarrassing." She stood up to go.

"Sit down, Lee," Sid told her.

"You're the one who wanted to come to this," she said. "I don't know why *I* have to stay."

"Because I want you to."

"I'll come back for you, Sid."

He took her arm and pulled her back into her chair. "I said sit down," he whispered. "You think I don't know why you want to leave? You're going to stay and see this till it's over."

Her face went pale and she said nothing, but sat like a stone now, hoping it would soon be over, knowing everything might soon be over.

From her seat above them, Laura had seen Lee rise to her feet. It must have been painful for her, Laura realized, to watch Art lose so badly. Is that why she had risen to go? And why had her husband forced her to stay? Did he know? Was he enjoying this? Laura sighed and tensed as she waited for the match to resume. Perhaps alone of all the people there she knew it wasn't over. She had sensed a calculated strategy in the way Art and his partner had lost, and she had also noticed when both Wharton and Tad had begun to miss their overheads. She shut her eyes and remembered how it had been when Art had been good, at the very top of his game—a smart, graceful player, a fierce competitor who never stuck to a losing game plan and who never quit under pressure. No, this match wasn't over, she knew, not by a long shot, and that realization made her fear for Tad, whose inexperience, at tennis and in life, could easily betray him now. She waited and watched, hardly daring even to breathe.

Before the start of the second set, Dan again confronted his partner. "Okay, Bonnell, it's our money," he said. "I don't give a shit about my two grand, but if you think I'm going to lose this way, you're crazy. For Christ's sake, man . . ."

Art stared him down. "Listen, you little weasel, you're not in your office now, screwing some poor asshole out of ten percent," he said. "This is *my* office and I'll call the shots here. Now, you lob your service returns, and that's all you do. After you lob, just get to one side of the court or the other, I don't care which. The main thing I want you to do this set, asshole, is stay out of my fucking way."

The agent's face went white, and there must have been a moment when he contemplated walking off the court, but as Art had figured, he chose instead not to lose face. Without another word he returned to the service line and play resumed.

366

At first it appeared that Wharton and Tad would win the second set as easily as they had the first. Despite two brilliant cutoffs at net by the pro, Dan's serves fell short and he was broken in the opening game. Five more people in the crowd got up to go, delaying play, but it was the mistake of their tennis-viewing lives, because, at one–love, with Tad serving, Art Bonnell began to play tennis.

The turnaround came on the opening point of the second game, when Tad mishit the first lob Dan threw up. Art slammed the boy's weak overhead so hard past Wharton at net that the lawyer appeared frozen in his tracks. And it was only the beginning. A stream of winners flowed off Art's racket and now, every time Dan lobbed, Tad and Jim Wharton couldn't seem to hit their overheads at all. After missing six in a row, in fact, Wharton began waiting for the ball to bounce so he could stroke it, only to find Art waiting for the shot at net to put it away. Tad managed to hold one of his service games, and Dan was broken a second time, but the second set went to Lefkowitz and Art, six–three.

As Tad, looking pale and determined, got ready to serve to open the third set, Art held up his hand and turned to the now enthralled audience. "I think it might be instructive for you all to understand what's happened here," Art said in a loud, firm voice. "I asked my partner, Dan, to lob in the first set, figuring that pretty soon our worthy opponents would begin to miss. It was a gamble, but it seems to be paying off. It might not have against top players, but there are different levels to this game. I once saw Bobby Riggs work this ploy against Don Budge, and there are no Don Budges on this court at the moment."

Art paused and noticed Bill Stevens grinning at him. "The third set is going to be a formality, and very boring for you," the pro continued, "unless, of course, I choose to make it interesting or Dan here screws me up by trying to play his rinky dink little game."

"You son of a bitch," Dan Lefkowitz said, as someone in the crowd laughed loudly.

"I love it," Charlie Wigham said. "What the hell's gotten into Bonnell?"

Laura knew. Nothing had gotten into him; it had always been there. She remembered her husband's fierce pride on the court, the way he had always played his best under the toughest conditions. She had forgotten the greatness in him, how she had sat and watched

367

him through all those big matches in the good days, and how she knew that he had played not only for himself and for her but also for the sheer competitive rapture of being the best and knowing it. He'd always had the champion's temperament, and once a winner, you were always a winner at some gut level, no matter what life could do to you. She looked at Tad now, and she was sick with fear for him.

Art ignored Dan Lefkowitz and continued to address the spectators. "What I'd rather do," he said, "is play Tad here one set of singles. You'll see some nice tennis, I promise you. To make it interesting, I'll offer him thirty points a game or five games—he can take his choice."

In the ensuing silence, Art turned to look at his opponents. "How about it, Tad? Or maybe it's up to you, Wharton?" Neither of them answered, so Art again addressed the viewers. "You should know that there's a little wager riding on the outcome of this match," he explained. "Bill Stevens here is holding the stakes. I'll go along with whatever our opponents decide."

"Let's play tennis," Wharton said.

"I don't consider what you play to be tennis," Art said. "It's work, that's all."

"I'll take the five games," Tad said, turning now to the lawyer. "Let me play him, Mr. Wharton."

The lawyer hesitated, then shrugged and walked off the court. He did not linger to see what would happen to his money, but kept on going to the clubhouse. Dan Lefkowitz flung his racket to the ground and went off to sit alone in a chair in one corner of the patio. "Are we ready now?" Bill Stevens asked.

It was brutal. Tad began by serving well, but Art hit winners off his best shots and completely dominated the court. Only twice did the boy get to deuce. Then, at five–all and deuce, a curious thing happened. With Tad hitting a second serve, Art hit the return like a bullet crosscourt. The boy lunged for it and sent up a weak, short lob, which Art smashed into the backhand corner for a winner. After hitting the shot, the pro grabbed his shoulder, but immediately let go, turned, and slowly walked back to receive again. Bill Stevens had noticed the grimace of pain on Art's face. "Art, are you all right?" he asked softly.

"I'm fine," the pro replied. "A little stitch, that's all. Serve, please."

Tad boomed a cannonball straight down the middle. Art took it on his backhand and lofted a deep lob that the boy hit out. "I thought we were going to play tennis," he snarled at his father.

"This is tennis, kid," Art said quietly. "And if you're going to play this game seriously, you'd better learn how to cope with junk artists. You think I'm going to feed into the strongest part of your game? You got a lot to learn. Balls, please."

All during the final game, Art served underhand slices, tossed up lobs, and hit chop and drop shots Tad simply couldn't put away. And all the time the pro kept up an instructive, teasing patter, as if he were back at his job of teaching beginners the fundamentals of the game. The tactic served only to prolong the set. Even so, it was all over in twenty minutes. Art had not only beaten the boy but also humiliated him, a spectacle that fascinated some and enchanted nobody. The crowd began to disperse in silence.

Only Laura did not move. She sat hunched over behind her dark glasses, tears running down her cheeks. *The crazy, dumb fool, to do this to himself and to his own son.* She wondered how bad it was, because only she and perhaps Bill Stevens, of all the people in the audience, had understood the significance of those last few points. No once had Art lifted his arm to above shoulder level. Not because he hadn't wanted to, but because he obviously couldn't.

Head down, Tad headed for the clubhouse, but his father's voice followed him out. "You don't know enough about hustling, kid," Art said. "You'd better learn, if you want to become a real bum like your old man. Next time, take the points, because that way at least you'll have a fifty-fifty chance. The other way, you're a goner against a more experienced player. Tad?"

But the boy kept on going. Terry was waiting for him on the patio, and she tried to speak to him, but he brushed past her. She started to follow him, but then thought better of it. She let him go, then sat down and cried.

Dan Lefkowitz got up from his seat and walked toward the pro. "Hell of a match," he said. "You're a hell of a player, Bonnell." He stuck out his hand.

Art ignored it and looked up at Bill Stevens, still rooted to his perch. "Mr. Stevens," he said, parodying the Oscar ceremonies, "the envelope, please."

"Boy, Art," the older man commented, handing him the bulky brown container, "that was quite a set. What got into you?"

"I thought it was about time I teach the people out here some real lessons," he said. "They're a little spoiled, and I got tired of all the bullshit." He took out two hundred-dollar bills and handed them to the older man. "Thanks, Bill."

"Listen, Bonnell—" the agent began.

"I don't want to talk to you," the pro said. "You're nothing." Without another word, he counted off the agent's share of the money, handed it to him, stuffed the envelope into one of his racket cases, picked up the rest of his gear, and quickly walked off the court toward his car.

"Now, that was really something," said Charlie Wigham, who had not moved from his courtside seat. "That was better than any tournament final I ever saw. I wouldn't have missed it for anything."

"I wish I understood more about tennis," Billie Farnsworth said.

"You don't have to, Billie," Charlie said. "You just have to know a little bit about life.

"That I figured out for myself," she said. "It's got to have torn him up to do that to his own son."

"Hello," Lee Harvey said, standing in the doorway. "Can I come in?"

"Please do." He stepped aside, and she entered. Nothing about the disorder in the room surprised her, because she had become accustomed to it by now, but the sight of the bulky brown envelope lying on his coffee table did. The flap was open, and wads of hundred-dollar bills were visible, bunched up against each other and spilling out across the table.

"Good God," she said, "how much was the bet?"

"Enough," he told her, "enough so I don't think I'll ever have to do it again."

"I had no idea."

"I think you saw my farewell appearance. I hope you enjoyed it."

"I'm not sure 'enjoyed' is the word," she said.

"No, I guess it isn't. How are you, Lee?"

"I'm okay. Please kiss me."

He did so, and she clung to him, but he soon gently disengaged himself. "Would you like anything? Coffee? Tea? A drink?"

She shook her head, and he could see she was close to tears but fighting very hard not to give way to them. "We're . . . we're leaving day after tomorrow," she said.

"So soon? I thought it was next week."

"The boys have to be back in school, and Sid wants to get back early."

"I see."

"You won't miss me, will you?"

"Yes, I'll miss you." He sat down heavily on his couch, behind the protective barrier of the coffee table full of money. He stared at the bills blankly. "I'm feeling a little worn out, Lee. I hope you understand."

She walked over to the living-room window, from where she could look down over the narrow rock-strewn, kelp-littered strip of beach that seemed so distant from the long curve of spotless Colony sand, not even visible from his little apartment. "Is it over, Arthur?" she asked, keeping her back turned to him.

"I think so."

"Just like that?" she asked. "You can say it so calmly? How can you be so calm?"

He knew she was keeping her back to him so he wouldn't have to witness or to cope with her tears. "Lee, I don't want to be unkind," he told her, "but this seems to by my day for telling the truth."

She turned back now to face him, where he sat, on the edge of the couch and behind the coffee table. She had dried her quick tears, but they still stained her cheeks. "Sid knows," she said. "I'm sure he knows. I don't know how. But he probably also knows I'm here. We drove home together, and I left him and came straight here. I don't care anymore."

"He'll forgive you."

"That's a rotten thing to say."

"You're right, I'm sorry. But it's true, isn't it?"

"I'll leave Sid. I'll leave him."

"No you won't, Lee. Why should you? You're not leaving Sid for anybody, least of all me."

"What are you talking about?"

"Lee, I'm fifty years old and I'm starting from scratch. You have the boys to think of—a whole life. Mine is nowhere."

"Arthur, I love you."

"You enjoy *being* in love with me."

"What's wrong with that?"

"Nothing. As a matter of fact, I enjoy it too. But it's not a life. You

371

already have a life, Lee, and I don't belong in it. You couldn't leave it even if you tried."

She was having a very bad time, and he was sorry about it, really sorry, but he knew it would do no good at all to take her in his arms; it would only delay the inevitable and hurt all the more later. So he refused to get up from his seat, and his weariness froze her in place. "I . . . I'd like to call you or write, if you'll let me," she said. "I mean, sometime . . . from back home."

"Why?"

"Just . . . just to find out how you are. To tell you how I am. Don't you want me to?"

"Sure," he lied.

"You'll miss me, you know."

"Of course I'll miss you," he said. "I'll always miss you. But it's over, and we both know it."

"It doesn't have to be."

"Yes, it does."

"Oh, Art . . ." she began. "I . . . I'd stay with you or come back to you, if you asked me."

"No you wouldn't, Lee," he said. "Or if you did, you'd pay too high a price for it. If you leave Sid now, he'll take the boys away from you, or try to, won't he?"

She nodded.

"So you see? We couldn't hack it together, not with all that weight on our backs. We couldn't make it, and we'd wind up gnawing on each other, just like we have ever since San Francisco."

She did not answer right away. "San Francisco was wonderful."

"Yes, it was."

"What will you do now?"

"I'm going into business," he said. "Remember the Meadows brothers? I told you about their offer."

"Oh, yes."

"Well, that's what this loot is for," he said, tapping the money on the table. "I paid very high interest on it."

"And what about Tad?"

"We have some talking to do," he said. "It'll be all right."

For the first time she noticed the way he sat, away from the back of the sofa and holding his right arm tightly against his side. "What's the matter with your arm?" she asked.

"It's my shoulder," he answered. "I can't play competitive tennis without a little medical help. Cortisone and novocaine. I began to feel it during that last set with Tad. The same old injury that screwed me up years ago. It's chronic, and there's nothing to be done about it now."

"So that's why you changed your game toward the end, the underhand serves and all that."

He nodded. "It went completely."

"And Sid thought you were just showing the boy up," she said. "He thought it was pretty crude. I didn't know enough about it to know. Are you okay?"

"I will be," he said. "Anyway, I've got some pills for it if it gets really bad."

She did not know what else to say to him. A killing silence filled the space and built a wall between them. Finally she forced a smile and said, "Well, I'll go now. Can I kiss you?"

He stood up, and this time he kissed her back. They held each other close, and then quickly, without another word or a backward glance, she ran out of the room and down the stairs. He waited until he could hear nothing, then he went into the bathroom for his codeine tablets. After swallowing two of them, he lay down on his bed and waited for the pain to ease.

37

After the fiasco with Jay R. Pomerantz, Charlie didn't think he could fall any lower, but he did. Ellie Hoad, Melvin Schwartz' process server, came up with another outfit, this one called Urban Investments. Without consulting Mel, Charlie allowed Hoad to set up an appointment for him and showed up there one afternoon. By this time Charlie figured he had nothing left to lose and was prepared to play the string out all the way. Even the poker game had turned sour on him, and he was down to his last fifteen hundred dollars, so, he reasoned, what did he have to lose?

Urban Investments, it turned out, operated out of a shabby-looking old building on Hollywood Boulevard that also housed an adult bookstore and movie theater screening eight-millimeter pornographic films. Charlie couldn't figure out whether this setup was part of the overall Urban operation, but he didn't really care either.

The two young but shifty-eyed smooth talkers who ushered him into an inner office, furnished exclusively in plastic and Naugehyde, were eager to help Charlie make his picture, even though they were not exactly in the business of producing. They offered, in effect, to co-sign a loan. They had money in a Swiss bank, they explained, and they'd give Charlie a letter guaranteeing to pay back any loan Charlie could negotiate from a bank or elsewhere. All they asked was that

Charlie deposit with them in escrow, as their fee, ten percent of whatever he managed to raise and two percent of his production budget immediately, "just to show your good faith." Charlie got up, shook their hands, thanked them, and said he would get back to them.

"It's a bunco racket," Mel immediately pointed out when Charlie clued him in. "Nobody in his right mind would lend money under such conditions."

"Why not?"

"Because, Charlie, these guys don't pledge to return the good-faith deposit, and you stand to lose up to ten grand, which you don't have and would have to raise through a personal loan yourself," Mel pointed out. "What are you? Crazy?"

Incredibly, Charlie actually heard himself arguing the possible merits of the arrangement with Mel, who stalled him long enough to check into Urban Investments. By the time he called Charlie back three days later, Mel was able to inform his client that Urban Investments didn't exist. The offices Charlie had visited had been rented for a month from the owner of the adult bookstore, who told Mel that the two men had represented themselves as movie producers and theater owners from Minneapolis who had come to Hollywood to look into a number of investment opportunities. They had skipped the day after Charlie's meeting with them.

The one mildly hopeful development during the first half of September came when Charlie wandered into the Century City office of a Chicago firm called Towers Financial Corporation and submitted his script to the executive manning the premises, Mervyn Friedman, an Old Hollywood dinosaur who had once directed musicals for Paramount and MGM. Friedman liked the script and told Charlie he was prepared to recommend to his home office that it finance the picture up to a total of eight hundred thousand dollars.

The only trouble with this arrangement, Mel was quick to point out, was that Towers didn't really finance movies. "What they do is provide interim financing," Mel explained, "which is a fancy way of saying that they'll lend you the money provided you can get somebody else to guarantee it by putting up a completion bond, as well as a firm agreement to buy the loan plus interest either eighteen months after theatrical release or thirty months from the first day of shooting, whichever comes first. You follow me, Charlie?"

"I follow you."

"And the interest they charge is high, like fourteen percent compounded monthly, and with all sorts of other little gouges that will actually get the rate up to around eighteen or twenty," Mel continued. "It's not a good deal, Charlie. It's mostly bullshit."

"Mel, at least it means I can go back to some people who've said no with something in hand," Charlie argued. "Right?"

"Right," Mel agreed, "if you like the feel of turds."

Charlie got back on the phone the rest of that week, but got nowhere. Then, one morning, Mickey Kramer called. "Charlie," he said, "I'm sorry it took me so long to get back to you. But I suppose Judy told you I've been away."

"Yes, she did, Mickey," Charlie said. "Only, she didn't say you'd be gone this long. And the day I saw you at the Racquet Club, you didn't say anything, so I figured—"

"I know, I know," Mickey Kramer interrupted him. "I was here two days, then had to go back up north. The deal I'm in up there turned out to be a lot more complicated than I thought. I've had a hassle with the Coastal Commission and all these environmental groups that don't want developments up there, you know how it is."

"Yeah, I guess I do, Mickey," Charlie said.

"Anyway, listen, I've been thinking about the deal," Mickey Kramer said, "and I think we can do it."

"No kidding, Mickey? That's great!"

"What I mean is, I think I know a way to do this," Mickey explained. "There's one condition."

"What's that?"

"Would you have any objection to taking on a black partner, or maybe a Chicano?" Mickey asked.

"No, of course not."

"Good. Meet me at the Malibu Pharmacy for a cup of coffee in twenty minutes and we'll talk," Mickey instructed him. "I've got to pick up some stuff for Judy, and I can lay the whole thing out for you in twenty minutes. Then, if you agree, we'll set up some meetings with you and your people and we'll get this project off the ground, okay?"

"Okay," Charlie said. "Twenty minutes."

Charlie tried not to allow himself too big a surge of hope after this conversation. After all, he'd been burned too many times this summer, and he tried not to let himself be swept away. He decided he would not even call Mel to tell him the possibly marvelous news until he'd heard exactly what Mickey Kramer had in mind. But still, it was hard not to feel at least a little optimism; Mickey Kramer was very rich, rich enough to finance the whole movie by himself if he wanted to. And what was he risking, anyway? Wasn't *Pale Moon Rising* a terrific project for somebody bright enough and innovative enough to see it? How could anyone lose money or entertain any serious doubts about the worth of the venture? Charlie asked himself reassuringly. Maybe the whole thing was going to come together for him, after all.

Mickey Kramer didn't waste much time enlightening Charlie. No sooner had the producer joined him in a small booth by the lunch counter than Mickey revealed what he meant by asking for the inclusion of a black or a Chicano into the deal. "The thing is, Charlie," he explained, "we can get some government help this way."

"I don't get it," Charlie said.

Mickey Kramer outlined the deal for him. By making *Pale Moon Rising* what Mickey called "a minority enterprise," the real-estate tycoon was positive he could pry funds loose from various federal and state programs designed to help the underprivileged. Of course, this would mean that Charlie would have to disappear into the background and allow some authentically ethnic type to figure as the picture's sole producer of record. "I know we can get a good deal of money by going this route," Mickey explained, "and maybe even most of it. How about it, Charlie?"

To Charlie's credit, it took him no more than a few seconds to make up his mind. "Mickey, I know this doesn't make much sense to you, as a businessman," he said. "I know you buy up land and develop it and your name isn't on anything that you do and that it isn't important to you either. But this is *my* movie, Mickey. This picture may never be made, but it'll always be *my* picture. And I'd rather it would never be made than give it away to somebody else to make." He fished into his pocket, dropped a dollar bill on the counter to pay for his coffee, and stood up, as Mickey Kramer stared at him, stunned by the force of his reaction. "And if you're really interested in helping blacks or Chicanos, Mickey, you don't do it by going down to Watts or the East L.A. barrio and waving a magic wand over somebody and making the guy a producer by virtue of some-

378

body else's sweat," Charlie continued. "If you really want to help ethnic minority groups, then help them to make their own movies, not mine." And he walked out of the pharmacy without waiting to hear anything else Mickey Kramer might wish to say to him on the subject.

Charlie did enjoy one good moment during the day. Later, after he'd told Mel about this conversation, his lawyer remained silent for a minute or two at the other end of the wire and then said, "You're a good man, Charlie Wigham. I'm proud to be your friend."

Two days after this meeting, Charlie was lying in bed idly leafing through *The Hollywood Reporter* when his attention was caught by a small ad. Some firm in Alabama was looking for a "dynamic person" who would move to Birmingham to "speak to large groups," as well as "direct/act in commercial films," all for a starting salary of four hundred dollars a week. Charlie read this ad through several times, then flung the paper aside and got up to get himself a second cup of coffee. When he came back to bed, he read through the ad twice more, then reached for the phone. As if on cue, it rang. "Hello?"

"Charlie, this is Mickey Kramer."

"Hello, Mickey."

"Listen, I want you to know I've been thinking over what you said to me the other day."

"Oh?"

"Yeah. And I want to tell you, Charlie, it makes perfect sense."

"Really?"

"Yeah, you were absolutely right."

"It was nothing personal, Mickey . . ."

"I know that, but you were right," Mickey continued, "and I've done some thinking about it."

"Well, that's fine, Mickey."

"And I'm going to do something," Mickey Kramer said. "I'm getting some people together at my house next week, Charlie, and I want you to come."

"What for?"

"I'm going to start a company to finance just the kind of films you were talking about," Mickey explained. "I think you hit on a terrific idea, Charlie. I mean, helping these underprivileged people make their own movies. I've talked it over with Judy and she agrees with me that it's a terrific idea. And I'm not doing it for the money, I want you to know that. This is going to be a nonprofit operation. I'd like you to come, too, Charlie, because you can give us some terrific input, and after all, it was your suggestion, wasn't it? I think you should get some of the credit. I'll let you know when the first meeting is. Meanwhile, I'm already structuring the financing, and I've got a name for the production company—American Arts. What do you think of it?"

Charlie had no chance to tell Mickey Kramer what he thought of it, because Mickey was already moving too fast for him. Without waiting for Charlie's answer, Mickey told him his other phones were ringing and he had to go, but he sure was grateful to Charlie for opening up his eyes to what was really needed in the film business these days . . . .

Charlie remained in bed most of the rest of that day and the next. He did not answer the ad for a filmmaker in Alabama. In fact, he did not answer not only the ad, but also the phone and the mail, as well. Toward the end of the second day, he called Melvin Schwartz.

"Where the hell have you been, Charlie?" Mel shouted at him. "I've called you three times today. Don't you answer your phone anymore? Don't you check your goddamn service?"

"Don't yell at me, Mel," Charlie said wearily. "I've been down, real down, the last two days. I was just calling to tell you I'm about ready to quit. I need a job."

"And why do you think I've been trying to reach you?" Mel asked. "Because I love the sound of your mad voice? Listen, Bud Lavin's been trying to get hold of you."

"What about?"

"The new Dan Gregory series, *Cain's Country*," the lawyer explained. "They're in big trouble with it. They're way over budget and they're running late. They want to fire the producer, and Gregory insists he wants you. I think I can get you a nice contract, Charlie. How about it?"

"I'll call Bud," Charlie said. "But listen, Mel?"

"Yeah?"

"This doesn't mean I'm giving up on the picture, you understand? I need the money, so I'll listen to what Lavin has to say. We postpone *Pale Moon Rising*."

"Your option's got three more months to go, you know that."

"Renew it, Mel."

"With what? You're broke."

"With part of the five thousand you're going to get for me as an advance from Gemini, got it?"

Melvin Schwartz laughed. "You're all right, Charlie," he said. "You're a real Hollywood hustler, after all."

38

Janet Morgan came walking quickly up from her end of the long hospital corridor toward the nurses' station, where Ann Warren, a trim-looking middle-aged woman with carefully coiffed gray hair, presided over a small kingdom of desks, typewriters, filing cabinets, and telephones. Janet seemed preoccupied about something, but waited until Ann had concluded a telephone conversation before inquiring after Dr. Ferrero's chart book and the order sheet for his patient, Evan Gilbert. "They must be there," Ann said, indicating the stack of clipboards and documents at one end of the counter. "What is it?"

"The same room. Don't they know?" Janet Morgan said, beginning her search. "They must know."

"What, Janet?"

"Why we stick all our terminal patients down at the end of that corridor. You'd think they'd know by now."

Marie, the young black girl on duty at the other end of the floor, came around the end of the counter in time to overhear this remark. "Honey, a hospital is no place to die," she said. "We stick 'em down at that end 'cause we got people in here we can cure, maybe. The dying, baby—they just clutter up the place."

"That will do, Marie," Ann said sharply. "Someone could hear you."

"Let 'em," Marie said, moving on. "Everybody knows anyway."

"The relatives don't know any such thing."

"It's horrible," Janet said.

"Don't let Marie upset you," Ann told her. "She has a wicked tongue, that one."

Janet found the chart for Evan Gilbert and glanced down the order sheet. "That's what I thought," she said. "This can't be right."

"What is it?" Ann asked.

Janet showed her the order sheet. "The dosage of amytal prescribed for this patient," she said. "Is that the right number?"

"With some of these doctors, you can't tell what they want," Ann Warren said, looking at the order. "That Dr. Wheeler, for instance—spider tracks. . . . Yes, this looks right, Janet."

"But that's a lethal dose, Mrs. Warren!"

Ann Warren seemed unmoved. "Ordinarily," she said, "but it depends on the patient."

"Shouldn't we call Dr. Ferrero?"

"I wouldn't. He'll be in very soon."

"But it's on the order sheet," Janet insisted. "Somebody else might handle it. I mean, mistakes do get made, don't they?"

"Yes, occasionally," the older woman admitted. "But I wouldn't worry about it now, Janet. Doctor usually handles this sort of thing himself."

Janet Morgan seemed undecided, but allowed herself to be convinced. After all, it was only her third week in the hospital, and it was her first job since graduating from nursing school. Who was she to question a doctor's judgment? Without another word she returned to her duties, while Ann Warren gazed thoughtfully after her, then picked up the phone to call Victor's house. But he had already left.

About half an hour later, Victor drove into the doctors' parking lot at Albert Mercer Memorial, parked, and walked quickly toward the hospital entrance. As he turned the corner, he noticed a small panel truck bearing the legend "Dateline News," but thought nothing of it.

The receptionist, a handsome woman in her thirties, looked up as

384

Victor passed her, heading for the elevators. She obviously liked him and smiled brightly. "Dr. Ferrero!" she said. "Hello, there! Sure is nice—"

But Victor ignored her. As soon as the first elevator arrived, he walked in and the door closed noiselessly on him. The receptionist seemed stunned by this unaccustomed rudeness. Victor Ferrero had a reputation in the hospital for being the kindest and cheeriest of men.

When Victor appeared on the third floor, Ann Warren happened to be alone at her station. She was obviously relieved to see him. "Good evening, doctor," she said, smiling. "Hello, Ann," Victor said, coming around behind the counter toward the stack of charts. "What's going on?"

"It's been quiet, actually."

Victor shuffled through his charts. "What we need to stimulate a little action around her is a good medieval plague. Cordoza come in?"

"Yes, sir. He's in intensive care."

"Nothing new since this morning? '

"No. He seems to be breathing a bit easier."

"Good. Now, on Gilbert . . ." Victor began, his eye caught by something on the patient's chart.

"Yes, sir?"

"I thought I specified 'No Code Blue,' " Victor said. "It should have been written on the order sheet."

Ann stood up and peered over his shoulder. "It wasn't?"

"I can't find it."

"Did you forget, doctor?"

"I must have," Victor answered, clearly annoyed. He scribbled on the pad. "Jesus, that's all I need, for some dim-witted nurse's aide to blunder in there, find my patient unconscious, and summon Dr. Kildare to revive him. Who's on call here tonight?"

"Dr. Goldstein."

"Okay. Now, on the medication—"

"Dr. Ferrero, we have a new girl on this floor," Ann Warren started to tell him. "She—"

But Victor was too absorbed in his own concerns and his charts to note Ann's mildly worried tone. He concentrated on his papers, absorbed in the minutiae of the scene he and Ann Warren had played

385

together so many times before, the real substance of their dialogue intelligible only to them, implicit beneath the banal, routine surface of their conversation. "'I know the patient well,'" he muttered to himself as he continued to scribble on Evan Gilbert's chart, "'and this is the dosage of medication he needs for comfort.' There."

"You'll have to stop by the pharmacy yourself, doctor," Ann told him quickly.

"Clayton again?"

Ann nodded. "Doctor—"

"That cautious bastard. Oh, well . . ." Victor finished writing and dropped the chart book back on the counter. "I'll look in on Cordoza first," he said, hurrying off once more toward the elevators.

Ann Warren again opened her mouth to speak, wondering whether she should tell him not only about the new girl but also about the interviewing team from that television station, but the doctor moved too fast for her. Before she could quite make up her mind, he was gone.

Downstairs, in the hospital cafeteria, Janet Morgan, her clean, pretty little mouth still full of apple pie, found herself staring incredulously at her new friend, Marie. She could not believe what this tall, handsome black girl with the caustic tongue and cynical eyes had just told her. Janet swallowed with difficulty and tried hard to make sense of it, but couldn't. "You mean some doctors actually leave orders knowing all the time they're not going to be carried out?"

Marie laughed. "You didn't know that?"

"No."

"What do they teach you in those nursing schools, anyway?"

"But why?"

"Honey, they got to get it all down in writing, you dig?" Marie explained.

"When I saw what he'd prescribed," Janet said, "I was sure he'd made a mistake."

Before continuing, Marie stole a quick look around the room, but satisfied herself they were out of anyone's earshot; the two women were alone at a corner table, and at this hour of the night, the cafeteria was nearly empty. "Look, they make mistakes, too," the black girl said. "Hell, an extra zero and you've killed somebody. Happens quite a lot. But the worst of it, honey, is when some of these patients *don't* die. When I used to work in the intensive-care unit, I'd get so depressed I'd go home sometimes and take it out on my family. Luke and I would fight and scream at each other. I cried all the time. I couldn't take it, so I got out of that."

"I always dreamed of being a nurse," Janet said, feeling her world beginning to crumble around her, "ever since I can remember."

"That's sweet," Marie said. "Me, I went into it because it was good money. Better than working as a waitress or a maid somewhere. You understand?"

"Yes. I'm sorry. We didn't have many blacks where I grew up, in Minnesota."

"Sorry? For what? I got no complaints," Marie said with a shrug. "I figure nobody owes me anything. I do my job, I get paid. That's it."

"I know I sound like some kind of idiot . . ."

"No, you don't, honey," Marie assured her. "You'll toughen up. You see enough patients trached or put on the respirator or hooked up to a transducer, a lot of tubes plugged into them just to keep 'em alive a little longer, you'll catch on. Anyway, you just do your job and you'll be all right."

"But if the doctor's made a mistake?"

"You catch the big ones and you forget about the little ones. Anyway, honey, what's wrong for one patient could be right for another, see?"

Janet seemed unconvinced. "Well . . . sure, but . . . I mean, I just can't get over the way we treat some of these patients," she tried to explain. "The obviously terminal ones . . ."

"You know what? When one of my patients was comatose or dying, it was a relief," the black girl said. "I used to fight with some of my doctors so they wouldn't prescribe a lot of unnecessary stuff or order all those treatments, just so they could turn around and tell the relatives later, 'See? We did this and we did that, we did everything we could.' Just to cover themselves. They'd call a Code Blue on some patient in my unit who wasn't going to make it anyway, we'd all *walk*. You know what I mean? We'd *walk* real slow, hoping we'd find that patient gone when we got there. Of course, in intensive care it's pretty hard to let them go. That kind of patient is better off in a regular ward."

"Like Mr. Gilbert, is that what you mean?" Janet asked.

"You're catching on."

Janet did not answer right away, but sipped her coffee, then glanced sharply up at Marie. "Then you don't think Dr. Ferrero made a mistake, do you?"

Marie abruptly stood up and began to stack dishes on her tray. "Honey, I don't answer that kind of question," she said. "You got to figure all that out for yourself. But I'll tell you one thing—Dr. Ferrero is a fine doctor, the best neurosurgeon we've got in this whole town, maybe. And a lot of people around here feel the way he does, but only about two percent have the guts he has." She headed for the exit, but delayed long enough to deliver a parting admonition. "You keep that in mind, honey, but don't tire yourself out thinking too much about it, know what I mean?"

For several minutes after Marie had gone, Janet remained in her seat, her head full of troubled, conflicting thoughts.

David Clayton, the pharmacist on duty, didn't want any trouble. He was a tall, thin, balding young man with mild brown eyes magnified by thick eyeglasses. "Look, Dr. Ferrero . . ." he protested.

"Dave, are you questioning my judgment!" Victor snapped. "Do you think you're qualified to do that?"

"This is twice the normal dose, Dr. Ferrero," Clayton insisted.

"So?"

"So I believe it may be lethal."

"And what would you consider normal, Dave?"

The pharmacist's puffy cheeks flushed with anger. What right did this guy have to push him around like this? "I'd consider five hundred milligrams a normal dose, Dr. Ferrero," he said. "This order is for a thousand. At the very least, we're in a twilight zone here."

"Jesus Christ, Dave—"

"Dr. Ferrero, I could have called the chief of medicine," the pharmacist said pointedly. "I waited for you."

This answer effectively disarmed Victor, who knew he had been unnecessarily rough on the man; he couldn't afford to push him any more. Even so, it was hard to have to play these time-consuming charades, in which all the players had to pretend innocence. There had to be a limit somewhere, Victor felt, and today he had come close to cracking it. But now, confronted by the reality of the alternative, he retreated. "I know, Dave," he said quietly, "you're on a spot here."

"Dr. Ferrero," David Clayton said, "I've been up before the Mortality Committee twice in the past four months. This is a lot of amytal for anyone."

Victor nodded glumly and began to play by the rules, spinnng, bobbing, and weaving as he danced. "Dave, I have a patient who is suffering and who needs sleep," he intoned. "He's become relatively immune. I know his metabolism. And I'm telling you that this is the dose of medication he needs for comfort." He paused, as if to take a little bow. "All right, Dave?"

The two men stared at each other, but Victor's composure held; too much depended on it, on this terrible need to play the game, however insane, by the rules. Finally the pharmacist nodded, again checked the order sheet Victor had handed him earlier, then turned and went to a shelf, where he began carefully scanning a long row of labeled bottles. Victor waited, never breaking character, his inner eye concentrated on the larger issue of the man dying alone in his room at the end of the third-floor corridor.

When Janet Morgan finally left the cafeteria after her dinner break, she was still upset over what Marie had told her and the conclusions she herself had begun to draw from the day's events. Lost in thought, she failed to notice the television news team coming around the corner and bumped head-on into Gail Hessian. "Oh, I'm so sorry!"

"It's okay," Gail said, smiling brightly. She was wearing a smart-looking pantsuit and Pan-Cake makeup. With her was a man with a small movie camera mounted on his shoulder and another one carrying bulky recording equipment. "We were looking for the cafeteria," Gail said.

"Oh, it's that way," Janet told her, indicating the far end of the floor, "through those swinging doors."

"Thanks," Gail said, as Janet, smiling weakly, now skirted the team on her way to the elevator.

"Hey, Gail, if we get hurt on this story," the sound man said, "at least we're in the right place."

"Boy, you could easily get lost in a hospital this size," the cameraman said. "I'll bet they misplace a lot of bodies in this joint."

"Come on, guys," Gail exhorted them as she led the way toward the cafeteria, "I'm starving. We'll grab a quick bite and see if we can wrap this up tonight."

Victor entered Evan Gilbert's room and paused just inside the door. This was not a visit he wanted to make. From where he stood he could look at Evan lying in bed, the I.V. bag in place and dripping life into his emaciated arm. The lower part of Gilbert's body lay motionless, but the rest of him seemed to be in constant movement. His hands twitched convulsively, and from time to time he would moan or make other unintelligible sounds. Though heavily sedated, it was clear to Victor that Evan was still in pain and in that less-than-human condition characteristic of people undergoing a long, drawn-out terminal illness.

Victor forced himself to approach the bed. As he did so, Evan's head moved and his eyes focused dimly on Victor, though the doctor couldn't be sure his old friend could actually consciously make out who he was. Evan's lips moved, but he was unable to speak. Victor took his hand and leaned down close to his face. "Evan . . ."

Barely audible, Evan's lips framed the single word, "Please . . ."

"Evan, it's all right," Victor said softly, "it's all right. You'll be asleep soon." And he moved quickly for the door.

Janet Morgan was alone at the nurses' station when Victor appeared from the end of the corridor, and moving briskly, came around behind the counter. "Where's Mrs. Warren?" he asked.

"She's on a break, doctor," the nurse answered. "Shall I page her?"

"No, it's all right," Victor said. "This won't take a minute."

"Miss Jacobs is with a patient, and Marie—"

"It's okay," Victor insisted, "I don't need anyone."

He went to the sink behind the station and began to prepare the amytal solution he clearly intended to administer to his patient. It made Janet Morgan very nervous, but she tried her best to keep busy and ignore what he was doing. When the phone rang, she snatched it up on the first ring. "Third floor. . . . No. . . . No, I haven't seen him. . . . Yes, thank you." She hung up and turned to glance at Victor, who was still methodically absorbed in his preparations at the sink.

Before he could finish, however, the calm, metallic voice of the hospital intercom paging system interrupted him. "Dr. Ferrero, stat five-oh-two," it called. "Dr. Ferrero, stat five-oh-two. Dr. Ferrero . . ."

Victor heard himself being paged and looked up. Moving quickly but not frantically, he placed the bottle containing the amytal solution on the shelf above the sink and walked briskly out toward the elevator bank. "Nurse!" he called out.

Janet Morgan jumped slightly. "Yes, doctor?"

"That's a Code Blue for me," Victor said. "Cordoza, my patient in five-oh-two. I've left the medication for Mr. Gilbert over the sink. I'll be back to give it to him myself. Don't let the I.V. nurse do it. Got that?"

"Yes, sir."

"And tell Mrs. Warren, when she gets back, where I am," he continued.

"Yes, sir."

He decided not to wait for an elevator, but headed now for the stairs. As he passed the elevators, the doors of one opened and disgorged Gail Hessian and her crew. Victor brushed past them. "Sorry," he said, and disappeared up the stairs.

"Everywhere we go," Gail said.

"Maybe an emergency," the cameraman said.

"I know that guy," Gail said, now approaching Janet Morgan. "What was that all about?"

"Oh, that was Dr. Ferrero," Janet said nervously. "One of his patients in intensive care. They just called a Code Blue."

"An emergency?"

Janet Morgan hesitated before answering. She seemed a bit confused, unaware, perhaps, of how much she was supposed to reveal concerning hospital procedures to these strangers.

"It's okay," Gail said. "I know Ferrero, from Malibu. We're from *Dateline News*, you ever watch us?"

"Oh, yes."

"We're filming a special, and we've been cleared and everything," Gail explained. "They must have told you."

"I guess so," Janet said vaguely.

"We want to do a short segment about nurses," Gail continued, "sort of a typical working day around a hospital, that kind of thing. You can be as general as you like. You mind if we hang around, ask a few questions?" Without waiting for the girl's answer, Gail turned to her crew. "Ed, why don't we get some footage on this area? It's a pretty typical ward."

"Right," the cameraman agreed as he and the sound man now began to set up.

Gail turned back to the nurse. "Has it been an unusually quiet time, would you say, or a very busy one for you around here?"

"Well, sort of normal, I guess," Janet Morgan answered. "Look, I'm very new here—"

"Good," Gail told her. "I haven't talked to anybody new on the job. You just go ahead and do whatever you have to do. I'll hang around and ask the questions, okay?" Without waiting for the nurse's consent, Gail suddenly thrust the mike of her tape recorder into the girl's face. "Okay, now, your name is . . . ?"

Suddenly conscious of the camera and the recording equipment, Janet Morgan stiffened. "Janet Morgan. Look, I—"

"Tell us a bit about yourself, Janet," Gail suggested. "Is this your first day on the job?"

"Oh, no. This is my third week."

"And why did you go into nursing?"

"I . . . I wanted to help," Janet Morgan said, staring with fascination now into the eye of the camera. "I guess I've always wanted to be a nurse. . . ."

It was nearly midnight when Victor got back to the third floor from his long struggle to save the life of his patient in the fifth-floor intensive-care unit. He looked exhausted to Ann Warren, who was alone at her desk and had been typing a report. Victor nodded to her and went straight to the sink where he had left the medication for Evan Gilbert. He washed and dried his hands, then rubbed his eyes. He made a visible effort to pull himself together, then retrieved the bottle of amytal solution and turned back toward Ann. "Ann, did you call my wife?" he asked.

"Yes, sir," the nurse said. "She said she was going over to Mrs. Gilbert's house later."

"Good. How is Mr. Gilbert?"

"He's in some pain. I told him you'd be in soon, but I'm not sure he understood me."

"Yes, I'm going to see him now," Victor said.

Ordinarily Ann Warren would have let him go, but tonight she seemed anxious to detain him, though, in his fatigue, he failed to notice. "How is Mr. Cordoza?" she asked.

"It was bad, Ann," he said, "but I think we pulled him through."

Again he started to head toward Gilbert's room, but she came out from behind the counter and took a few steps after him. "Dr. Ferrero . . ." she began.

Puzzled, he looked at her. "Yes?"

"You're very tired," the nurse said. "I can take care of Mr. Gilbert. Why don't you go home?"

Victor stared uncomprehendingly at her. "Ann, it's all right, really," he assured her. "No problem."

"You've had some calls," she tried to explain. "What I mean, Dr. Ferrero—we have a TV crew in here, and—"

Gail Hessian, who had apparently been waiting for him in a small lounge around the corner, now appeared. She was alone this time, but evidently eager to talk to him. "Oh, Dr. Ferrero," she called out, "I've been waiting for you. Remember me? Gail Hessian, *Dateline News*. We met a few weeks ago, in Malibu."

"Yes?"

"I wanted to speak to you about your patient Evan Gilbert," she said. "He's here, I was told."

Amazed, Victor stared at Ann. He started to speak, but seemed unable to.

"They interviewed Janet," the nurse began. "I don't know what she told them."

Gail was fiddling now with the dials on her portable tape recorder, which she had slung around her neck. "I'd just like some statement from you about his condition," she said, "I understand he's on the critical list. When Miss Morgan told me, I telephoned the story in to the station, and we've already carried it on the eleven-o'clock news. I'm just doing a follow-up."

"Miss Morgan told you . . ." Victor muttered. "Told you . . ."

"I really just sort of found out by accident," Gail explained, "and they asked me to stay on and get a statement from you. You do remember me, I hope? Gail Hessian. We've been doing this special on the hospital and sort of lucked into this one—"

"I'm sorry," Victor snapped, "I have no statements to make about any of my patients."

Gail ignored him and thrust the mike into his face. "Well, I understand you're also an old friend of Mr. Gilbert's."

"That's right," Victor answered. "Now, if you'll excuse me . . ."

He attempted to brush past her, but, still holding her mike out in front of her like a dagger, she followed him. "Dr. Ferrero, Evan Gilbert is a famous man," she said. "You can't expect his illness not to be reported. It's news."

"I don't discuss my patients with the press," Victor said, turning to prevent her, if he could, from following him. "Now, please, Miss Hessian . . ." He again pushed the mike away from his face.

"But, Dr. Ferrero, it's already been on the air," Gail explained. "The papers will pick it up, so will the other news programs. Haven't you been contacted already?"

"No," Victor answered, staring past Gail toward Ann Warren, who was gazing at him in alarm.

"Doctor, there were two calls for you," the nurse said. "Channel Two news, and also one from the *Times*."

"Dr. Ferrero, Miss Morgan seemed very upset," Gail Hessian stated. "She said Mr. Gilbert was very ill and being very heavily sedated. Do you have any comment to make on that?"

Victor could not answer. Stunned by the enormity of what had occurred in his absence, he could only look at Ann, who was also now visibly upset. Finally he again confronted the anchor woman. "Miss . . . ?"

"Hessian, Gail Hessian. I'm sorry this comes as a surprise, and I know it's very late . . ."

"Never mind, Miss Hessian," Victor said. "If you'll leave your tape recorder with Mrs. Warren here and take no notes, I'll give you a statement. Off the record."

"Well, I don't know . . ." Gail began to protest.

"It's the only condition under which I'll talk to you," he said. "I have to protect my patients. I don't have Mr. Gilbert's permission to talk to you."

Gail hesitated, then yielded. "Well, all right," she conceded. She took the tape machine from around her shoulder and set it down on the end of the counter beside Ann Warren.

Without another word, Victor led Gail down the corridor to Evan Gilbert's room. He opened the door and ushered her inside. What she found in there pinned her against the wall, near the door. Victor quietly and efficiently checked his patient's condition, then turned back to the reporter. "As you can tell, I'm sure, Mr. Gilbert himself cannot give an interview," he said, opening the door and ushering her now out of the room. "This way, please . . ."

Victor led her now to the small waiting room around the corner from the nurses' station, where Gail had waited for him. Luckily, it was empty. Gail sank into a chair and pressed a handkerchief to her nose and mouth, fighting the wave of nausea that had engulfed her.

394

She was pale and sweating slightly. Victor ignored her distress. He lit a cigarette, then went to the only window in the room, from where he could stare out into the night. When he spoke, his voice was soft, matter-of-fact, devoid of cruelty or malice.

"You use X-ray therapy at first, and it helps, for a while," he said. "Then, because of the therapy, the patient begins passing blood in his urine. He develops severe colitis, which means that he has to move his bowels about once an hour. The disease itself also cuts off sexual function. That comes before you lose the ability to walk. Eventually, you lose all control of your bladder and bowel functions, but by then, of course, you can't get around at all." He paused long enough to glance back at her. "Can you imagine, Miss Hessian, what it is like for a human being with any pride in himself to lose all control of his bladder?"

Gail started to rise, but he stopped her. "Please, I haven't finished," he said. "do you know what a mass reflex is?"

The reporter shook her head helplessly.

"You go into a tremendous spasm," Victor explained in the same calm, detached voice. "Your legs draw up and you defecate and urinate all at the same time. It can be caused simply by striking any part of the patient's leg. It's another side effect of this disease. We try to prevent that and control it by using catheters and enemas."

Again he paused, but went on gazing at her, pinned in horror to her seat. "The odor that made you ill, Miss Hessian," he resumed, "was caused by something else. All patients who have been bedridden for a month and a half or more and can't move by themselves develop decubitus ulcers. Their bones quite literally wear through their skin. It leaves a big open hole and it stinks like hell. Nothing a Kenneth Galbraith or an Evan Gilbert would tolerate, you see."

Gail stared up at him, the handkerchief still clutched to her mouth. "I'm sorry," Victor said. "We spend a great deal of time in my profession hiding the truth from people. Since you profess to be in the business of telling the truth, regardless of any possible consequence, I thought you ought to hear it, at least my version of it."

Victor now savagely stubbed the butt of his cigarette out on the windowsill, then flung it into the wastebasket. Gail managed to get to her feet. "It's not your fault," Victor told her, "but you know now what's happened here, don't you?"

Without answering him, Gail got as far as the door, but he

395

reached out, took her arm, and pulled her back to face him. His control was badly off now, and he had begun to shake, but he was determined to finish what he had to tell her. It was the only release he could now permit himself. "What did you think death was like, Miss Hessian? The way it's portrayed on your TV screen between commercials? With the victim either lying there out of close-up range or with the patient snuggled down between clean white sheets, looking pale but beautiful, surrounded by loved ones and waited on hand and foot by cheerful, handsome young doctors and nurses in crisp starched uniforms, and always time for a graceful deathbed speech? Evan Gilbert wants to die, Miss Hessian, and now he'll go on living, if that's what you call it, for another two or three or maybe four days, maybe for as long as we can keep him breathing."

Gail finally broke away from him and ran out into the corridor. He made no attempt to follow her. Drained of every emotion now but grief, he leaned against the wall of the waiting room and wept.

Dorothy was with Jennifer when the call came from the hospital, sometime after midnight. The two women had been waiting for it, and Dorothy had expected to answer it, but at the first ring Jennifer jumped to her feet and ran for the phone. She listened in silence for a few moments, then turned, ashen-faced, toward the other woman. When Dorothy took the receiver from her, Jennifer ran out of the room.

It was Victor at the other end of the line. "Dottie?"

"Yes. What's wrong?"

"Honey, stay with Jennifer tonight," Victor said. "Don't let her do anything rash, and try to keep her away from the hospital. I'm staying over here. I have to attend to Evan as best I can."

"Evan? Evan's . . . Victor, what's happened?"

"I can't tell you on the phone," he said. "I'm trying to help Evan any way I can. There's a news team in here, and Evan's presence has leaked out. All I can do now is make him as comfortable as I can, do you understand?"

"Yes," Dorothy answered, sick at heart.

"Stay with Jenny, sweetheart," Victor repeated. "I don't want to have to worry about her, too."

After she hung up, Dorothy called out for Jennifer, but got no answer. She looked for her through the house and found her upstairs. She was getting dressed, and Evan's .38-caliber revolver was lying on the bed beside her nightgown. "No, Jenny, you can't," Dorothy said.

Wide-eyed with terror, the younger woman stared at her. "It's up to me now," she said.

"No. No, it isn't, Jenny." Dorothy walked over to her and took her in her arms. She held her closely, providing as much comfort as she could, until at last the younger woman's despair settled itself into grief, which at least was a more familiar emotion and an easier one to cope with.

39

The last Wednesday in September began badly for Jim Wharton with the appearance on the front page of the Los Angeles *Times* of a long story by one Bruce Johnson, a Sacramento journalist, concerning the odd history and goings-on at Rancho El Mirador. A lot of the material in the story was old stuff rehashed by the reporter to make it seem new, but one aspect of the piece disturbed Jim. It linked Morton Lewis, the attorney general of California, to a petty hood named Pinky Baldo, whose decomposed body had been found only three days earlier in the middle of the Nevada desert, about twenty miles south of Lake Mead. Baldo had been shot three times through the back of the head and left to rot in the open. He had last been seen alive at the Las Vegas airport, where he had been met by two unidentified men and driven away, presumably to his death.

Baldo had been well-known to a number of law-enforcement agencies, both local and federal. Public testimony before a 1970 Chicago grand jury investigating links between horse racing and organized crime had described Baldo as a part-time bookie and, more importantly, as a bag man specializing in carrying skimmed funds from Las Vegas casinos to Chicago companies with interests in various sporting ventures and real-estate developments all over the country, including the corporation set up to finance and build Rancho El Mirador.

In 1974 Baldo had been a guest at Rancho El Mirador at the same time that Morton Lewis had stayed there. He and Lewis had also reportedly been seen in Las Vegas together on several occasions. In 1976 a California investigation into Baldo's Los Angeles interests, including alleged secret stock acquisitions in Hollywood Park racetrack on behalf of parties unknown, had been vigorously opposed by Morton Lewis' office, and it had also been common knowledge that Baldo, through several fronts and aliases, had lent Morton Lewis money. In 1977 Lewis' office had again attempted to put off or kill another series of hearings in which Baldo was to have been asked to testify concerning his activities in California.

Lewis' office had not come out openly in Baldo's behalf, but had only backed off from opposing the hearings when the attorney general's own investigators had threatened to inform the press of his reluctance to support actions against the reputed hood. Baldo had never appeared at these hearings, and no firm links between him and California interests had been proven, but the circumstantial evidence was certainly significant, the article pointed out, and worthy of further probing.

No sooner had he read the piece than Jim Wharton attempted to contact the attorney general's office, but without success. When the whole morning passed and his own phone had failed to ring, Jim decided he would have to go to Chicago. Something had gone wrong, he knew, but he couldn't figure out exactly what, and this troubled him. Jim Wharton was used to being on top of events, not at their mercy. He telephoned Chicago, could find no one he knew, but left a message that he would be coming in shortly for a meeting.

He sat at his desk for over an hour after lunch, trying to think the matter through, but none of it added up satisfactorily in his head. He did not like the silence out of Chicago, and he asked himself whether, somewhere along the line, he had miscalculated. He tried to imagine how these recent events were being interpreted back there. Would they blame him? No, how could they? The advice he'd been giving from the beginning on Rancho El Mirador had been absolutely correct, and they had ignored it, at heavy cost. Could they have interpreted his advice as too cautious, especially in regard to the recurrent outbursts of bad publicity from down there? He didn't see how. He had yet to be proven wrong. Caution was not to be confused with softness; surely they could see that. Well, the old hands in Chicago would see it and approve. It was these new men, the faceless computerized men like Kerrigan, whom Jim couldn't quite read. They were the source of his present uneasiness. Yes, he would have to be more careful still with the Kerrigans and cover himself better with them. His contempt for Kerrigan might have been too obvious to the younger man, and that could conceivably make him dangerous. After all, Kerrigan was on the spot, while Jim was outside the mainstream of decision-making. That, too, was a factor he could never lose sight of, and one that had to be taken into careful consideration.

One thing Jim knew with absolute certainty, and that was that somebody somewhere had fed this damn reporter a crucial piece of information—the stuff about Lewis—but who? Certainly not anyone in Chicago or Las Vegas. As for Baldo, who had killed him? Lewis' people, perhaps? The attorney general would undoubtedly have wanted Baldo eliminated, but he couldn't have engineered the job himself, not with Wharton's group holding such compromising photographs as evidence of the Baldo-Lewis linkage. No, Jim knew there were other forces at work here. Clearly, most of the reporter's information had come from Pete Hester and maybe one or two others involved in past investigations of Rancho El Mirador. But the question of Baldo was important, perhaps pivotal. Could the man's death be entirely unconnected to Rancho El Mirador and the continuing brouhaha down there? Most probably. Pinky Baldo had always had his sticky fingers in a lot of juicy pies, and he could have pulled out too big a plum for himself.

But what was going on back in Chicago? The situation there and his inability to break the barrier of silence had made Jim increasingly uncomfortable. What had Dudley Kerrigan told his people back there after their last meeting? Obviously, the only thing to do was to go and find out.

Jim called Donna Smith into his office. The woman, tall and looking trimly severe, as ever, shut the door behind her as she entered. "Donna, book me into Chicago, will you?"

"When? Tonight?"

"Yeah." The woman turned to leave, but Jim had a second impulse. "Wait a minute."

"Yes, sir."

"Book me out in the morning, the first available flight. I don't care what airline. And wire Mr. Kerrigan my exact arrival time, please."

"Yes, sir. Anything else?"

"No. But no more calls today. I'm leaving in a few minutes."

"Miss Hessian called while you were on the phone," the woman said. "Shall I cancel your afternoon appointment?"

"No. Did she say what she wanted?"

"No."

"Okay. Thanks."

Donna Smith, who had been with Jim Wharton for ten years and was the highest-paid private secretary in town, left the room quickly and quietly, making sure to close the door firmly behind her, as always. Donna Smith knew nothing about Jim Wharton; she only executed orders, and she asked no questions. She had a brother in Chicago who had killed an off-duty cop in a barroom brawl and whom Jim had managed to get released after doing only two and a half years, and she was fanatically loyal to the lawyer. She was perfect, absolutely perfect.

Jim waited a moment, then picked up his private line and dialed Gail at home. She had taken the day off, he knew, ostensibly to read through the first draft of Williams' manuscript. "Gail?"

"Oh, Jim," she said. "I tried to reach you."

"I know. I'm seeing you, aren't I?"

"I can't today."

"Yes, you can, Gail. I've been counting on it."

"Jim, I have so much to do."

"It can wait. I put off an urgent trip for you. I'll see you at two-thirty, as we planned."

"But, Jim—"

"Gail, let me tell you what I want you to do. Are you listening?"

"Yes."

He could hear the tremor in her suddenly docile, servile tone, and it made him lustful for her. "You are to come to me naked, Gail," he said. "You are to shave yourself. Do you understand?"

"Yes, Jim."

"You can wear a coat and sandals to come to me, and that's all. Is that clear?"

"Yes."

"You will get there before me," he continued in a soft, hoarse voice. "You will strip, and you will kneel on the floor, facing the door. You will find a hood on the bed. Put it on and tie it around your neck. When I arrive, I want to find you prepared to receive me."

"Yes."

"Good." And he hung up. This would be the best session yet, he knew, the most rewarding, the most fulfilling for both of them. Thank God, he thought in passing, that Chicago knew nothing of his personal life. Or did they? No, impossible. He had been absolutely, scrupulously careful, always. In Chicago it would have been interpreted as a weakness, a possibly fatal flaw. They would not tolerate it. It would have made him too vulnerable in their eyes. Jim yawned, stretched, glanced at his watch, got up from his desk, and stepped into his adjoining private bathroom to clean up and get ready.

Late that afternoon, on his drive up the coast toward Malibu, Jim Wharton failed to notice that he was being followed at a safe distance, as he had been off and on for days now, by the two men in the blue Oldsmobile. By the time Jim reached the Malibu Canyon traffic light and coasted into the left-turn lane that would lead him back toward the Colony main gate, however, the blue Oldsmobile had dropped out of sight. It had parked on the highway, about a mile south of the Colony gate. Dressed in matching brown jogging suits that looked very new, the two men who had been in the car now made their way down toward the public beach, where the hardiest of the day's surfers were still challenging a choppy four-foot swell. When they reached the tideline, the joggers turned and began to trot slowly together on the hard sand up toward the southern tip of the Colony crescent, where the houses crowded together facing the ocean and the smog line of the horizon.

Mary Wharton was alone in the house when Jim walked in. She was sitting in the living room, with the blinds drawn, and obviously drunk. She called out to him, but he ignored her and went upstairs to shower and to change. He felt at peace with himself, the feel of

403

Gail's flesh still in his hands and the sound of her moans of pain and pleasure still in his ears.

When Jim came down, nearly an hour later, Mary was still sitting there, but seemed to be asleep. Her head rested against the back of her chair, and one arm dangled toward the floor. Jim headed for the kitchen for ice, but something in the way his wife looked, sitting there like that, so motionless and relaxed, suddenly struck him as peculiar. He turned back and poked his head into the room. "Mary?" he called out.

She did not answer or move. In the gloom he couldn't even be certain she was breathing, so he started toward her. "What the hell . . ."

The short, stocky man, who was wearing a brown jogging suit and a ski mask, stepped out from the corner behind the door and jammed a gun up into his ribs from the back. "Sit down," he whispered.

Jim immediately swung his right arm back and knocked the gun aside. He lunged for it, glimpsing now, even as he did so, the small bloodstain just above Mary's jawbone where the bullet had gone in. He reached the gun before his assailant did and grabbed it, but it was his last conscious act. The tall man, also in a brown jogging suit and wearing a mask, had risen from behind the sofa, taken dead aim, and pumped four shots into Jim Wharton's broad back. With a single rasping gasp the lawyer fell forward on his face and lay still. *Oh, Jesus Christ, they knew, one goddamn mistake . . .* Jim Wharton coughed up his life and lay still. The sound of his falling body had made more noise than the shots, which had been muffled by the long silencer clamped to the muzzle of the assassin's gun, a .25-calibre pistol of European make.

"You almost blew it," the tall man said.

"He's a big motherfucker," the short one answered.

"Okay, now we wait. Check the doors."

"I already done that."

"Okay, then help me clean up. And let's get these two over here, behind the sofa, just in case."

"You bring the cards?"

"Yeah, yeah, we'll play. We do this first, then we'll play. Only, no lights."

"I brought a flashlight."

"You're a fucking degenerate, you know that?"

"Yeah. Just because you can't beat me."

"Here, give me a hand now, and shut up."

They pulled the bodies of Jim and Mary Wharton over behind the sofa, from where they could not be seen by anyone entering the house. Julie was away, these men knew, and it was the maid's day off. But you could never be absolutely sure, and it was better not to take chances. These two men were very good at their profession. In fact, they were the best, and they were very expensive. They had never yet made a mistake, and they weren't about to make one now. They carefully cleaned up the room and scrubbed the carpet and the floor before they sat down in the darkened, windowless hallway to play cards. They played gin rummy in silence, for fifty cents a point.

40

"I've written to Tad," Art said. "I've tried to make him understand."

"I think he does," Laura answered. "He didn't for a while, but I think he does now. It was very hard for him, after what happened."

"Yeah, I know," Art said. "I didn't want to do it that way. I didn't want to make him look bad . . ."

"I know you didn't," she said. "He loves you, Arthur. He's always admired you. It seems strange that you had to hurt your own son so badly over something so trivial."

"It wasn't trivial," he objected, "not to me."

"You mean the money? You could have borrowed it."

"Maybe, maybe not," he said. "But more than the money, I guess I got tired of being used, of being nothing to anyone."

"Including yourself, Arthur?"

He nodded. "Yeah. I was somebody once. I liked the feeling. I was damn good, and I'd forgotten what it meant. I guess I'd lost my pride."

"Anyway, you know Tad, he's just like you," she said. "He has a lot of that stubborn pride of yours. It takes him so long to get over things. Thank God for Terry."

"Really? He's still seeing her?"

"Oh, yes. She's back in college now, but they write each other every day, I hear, and the phone calls . . ."

"I can imagine."

"I hope so, because you'll be getting the bills."

"Oh-oh."

"Next year they want to go to the same school, either Santa Cruz or maybe down to La Jolla," she said. "Anyway, she's a terrific girl. I'm so glad for them. Tad has a lot of crazy ideas, you know. He's a little like you. He lives for the big moment. He doesn't plan or look ahead. She's good for him that way. He's still thinking of going to medical school."

"I know."

"It will cost a lot of money, Arthur."

"I know that, too. Between us I guess we'll manage. You're doing okay, aren't you?"

She nodded. "Yes. And I love it. But it's not a lot of money. How are you going to get along without teaching?"

"It's going to be rough for a while," he admitted. "But I'm really high on this venture for the long run. I'm working six months in the store, you know, finding out what it's all about. After that, I'll take over the new sports line we're launching. It could be a big thing for me, and I have a one-third interest in it. It'll mean a lot of traveling, at first."

"You never minded that," she said. "I was the one who hated it. It'll be like old times for you."

"I don't know, Laura. Mainly, it's a good chance for me. It's something I want and I think I can do. You understand, don't you?"

"Yes. Just as I hope you understand about me."

"I guess, these past few years, understanding hasn't been my strong point," he said. "We . . . I guess I mean *I* drifted for a long time. It's easy to do, isn't it? Out in all that sunshine and the lazy, easy days . . ."

How strange it was to be sitting here, just the two of them, in this slick, impersonal, rather noisy restaurant on Wilshire, halfway between his downtown office and hers in Beverly Hills, conversing like old friends who hadn't seen each other for a long time. Their conversation had a chatty, intimate quality, very friendly but a little cautious, a little distant, as if too much of the past, especially the recent part of it, could not yet be safely exhumed; better to stick to older patterns, to remain within the conventions that bounded friendly chatter and limited the risks, maintained a little distance. Above all, it was important to be kind, to gloss over old hurts, to ignore the more serious wounds, to be, if nothing else, the most loving of old friends. Out of such an effort, the absence of grief and the reluctance to inflict pain could be, if not guaranteed, at least aimed for.

"Do you still want a divorce?" he asked her over coffee.

"I don't know," she said. "I have no plans right now to get remarried, do you?"

He laughed. "God, no! I never was the marrying kind."

"Do you hear from Lee?"

"She wrote me. I haven't answered."

"Are you going to?"

"Yes. I don't know what I'm going to say yet."

"Do you care for her?"

"Yes, I guess so. But she and Sid are sort of permanent. They're coming back here next summer."

"Really?" Laura asked, astonished.

"Yeah. They're looking for a house to buy. They want to live in Malibu, preferably in the Colony."

"Then you and Lee can see each other."

"No," he said, smiling. "I don't want that, and neither does she. And now that I'm living in town, it'll be easier for both of us. It's over, Laura. It was a big thing, but it's over. And Lee's a nice person. She really helped. I needed something, and she was there, for a while, at least. I'm only sorry it hurt you. I'll always be sorry about that, but I don't want to have to lie about what Lee meant to me, either. Are you seeing Alcorn?"

She nodded. "Yes. But it's not what you think."

"What do I think?"

"I mean, he *is* my boss, but that's not why I'm seeing him."

"Laura, I don't think anything about it. I mean, I'd never knock it just because he's your boss."

"You said something to Tad—"

"That's when I was angry," he explained. "I wanted to hurt. It didn't mean anything. You happy with this guy?"

"Yes. He's a nice man. We see each other now two or three times a week."

He accepted that and sipped his coffee slowly, before he said, "I suppose we should get a legal separation, don't you?"

"I suppose."

"There isn't much to discuss financially, except the house. What do you want to do about it?"

"If Tad goes on to medical school, we'll have to sell it," she said. "Till then I guess I'll go on living there. Is that okay with you?"

"Yeah, of course. Oh, about Alcorn . . ." But he did not quite know how to finish that sentence, so she had to finish it for him.

"He doesn't stay there with me," she said. "I stay with him in town. Tad knows all about it now."

He nodded slowly, then called for the check.

"We'll split it," she said, reaching for her purse.

"I was going to ask you," he said, "whether you'd ever want to see me again."

She looked up, surprised. "Are you asking me for a date, Arthur?"

He grinned. "Sounds funny, doesn't it? No, I guess I meant a dinner or lunch every now and then. Just to talk."

"Well, sure."

"I guess I should apologize, shouldn't I?"

"For what?"

"The failure of our marriage."

"It wasn't exactly a failure, was it?" she answered. "We have Tad to show for it."

"Yeah, you're right. And a lot of wonderful years. At least, I think they were wonderful."

"They were," she said. "They were fine."

As they walked together toward their cars in the underground parking level of the building, he was careful not to touch her, but he couldn't resist verbalizing the thought that had nagged at him for weeks. "I bet we'd have made it," he said, "if we hadn't moved to Malibu."

"What makes you think so, Arthur?"

"I don't know. Just a feeling I have. Everything is too easy in this town, and especially out there," he said. "You drift from day to day, without realizing what's missing or where you're going wrong, and suddenly one day you wake up and everything's changed and it's too late to do anything about it."

"That's not Malibu, that's just life," she said.

He shook his head. "I don't know. It's all so painless. Whatever you want, it's all there, and it's so easy to just accept and go along. Everything slips away without your being aware of it. It's here and it's gone. I look back over these last five years, and it seems like yesterday we got here, and now it doesn't mean anything. Nothing happened, no single bad thing I can remember, but somehow everything fell apart."

She turned to him to say good-bye, but did not touch him. "Call Tad, if he doesn't call you," she said. "I think he wants to hear from you."

"Yeah, I will. So long. We'll be in touch."

They got into their separate cars and drove out of the garage in single file, then in opposite directions, to their new careers and their new lives. The long Malibu summer was over for both of them.

VII

Winter Epilogue

Billie Farnsworth

It's been raining steadily now for nearly two months, and the hillsides, bare from the brushfires of last October, have been sliding away. Pacific Coast Highway is a mess and has been closed for weeks. First the mud flowed down in thick streams that pushed right through the sandbags people piled up in an effort to save their beach houses from being inundated; then the big boulders started coming down, banging across the highway and crashing into cars and buildings. Most of the time the road has been closed and people have had to take the long way around to get to and from work, through the canyons to the Valley, and then down the Ventura and San Diego freeways. Some people, like Laura Bonnell, have preferred to stay in town rather than travel this long route every day. Others, the ones with two cars, now park on on each side of the roughly mile-long stretch where the highway is closed, walk through, and drive away.

For those of us who don't have to go in and get out every day, it's been kind of fun, a real adventure. One of the joys of living in Malibu is this struggle with nature. Since I moved out here twenty years ago, we've been through four major brushfires, two earthquakes, three floods, and more earth and mud slides than I can count. Every time something happens, it seems to happen in Malibu. I have a friend back East who lives in New York, and whenever she reads or hears about what she describes as the annual Malibu winter carnival, she calls me up and asks me how I can go on living in such a barbarous, dangerous place. This from a woman who won't open her door without first looking through a peephole and who every day of her life has to cope with trash on the sidewalks, garbage in the streets, all kinds of strikes, and is afraid to take the subway even at midday. I tell her I'd rather have to cope with natural disasters, which at least are impersonal and involve the whole community, than the savagery of jungle survival in a big city like New York, which they ought to put a big barbed-wire fence around with watchtowers to keep the animals in.

There's a good side, too, to whatever happens in Malibu. When the highway is shut down, the whole area becomes a lot like it was when I first moved out here. With almost no cars on the road, the tempo of life becomes truly rural and delightful. People run and bicycle along the highways, everything slows down, and there's less noise and pollution. Kids ride their horses down to the beach again, and I like to think I can hear old Mrs. Rindge cackling with glee at night when the wind blows through the canyons and the rain comes beating down. I like to think of the fires and the winter storms as Mrs. Rindge's revenge for the rape of the old Rancho Malibu that she fought so long and so hard to prevent.

The colony has never been too much affected by Malibu's natural disasters. The brushfires don't reach the Colony gate, the big houses on the sand don't shake much during the earthquakes, and the floods and slides pass it by. This year, however, has been an exception. The heavy rains have come up from the south, from a huge trough of low pressure created by a clash of northern cold air with tropical storms boiling up from the Mexican coast, and with the freak weather came the huge tides that undermined the Carey house and a few of the other older Colony mansions resting on the flat ground instead of on pilings, like the newer ones. Most of the beach down at our end has been washed away, and for three nights the waves pounded against my back windows, which luckily held. The whole rear end of the Carey place has been bashed in, completing the work of the Carey children over the years, while other people have lost teahouses, patios, and sun decks.

We had to bring in bulldozers and truckloads of sand. The governor even called out the National Guard last week. Burgess Meredith, dressed up like Spencer Tracy in *Captains Courageous*, went on TV to ramble on about that old devil sea, while everybody was pitching in to keep his gazebo from being pounded to bits. Mostly, the soldiers helped everybody in the Colony, between forays for beer to the local supermarkets, which pissed off a lot of other Malibu residents, especially those fighting off the mud slides and rocks along the highway. They said they never saw a guardsman and got no help at all. Jerry Brown will make a great president; he knows whose special interests to defend and where the money comes from.

It's funny about the Carey house. I guess it's become the Colony white elephant and will never be bought, at least until the Carey heirs get together and either decide to fix it up or come down in price. I almost had it sold to the Harveys, who have decided to move out here permanently and wrote me three weeks ago, but they bought the Ferrero place instead, and I can't say I blame them, even though they bought directly from the owners and I got no commission on that one. It's really a nice house and in very good shape.

Victor's taken a teaching post at Columbia Presbyterian back in New York, and they'll be moving out in June, after the school year. He's sold everything in California, including his practice, and I understand he and Dottie are taking a long vacation together in Europe. They're going to a lot of places they've never been to and, according to the Kramers, are having a wonderful time. Victor never did like Malibu much, and he wasn't really our kind of guy, if you really think about it, though I always liked Dottie. She's very square, a doctor's wife through and through, but also very nice. Terry, I hear, is staying. She's still in school and all involved with young Tad Bonnell. She'll never leave Malibu, I don't think. It's such a great place for kids, and if you grow up here, no other place ever seems quite as good to live in. Poor Michael is going to hate it in New England, where I hear they're going to send him to boarding school.

The Harveys will get back just in time for the summer fun and games, but I can't imagine next season being quite as dramatic as last. Wilson Mahoney probably won't be around again, and Rich Bentley's moved to Santa Barbara, where, I guess, the wives are equally accessible and his reputation as a lousy lover hasn't preceded him. Mickey Kramer, who succeeded Jim Wharton as president of the Malibu Colony Association, says he's going to try to put a lid on some of the wilder doings this year, and he's asked the Association members not to rent their houses to rock groups or movie people with wild reputations, though just how he plans to get anyone to comply with that request is something else. People rent their places for the summer to get as much money as they can, and the rock and movie people will pay just about anything. I've already got the Wharton home rented to this producer Bud Lavin for twenty grand just for July and August, which will help poor Julie out, since she's alone now and the Wharton estate is all tied up in complicated litigation and, I hear, some kind of criminal investigation.

I still can't get over how Mary and Jim Wharton died. What were they doing, where were they going that late at night and so fast through Malibu Canyon? Either Jim missed the turn completely or Mary had been drinking and grabbed the wheel, which certainly figures. Anyway, the car went off the embankment and through that flimsy little retaining wall, the same spot Dee and I almost bought it last summer, and plunged down to the bottom of the canyon. It turned over several times and exploded, so at least they couldn't have suffered much. They were probably killed right away. But where were they off to, and why? Jim was leaving for Chicago the next morning, and Mary never went anywhere with him anymore. Wharton's secretary left town herself the next day, and nobody knows where she went to either.

The strangest part of all is that Wally, who was on duty at the gate that night, remembers Jim driving out, and he swears there were at least three people in the car at the time. He doesn't think Jim was even driving, but he can't be absolutely sure. We all know Jim was supposed to have been linked to the Mafia or something when he first moved out here, but then, you hear all kinds of things about people all the time. It's fun to gossip about, but nothing you can prove. He did have something to do with that Rancho El Mirador place down around Del Mar, but it's all speculation and hearsay. I always liked Jim. He was a shit, but right up front about it. I didn't see much of Mary. She got to be too much of a lush at the end.

The tennis tournaments won't be the same without Jim, but no one's irreplaceable, not even Art Bonnell, who was good at running them. Bill Stevens, who's sort of the local hotshot pro now, will be in charge this year, and I suppose he'll do a good job. They say he's a very good teacher and a nice guy. Dee tells me he's also a terrific lay, but then, she thought Rich was good when she first went to bed with him. Dee is an optimist and a terrible reporter. And she thinks, after my fiasco with the swingers last summer, that I'm a prude!

I don't know. Maybe I'll just read a lot this summer. Maybe that new book coming out in July by Gail Hessian. She wrote it right here in Malibu, though the word is she had a lot of professional help. Too bad the network let her go. I always liked her casual style on the air, though Barbara Walters she wasn't. I wonder if I'm still up to all the summer partying now? With my son, Dave, getting married, I'll be a goddamn granny pretty soon. The thing is, I don't feel old. Malibu is a place that keeps you young. It's kind of a Lost Horizon. I guess if you ever leave it, you age overnight, and I sure as hell have no plans to do that.